THE *Sweet* LIFE

ALSO BY FRANCINE PASCAL

Sweet Valley Confidential: Ten Years Later

SERIES
Sweet Valley High
Sweet Valley Twins
Sweet Valley Kids
Sweet Valley University
Fearless

YOUNG ADULT NOVELS
Hangin' Out with Cici (My Mother Was Never a Kid)
My First Love and Other Disasters
Love and Betrayal
Hand-Me-Down Kid
The Ruling Class

ADULT NOVELS
Save Johanna
If Wishes Were Horses . . . (La Villa)
Little Crew of Butchers

NONFICTION
The Strange Case of Patty Hearst (with John Pascal)

THEATER
George M! (with Michael Stewart and John Pascal)

THE *Sweet* LIFE

THE SERIAL

THE SWEET LIFE
by Francine Pascal

LIES AND OMISSIONS
TOO MANY DOUBTS
SECRETS AND SEDUCTIONS
CUTTING THE TIES
BITTERSWEET

by Francine Pascal
with Cara Lockwood

ST. MARTIN'S PRESS
NEW YORK

THE SWEET LIFE: THE SERIAL. Copyright © 2012 by Francine Pascal. All rights reserved. Printed in the United States of America. For information, address St. Martin's Press, 175 Fifth Avenue, New York, N.Y. 10010.

www.stmartins.com

Sweet Valley® is a registered trademark of Francine Pascal.

The six episodes that comprise this book were originally published as e-books in separate installments.

ISBN 978-1-250-02388-9 (hardcover)
ISBN 978-1-250-02389-6 (e-book)

First Edition: November 2012

10 9 8 7 6 5 4 3 2 1

To my dearest, loving daughters,

Laurie and Susan.

And as always, Jamie.

Acknowledgments

With gratitude to my agent, Amy Berkower, and my publisher, Dan Weiss, who together came up with the inspired and original idea of an e-book serial of novellas. And to my editor, Hilary Rubin Teeman, who helped make it possible.

And thanks to others who were so helpful along the way, giving me valuable information, editorial suggestions, checking my facts, my music, current references, and so many other things about thirty-year-olds that I have forgotten: Taryn Adler, Molly Wenk, Sandy Mendelson, Ken Gross, Hilary Bloom, John Carmen, Alice Wenk, and Susan Stevenson Brown. And to my writing partner, Cara Lockwood.

And just for being my family: Mia and Nicole Johansson, Thomas Wenk, and Anders Johansson.

EPISODE 1

The Sweet Life

1

"They're ready for you," Katy Johnson, Jessica Wakefield's assistant/ savior, said as she peeked into Jessica's double-windowed corner office, iPad in hand. Katy was wearing one of the new red lipsticks Revlon was introducing. It showed up brilliantly against her deep brown skin.

"Come in. I'm crazed; they're going to hate it."

"No way," Katy said, stepping into her boss's office. "They're gonna love it. They so love everything you do. Did you forget you're the resident genius?"

"Yeah, right. As long as you don't tell."

Jessica was convinced that she would drown under everything if it weren't for Katy. Six-foot-tall Katy, who claimed Watusi somewhere in her background, came closer than anyone else to knowing how vulnerable Jessica really was. What she didn't know was how much Jessica worried that if ever Katy left, she'd write a tell-all book about her, and everyone would know that half the time the Queen of Green was scared shitless and had no clue what she was actually doing.

The meeting today was for her to present her latest project. This time for Revlon. They'd just started a new line of green cosmetics, and she'd been tapped to do the big intro gala. Everyone, all the big shots, was waiting in the meeting room for the Jessica Show.

In three years, from part-time assistant to nobody, Jessica had become a vice president of the My Face Is Green marketing company, now re-named VertPlus.net.

It was a green marketing and promotion company owned by George Fowler, her best friend Lila's father. Originally based in Sweet Valley, but now with offices in Chicago and New York, as well, the company special-ized in introducing new green cosmetics for the popular market. It was a little idea Mr. Fowler had hit on at the right time and place and that in the last five years had exploded onto the national consciousness.

Right from her first week there—actually, from her first day—Jessica knew the job was made for her. It was as if she had the idea gene. Ideas just popped up naturally, practically jumping out of her head.

And the weird thing was, she was usually right. Like the first cam-paign she did for Almay. She did a whole big splash costume party in L.A., and every local magazine and newspaper covered it. Even some national media ran stories.

It all started with a face mask she found made out of seaweed. She made it the center of the promotion and threw a fabulous Marie Antoinette—themed, seaweed-masked ball that everyone had just loved.

The mask even sort of worked. Well, it was no worse than most of the cure-all creams out there. Whatever. It earned her the title Queen of Green. Perfect.

Besides her anxiety about the possible tell-all, Jessica worried that what-ever magic genius she seemed to have would one day vanish into the same place it came from—nowhere.

Right now was no time to worry about that. She had her first Revlon presentation today. And it was far-out.

Katy said she loved it, but Katy could be far-out, too.

A touch of panic hit Jessica as she rolled up the new Revlon invitation layout, rubber-banded it, and stuck it in the corner of her fake-fur lap-top case (made specially for her), which was jammed full with papers already. She grabbed more papers and stuffed them in alongside, and then, holding the bag right at the edge of her desk, swept myriad makeup samples from every corner of the glass top of her personally designed desk, where the only thing you could ever find were your feet underneath it, into the overflowing bag. Not everything she got from her idea gene was perfect.

"Do you need all that?" Katy asked.

"I'm cutting out right from the meeting. I am so going to be late, Todd will kill me."

Katy handed her a large envelope. "The photos?"

"Oh, God, I'm such a wreck, I would have forgotten."

Together she and Katy walked down the hall toward the meeting room, shoulders back, heads high—very high in Katy's case—trying to look invincible.

The meeting was in the grand conference room and was packed with everyone from the top execs of VertPlus.net to the heads of Revlon's marketing department. No one wanted to miss a Queen of Green presentation.

As prearranged, Katy stood in the back.

Jessica knew that not everyone loved her. There was some serious jealousy, especially from the original marketing side. They had been swept aside by Jessica's new promotion group and sorely resented it. Especially Tracy Courtright, an elegant middle-aged woman who had been with the company since it first started. As the former top dog in marketing, she was devastated to find that her work now consisted mainly of carrying out Jessica's ideas.

The minute Jessica walked into the meeting room, the enthusiasm could be felt. She was, after all, Jessica, the star.

But a star can fall. And Tracy Courtright was ready to give her the necessary shove at the first opportunity.

Michael Wilson, the executive vice president of the Sweet Valley office, introduced Jessica.

She stood up and looked around, confident and comfortable as the beautiful blond-haired prom queen she had always been. All jitters vanished; this was her territory.

Jessica wasted no time. "Simply put, I'm taking the green out of Sissyland, Organicville, and Priustown, and from now on, it's gonna be down and dirty!"

She didn't have to wait long for the approval response; it came instantly in big smiles and enthusiastic head nodding. They liked it. Better than that, they loved it. Now she turned directly to Reggie Weiner, the head of marketing for Revlon.

"I'm calling it MeanGreen and it's going to be all those fabulous off-the-charts colors your people have come up with. For anyone who hasn't seen them yet, they're twice the depth of what's out there now. Like reds that stop just short of black and pinks that are so bright they're electric."

There were even more smiles. Especially from the Revlon group.

"I've added a little contribution that you might find interesting. Whatever you're wearing on your lips is also your eyeliner."

"Ugh." Tracy Courtright practically jumped out of her chair. "Red eyes?"

"I know the eyeliner part sounds scary, but I promise it's not. It's totally subtle. Just a hint of a connection. But the lips and the nails—they are definitely scary."

She could see that some in her audience were a little put off by the eyeliner idea, but Jessica wasn't worried. Geniuses are allowed to take that extra leap sometimes. She could lose the eyeliner easily because the pièce de résistance was her gala idea. That was the Jessica touch they were all waiting for.

"I just want you to take a look at the costumes for the MeanGreen gala."

Jessica picked up the large envelope next to her chair. She opened it and slid out the photographs. She kept one and started handing out the others.

"There will be fifteen models. This is the first one," she said, holding up a picture of a stunning model dressed completely in green paint.

Before anyone else could respond, from her positioned place in the back of the room, Katy jumped in. "It's totally fantastic!"

Everyone turned. "If you didn't see the zippers," she continued, "and the flowers on the thongs, you would swear it was paint on naked skin."

"It really does look like she's naked," one of the Revlon people added.

A murmur of agreement went through the audience.

"Absolutely," someone else said.

"She is," said Jessica.

"No way." Back to Katy in the back with her important line. "I can see the whole zipper down her side. And the thongs with the flowers . . ." And then, as if she had just caught on, "Oh, my God, I can't believe it!"

"You better believe it." Jessica gave the punch line: "Trompe l'oeil."

Jaws dropped. "The thongs and the zippers are painted on. The models will actually be totally nude under the paint. A definite knockout when the media finds out, which I'll make sure they do. But not till the end."

By now everyone was craning to catch a glimpse of the pictures. It was a sensation. Neighbors were poking neighbors to make sure everyone got it, and then someone in the back suspiciously close to Katy (maybe it even was Katy) started to clap. And everyone picked it up. Almost everyone.

"I'm not sure we can do such a thing. I mean, after all, naked? Revlon?" Tracy looked to Weiner, expecting support, but all she got was an Obama "Yes, we can."

Michael Wilson stood up. "Brilliant! This could be bigger than the mask gala. Thank you, Jessica, and your fabulous team." He motioned in the direction of the seven-man promotion section, thereby closing out any further objections.

Tracy Courtright was on her feet again. "We just had a gala. I think we used that up."

Jessica was ready. "This isn't just a gala. It's a dinner at Vert Farmhouse with chef Jean Pierre, and everything on the menu is sustainable, homegrown organic from their own acreage—"

"Not exactly earthshaking. Organic food."

"—and an outdoor concert with a hot live band that is still a secret." Jessica pulled that out of nowhere. Well, Liam O'Connor, her movie star friend, would help. Whatever. For the moment, it shut up Madame Courtright. But from experience she knew it was only momentary.

"Thank you, everybody," Jessica said. "I would love to stay and listen to more, but I really am late." She scooped up her laptop bag and, like the star she was, left them wanting more.

These were the times when she absolutely loved her work. Sometimes, hours would pass in the day when she didn't think about anything else. Not even Jake, her two-year-old. Of course, she was always there if he needed her. One call and she'd be out the door.

She checked her watch. It was six thirty, and by the time she got home she'd be almost an hour late and Todd would be furious.

"Jessica." Michael Wilson followed her out the door. "This will only take a couple of minutes."

She really liked Mike. He was a great boss, about thirty-seven and very good to look at. He was also single. And sort of interested in her, maybe more than sort of, but he kept his distance. If you didn't know the situation, you wouldn't, except everyone in the office did already. Gossip, that's what coffee machines were for.

"What's up?" Jessica asked.

"We should talk about the green paint stuff."

"I was just on my way out. I'm really late."

Now here was the running problem: the mother/wife stuff. At the office, they didn't want to think about her personal obligations. And she couldn't look like she was letting them cut into her work. Not a whole lot different from Todd's problem with her, only inverted.

Which kept her always teetering on the brink between crazy and balanced.

"You can't give me ten minutes?"

"Can't." Being a pro, she took the coward's way out. "Theater tickets."

And it worked.

"Oh, sure. It can hold till tomorrow. Enjoy the show."

Theater tickets he understood. Motherhood, not so.

"See ya." She caught a glimpse of Katy's knowing look, winked, and was out the door.

And inside of three minutes, she was in front of her silver BMW that was waiting in its own parking space, the one with her name printed on the wall: JESSICA WAKEFIELD-WILKINS. As much as she pitched "going green" at work, she would never be caught dead driving a Prius!

She was very late, but luckily there wasn't much traffic, and inside of twenty minutes flat she was home in Sweet Valley Heights.

She left the car on the street in front of her town house, which looked exactly like every other one on the block. The only thing they let you choose was the color of the front door. Being Jessica Wakefield, she chose pink. Yves Saint Laurent Pink Ice number 22, to be specific. No one ever had trouble finding Jessica.

As soon as she opened the car door, she heard her son's squeals of terror and delight. She could see the monster box game through the window. A moment of silence and then Jake's favorite two-year-old word: "More!" And by the time she got to the door, he was squealing again.

She opened the door and Jake saw her. He was torn. He loved his mommy, but he loved the game, too. Todd was on the floor with him, holding a cardboard box over his head, ready to raise it and make the big growl noise that had delighted Jake for months now. Todd's face was turned away from her, but she knew he had to be pissed.

She watched Todd raise the box in one grand finale of monster roar, get the expected scream of joy, and put the box down on the floor and free Jake to run to his mother.

Jessica scooped her precious baby into her arms and covered him with kisses. The chill coming from Todd, who was on his feet now, folding up the cherished box that was practically collapsing on its own from overuse, was almost palpable.

If she could just keep kissing Jake, she could postpone the bad part that was coming. But unfortunately she couldn't because Jake was squirming out of her arms, rushing to get back to the game. But the game was over.

For her, too.

"I have to be in L.A. for the game tonight. You knew that. I'm never going to make it by eight."

"I'm really sorry. I just didn't realize and I had that big meeting . . ."

"And I have a game . . ."

"And I had a meeting," she shot back.

Todd turned away from Jake and in a whisper that was as piercing as a hiss, said, "Another half hour and I'd have put him to bed and he'd have missed seeing his mother for the whole goddamn day because her work was more important than her kid!"

"That is so unfair!" She answered him in that same sizzle of words. "How many times do you miss putting him to bed?"

"I'm not his mother!"

"You're his father and that's just the same and—"

"Forget it." He cut her off before it got even nastier. Both were suddenly aware that Jake was listening.

It was the two-year running argument that never got solved and only turned into more vicious accusations that cut deep and left scars that might not ever heal. "I left his clothes on his dresser."

Jake was trying to reassemble the box, but Todd took it from him gently. "Mommy will save the box and we'll do it again when I come next Wednesday. First thing, okay, buddy?"

"Now," Jake said, even though at just two he knew it wouldn't be now. But that didn't stop him from hoping.

Todd kissed the top of his son's head, said, "See ya," and went toward the door. The walk took only a few seconds, but they were heavy with emotions: anger, hurt, and the twinge of regret. And somewhere in there, love. On both sides. Albeit the leaving was easier now than it had been that first time. But still painful.

He couldn't turn around and look at her. That would be too hard.

And no matter what had happened in these last four months, when Jessica looked at Todd, she was still excited by that tall, gorgeous man with the silky blondish brown hair, the errant piece that kept slipping over his forehead only to be swept back in that familiar gesture she'd been watching for all those years. She remembered how she and Elizabeth used to make fun of it, but now every time she saw him do it, her stomach clenched.

No question but that he still had the body of the fabulous basketball player he was in high school. A body she'd grown to know so well. And even now longed to feel against hers, to feel the warmth of him touching her, his arms tight around her, holding her, loving her. She knew he didn't feel that way about her anymore; he was too angry. He felt he'd been tricked. She wasn't the woman he had fallen in love with.

And he was right. She had changed and grown. Why wasn't that good?

And why was it still so weird seeing him but not being with him, even though they'd been separated more than four months?

They didn't argue about why anymore. Nobody was defending his or her side, it was not as if an explanation would change anything anyway. In fact, they hardly said anything except what had to be said about Jake. Even that was uncomfortable and awkward, and loaded with lots of unsaid stuff that stuck in the throat.

She didn't ask him about his work, and he certainly didn't ask her about hers. That was the last thing he'd ask. This guy who was always complaining in the beginning that she didn't "do anything." And then when she started doing so well at her job, he seemed happy until it hit him that it wasn't just another one of her phases and that maybe it was going to be a big deal. And being a mother and a wife wasn't going to divert her.

She always felt that she had given up almost everything for him, most important, the closest person in the world, her twin, Elizabeth. And what did he give up for her? Nothing comparable. Okay, that was probably unfair, but still, what he gave up didn't come close to what she had given up. She'd given up love for love. That was the hardest sacrifice.

All she asked was that he understand that this was the way her life was now! Well, maybe not *all* she asked, but still, this was the way it was going to be, and too bad for him if he couldn't accept it.

Except what sucked was that the real "too bad" was for Jake. She still got sick to her stomach about what she was doing to her baby, but it wasn't just Jessica, it was Todd, too. Actually, she felt it was mostly Todd. Jealousy, that's what it was. It was a response she'd never expected and he would never admit. In fact, his whole attitude about her career was so retro. Were they really back to where the woman had to stay home with the children or have some kind of unimportant job that was totally second to her husband's and could be dropped whenever he needed it to be?

Jessica knew she could work and succeed and be as good a parent as he was. That was the difference—she wanted him to measure being a father on the same scale as being a mother. So far, he couldn't seem to do that. Or just wouldn't.

Maybe that was a reach, but she'd made up her mind it was the goal she was aiming for.

Todd had underestimated her. Everyone had, herself included. And now they were all waking up. Todd especially. She was so not his "old Jessica," and he really was feeling threatened.

All the signs were there: She was probably going to be very successful, possibly more than he was. Shallow Jessica Wakefield, the lightweight, was not so lightweight anymore.

And he better watch, because this Jessica was only starting to climb!

Oh, God! It hit her: Did Jake eat?

She texted Todd. He shot back: R U KIDDING? I DON'T NEGLECT MY SON.

Oh, like I do? She rolled her eyes and didn't even bother responding.

Instead she texted her sister, who answered right away: BRINGING DINNER.

Her identical twin lived part-time in a penthouse in Beverly Hills and the other part, mostly weekends, in a mansion in Sweet Valley Hills about fifteen minutes away from Jessica—fifteen minutes and four million dollars away. Dinner from the mansion was the best takeout in all of Southern California, maybe the whole state. Yvonne Dechamps, her fancy French master chef, prepared it.

The whole situation was so unlike her down-to-earth, unpretentious, best-friend-anybody-could-ever-have-in-the-world Lizzie, but she was getting used to it. Living with Bruce Patman, who, in the last three years (thanks to his own dotcom stuff and family real estate investments) had become a multimillionaire. Actually, maybe even a billionaire, heading his own multimillion-dollar charitable foundation and an important social impact company and becoming, at thirty, a force to be reckoned with, possibly a kingmaker, maybe even a king himself.

Incredibly enough, Jessica was not envious. Not to misunderstand, she was still Jessica Wakefield, very competitive and self-absorbed and never bothering to hide it. But now she was too busy succeeding to waste time on envy.

As far as being self-absorbed, that worked because Jake was a part of her, so he never lost out. Todd was, too, when he was. And in a unique way, so was Elizabeth. Even after what had happened. No question that a lot of people might wonder, "So how could you do what you did to her? How could you marry your sister's ex-boyfriend?"

It was still too hard a question for her to answer. Would love be a good enough answer? How ironic, all that pain they'd suffered was for nothing. Everything she gave up so much for was gone.

She felt like her sister had forgiven her. Maybe not completely, maybe never completely, but enough so that Lizzie could love her again.

Me. Me. Me. See, she was still Jessica Wakefield.

2

Mme Dechamps was happy that someone was going to eat her exquisite boeuf bourguignon. Elizabeth had tried to tell her in a very subtle way, in her not-so-stellar French, that she didn't eat red meat, but it didn't seem to register, so she mentioned it a couple more times. Mme Dechamps seemed to get the red part, enough so that she never made anything with tomatoes or tomato sauce for Elizabeth. But it was too late to say it again, so she'd just push the meat around on her plate until it was partly hidden. That's what came from pretending to understand more French than she did with all that smiling and nodding her head in agreement with anything the chef said.

Bruce just figured she was back to meat again, and he was happy. For some reason, people who ate meat seemed to want everyone else to eat it, too. Elizabeth didn't tell him about the miscommunication because she knew how proud he was of her "fluent" French. It was actually not a problem because most of the time Mme Dechamps cooked fish and chicken and lots of veggies.

Tonight's bourguignon would go straight to Jessica, who, conscientious and green as she was inside the office, ate everything outside—organic or not.

As soon as Jessica heard the car, she shouted, "The door's open."

The first person Elizabeth saw was her adorable nephew, Jake, sitting in the middle of the living room floor concentrating on building skyscrapers with his Legos.

"Hey, munchkin," she said, holding out her arms.

The baby looked up with that flash of confusion, just long enough for the penny to drop and register "Not Mommy." The flash was down to a nanosecond and on its way to a picosecond, and soon it wouldn't be there at all. Instantly, she'd be Zizzie. Even if it was only for a moment, she had to admit she liked being mistaken for Mommy.

Jake flung the Legos away and rushed into his aunt's arms, giving her just enough time to put down her food delivery and scoop him up. She was totally hung up on her nephew.

"In the kitchen!" Jessica called out. "Hit the stereo when you pass!"

Elizabeth grabbed the food package and, with Jake in her arms, turned on the music with her elbow and headed into the kitchen. Pop music started playing and Jake happily bopped his head to the beat.

Jessica was still in her office clothes, but barefoot, standing in the middle of the kitchen with a glass of wine in one hand and pouring another glass for her sister.

Jessica's office clothes were Elizabeth's party clothes. Today it was a hot little dark pink DVF minidress with a deep V back. Off the hook the whole dress couldn't have weighed more than two ounces. Her hair was parted in the center with cascades of blond flowing on either side of her face, just the way she'd worn it for her wedding. Her Jimmy Choo heels, which she had kicked over into the corner, were woven with the thinnest pink and silver threads, which if she were wearing them, would make her about five inches taller than her sister.

Even though they were identical twins, Elizabeth always felt that even if she wore exactly the same clothes, she could never look like Jessica. She didn't have that delicacy, that ethereal quality. In fact, she never felt ethereal; she felt sturdy and solid. The closest she'd ever come to delicate was when she was with Bruce. He always treated her so gently, like she was breakable. And with him, she liked it.

It had been thirty years, and she still didn't get how people, even ones who knew them well, could mix them up. Todd never did. Bruce didn't, and soon Jake wouldn't. Maybe men could differentiate better, except their dad, Ned Wakefield, could still get them confused. They might or might not try to fool him, and it might or might not have been his private game with them.

For Elizabeth, Jessica had been the constant in her life, even before they were born, with the exception of that terrible time with Todd three years ago. Even then she was a constant, albeit a terrible one. That time was brutal, the worst she'd ever gone through in her life. After what Jessica did to her with Todd, she never thought she would be able to love her again. But as angry and as hurt as she was, and as much as she detested her sister (the way you can detest only someone you love), it happened.

The rapprochement was not something that could be explained; it just had to be felt. In fact, neither one wanted to explain it because it was too hard for other people to understand. Elizabeth knew that someday someone would say Jessica didn't deserve to be forgiven, that she had stolen the love of Elizabeth's life. And then Elizabeth would have to hate *them*.

All she knew now was that with Jessica, wherever she was, she was home. It was different with Todd. She didn't think she would ever find the right place for him in her life. And it was especially difficult now, since the separation.

She still choked up when she saw him, but it wasn't about love, she was definitely not in love with him anymore. In fact, compared to the passion she had for Bruce, it might have stopped being love and started being habit longer ago than she realized. Sometimes she wondered what would have happened to her and Todd after the passion dripped out and they were just good friends. Would someone else have come along, like maybe Bruce? That could have been a major problem.

So, if it wasn't hate she felt for Todd, maybe she just felt plain old uncomfortable. Weird.

Fortunately, she didn't see him often. But whenever she did, it was too much. Ironically, Todd and Elizabeth both wrote for the *L.A. Tribune*. He wrote a sports column, and she wrote a kind of general "foibles of life" column for the paper and her blog. She was at the office less often now that she often e-mailed her column in, so thankfully they hardly ever ran into each other at work.

Her blog belonged to the paper, but she had created it. It was the place she could converse interactively with her readers. It covered L.A. and its suburbs, including Sweet Valley, but mostly she covered Los Angeles, where the action was.

When they were growing up, Sweet Valley was its own world. Now it was just a suburb of L.A., which, with improved roads, was only an hour away. Forty-five nauseating minutes if you were in Jessica's BMW.

Mostly now she ran into Todd only when it was about Jake. She'd had to pick up her nephew at his apartment a few times when Todd had a game to cover and Jessica had to work late. *Weird* wasn't a strong enough word to describe what that felt like.

"Is Bruce home tonight?" Jessica asked Elizabeth.

Bruce Patman was the man Elizabeth loved and the man she lived with. Typical of small-town life, she'd known him forever. And for the first part of forever, couldn't stand him. But in college, he'd lost his parents in a horrendous car accident, and it was a huge wake-up call for him. He'd changed completely, and Elizabeth was there for it. In fact, he became her best friend. And then three years ago, after the Todd debacle, she fell in love with Bruce. He was still her best friend, but now way more.

"No," she told Jessica, "he's in L.A. at a Lakers game."

"Todd is covering it," she said, picking Jake up out of the pantry and dislodging the spaghetti box from his tiny fists, but not before he had a chance to empty half of it on the floor.

"Well, it's not like they're going to share a ride. Ever." Bruce was not big with forgiving when it came to Todd. Even though, ironically, you could say he owed him his happiness now.

Elizabeth bent down to help Jessica pick up the loose spaghetti, then stopped for a second while Jessica decided whether to throw it away or put it back in the box.

It was her last box. They stuffed it back in.

"How's the baby?" Jessica said, taking a couple of strands out of Jake's mouth.

The baby belonged to their brother, Steven, and Aaron Dallas, his partner. A four-month-old daughter, Emma. A year ago they had hired a woman named Linda Carson from San Diego as a surrogate mother to add her eggs to their sperm and carry their baby. Short of a DNA test, which they both promised never to do, neither would ever know who was the biological father. It didn't matter. They would both be the father.

Given enough money, Linda, with her silky Scandinavian blond hair, expensive tastes, and, according to Jessica, bitch eyes (she was not a favorite of either twin), had signed papers giving over the baby completely to Steven and Aaron.

"I saw Emma yesterday and she is delicious. Gorgeous, actually, but she does run the show. Steven is a bit clumpy at taking care of her, but Aaron is fantastic."

"All that playing with dolls when he was a little boy finally paid off."

"Don't say that."

"Are you kidding? That's what he says."

"Have they decided who the stay-at-home dad is going to be?"

"Nope, still talking it out. That's the problem, they both want to be. Maybe I should tell them to come over to my house. Give Todd a few lessons."

"What about you?"

"Low blow, Sis."

"I only meant it must be so hard to divide up the parenting jobs."

"You didn't mean that. It's like you're taking Todd's side."

"I'm absolutely not." The silence hung in the air. "Hey, let's not go there. I'd rather talk about something dumb like Lila and the *True Housewives* thing."

"Me, too. So what's happening?"

"She's really trying out and she thinks she's got a shot. Don't you ever read my tweets?"

"I've been so busy what with the new—"

"Save it for Todd."

"Hey!"

"My bad. Sorry, that wasn't nice. But sometimes your whole work thing can be a little much."

"Oh, are you jealous of the lesser sister?"

"Am I? I don't want to be. I'm sorry, Jess, I feel terrible. I'm really proud of you, but I guess maybe I'm a little jealous of how important your work is to you. I'm not used to being so far down on the list."

"You think I'm too involved in my work, don't you?"

"I absolutely did not say that. Well, I don't know. Maybe you are sort of a bit."

"Okay, okay, I hear you, but that's enough. Back to Lila."

Elizabeth put up her hands in surrender. "Sorry."

Their unique relationship allowed the sisters the freedom to tread on each other's territory and still survive. But instinctively they knew when to get off.

"Would Lila be a perfect True Housewife or what?" And Elizabeth was off.

"I would be, too, but it's just way too superficial; I'm past that stage in my life."

"What about me? Think I could be a True Housewife?"

"I can just see that: Elizabeth, the housemother with everyone lining up to complain and confess to you. A kind of *Dr. Phil* meets *True Housewives*. Suddenly they're talking about morals and ethics and everyone is changing the channel."

"I know you don't read it, but my blog is really edgy now."

"I know it is, and I absolutely read it. It's definitely got edge. Got a ghost-writer? You can tell me."

"Hey, if there's a new Jessica, how about a new Elizabeth?"

"Sleeping with two guys in New York three years ago does not make you a new person!"

"Come on! It was a start. You never said anything to Caroline Pearce, did you?"

"Three years ago, Lizzie!"

"I know. I just hate to be in her mouth. I don't know where she gets her dirt. It's actually incredible. Not that I read her blog."

"Yeah, right."

"She knows I can't stand Enid, so she calls me if there is any dirt."

"And you listen."

"Can't resist. She told me a little item about the holier-than-thou Dr. Enid Rollins and Brad Jones, the married pool salesman."

"Tell. Tell."

"Let's just say it involves leather straps and an examining table . . ."

"Keep going!"

Elizabeth recounted the whole gossip bit. Apparently the esteemed Dr. Rollins (her ex–best friend from high school) had been secretly having Jones over for afternoon trysts in her office. She was Sweet Valley's leading gynecologist, and if you met her, she wouldn't let you forget that. Modesty was not exactly her strong point. And by the way, Mrs. Jones was one of her patients.

"So guess who just happened to be ten minutes early for her appointment and walks in on them? According to Big Mouth Pearce—and God knows how she finds out these things—the long-suffering wife walks in on them playing kidnapped patient, stirrups, leather straps, and all. Do you love it? Think Caroline'll blog it?"

"I see the tweet now. 'Forget appointments with Dr. Rollins, Jones has got her all tied up.'"

"Or 'Pool salesman found floating in his last sale. And I mean last.'"

These were their best times together. Just talking about everything and nothing. It was something they had together that they could never have with anyone else, ever. Neither one. That's why what had happened had been so horrendous and why they'd vowed that nothing like that could ever happen again.

Jessica put Jake to bed, and the sisters ate dinner and listened to lots of upbeat dance music—giggling and shaking their hips as they did the dishes. They both had the same taste in music and both loved everything on the top 100 chart—especially the songs that got them moving.

Jessica told her about her triumph at the meeting, and from there they went on gossiping and laughing and didn't stop until nearly midnight.

Elizabeth reached for her purse, but Jessica put up her hand to stop her.

"Wait! I totally forgot I have presents for you!" She grabbed her over-stuffed laptop bag and emptied it on the cocktail table.

Tons of Estée Lauder blush and bronzer and mascaras and even high-end makeup brushes that probably cost a fortune at the department stores came pouring out.

"I cannot believe you get all of this for free," Elizabeth said. After the success of My Face Is Green promotions, every leading makeup company was dying to get on board with VertPlus.net.

"Shush." Jessica put her finger to her lips and shoved some Clinique eye shadow into Elizabeth's purse. "Definitely take this." In went a large Yves Saint Laurent palette.

Elizabeth couldn't resist the Chanel Glossimer lip glosses and all of the gorgeous Dior shadows that she would probably never use.

"What about this eyeliner? It's the Bobbi Brown gel stuff that I swear by."

"Okay." She took that, too. "I'm never going to wear half of this, but I just love to have it. Shades of all those teenage years when we lived for makeup. Remember how our drawers were crammed with all this junk? Mom used to go nuts about getting us to get rid of it."

Jessica got enough makeup every day to open her own store. She was always giving it away, but sometimes it was even more than she could give away.

Elizabeth said she should donate it.

"Oh, my God! Like to a children's hospital?"

"Yeah, right."

"No! I'm serious. Can you just picture all those little girls knee-deep in makeup? The smiles on their faces. And it's okay because it's all organic. Nothing to hurt them. I'm doing it! And I'll do a little video and throw it into the new Revlon promotion. Just a little something for Tracy Courtright to choke on."

"You really are fabulous!"

"Maybe a little."

That tickled both of them. How they loved being together.

"Wanna stay over?" Jessica asked, like the little sister she still was.

But Elizabeth said she couldn't because she had an early interview.

She did have an interview, but in the old days she'd have rearranged it. But those days of dropping everything for Jessica were over. She felt like she had to keep proving that to herself.

That was one of the biggest "new" Elizabeth changes. Although if she really felt Jessica needed her, she would, but she knew tonight it was just the company.

The separation with Todd was hard on Jessica, and even though she'd explained the breakup over and over again and they'd talked it to death, Elizabeth still felt it didn't look final. And she thought that neither Todd nor Jessica knew what they were doing, but for now both were too angry and proud to admit it.

Elizabeth warned her sister that time could be a big danger. With both of them out there, who knew what could happen.

Elizabeth didn't tell Jessica the gossip she'd heard at the paper about the new writer from San Diego who was making a play for Todd. Not so unusual. Todd was hot. And the nasty word was he wasn't putting up a big fight.

That brought up the eternal question best friends ask themselves: "Do I tell?" But with twin sisters, it's even worse. For the moment, she had decided to wait and see what happened. Right now it was only a rumor.

She knew there was gossip about Jessica, too, starting with Elizabeth's nonfriend from New York, Liam O'Connor, the New York actor. He'd moved to L.A. and was getting parts in movies. In fact, you could say he was a real star. He had been on a couple of HBO series and actually wasn't a bad actor. People were talking about him. Caroline had him all over her blog.

Of course, it didn't hurt that he was totally gorgeous. And crazy about Jessica right from the first time he'd laid eyes on her at their grandmother's birthday dinner three years ago, before her marriage to Todd. It was a memorable evening that turned into an explosion of drama the Sweet Valley Country Club had probably never seen before, certainly not from the well-mannered Wakefields. That night Liam went nuts for Jessica, and it hadn't changed.

In fact, too crazy. It was like he was mesmerized.

Elizabeth had been furious with him that night, but when fate happens, there's little that can be done about it. Once Jessica was separated, there was no stopping Liam. The e-mails, the texts, the phone calls, and he'd even shown up a couple of times without warning. With flowers, but still . . .

Jessica didn't seem so disturbed, but Elizabeth didn't like it. It felt a little creepy, like borderline stalking. But for the very desirable Jessica who was used to over-the-top attention, it could be a little annoying but mostly kind of flattering. Besides, when Elizabeth mentioned it to her sister, her answer was that he was too gorgeous to be a stalker.

Truth was that she didn't think Jessica was into either Liam or the VP Michael from her office who, rumor also said, had the hots for her. Maybe it wasn't really over with Todd.

⌣

By the time Elizabeth got home, it was twelve thirty and Bruce's Ferrari was in their five-car garage that also held Elizabeth's car and the Bentley for when they used the driver who doubled as a handyman but looked to Elizabeth like a butler that Bruce swore he wasn't. She told him if he was, she was definitely going to need a lady's maid.

That left two more spaces free, but from Bruce's car habits, they wouldn't stay empty long.

The house was definitely not a McMansion. There was nothing Mc about the fabulous Gehry-designed structure. On the outside, it was a modern museum piece, but inside, it was actually a home. Bruce had started it as soon as Elizabeth had moved back to Sweet Valley, and they'd been in it for more than a year now. *Architectural Digest* had done a piece on it the minute it was finished. They wanted shots of Elizabeth and Bruce together, eating or just hanging out in the living room, but Elizabeth wasn't ready for so much attention, so they ran the piece with just Bruce. He was really the star, anyway.

Elizabeth had very little hand in the decoration, not her strong suit, so she leaned on Bruce with some help from Jessica. She had pushed that because she wanted them to be friends. It helped, but there was still a long way to go.

Unbeknownst to Elizabeth then and even now, Bruce had been aware of Todd and Jessica's affair their senior year in college, and even though it might have cleared a place for him with Elizabeth, he stayed silent. The idea of being the one to hurt the woman he loved was inconceivable to him.

Ironically, as it turned out, it was Jessica's malevolence that brought them together. Not a selling point that Elizabeth would ever use.

⌣

"Hey, babe." Bruce was waiting for her in his study. They each had a study. Elizabeth was never sure what to do with hers since she carried her laptop with her and just set it down wherever she was. Which was not often in her study, so sometimes she would just push things around to make it look used.

It was not like Elizabeth had grown up disadvantaged, because she hadn't. They had a nice house, even had a pool, and when she was sixteen, she and Jessica got a car to share. But Bruce's money was extreme. Not that she was complaining, except that sometimes she felt like she was living completely outside her experience and maybe she did need a lady's maid.

Outside her experience was like what had happened with the Mary Cassatt painting. She had seen it at a gallery opening and said she loved it. So Bruce secretly bought it for her, just like that—had to be a couple of million dollars—and while she was at work had it hung in her study. Of course, she went nuts when she saw it, stunned, delighted, and figured it had to be a copy, right? But he said, no. "You mean this isn't a copy?" And on and on until he finally said, "You're going to have to get used to this kind of life."

Not exactly a punishment. But it wasn't that easy.

They had had long conversations about it, and she told him that she felt threatened by demands of this kind of life that sucked up everything in its path, including her independence. She was expected to participate in everything that involved the Patman Foundation and the social world of charities and big money. It didn't leave much room for her life, and that led to more talk about marriage, and from there they went into children and back again to money and independence and then they usually ended up making love, and that took their mind off everything else.

She was trying to adjust. Which sounded like a joke, trying to adjust to living like a millionaire. But most of the time, except for the tuxedos and gowns, she felt like she had been dropped into an old 1930s movie. And she couldn't always resist making fun of it, which was not always so funny to Bruce.

Meanwhile, she owned a real Mary Cassatt. And sometimes when she was in her study and Norah Jones was playing softly in the background, singing about being in love and never surrendering, and Elizabeth was not studying or even reading, she just sat in her little-used custom-made desk chair staring at the enchanting little girl in the painting and loving her.

⌣

She followed Bruce's voice into his study, which he had designed himself in custom-built iron-and-glass furniture. On the wall over the fireplace he had a Warhol of his mother and an early Jackson Pollock, and a Bruno Romeda sculpture on the mantel.

Standing there, looking sexy and handsome with his slightly too long dark hair and navy blue eyes, he looked like an expensive watch ad in *Esquire*.

Elizabeth looked at him and thought that despite his money, she was completely and totally in love with this guy. Nobody but Jessica would understand such a weird idea.

Sometimes she'd think how much easier it would have been if they'd never come back to Sweet Valley, but then she wouldn't have her sister. And after all that had happened, she knew now that she would always need her. And Jessica would always feel the same.

You were supposed to outgrow the need for siblings, but nobody said anything about twins.

"How was the game?"

"Lakers won by two points. Kobe took a shot in the last three seconds and made it. He's clutch. We were down by one with three seconds left, and Kobe shoots a three-pointer to win by two."

"Todd was covering it." She could see the next question, so she answered it before he asked. "Jessica told me."

Would there ever come a time when the mention of Todd's name would just be part of a sentence? "Did you see him?" she asked.

"You can't exactly miss him, he was right in front of the press box. I think he had someone with him."

"A dark-haired woman?"

"Yeah, good-looking. You know her?"

"Not really. She's a new writer at the *Trib*. I think her name is Sarah something. Business section, someone said."

"So?"

"So, nothing's happening that I know of. Unless you mean office gossip."

"I'll take it." Especially if it wasn't good. It was rare to see that side of Bruce, like the old Bruce and not so nice.

"She wants him," Elizabeth said.

Sometimes, she thought, the only way Bruce would ever forgive Todd is if he saved their daughter's life. Not easy, considering they didn't have one.

Maybe then she, too, would forgive Todd. Maybe.

Bruce took a bottle of Cristal champagne out of the bar fridge and popped it.

"We're celebrating?" Elizabeth asked, trying to read his face. "You got the land?"

Bruce smiled and filled two flutes. "Patman Social Impact Group, Limited, now owns all 1,860 acres."

Along with the Patman Foundation, Bruce had started Patman Social Impact Group just two years ago, and so far they had invested in projects that built waste-product renewal plants and others that worked on experimental methods of cleaning water. The waste-product plant was already showing a profit.

"What about WNG?" His competitor for this land deal, Warner Natural Gas, had been fighting him for the last year. "Did they just give up?"

"They had no choice. Now all I need is EPA approval and they're out."

"Fabulous!" she said, lifting her glass. "You're incredible. I thought they'd never give up."

"I was a little surprised, too. They backed off more easily than I expected."

"I don't like that."

"What, them giving up?"

"Easily? No. Not Rick Warner. He has to have something up his sleeve."

"There are no more tricks left. We get that approval and it's over. What?"

"Rick Warner is an underhanded, conniving creep. You ever read his interviews? 'I never lose.' "

"Well, he just never came up against Bruce Patman before."

"I hope you're right. In the meantime, you're going to have a lot of very grateful people between San Diego and L.A. with lower electricity rates, cleaner air, and unpolluted water. True they're going to have to look at a lot of windmills. You're going to get a lot of phone calls from Darko."

Darko Crowitz was a big mover and shaker in the California Democratic Party. He'd been after Bruce for the last three years. First as a donor and lately as a possible candidate for anything he wanted. But Bruce didn't want anything right now.

"I already got four e-mails and five tweets."

"So?"

"So nothing. I told him I'm not running for anything—"

"For the fiftieth time. This is a real coup, Bruce. That land is a natural-gas bonanza. I can hardly believe Rick Warner walked away . . ."

"There was nothing else he could do. Not to worry, we're safe."

"This feels like one of those horror movies where they always say, 'It's okay, you wait here and I'll . . .' whatever, and then as soon as their back is turned, the monster comes out of nowhere."

"Liz, you underestimate my strength."

"Bruce . . ."

"Liz. It's really okay. The guy even called to say congratulations. I happen to know they found what they wanted just north of San Francisco. Come on, let's just celebrate."

"To my own Don Quixote!"

Elizabeth kissed her hero and together they raised their glasses and drank the glorious Cristal. It was so good they did it again. By the third glass they were feeling so good they were running out of people to toast.

"By the way," Bruce said, "I forgot to tell you. Missy LeGrange called about you being on the benefit committee for the greyhound dinner. I said yes."

"Ugh."

"Come on, don't be like that."

"I can't help it. It's brutal."

"They're nice dogs."

"The dogs are fine, it's Missy and her friends I can't stand. They're fake and totally insufferable. And the idea of working with Missy makes me want to gag."

"Okay, then just do it for me. I've known her all my life."

This was a running problem for Elizabeth: his world, her world, and the "do it for me" stuff. She was not exactly a fish out of water, though at times more like a fish drowning in the water. And it was getting worse. Everyone wanted Bruce Patman. And after this deal, he'd be a rock star.

"Come on, she's like a sister to me."

"Yeah, right. Sister. I don't think so."

"Jealous?"

"Absolutely not. Well, maybe a little."

"Hey, screw Missy." He wiggled his index finger in a *come here* gesture.

After three years, she knew that look, and with a little heel kick pushed the door closed behind her. Nothing Goody Two-Shoes about that sexy walk over to him.

He waited.

Now she was in charge. She moved up close, carefully not touching but just inside the heat of his aura, and before he could put his arms around her, she started to unbutton his shirt. He dropped his arms to his sides and just waited.

She loved undressing him and loved the crisp, clean shirts he wore, always the softest cotton, handmade in London. And she loved the smell of him. By now, late in the day, the cologne had disappeared, but the fresh smell of soap was awakened by the light sweat on his skin.

She opened his belt and unzipped his pants. He didn't move. He was no longer looking at her. His head was raised and his eyes had found some other dimension. Her head was against his chest and she could feel his pounding heart.

His body was still, but the expectancy was almost tangible. Their breath was the only sound in the silent room, his deep and long, hers quieter.

He waited, as if to move would break the spell. With her hand she slid his pants down over his hips and then the sexy briefs she'd bought him. From his flat, hard stomach down, he was naked.

His skin was hot and smooth, and she could feel the intensity of his need. And now hers, flooding her body with waves of heat and longing.

Nothing, she thought, had ever been so powerful as the love she felt for this man.

3

For Lila Fowler to get up, get dressed, makeup and all (all meaning her diamond wedding ring, her four-carat engagement ring, earrings, and the thinnest gold chain necklace dotted with ten quarter-carat diamonds), and be someplace outside of her own bedroom by nine o'clock in the morning had to be an emergency call from the hospital, an earthquake, or an interview for *The True Housewives of Sweet Valley*.

Not only was she on time for the interview, she was ten minutes early. When Lila wanted something badly enough, there was no stopping her.

And she wanted this very badly. If she were a True Housewife, then maybe her father would stop carrying on about her best friend, Jessica "the genius" Wakefield. Not that Jessica didn't deserve it, because she *was* doing fabulous work, but between her father's boasting about Jessica and his son-in-law, Ken Matthews, the great NFL quarterback, there simply wasn't any room for his own daughter.

No wonder with all her nonaccomplishments she was treated so second-rate. Well, this was an accomplishment that was going to be all hers. Superboastable!

Lila Fowler Matthews was meant to be a True Housewife. No matter what.

The interviews were taking place at the new Patman Building on the corner of Main Street and Marshal Drive.

Lila valet-parked her Maserati, and with one last check in the mirror, refreshed her lipstick, touched up her eyeliner, and was ready to roll.

The interviews were on the fifth floor of the palatial offices of StarFinder Productions. The secretary directed her to the waiting area where, to Lila's dismay, at least fifteen other women were waiting, all perfectly made-up and appropriately overdressed.

But Lila was happy to see only one other woman with dark hair like hers. And it was not really like hers, not by a long shot, since it was shoe-polish black and hung down to her elbows limply like a rug with bad fringes. No competition for her newly darkened, shiny brown hair with just the slightest glint of auburn. No more stick straight for Lila. She'd moved over to soft waves and had it cut to a classy new length just below her shoulders. The other nonblonde had short, curly red hair and looked like she should be teaching crop rotation in Zambia.

All the rest were—yawn—blondes. Exactly why Lila had changed her hair color. Brunettes, she told Jessica, were becoming an endangered species.

By the time Lila was called, it was nearly noon and she'd had to refresh her makeup two times.

She was directed into a room with three production people, two men and a woman. The three were seated behind a rectangular table facing one tall stool for the interviewee.

They didn't even bother to introduce themselves. At this point it was just a cattle call.

One look and Lila knew her hair choice was perfect. The one woman, plain, about forty, and a tiny bit plump, had brown hair. One of the men, he looked about thirty, had light blond hair and the other, older man, had short gray hair.

Lila might have been deficient in certain disciplines, but when it came to knowing what appealed to people, sexually or otherwise, she overflowed with skill.

Blond men were often turned on by their opposites, dark-haired women. The brown-haired woman would identify with Lila, imagining that they were the same type. Hardly, but anyone can dream, can't she? As for the older guy, her sex appeal would work, and that had always been Lila's strongest suit anyway.

Figuring him for the power, she made a point of focusing on him right away. Since he was older and unattractive, she figured he needed the attention most.

And she gave it to him, subtle enough that the other two didn't feel left out.

The first questions were easy: name, age, where did she live, etc., and all those nonthinking answers designed to put a person at ease. Of course, Lila knew they were not interested in those facts; they already had them. They were watching her when she was supposedly not trying.

But Lila was always trying. Always on. The trick was to give them that sweet spot between sexy, smart, fun, and outrageous.

Lots of women fit that bill, especially the ones trying out for this show, so Lila knew she needed a special niche, and with her well-hidden smarts she thought she'd found it. Additionally, it would be easy because she didn't have to put it on, it was that close to the truth, though Lila wasn't introspective enough to know it. She thought she was pretending. It worked either way.

While all these advantaged women were trying to show how unspoiled they were, Lila would do just the opposite.

Spoiled rotten and proud of it. Her niche.

"So, Lila," said the brown-haired woman who thought she was Lila, "what are you passionate about?"

"Lots of things. I'm a very passionate person." Looking right at the old gray hair and in a voice at once both proud and intimate, she said, "When I think passion, I think sex. But doesn't everyone?" And then she allowed herself the tiniest smile. "Well, right after world peace."

They all smiled back. They were on her side already. "And I'm passionate about myself, about the way I look. I love my brown hair. I am so done with blondes." And right to the brown-haired woman: "We may be the only two left."

More smiles.

"And style. That's a real passion with me. I think I could have been a designer, but you have to get up too early in the morning for that. I hate early mornings. I love clothes, I could shop all day and I'm very good at it, but I can't start before eleven. And jewelry. Love it. But it has to be real, obviously. And gossip. Sitting around with my girlfriends and dissecting everybody's lives; what could be better? I see it as kind of like group therapy, only meaner. But it's totally honest, so it can be really helpful when the tears stop.

"Fabulous cars, starting with my Maserati, my beautiful home, gorgeous bling, and every shoe I ever loved. I have a passion for new experiences. And I like risk. Perfection is my god. I'm not interested if it's not perfect. And it's not easy to be perfect for me. And . . ."

"And?" The blond man was completely hooked.

With a look just for him: ". . . and my husband, of course."

"Your husband?"

"Ken Matthews. You've heard of him?"

"The NFL quarterback?"

"The same."

"I thought I read on PearcingBitches.com that you two were separated."

"I tried, but he just wouldn't go away."

The gray-haired man asked what was the craziest thing she'd ever done. And then leaned forward, waiting to inhale every word.

"Are we talking HBO or network?"

"Let's start with HBO."

"Well, I have this really close girlfriend—"

The brown-haired woman interrupted. "Let's keep it more network, huh?"

"No problem. The craziest thing was one time when Ken was in Miami. I don't know, it was some big game."

"The Super Bowl?" Blond guy was hanging on every word.

"That sounds right. Anyway, he wasn't home and it was just me and I was really bored. I mean totally wiped out looking at the same things all the time, the house, the furniture, the pool . . . So I sold it."

"The house?" all three said at once.

"Yeah, I sold the house."

"What did he say when he came home?" The gray hair, the power, was caught.

"What he always says: 'Whatever Baby wants, Baby gets.'"

4

Jessica had been trying to call Elizabeth all morning. She was not answering her cell. She texted her four times and still no word.

Sarah Miller: Caroline Pearce had casually dropped that one on Jessica. She was the "hot" new writer from the *San Diego Union-Tribune* at the *L.A. Tribune* covering Sweet Valley and environs for the business section. According to Caroline, she was looking to hook up with Todd and he had taken her to the last Lakers game.

Jessica knew that Bruce had been there, so he would have to have seen her and he definitely would have told Elizabeth, who never mentioned it to her. Jessica figured Lizzie would have known why she was calling and that was why she wasn't answering.

It was not like Jessica thought Todd should be a monk, but this was so in her face. Couldn't he like find somebody in L.A.?

It was different with Michael Wilson being here in Sweet Valley because he was her boss, and as for Liam O'Connor, well, that's exactly what she meant, he was in L.A.

Of course, she immediately Googled Sarah Miller.

The photo was a newspaper shot, dark and grainy, but she could still see that Sarah was good-looking in a kind of tomboyish way. She had short dark hair, like a guy's long haircut, the kind that looks like you just run your hands through and don't even comb. Her eyes were big, a good shape with long lashes and no makeup. It was hard to tell the color, but they looked dark. Sarah Miller was just about as far away from the Jessica look as you could get. Far enough so that it was practically an insult.

Sarah's background was no big deal, born in Chicago, University of Chicago, and then a master's at Northwestern. Worked on some Chicago papers Jessica had never heard of and then the *San Diego Union-Trib* just before coming here. But the best part, she was thirty-five. That was five years older than Jessica, which meant she was five years older than Todd.

She went through some of her articles and found one on the business of going green. It was a lot about fuel and emissions and even a couple of long paragraphs on makeup.

No new information, actually, really familiar stuff. Stuff she'd read before. Stuff she herself had said in many interviews.

And there were some other articles about the cosmetics industry going green. No new information, but they were weirdly familiar.

In fact, she totally had read the exact same thing before and was trying to think of where. How could that be?

Elizabeth finally texted her back. She was just finishing an interview. TEXT U IN 10.

No way she was going to do this back-and-forth over text. She waited ten minutes and then dialed.

Right off, Jessica said, "So, when were you going to tell me?"

"What?"

"Sarah Miller."

"Oh."

"Oh?"

"I don't know anything except Bruce saw her in the press box at the Lakers game."

"And she was with Todd?"

"He thinks so."

"He *thinks* so?"

"Okay, he knows. I heard it at the paper, too. It's no big deal, it's just a rumor. Besides . . ."

"What else?"

"Nothing."

"Okay, I'm hanging up." And she did. So like ten seconds later, Elizabeth texted her back: WANNA TALK?

Jessica texted her that she was done, then shoved the phone in her desk drawer and slammed it shut.

She hardly got any work done for the rest of the day, and at about four, she picked up her laptop, grabbed the phone and her bag, and left. Katy, her assistant, asked if anything was wrong. Jessica said no and shot past her.

Like she did when she was really upset, she drove to the beach and took a long walk, all the while playing scenarios in her head of running into Sarah Miller with Todd. She rehearsed about twenty different smart comments she could make and then, just when she was getting totally bored, it hit her. Where she saw those paragraphs.

She had to get home and find the first piece. It was a magazine article from some small green magazine from a weird place like Denver or Dallas. They had sent the piece to her because she was on a green mailing list. She'd never heard of the magazine. And hadn't seen it since.

Jake was still out with the nanny when she got home. She spent the next couple of hours searching every green magazine in the West, and there were tons. Green was *the* business today.

She went through everything she could find in Denver and Dallas, but nothing looked familiar. Maybe it was San Antonio; that could be the right place.

And sure enough it was. She recognized the name, *Green with Beauty*. It had to be last year, maybe around the summer because she remembered it dealt with sun creams and summer makeup. And it was more than familiar; it was Jessica's *very own words* from an interview she had given for *The Boston Globe*. Damn!

Just as she started to read the articles, Jake came back from his walk. He was delighted to see his mommy home so early. Naturally she had to stop what she was doing and scoop him up in her arms.

He had a long, involved story in his adorable two-year-old language, which she understood perfectly. It was all about a lost dog in the park and how he wanted to bring it home. He was the sweetest.

Liza, the nanny, stood there looking so proud of her charge. They both agreed he was totally brilliant.

"Is that absolutely amazing or what?" Jessica said. "Wanting to bring a little lost dog home." She was glowing. "Isn't he the best, the kindest little boy?"

"He is. But that wasn't exactly the story."

"What was it?"

"More like he stepped in dog poop."

"Eww!" Jessica held her son out to Liza, who took him, holding him high in the air. It was too late for Jessica. "I'm going to have to change my skirt. Maybe you should have taken off his shoes before . . ." And then she stopped herself. Nannies were very hard to find.

"Sorry," Liza said as she carried Jake into his bedroom for the overdue change.

Jessica dropped her skirt, rolled it up, and dumped it in the laundry room. She had to get back to those articles.

She found the interview she had given two years ago to a writer from the Boston paper who was most definitely not Sarah Miller. The first part wasn't interesting, but when it got to makeup, it knocked her out.

It was word for word what Sarah Miller had written in the *Tribune* just last week. Word-for-word Jessica Wakefield but under the Sarah Miller byline, with no quotes. Hey, you didn't have to be a journalist to know plagiarism when you saw it. And she was totally seeing it now.

She was stealing Jessica's words and her husband!

Jessica texted Elizabeth that she had to get there now.

Of course, Elizabeth texted her right back: WHAT'S WRONG?

NOTHING. I JUST HAVE TO SHOW YOU SOMETHING YOU'RE GOING TO WANT TO SEE.

They did the whole tell-me-no-I-gotta-show-you, and then finally Elizabeth texted: OKAY.

Elizabeth was shocked. Plagiarism was a real no-no. Once she saw that article, they started going through all of Miller's stuff and found another quote Jessica had given in an interview last year for the *Morning Star,* a local paper in Billings, Montana. Not only did Sarah use her words, but again she used them without credit.

"She's out of control," Elizabeth said.

"So what are you going to do?" Jessica asked.

"Me? Why is this on me?"

"Because it's your paper. You're the journalist."

"Maybe you should say something to Todd."

"Are you nuts? Coming from me? That's beautiful."

"Okay, bad idea. First I should check and see if this is a habit or if she just forgot to give credit."

"How?"

"I just run it through LexisNexis and you get instant feedback."

"Do it now."

"Stop drooling," she said, and took Jessica's laptop and ran Miller's last few articles through the site.

And like in no time it came back. Positive. "This bitch has a bad habit," Jessica said.

"Yeah, but I can't do this," Elizabeth said.

"What if I send them anonymously to the editor?"

"They won't open anonymous e-mails. I suppose I could say something to Sarah. Give her a chance to defend herself, but actually, it's too many times to defend."

They went back and forth about who should do it, and then Jessica said, "Hey, look, I'm the green professional. She's in my field. And in fact, some of them are my own words. It's only natural for me to, you know, like . . ."

"Turn her in?"

"Yeah, turn her in."

Jessica sent copies of Sarah Miller's plagiarized pieces along with the original works to Walt Tyndale, the managing editor of the paper. And she sent them under her own name. That was two weeks ago, and she'd just heard today, from Caroline, of course, that Miller had been fired.

Now Jessica knew it was only a matter of time before Todd came charging into the house.

In fact, his Audi had just pulled up in front. It was like déjà vu. Just like that other time, more than three years ago, when she was waiting at this very same window for Regan, her furious ex-husband, to come. Then, Todd was her protector. Now the tables were turned and she thought she could use Regan. Luckily, Jake was out with Liza.

She opened the door before he could burst through, but he managed to burst through anyway; he was livid.

"Before you say anything"—she held up her hand to stop him—"I want you to know that yes, I did Google her. I think it's only right to want to know who might be hanging out with your child. I only accidentally found the plagiarism."

"Did you know she got fired?"

They were about to be in the full heat of an argument, and it wasn't even about them. Todd's anger was frightening, not that she was physically afraid of him. Never! But just seeing the passion that this woman had stirred up in him scared her. It meant she might really be losing him. Dumb to say about someone you're separated from. And she had wanted that separation, too.

Still, all along she was thinking neither of them had really made up their minds. But maybe she was wrong. Maybe this Sarah Miller person was what was going to finish them.

"No, I didn't know she was fired," she lied. "I just thought they'd give her a warning or something."

"Bullshit! You just wanted to get her out of the way because you knew I was seeing her."

Suddenly he stopped and looked around. "Where's Jake?"

"Out with Liza."

Now he could go full steam.

And he did. "You're conniving and devious and you always were. I should have known—"

"I am not. And what does that mean, anyway, you 'should have known'?"

"That accidental thing that happened all those years ago at the party when you pretended to be Elizabeth. You planned it, didn't you?"

"How could you say that? That destroys everything about us."

"Maybe everything about us was a fraud, all set up by you."

"And you were totally innocent, right?"

"How could you do this to Sarah, a person who never did anything bad to you?"

"Answer me! You were innocent, right! It was all my fault. I seduced you! There was no love, it was all sex."

"I don't want to talk about that."

"Is this what you've been thinking all this time? That you got tricked?"

"This is not about us. This is about ruining a person's career out of jealousy. And obviously, since career is the most important thing in your life, you knew how it would destroy her. Only you could do something as rotten as this."

"First of all, I am *so* not jealous. Second, cry me a river for Sarah Miller, a plagiarist criminal who got caught. You want to fuck that bitch? Go ahead, who cares!"

"You're the bitch! And I'll fuck whomever I please."

"And I will, too!"

"Good luck to that poor sucker!"

That was his exit line. He spun around and charged out of the house.

All she could do was to whisper after him, "I hate you!"

Even in their worst fights, he'd never said anything like that before, accusing her of tricking him, that everything about their love was her manipulation.

Now she knew it was really over. He'd killed it. Maybe she was dumb to think that there was something left; that a love like theirs that had survived such awful obstacles was somehow indestructible and in some way they would put it back together.

And now she couldn't tell the one person in the world she needed to tell. She was desperate for Elizabeth's comfort from those terrible accusations. But it would be more than horrendous if Elizabeth ever found out the truth of how Todd and Jessica had started. Instead, Jessica had always left out the lurid details and allowed Elizabeth to think it had been some kind of hidden attraction they'd had for each other.

He thought she'd tricked him. It wasn't true. It wasn't a plan. It had just happened. Or had it?

Her heart was broken.

6

Todd headed straight for Sarah Miller's studio apartment.

It was obvious from her swollen red eyes that she had been crying. Combine that with her petite body and attractive boyish looks, then add her freckled face, sans makeup and streaked with tears, and she looked heartbreakingly vulnerable.

Sarah threw herself into Todd's arms, and he held her while she sobbed.

"Oh, God," he said. "I'm so sorry. I never thought she could be such a bitch. I don't know what to do. Do you want me to talk to Walt?"

"No, leave it. It's over. Even if he were to forgive the mistake, my reputation here is ruined. Nobody would ever look at my work the same way. And it doesn't matter that it was just one little mistake."

"You're wrong. That could happen to anyone, you just forgot to give credit. Just some stupid quotes, that's all. Did you explain that to him?"

"He wouldn't even listen. Said that subject never has room for any explanation. It's the equivalent of murder in journalism, and if I never ask him for a recommendation, he will never have to mention it. Doesn't matter. Thanks to your wife, everyone knows anyway."

Sarah pulled away from Todd and walked over to the unmade bed. She sank down on the edge and buried her face in her hands, weeping. "Why would she do this to me? I never did anything to her. I don't even know her."

"It's because of me," Todd said, sitting down next to her, taking her in his arms and holding her gently against his chest. He kissed the top of her head tenderly, the way you do to comfort a child.

"But you said it was over. Everyone says she's seeing other guys. Why does she care like that?"

"Because she's jealous and selfish. It's not enough that she doesn't want me, nobody else can have me, either."

"But to ruin my life for just one simple mistake . . ."

"That's who she is. I knew it for years, but I just got blinded. My own stupid-ass fault." He held Sarah closer. "I don't know what to say. It's my fault. I fucked up your life and I'm so sorry. What can I do?"

Sarah moved deeper into his arms. "Just hold me," she said, sliding her arms around him and turning her face up to his. Tearful as she was, her lips softened and opened slightly, erasing all traces of anything boyish, leaving only the fullness of woman.

Todd leaned down, touching his lips lightly to hers, and she became alive. Her whole body responded, wiping out any hurt and anguish, leaving only heat and longing.

And the vehemence that Todd felt was released in passion, and he pressed his mouth to hers, hard with anger and need. Four months of need.

And the sting of revenge.

But Sarah was aware only of how much she wanted this guy. And the response she felt from him, the body heat and the deep breaths, was all she needed to tell her that he wanted her, too.

He pushed her down on the bed as she pulled off her T-shirt and shoved down her sweats. She saw him registering that she had been naked under her clothes.

She reached up to unbutton his shirt, but he pulled away.

Sensing second thoughts, she began to caress herself, her fingers playing lightly over her small but firm breasts, circling her nipples. With one hand resting on her breast, she moved the other, tracing a line down across her stomach. She watched Todd, who didn't move. Only his eyes were connected to her, watching as she moved her fingers gently over her thighs.

She could hear the speed of his breath and closed her eyes, waiting for his touch.

But the touch didn't come.

Instead, he stood up and mumbled, "I'm so sorry," rushing out the door before she could even register that he was gone.

7

Jessica couldn't call the one person in the world whom she needed most. Her Lizzie. Instead, she just sat in the living room waiting for Liza to come home with Jake. She desperately needed her baby now.

When the doorbell rang, she knew it wasn't Liza, who had her own key. Maybe . . .

Was it possible that Todd had cooled down and realized that what he had said was cruel and wrong, and he'd come back to apologize? Then she could explain and maybe this was exactly what they both needed to make them really sit down and talk and find a way.

Find a way. They had to find a way . . .

But it wasn't Todd. It was the last person she wanted to see now. Well, maybe not the *last* person, that would be Caroline Pearce, and this was only Lila.

No stopping Lila. She burst in, practically dancing. Actually, she *was* dancing. With her newly dyed hair flying, she was spinning and whirling around the room. And all this on seven-inch heels.

"I got it! I got it! They want me. Look at me! I'm a True Housewife!"

Which is about the closest Lila would ever come to being any kind of housewife.

Even though Jessica was totally miserable and disheartened *and* felt like shit, she put on a brave face for her friend.

"That's amazing! Awesome! Tell me everything."

"Well, they called me about an hour ago, and I was like, what kind of stupid excuse are they going to give me for why I'm not a True Housewife, which is totally wrong because I am the perfect housewife. And then she says, 'We want you,' and I freaked. And Ken wasn't even home and I couldn't find him anywhere and I texted you but you didn't answer, so I'm here. Is this incredible or what?"

Actually, it was so not incredible. "I knew it." And she sort of did. Lila *was* absolutely perfect. "So when is it going to happen?"

"Right away, practically. They're going to do a test day tomorrow at the house with me and Ken and a couple of the girls from the cast. Can you believe this?"

"Are you really okay with everybody seeing inside your life like that?"

All she could think was how she would hate anybody seeing what just happened with Todd. She was never as private as Elizabeth, but still, the thought of millions of people judging her and gossiping about the two of them was horrendous. She would hate it.

And then she began to think about what they'd said at the end about sleeping with other people. Jessica hadn't and was almost positive that Todd hadn't, either.

Yet.

Lila was going on about how fabulous her new life was going to be, and even though Jessica heard her, the words just slid off her mind, unregistered. All she could think of was Todd making love to that lying, cheating, plagiarizing bitch.

Elizabeth was in the shower when Bruce poked his head into the bathroom.

"Missy is on the phone. She wants to go over tables with you."

"Ugh!"

"I heard you. And stop rolling your eyes."

"You cannot possibly see my eyes."

"Still. Stop rolling them. She's only trying to be friendly."

Bruce was smart enough to close the door before Elizabeth gave him her real opinion of Missy LeGrange for the umpteenth time. This was the running disagreement. Missy was an impossible snob. Bruce knew it, but he was stuck between a rock and a hard place. The rock was that his family, and hers, had been members of the Harrison Club for ninety years.

The founders, including Bruce and Missy's ancestors, all had lineage that went back to William Henry Harrison, the ninth president of the United States. Bruce never even mentioned it, but Missy never stopped talking about Harrison like he was her favorite uncle. The fact that he served only one month in office didn't shut her up.

The Patmans and the LeGranges were as close as family starting with their great-grandparents, so Bruce had known Missy all his life.

When Bruce's parents died, Thomas LeGrange, Missy's father, was the executor of the Patman estate. Even now Bruce still felt an allegiance and an affection for the LeGranges.

In fact, the families, his parents included, had been hoping for a stronger alliance than just friendship when the kids were teenagers, and then later when Missy came back from her years in boarding school and college in the East. Except by the time she returned, Elizabeth had come along. But it hadn't sunk into Missy's head yet. And her family? Forget it. They thought if they pretended Elizabeth wasn't there, maybe she wouldn't be. Yeah, right.

So yes, she was rolling her eyes.

Bruce poked his head in again. "Should I say you'll call her back?"

She loved Bruce and she couldn't be mean to him. "Yes. Give me half an hour."

He closed the door as she stepped out of the shower, grabbed the towel, and wrapped it around her waist, but not before Bruce, fully dressed, stepped back into the steamy bathroom and unwrapped her.

"I told her an hour."

"This steam is going to wilt you."

"Not really," he said, sliding off his jacket, flinging it over the vanity, and gently releasing her towel. "Not wilted at all."

⌒

"Your phone is ringing," Elizabeth whispered into his ear.

"Let it."

"It's the third time. Maybe it's important."

"Okay. Don't move," he said, grabbing a towel and slipping into the bedroom.

Elizabeth looked in the foggy mirror. Her hair was still dripping and now beginning to curl. Should she blow dry it or just wear it loose and kind of curly? Those were her thoughts until she heard Bruce's shout: "That's a goddamn lie!"

She cracked the door and poked her head out. Bruce was standing in the middle of the room, naked but for the towel around his waist. She could see he was furious.

"What's wrong?" she whispered.

He made a *hold on* sign and then in a quieter voice said, "Call Ben. Tell him to get here now."

He listened for a moment and then, in a very uncharacteristic non-Bruce manner, said, "I don't give a shit. I want him here now!" And slammed the phone shut and sat down hard on the bed.

Elizabeth opened the bathroom door. "Who was that?"

"Dean, my PA."

"What happened?" By now Elizabeth had grabbed her robe and was beside him.

"I don't know. I only have a piece of the story. Some intern . . ."

"Oh, no . . ."

"Yes. This girl is saying that I forced sex on her. I don't even know who the hell she is. It's crazy."

"Where is she?"

"They don't know. They didn't get it from the girl. From what Dean said, it was from her priest."

He switched on the TV and there it was. *"Bruce Patman, billionaire head of the esteemed Patman Foundation and the Patman Social Impact Group, was accused today of sexual assault of an intern working for his foundation this past summer. The alleged attack happened at the Charm Bar in downtown Sweet Valley. The accusation came to light through the young woman's priest. Ben Bookman, Patman's attorney, immediately denied the allegations."*

Elizabeth turned off the TV.

"It's a lie." Bruce looked right at Elizabeth, his face stricken. "Never happened. I swear."

"This is crazy."

"I don't even know who this girl could be. I can barely remember any of the interns this summer. They each work for two weeks and then there's another one. They just come and go. All I do is go down there and say hello and give them a little introductory speech."

"Was there one you had contact with?"

"Let me just set this straight. Yeah, I talk to some of them, a couple I've helped or had the office do whatever for them, but nothing more. Never anything where I met them privately. This is just a wild accusation that has no basis. I'm almost not worried because it's got no possibility. It's just a disturbed young woman making something out of thin air. That's what they'll find. She's mental."

"Maybe, but it comes from her priest. That's not good."

"So she lied to him."

"I'm going to go down to the paper and find out who's covering the story and what they have. And how come a priest is revealing a confession."

"Ben is coming. Don't you want to wait and see what he has to say?"

"I can find out more on my own."

"Liz . . ." Bruce stood up and walked over to her. There was no way to hide his despair. And there was only one question and he couldn't ask it.

But Elizabeth answered anyway. "You don't have to say anything more. I believe you."

He closed his eyes and let out a deep breath in relief. She went to him and put her arms around him. He just stood there, arms at his sides, in shock.

There was a second question, which neither of them wanted to ask, but it had to be asked.

It was the hated good-wife question: *Will you stand by me?* Despite the fact that they weren't married, they were, after all, partners, having lived together for the past three years.

Bruce hit it first and even smiled. "I can just see you doing the good-wife face. It's a snap—you just pretend you got a bad oyster. And it happens to be standing right next to you."

"How about if I winked?"

"Or gave one of those *yeah, sure* faces?"

More seriously, she said, "You know if you needed me . . ."

"No way. If I needed you there, then I really wouldn't let you do it."

"If I'm all over TV, that would be the end of any investigation I could do. And I know you won't agree, but I swear this smells like Warner to me."

Elizabeth threw on her jeans and sweatshirt. The hair would stay curly. In less than five minutes, she was ready to go.

He was still standing frozen in the middle of the room, looking miserable.

"Should I wait with you?"

He seemed to come to at the sound of her voice. "No, it's okay. Go see what you can dig up."

Just as Elizabeth turned to leave, her phone vibrated. It was a text from Jessica.

NEED U. NEED U. MY HOUSE. NOW. PLS NO PHONE.

"It's Jess. She wants to see me right away. Says not to call. She must have some information. I'll stop there first."

"Okay, call me."

Elizabeth left the bedroom, but when she turned to close the door, she saw Bruce as she hadn't seen him since that terrible time in the hospital when his parents died.

She didn't consider for an instant the possibility of his guilt. She was sure that there was only one guilty person in this farce—and that was Rick Warner.

And she would find the proof and expose him for the corrupt, vicious bastard he was.

It seemed like Jessica was always at the same stupid window waiting for something enormous to happen in her life. Now she was waiting for Liz like she was going to save her. Well, she usually did, but this was beyond even her magic.

There was a paint splotch she remembered seeing three years ago when she was sitting there waiting for her ex-husband, Regan. She remembered thinking how easily she could scrape it off with a kitchen knife. But it was still there like a lot of other things she had planned to fix in the apartment but she'd got distracted with Jake and her work and hadn't. Was this a sign that she wasn't fully committed to her life with Todd?

She decided she was going to do it right now. She got a sharp nonserrated knife from the kitchen drawer, and just when she was about to start, the doorbell rang. It was an Elizabeth ring, short and light. And so sweet and undemanding. *I love her,* she thought.

She opened the door and Elizabeth jerked back, her eyes practically popping out of her head.

"Oh, my God!"

"What?" Jessica said.

"The knife!"

Of course, she was standing there with this four-inch knife hanging from her hand. "Oh, sorry. I totally forgot I had it."

"Um, *why* do you have it? What's going on?"

And she explained about the paint splotch on the windowsill. Elizabeth still looked quizzical, so Jessica showed her. "What did you think?"

"I don't know. I get these frantic texts and I rush here and you're standing there with a knife. Naturally, I'm not thinking paint splotches. So it's not about Bruce?"

"No. It's about Todd. We had this horrendous blowup and he said the most horrible things."

"Like what?"

No way Jessica could tell her what he said about how they started their affair, so she went straight into the Sarah thing.

"Like he said I lied about Sarah Miller and purposely did it to stop him from hooking up with her. And how I apparently ruined her life and that I'm such a bitch and blah blah blah. That's when I lost it and said something like if you're so crazy about her, why don't you sleep with her. Not exactly sleep with her, more like—"

"I get it."

"He said I'll sleep with whoever I want, and I freaked out and shouted back how I would, too. And please don't say, 'Well, you *are* separated.'"

"I wasn't going to say that. I know it sounds dumb, but I never felt like this was a real separation. To me it was like if one of you just backed down and said the right words, I knew you would both—"

"Well, no one did, and now it's really going to be over. He's going to sleep with that bitch just to spite me. And then I'll get back at him and it will just be totally finished."

"Then you have to end this craziness right now. Call him. Sit down with him and talk it out. Make it a nonstop negotiation where nobody leaves until you work it out."

"I can't."

"Why not? You love him, don't you?"

"Yes, but . . ."

"But what?"

"From the things he said, I could tell it won't work. He doesn't love me. He blames me for everything. If he does sleep with her . . ." She couldn't go on.

"And then you sleep with someone?"

"It's just different for a man."

"Like you can handle it and he can't?"

"Yes."

"That's crazy."

"But it isn't. Men fall in love, at least they think they do. Everyone thinks it's just the opposite, but they're wrong. Like I could sleep with Liam and it wouldn't make any difference. I'm never going to fall in love with him. But I can just see what will happen with Todd. Because of what he thinks I did to Sarah's life, he's going to feel somehow responsible for her, which brings out his macho-hero-protector side, and from there it's not a big step to thinking it's love and . . ."

"Wild theory, Jess, something I really don't have time for now."

"What's wrong? Oh, God, Bruce! Oh, I'm so sorry, Lizzie. You said something about him and I just went into my own thing. Is he okay? What's wrong?"

"Obviously you haven't turned on your television."

"What are you talking about?"

"Bruce. He's been accused of forcing sex on an intern."

"That's crazy! He should deny it."

"Not so easy. People have seen that story so many times and it always turns out they're guilty."

An instant change came over Jessica. Elizabeth, unaccustomed to seeing Jessica at work, was transfixed by the change from grieving wife to professional image maker taking charge.

"Okay, what's he done so far?"

"What do you mean? He just found out. He was waiting for Ben. Meanwhile, I'm going down to the paper to see who's covering it and what I can find out."

"Okay, but we can't lose a minute. I'm going over to your place right now."

"What are you talking about?"

"Crisis intervention. That's what it's all about now. Remember Amanda Knox? PR. That's what saved her."

Jessica grabbed her jacket and laptop and stopped. "What do you think? Bad jacket?"

"Who cares! Just go!" Elizabeth said, opening the front door. As she did, Liza and Jake came bursting into the house. Jake had a string with three giant balloons that were practically lifting him off the floor.

"Look, Mommy!"

And then there was that momentary confusion as he looked from Elizabeth to Jessica, which was always amusing and would have been now if they weren't both so crazed.

Jessica picked up Jake for a giant hug. And for Liza, a stream of instructions and that she'd be back by nine.

Elizabeth gave Jake a kiss and a squeeze, and she and Jessica were out the door.

"Mommy, I'm gonna fly! Call Daddy, tell him!"

"I will, sugar, I will!" she called back as she rushed to her car. If only she could tell Daddy.

And to Elizabeth: "Text me if you get anything."

10

Jessica made the twenty-minute trip to Bruce's house in her usual twelve minutes, since there was no one sitting next to her complaining about her driving.

Bruce was in his study with Ben Bookman, his attorney, when she came in.

"Liz left already," he said when he saw her. "Do you have any new information?"

"No."

"Then why are you here?"

"Are you kidding? To save you."

"Thanks, but it's going to take more than green makeup to save me."

"You are so right. Crisis management is what you need. Just close your eyes and pretend you're Amanda Knox and leave the rest to me."

"Jess, I'm not in the mood."

"I'm not kidding. This is my specialty. Making people love what I want them to love. In this case it's going to be you. Have you issued a statement yet?"

Bruce wasn't used to this take-charge working Jessica, but he was so devastated by what had happened he was almost punch-drunk, ready to follow anyone, even his nutty, putative sister-in-law.

"No, I haven't said anything yet. I don't even know what they're talking about. This intern said I picked her up in a bar and tried to force her to have sex with me."

"It's good you didn't say anything yet. The first announcement is the one that counts. Everything else comes off that. If that one's no good, you turn into a political hack dribbling out pieces and then changing them. We have to prepare your statement."

"I was just working on that with Bruce," Ben said. This was so outside his normal law practice he was grateful for any help he could get. But Jessica was in her métier and she was good. Now she even had Bruce's full attention. It wasn't the Jessica he was used to, but he was desperate and she seemed to know what she was doing. She was a professional.

"I have to hear the story from the beginning. Every detail."

"Should I go?" Ben asked.

"No," Jessica said. She could see that he was impressed with her. And besides, he was cuter than she remembered. "We need you."

The three of them sat down and Jessica opened her laptop and began taking notes.

"Do you know who this intern is?"

"No. That's what's so weird."

"You mean you never were in a bar with any intern?"

"If this is the incident at Charm in July, there was no intern."

"But there was an incident?"

Jessica realized that this was going to be harder than she'd expected. After all, her sister was in love with this man and she was maybe going to find out things she didn't want to know.

"There was no intern. I had a meeting with Alan Bloom in the Charm at around six that night. I remember it clearly because I had just sat down when the bartender accidentally spilled some gooey pink drink on me. It got all over my jacket. He apologized profusely and told me there was an attendant in the men's room with some cleaning fluid who could get it off before it stained permanently.

"I told him that if someone named Alan came looking for Bruce, please tell him I'll be right back, and I went to the men's room, which if I remember correctly, was down a corridor on the far side of the bar.

"There was no attendant, so I just cleaned it up the best I could. When I came out, there was this girl standing outside the ladies' room, sobbing. I asked if I could help. All she would say was she was scared. I said for her to come sit down and tell me what was wrong. I walked her back into the bar and she sat down and I bought her a Coke, I think it was a Coke. I know I had a Perrier because the bartender said at least that wouldn't stain.

"And then she told me this nightmare story about how her father had been abusing her. I asked how long that had been going on, but she clammed up, too embarrassed to tell me. The thing was, she was scared to go home because he was angry at her for forgetting to . . . I can't remember what it was that she didn't do, but she was really frightened."

"Back up a little. Was the meeting with Alan set up by e-mail or text?" Ben asked. "It would be good to dig that up."

"Neither one. He sent me a note. Just the fact that he didn't e-mail me made me think it was serious and very private."

"Not good, but Alan can corroborate," Jessica said. "Then what happened?"

"Actually, I offered to get her in touch with you, Ben, but she didn't want that. Then I suggested a women's shelter. Said I would call, but she said she would do it herself. She found the number and called."

"On your phone?"

"I don't think so. I think she did it on her own phone. Here's where it gets a little complicated."

Jessica dreaded that complication. It could only be compromising.

"Go on," she said, trying not to sound as cold as she felt.

"That's just it. I really can't."

"What do you mean?" Ben asked.

"I wasn't feeling well. Something from lunch didn't agree with me. I felt sick to my stomach and dizzy like I had to lie down. I think the bartender walked me into some empty office with a couch. The next thing I knew it was after nine and I was feeling better, so I got up and went home."

"That was it. You didn't see anyone? The girl was gone?"

"Actually, I did thank the bartender for helping me and asked about the girl. He said she left. That's all he knew."

"How much of this did you tell Lizzie?"

"Nothing, really. She wasn't home when I got there. I still wasn't feeling great, so I went right to bed and slept through the night."

"Hold on," said Jessica. "Let me e-mail this stuff to Lizzie so she's got something to work with."

She copied her notes to her e-mail and sent them off to Elizabeth.

"Did you tell Elizabeth in the morning what happened?" Ben asked.

"It was one of those mornings where she was rushing like mad for an interview in L.A. or someplace and all I said was that I thought I'd had food poisoning last night, but I was okay now. That's all we had time for, and then she was gone."

"What about Alan?"

"I stopped by his office that morning and asked if everything was okay. He said absolutely and I figured he'd changed his mind about talking to me. I thought it was a little strange that he didn't show up and didn't apologize, but maybe he was too embarrassed. Whatever, I let it go."

"Did you tell Lizzie about Alan or anything?"

"I don't think so. I was going straight from work to a benefit dinner, I think it was the American Theatre Wing, but I can check that. Anyway, I knew Liz wouldn't be home until late. The thing with the girl was sad but short. I figured I'd tell her later. I don't know if I ever did. It wasn't a big deal, and I didn't want to come off making myself sound like some kind of hero. You just help somebody and that's it."

"I should text Lizzie Alan's name so she can get in touch with him." Jessica took out her phone.

"Wait a minute. Maybe he doesn't have to be involved. Obviously, it was something very sensitive . . ."

"You're going to need him to corroborate the meeting," Ben said.

"Maybe it's not going to go that far."

"It will," Jessica said, and Bruce had that sick feeling in his stomach because he knew she was right.

"Can you describe the girl?" Jessica asked.

"Young, maybe about twenty or so. Blond, pretty, petite. I don't really remember anything special about her."

"Do you know who she was waiting for or why she was in the bar?" Jessica asked.

"No, and I don't remember asking. All I knew was that she was terrified and I wanted to help her."

"Okay, we'll have to refine that, but first two things: I have to set up a Web site for you, and I'm going to need people, mostly women, for character witnesses. They should be celebrities, the right kind. Like Susan Sarandon or Angelina Jolie, you know, women's activist types. Do you know any?"

Bruce put his head in his hands and just sat like that for a moment, then looked up hopelessly. "God, this is a nightmare."

"I know, but I need some names. We have to come in fast with this before cable news brings in those talking heads who don't like you anyway. Come on, think. I need a list."

In the next twenty minutes, they came up with a list of fifteen real possibilities. The phone never stopped ringing. But no one picked it up.

Jessica texted the names to Katy at the office and asked her to find their contacts.

Ben left to go back to his office, and Jessica stayed with Bruce while he went over what in PR-speak is called the "essentials," a kind of relentless cross-examination of the events with as many details as he could remember.

Jessica loved the way she was handling this. Like how many times do you get to use your talent to save someone's life? Well, reputation anyway.

Actually, she was using that same idea bank in her head she depended on for her makeup promotions. Except nobody was going to be naked. She hoped.

Since the *Tribune* was a morning paper, the city room was quiet now. It was only a bureau anyway. The main office was in L.A., so there were never more than fifteen or so people there at any one time.

By the time Elizabeth got to her desk, her e-mail from Jessica was on her computer and her text about Alan Bloom was on her phone. She immediately called him. He wasn't at the office, but she tracked him down at home. He had heard the news about Bruce and was very upset.

"There's no way this is Bruce. She must be some kind of nut. We get a lot of interns and though we ask for recommendations, sometimes you get a lemon."

"He really didn't want to bring you into this, but I told him there was no choice."

"Are you kidding? I'd do anything for that guy. He's great."

"Good, because it was all supposed to have happened on the night you were meeting him at that bar, Charm."

"When would that have been?"

"Sometime in July."

"Offhand I don't remember that meeting, but I can look it up in my e-mail."

"It won't be in your e-mail. It was private, so you sent him a note."

"A note? You sure it was from me?"

There was a silence on the phone. It lasted an uncomfortably long few seconds, and then Elizabeth said, "Look, I don't have to know the reason, just that you planned to meet and what time and why you didn't show."

"Actually, I don't remember, but I can look it up in my diary . . ."

"Alan, this is important. You must remember."

"Can I get back to you?"

"Are you saying there was no meeting?"

"Oh, shit."

"I have to know before someone else does."

"I would remember sending a note. And I would never make an appointment with Bruce and not show."

"That's okay, Alan. Let me get back to you later."

Elizabeth hung up and with a sinking feeling texted Jessica and Bruce: ALAN NEVER SET UP ANY MEETING.

An instant later her phone rang. It was Bruce.

"Of course he did. This is getting even crazier. I remember the note 'cause it was weird that he didn't e-mail."

"It's okay. Let me talk to Andy Marker. He's the reporter covering the story. He'll be back in few minutes. Did you talk to anyone yet?"

"You mean the press? No. We haven't answered the phone. Here, talk to Jessica."

He handed the phone to Jessica. "We're still putting things together. I need more information. Can you try to find that priest and the bartender?"

"I'll try right after I see what Andy's got. Actually, I see him now. Talk to you later."

Elizabeth closed her phone and called out to Andy across the city room. He saw her and made his way over to her desk.

"I don't know, Liz, this is bad. And it's weird talking to you about the guy you're living with."

"Give me a break, Andy. Look, he's innocent, I know it, but that's not going to matter when it goes viral and we have no counterattack. He'll be destroyed, that's all. I can't watch that without doing everything I can. I mean, I love this guy. Please help me."

"Sure, Liz, but it doesn't look good. They're not telling anyone who the girl is, just that she was one of the summer interns. The cops took the July list, but I asked around and found a couple of interns who worked there in August. Everybody likes Bruce and they want to help."

"Can you give me their names so I can talk to them? And what about the bartender, anyone talk to him yet?"

"Not yet."

"And the priest?"

"Nobody's giving that out, but I lucked into it through a friend. It's Father Riley over at All Saints on Highland Avenue in Sherman Oaks. But it's almost impossible to get to him."

"Thanks, Andy, I really appreciate this."

"Good luck."

Elizabeth texted Bruce that she was going to try to find the bartender. She grabbed her laptop and left the office.

There were only a few people at their desks, and they watched her leave, silently. They were on her side, but everyone knew from experience that generally these things turn out to be just as bad as they look.

With time out for a few frantic phone calls about the concert with naked green people, Jessica helped Bruce put together a statement for the press and his Web site. It was simple: He denied everything as vicious lies, said his people were looking into the accusations, and as soon as they found the real story, he would answer all questions.

"Try not to look sexy. Give them a serious but friendly face." Jessica did her serious-friendly imitation that still looked sexy. "Try it."

"Jess, please, enough. All I can be is me."

It was after seven in the evening when Jessica left to go home to try to set up the celebrities who would attest to Bruce's character. Turned out that even people Katy hadn't asked, when they found out, had called and offered their help.

The Bruce crisis had nearly wiped out the Todd mess, but as soon as Jessica stepped into her house, all the misery flooded back. She wondered if Todd had called about Bruce or anything.

But he hadn't. Jake was asleep, and she paid Liza and let her go. She would be home all evening trying to line up people willing to go on TV or the Web to speak up for Bruce. Katy had e-mailed her all their private numbers.

What if he really did it?

No way. Jessica didn't waver. The Bruce she knew today would never do that, never force himself on a woman. And besides, he really did love her sister. He had waited for her for years, like practically biblically, and wouldn't screw it up now.

But this was just Jessica's intuition. Elizabeth would have to find out the facts because other people were always ready to believe the worst. Her job was to make them believe the best, no matter what.

She grabbed a cup of coffee and started dialing.

11

The Charm Bar was crowded with after-work people who didn't want to go home.

Elizabeth identified herself as a reporter from the *L.A. Tribune* covering the Bruce Patman story and asked for the bartender who had been there that night.

"That's Jackson. He doesn't work here anymore."

Elizabeth's investigative antennae shot up. If it really was a Rick Warner setup—and she prayed it was—the disappearing bartender would fit right in.

"And you probably don't know where he is now?"

"Actually, I do. He's over at Friday's on Riverhead."

That wasn't what she was expecting, or hoping for. She thanked him and headed over to Friday's.

She found Jackson working the bar, and he was very forthcoming. Maybe too forthcoming.

"Hi, I'm Liz from the *L.A. Trib,* could I ask you some questions?" she said, purposely giving only her sobriquet. Sweet Valley was a small town, and Bruce was a big guy, which made her a little too well known.

"I've been expecting you guys. Boy, that's some story, isn't it?"

"Can you tell me from the beginning whatever you remember about that night?"

"Sure. I remember a lot because I recognized Patman and I'd always thought he was a good guy."

"From the beginning, please. He was waiting at the bar for someone? Right? Do you remember if he was drinking?"

"Yeah, he was. I remember because he had Johnny Walker neat, like the Europeans. And he had a few. If he was waiting for someone, I wouldn't know that."

"Then what?" Despite the heavy air-conditioning, Elizabeth was beginning to feel very warm. Johnny Walker neat was Bruce's drink.

"Then this young girl sits down a few seats away . . ."

"Yeah . . ."

"And he begins working on her."

"What do you mean?"

"Trying to pick her up. But she wasn't too hot on him. Guess she didn't know what a big shot he was. And rich, too."

Maybe it was a mistake for Elizabeth to do this, but she felt she had to, for Bruce. And for herself. But it didn't stop her stomach from dropping.

"Go on."

"Like I said, she wasn't responding like he wanted. In fact, he looked a little annoyed. Tried to buy her a drink, but she didn't take him up on it. Next time I looked, she wasn't there. I figured she'd had enough and left, but her jacket was still there so she must have gone to the ladies'."

"You have a good memory."

"Yeah, well, when you see a big shot like Patman getting turned down, you remember it."

"What happened then?" For no reason, she hated this man. Something about him was ugly. Or maybe it was just what he was saying. Or maybe the ugly was Bruce. No. She could never believe that.

"He got up and headed in the direction of the restrooms. I wasn't really watching, but the next thing I see is the girl comes back and she looks really upset, like maybe she's been crying, and she grabs her jacket and leaves. More like runs out."

"And Patman?"

"Never saw him again. Until the pictures today all over the TV. Anything else?"

"Not right now. And thanks." Elizabeth couldn't get out of there fast enough.

Nothing matched. Not the story and not Bruce himself. No way. It was like he was talking about someone else. Someone she didn't know at all.

The bartender had to be lying. But why? Right now she had to find that priest. But there was no way she was going to find him at this hour. Her best bet was to wait until tomorrow and catch him at church.

The priest would give her the real story.

12

Meanwhile, way earlier that same day, at six o'clock in the morning, when Bruce's world was just about to collapse, the first *True Housewives* cameras were rolling into the Matthewses' villa, carving deep wheel tracks in the Persian rugs. They were followed by two more cameras and a lighting bank. One of the extension poles for the lights had knocked off a lampshade and rammed it into a Brancusi sculpture, ripping the shade beyond repair. A moment later an overweight cameraman had managed to spill his coffee on a yellow satin Regency armchair. No one said a word.

All this was a small price to pay for being on nationwide television, or so thought Lila Fowler Matthews, who was about to be filmed for the latest *True Housewives* franchise.

Bringing in all the equipment took a good forty-five minutes, and as every new worker came in, he—and it was mostly men—had to stop to talk to Ken Matthews, NFL star. No one looked at Lila, and when the director came in he never even acknowledged her. All he wanted to know was did Ken think they had a chance at the Super Bowl.

Lila was pretty used to the attention Ken got, but now with this series, finally, she would be the star.

By seven thirty more than forty people were in her house setting up lights and cameras, moving furniture around, and in general taking over. By eight o'clock, the three other True Housewives had arrived and the cameras were rolling. Like Lila, the others were all new to the show.

She recognized one of the blondes from the tryouts. She was memorable, too, because of her ample Kim Kardashianesque figure, unusual in True Housewives terms. Other than the blonde, True Housewives rarely hit more than a size-eight dress. Ashley Morgan was no smaller than a twelve but so perfectly proportioned that there was no place to take off even an ounce.

"I'm gonna grab some breakfast in town," Ken said, reaching for his jacket. "See you later."

"Right," Lila said, raising her hand in a half wave but barely looking away from the camera.

"No way." Eric Sander, the director, blocked Ken's way. "We need you."

"Me? What for?"

"Are you kidding? You're the draw. And Lila, pay no attention to the cameras; don't worry, they'll find you."

Lila was not used to being overruled or directed. She quickly turned her face away from the camera to the hall mirror. The reflected image was tight and controlled and very displeased. She said nothing.

But the luscious Ashley Morgan did. "You can't leave now. We haven't even met," she cooed, putting out her perfectly manicured hand not for a shake but for a warm, gentle hold, a hold that lasted long enough for a sexy *I want you* smile to register the promised intimacy intended. Long enough for Lila to get it, too.

Again, she said nothing.

"Nice to meet you," said Ken Matthews, always one of the warmest, friendliest, most unpretentious NFL stars you could ever meet.

"Baby." Lila finally spoke up, still keeping her face from the camera. "I'd love something cold to drink and maybe some of the other guys would, too."

"Sure," Ken said. "I'll get Ida to fix a pitcher of lemonade."

Without another word, he headed into the kitchen to fill the order.

Lila turned to Ashley with a *don't fuck with me* smile.

It bounced right off. Ashley Morgan would need a lot of watching. But Lila wasn't worried; she had her man all wrapped up.

Eric, the director, didn't miss the little exchange. He knew just how useful, with the right encouragement, it could be.

Under the big brother lenses of the cameras, the girls were all formally introduced and a PA led them over to the couch for a little meet-and-greet time.

Immediately, Ashley took the big armchair that had all the earmarks of the house owner's favorite spot. Devone Waters, an African American with a great body and gorgeous brown eyes and a look that said, *This can't be real and what am I doing here?* sat down on the far end of the couch. Marina Delgardo, an Eva Longoria spitfire type took the other end of the couch, leaving Lila the choice between the center of the couch or a little pull-up chair.

She took the chair and positioned it so that it was the focus of the group and, more important, of the camera.

"So nice to have you all here," she started, immediately taking charge. "I know we're going to be like the best friends ever. In fact, I love you all already."

Marina, still in the thrall of delight and pleasure at having been chosen, responded immediately with a blazing white-toothed smile. Devone still looked like *Why in the hell did I decide to say yes to this?* but Ashley's response was the most telling. "I think this is going to be very interesting, don't you?" looking directly at Lila.

Lila returned the look, armed but silent.

"Are you all married?" Marina asked.

"Obviously, I am." Lila managed to do a slight eye roll.

"Me, too," Marina added, and Devone nodded in agreement. They all turned to Ashley.

"Happily divorced from the creep."

"Because?" Lila asked. If this was going to be a no-holds-barred relationship, she'd better start now.

"A creep is a creep even if he's rich. It may not help in the marriage, but it sure does in the divorce."

"Like how much does it help?" Marina was very interested.

Ashley smiled but didn't answer. All she did was hold out her hand with a rock almost as big as her knuckle.

"But I want to know like how was he a creep." Lila was relentless. "Sexually, I take it."

"Are you kidding? That would have been refreshing. No, he was just plain gross."

"Like how?" Now Devone was hooked.

"How about never changes his boxers, which by the way, come down to his knees and are covered in gross holes, doesn't go near soap, thinks dirty nails are a sign of a regular guy, and deodorant is only for gays. And that's only the stuff you see."

"And the stuff you don't see?"

"Ugh." Devone shook her head and shivered, sorry she'd asked. "Don't even tell me."

Marina jumped right in, "Michael changes his underwear, but he likes little pink ones better."

"You're kidding." Devone was shocked. "You mean he wears your underwear?"

"Thongs? No way. Just silky pink full underwear. He buys his in lingerie boutiques and pretends it's for his wife. He says it's the most comfortable and nobody sees it but me."

"So what do you think?"

"At least, like I said, he changes them every day."

"So"—Ashley turned to her hostess—"how in the world did you manage to snare that gorgeous guy?"

"That gorgeous guy had nothing but looks when I married him. Flat broke. And not even playing football. In fact, an all-around loser before I gave him the Lila touch."

"And where exactly was that touch? Let me guess," Marina jumped right in.

"It's not hard. I mean really not hard."

Devone's eyes were spinning. "This is brutal, don't you think? I mean, this guy's your husband."

"That means I can say what I want."

"So can he say whatever he wants about you?"

"I'd like to see him try."

By now the object of the conversation was back with the lemonade and everybody got quiet like it wasn't going to be on the show. But of course, it would be.

Ken and Ida, the housekeeper, were each carrying a tray of frosty glasses.

Ashley was up in a flash, giving the camera a full rear view as she took the tray from Ken. "You can't spoil my picture of my favorite quarterback."

It was hard to tell if Ken was amused or flattered, but Lila went for the latter and quashed it immediately.

"Baby, the guys are waiting for you inside. Help Ida give out the drinks, will you, sweetie?"

Nice as the attention was from Ashley, Lila trumped all. Since the separation that wasn't a separation because he'd never left, Ken was more besotted with Lila than ever.

With Ida in tow, Ken headed into the crowded front of the house where the action was in full steam.

One camera followed.

Lila gave Ashley a *don't even bother trying* look but was surprised when Ashley got up and followed Ken into the other room.

The second camera followed her.

It wouldn't look good for Lila to race after her, so she just kept seated and steamed.

Devone, an occasional freelance writer for local magazines, was beginning to enjoy herself. Maybe this would be more fun than she'd expected. Additionally, she could see at least one good, salable piece for maybe *Star, Us Weekly,* or one of those magazines.

Lila was so furious she could barely concentrate on the conversation and finally had to excuse herself and follow Ashley.

Marina looked at Devone. Both knew they couldn't miss this and headed out after Lila.

When Lila got to the front room, it was just as she expected. Ashley was practically crawling up Ken's arm.

Anticipating interesting action, the second camera turned on Lila with just enough of Ashley and Ken in the background to set the story.

Lila knew this had to be handled delicately. Too much of a response would make her look desperate, but too little would put Ashley off only for the moment. Lila had to show control without looking controlling.

"Sweetie?"

Ken turned immediately on hearing his master's voice, barely noticing that the move made Ashley's hands slip off his arm.

"What's up, Baby?"

Lila gave the adorable little shrug that so nauseated her new friends but thoroughly charmed Ken.

It was a shrug that said *Baby needs you, and if you want to get fucked later, you better come here.*

Ken, always up for Lila, was instantly at her side.

The camera caught everything, even the shrug. And so did Ashley, but she wasn't discouraged. She had faced greater challenges. In fact, she loved a good fight and rarely ever lost.

Eric, ever the director, stepped in.

"Ken, it might be nice if you showed the girls"—despite the fact that there were no girls per se there, he always used that term, though never boys for men—"the house. Go on, Ashley, you can be first."

Lila was smart enough to know that Eric was setting her up and took it in her court. "Go on, sweetie. You can start with our bedroom." A thinly veiled reminder of possibilities to be given or denied.

Ashley was back on Ken's arm as the camera followed them toward the bedrooms.

Meanwhile, the other camera searched Lila's face for a reaction but found none. By now, Lila knew just what Eric's plan was.

And she began to formulate her own.

Under the eye of the camera, Ashley blossomed. She oohed and aahed at every corner of the overdone silk and satin bedroom that had no hint of a male touch. Like their marriage, Ashley guessed.

Ashley saw easy pickings. And she didn't even have to pretend the attraction.

Lila Fowler Matthews understood what was really at stake, and it wasn't her husband. That was a sure thing. The real prize was a solid position on the show, the star of the new *True Housewives of Sweet Valley*. And in order to get that, she had to be the knockout standout. And she wasn't going to get it by being the most beautiful, though she was great-looking, because Devone was perfection. And no one was more spirited and feisty than Marina; she had the firecracker bit all wrapped up. And absolutely top billing for sexiest had to go to Ashley. So what was left? The best of all: the spoiled bitch!

Lila saw herself as basically a good person who was honest enough to admit she might be a tiny bit self-centered. She felt she was a loving friend and pretty honest and kind of generous and more or less faithful. That would all have to go.

There would be no more sweet-as-pie welcome-to-my-home-I-love-you-all stuff, and certainly no more Kenny sweetie, could you get me a whatever. Being a bitch was a full-time job.

Starting right now.

With the camera still waiting for her reaction to the Ashley-Ken house tour, she turned to Marina and said, "No offense, but could you not put that glass down on my Duncan Phyfe table?"

The very surprised and offended Marina, who was still holding the glass and had no intention of putting it down, said, "I would never."

"Whatever," Lila answered as bitchily as she could.

Turning to Eric, Lila said, "Why don't I show the girls around? Ken takes forever to do anything. He's probably still talking Ashley's ear off. And boring her. By now she's dying to be saved."

Without waiting for Eric's answer, Lila led the other two women to the winding staircase.

"Devone, please try not to touch the walls," she said, as if her exquisite coffee color would come off. "They smudge so easily."

Devone, smart as she was, was speechless as she walked up the steps behind Lila, actually careful not to touch the walls.

The camera didn't miss a thing.

"You know, of course, Ashley didn't really leave her husband. He left her," Lila said in the middle of an explanation of how the silk screens that surrounded the eighteenth-century bed were designed and handmade by the Chinese artist Wong Lu, whose work was in the Shanghai Museum. "He was having an affair with the babysitter. In her bed."

For a moment Devone thought she was talking about the artist. "Wong Lu?"

"No," Lila said impatiently. "Ashley's husband, the creep."

"How do you know?"

"Facebook."

Without waiting for their response, Lila led them into the master bedroom, where Ashley was still trying to seduce Ken by way of a million football questions.

"Is he still boring you with his football stories?" Lila asked on entering the room.

"Not at all," said Ashley. "I'm actually fascinated."

"Sweetie, why don't you go fascinate the guys downstairs?"

"Sure. I was just answering some questions."

"Like go, okay?"

Ken looked at her quizzically. Lila could be pushy sometimes, but this was a little much. Still, he figured she was nervous, this being the first day and all, and like always, he only wanted to help her.

"Hope I answered your questions," Ken said to Ashley.

"*Why* are you still here?" Lila said as bitchily as possible.

Ken wasn't the only one surprised. He looked around, shrugged, and left.

"Can he be a pain in the ass or what? It's like sometimes I look at him and think, *I am way done,* but then, he *is* gorgeous. We've been sort of separated on and off forever, but he just never leaves."

The other three looked at each other. Even Ashley was uncomfortable, which was rare. No one said anything, but everyone was thinking, *Doesn't she know she's on camera?*

But of course Lila did know, and it was only fueling her. She turned to Ashley, "Bet your creep isn't as good-looking as my creep."

Devone couldn't hold herself back. "This is all recorded, Lila. I mean, Ken is going to see it."

"Not to worry. I'm Baby and Baby can do no wrong," Lila said, leading the others out of the bedroom for the rest of the tour.

Ashley felt she was doing a good deed giving a little pleasure to this poor, mistreated (and super hot) guy when she took Ken aside and whispered maybe they could meet later someplace where there weren't so many people, like her penthouse.

Unfortunately, Lila was watching for just this possibility. In fact, she practically set it up.

"Excuse me!" said the Star Bitch, pushing herself between the lovers manqué. Though she hadn't heard the words, she had gotten the message. "Excuse me, but are you trying to hook up with my husband?"

Ashley gave it right back to her. "Someone should. Obviously, you don't."

Ken, never known for being quick on the draw, just stood there stunned. He knew Lila could have some lip, but this was too much.

Devone stepped in. "Hey, you guys, this is only the first day. Relax."

"Yeah, right, except it's not your husband, so mind your own business," Lila snapped at her.

"That's not the way it works," Devone said, trying to be reasonable and very aware of the camera. "We're supposed to be a group, like friends. Maybe Ashley was out of line, but still—"

"Out of line propositioning my husband? You think? Should I just wait for her to start screwing him right here?"

Still trying for mediation, Devone said, "I don't know what happened, but it seems like Ashley should either explain or apologize."

But Ashley was not one to fold easily. "You have no clue what happened, so please do not give me advice."

"Sor-*ry*."

"Apology accepted."

"That was not an apology." Devone was not a pushover, either. "You're making us all look totally shitty."

"Kenny, baby, you're excused." Lila pointed to the other room the way you would direct a dog, but fortunately Ken didn't see. He had already turned away and was walking out. Storming out would be closer to it.

"So now what are we supposed to do?" Lila asked Eric.

"I think you might want to try to put this thing together. Devone is right, you're supposed to be a group of friends."

Lila almost laughed. "Like I would ever actually pick these girls for friends?"

"I beg your pardon," said Marina, who had been quietly watching the action but now clearly saw the danger. If they couldn't find some connection, they would all get kicked out.

"You're not exactly my first choice, either, but if this is going to work we have to have some kind of relationship." She directed this to Lila and Ashley.

The idea of not being a True Housewife hit home, and suddenly, with the exception of Lila, they all softened up. But Lila had to keep her Star Bitch position. Every show needed one. She expected some trouble with Ken later, but she could handle that.

Whatever happened, she had to be a True Housewife. She'd been dreaming of this since the show first started. She knew she was made for it. All that drifting around, trying one thing after another and losing interest almost immediately, was over. This was it. And no matter what it cost, she wasn't going to lose it.

⌒

The rest of the day went along with the others trying to be good friends, listening to problems and enjoying each other. With the exception of Lila, who never let down her bitch act. It got to the point where everyone was watching and waiting for her. She *was* the star. And she could feel Eric's pleasure.

Ken had disappeared for the rest of the day, and though Eric tried to find him, he couldn't.

The Housewives were busy gossiping and making plans for a big Happy Divorce party for Ashley when the final papers came through in two weeks.

Just to keep things interesting, Eric suggested they have it at Lila's.

"My pleasure," she said, rolling her eyes.

Never once all day did Lila let down her bitch persona, even at the cost of saying some very nasty things about her marriage. Everyone was riveted to her, waiting for some other awful revelation.

And for the most part, they got it.

⌣

At six that evening, it was a wrap, and Eric offered to show them a few of the early rushes.

Everyone found places on the chairs, the couches, and the floor in the living room to watch.

Even Ken showed up. Discreetly standing in the back.

The rushes started, and Lila, the bitch, was indeed the star. There were even gasps at some of her comments, especially those about her marriage.

Ken disappeared before it was over.

The cameras and lights and all the other equipment were loaded into the trucks, and part of the crew stayed on a little while to clean up. By the time they had finished, it looked like no one had been there. Even the tracks in the carpet had magically disappeared.

Lila was delighted. Eric was delighted. Ashley not so, but Marina was pleased, and Devone a little embarrassed but overall okay.

The next shoot was set for four days later.

The minute they were all out of the house, the very thrilled Lila started up the stairs, searching for her husband.

But she didn't get to the third step when Ken appeared at the top of the stairs, suitcase in hand.

"Where are you going? I'm a success. We have to celebrate." She could barely keep from jumping up and down.

"No, you're not. You're a first-class bitch and I'm finished!" He didn't even stop to look at her as he passed on his way to the front door.

"No! Wait! You don't understand. I only did that for the show. I didn't mean any of those things I said about you. It was just a part I was playing. Like it was a joke."

"No, Lila, it was you. And I was a jerk for thinking there was ever anything left in our marriage."

"Kenny, it's not me. I was just pretending to be a bitch."

"Not pretending."

"Where are you going? You can't leave now. They're not going to use me without you. I'll lose everything I ever wanted. Please . . . please . . ." she begged.

Ken looked at Lila sitting on the bottom step, tears streaming down her face, pleading, but he didn't say a word.

He didn't have to. The line was already there, hanging in the air.

Frankly, my dear, I don't give a damn.

And the door closed behind him.

13

The next morning, before eight thirty, Jessica's doorbell rang. It had to be the press, she thought. But it couldn't be; so far they didn't know about her involvement. Who could be ringing her doorbell before nine on a Saturday?

Even Jake was still sleeping.

Too early to be good news.

Oh, my God, she thought, it had to be Todd.

Of course, he was sorry for what he had said yesterday. And she was sorry, too. Sorry for lots of things. How could they both be so dumb? So stupid and stubborn.

At this point she didn't care what had happened. All she wanted was that this separation be over. And everything back to like it was when it was so good. And with this Bruce thing, the family really needed to be together. She needed him.

Convinced it was Todd, she decided against the robe. She'd go with the just-up-from-bed look, tousled hair and bare feet. One check in the mirror and she whipped off the old T-shirt she wore to bed and threw on a sexy little silk thing that was barely shirt length, and smiling with excitement rushed to the door. She just wanted to throw her arms around him.

And that's what she was feeling when she threw open the door.

But it wasn't Todd. Not at all. It was Caroline Pearce. And not in her real estate broker power suit. She was in whatever she could throw on fast enough to be the first to get the hot news.

So not good, Jessica thought.

Her hand was still on the door. She could just swing it hard, slam it right in Caroline's ugly face. Shut out the vicious miserable gossip she was about to spew out.

"Hey, I was just in the neighborhood . . ."

Liar! Caroline was the best excuse for killing the messenger. Why had no one done it in all these years? Because she'd had cancer and it might come back? What if they couldn't wait that long? Jessica certainly was not inviting her in, so she just stood there, blocking the doorway, waiting.

"Do you have time for a little coffee?" Caroline was totally insensitive.

"No."

"If I'm disturbing you . . ."

"Mommy!"

Jessica knew Caroline couldn't have arranged this with Jake, but the timing was perfect.

"Come in." She had no choice. She had to go to Jake. "I'm coming, baby-cakes."

She took her time changing the baby and dressing him and doing good-morning hugs. How long could she put off Caroline?

Not too long because as dumb and tactless as Caroline was, she might say whatever ugly rumor it was in front of Jake. She didn't know what it was, but she knew that she didn't want it said in front of her baby.

Jessica put Jake down in front of *Dora the Explorer,* his favorite DVD, which would give her a good ten minutes.

By the time she got into the kitchen, Caroline had helped herself to coffee and was about to pop in a piece of toast as if it were her own house. Jessica took the bread right out of her hand.

"Okay, let's hear it."

"Bruce or Todd?"

"Just so you know right off, anything Bruce is out of bounds."

"Okay. Todd, then. You know me, how I just can't stand how unfair it is to keep important, life-altering information from the person most involved."

Here she comes flapping her wings on the side of the angels. Jessica knew it was going to be totally obnoxious. But she had to bite.

"Go on."

"It's like the stuff nobody tells you because they don't want to hurt you?"

"Yeah, I know. You're wonderful and you're only doing it because being fair is so important to you, blah blah blah."

"Hey, if you don't want to hear—"

"Just say it."

"They're a couple."

"That's it?"

"There's more. My source says he's serious about Sarah. According to her, it's more than just a hookup."

"Okay, give me back my coffee and get out of here." Jessica actually took the mug from Caroline's hand and slammed it down on the counter.

"Well, you're welcome!" Caroline said.

"Good-bye." With not such gentle shoves, Jessica eased her out of the house.

Nobody could ever win with Caroline. How come people still didn't know that?

And me, Jessica thought, stupid enough to think Todd was coming to apologize. Why would he apologize when he thinks all those lies he said the other day are true?

Even though it was still before nine, Jessica texted Elizabeth. R U UP? CALL.

Moments later, the phone rang.

"Caroline was here," Jessica said.

"Of course. Did she have anything about Bruce?"

"I told her I wasn't going to talk about him. Mostly she brought me some garbage about Todd."

"Like?"

"Not worth hearing. What did you get last night?"

"Not much."

"Like . . ."

"The bartender's story doesn't match."

"So he's lying. Now you have to find out why he's lying."

"*If* he's lying."

"Lizzie, what are you saying?"

"I don't know."

"Wait. Go back. What do you mean, *if* he's lying?"

"The story was so weird. Alan Bloom said he never had a meeting with Bruce. The bartender told a whole different story."

"Hey, I don't care what they say, you know Bruce."

"Yes, and you know Todd."

"It's different. Caroline said they're a couple. Made it sound like he's sleeping with that plagiarizer bitch."

"You don't know that. Neither does Caroline."

"Yes, I do. 'Cause I gave him permission. I mean, you should have heard what he said. It's really over now. And you know what? I like it this way. He made up my mind for me."

"Come on, Jess."

"I'm so done."

"Maybe I should come over . . ."

"Forget it. You have enough happening. Besides, I have to set up Bruce's Web site and get the quotes from the celebrities. I'm going to call a couple of people on the magazines and some TV shows like *ET*. See what I can set up for him. But not Bruce himself. I think it's a little early for him to go on TV."

"You're great, Jess. I really appreciate what you're doing. I know this is a bad time for you . . ."

"Are you kidding? I'm showing off my big talent so you know it's not just for lipstick. Come on, Lizzie, he's family. Besides, just so you know

I'm moving on. I have a date with Liam tonight. And don't say anything."
She didn't, but she would momentarily.

"Okay, but . . ."

"Okay, say it."

"He's a little obsessive, don't you think?"

"Because he's crazy about me? I think he's great and he thinks I'm incredible, which is just what I need right now. And besides, he's going to be a big star. What have I got to lose?"

"I guess you're right. Go out. Forget about all this."

"Time to move on, right?"

"I guess."

"It is. It's time to hook up with someone else, and I'm thinking Liam is my someone else. And the kicker?"

"What?"

"Todd hates him."

14

Elizabeth was down at All Saints by ten o'clock in the morning, just as the first Bible class was ending. She waited for Father Riley to come out.

The priest, a nice-looking young man, emerged, leading his class of children out to waiting parents.

"Excuse me," Elizabeth said, "Father Riley?"

"Yes. Can I help you?"

"I'm from the *L.A. Tribune*. Could I have a couple of words with you about the Patman story?"

"How did you get my name?"

"A friend. I may be the first, but I'm not going to be the last. Have you spoken to anyone else?"

"No. And I can't talk to you about anything my parishioners say."

"I'm not surprised. In fact, I thought priests couldn't talk about what people said in confession."

"We can't. And I would never, but in this case it wasn't in confession, and the young woman asked me to speak out."

"Why?"

"Because she didn't want to see it happen to other young women. This man is an important, powerful person, and he takes advantage of his position."

"Still that's unusual, isn't it? Being asked to tell what you heard?"

"It is, but she wanted me to, and I agreed with her. This man should be stopped."

"What if she's not telling the truth?"

"I have no reason to doubt her."

"Is she a regular churchgoer?"

"I'm sorry, but I told you I can't talk about my parishioners. If you'll excuse me . . ."

With that he turned and walked down toward the offices.

Elizabeth knew she couldn't get anything more out of the priest. She would have to find the girl.

Elizabeth and Bruce had been texting back and forth all morning. She didn't want to give him too many details because, ultimately, texts and e-mails are not private.

Bruce's texts were mostly about the paparazzi who were storming the gates. Until he had his statement ready, he was staying put. Jessica was running that show. And he was letting her.

The intern lists for July had been confiscated by the police, but because of the unique connection—it *was,* after all, Bruce's foundation—Elizabeth was able to see the August and September lists.

She chose Renada Leight, a student at Cal State Northridge who worked in the Sweet Valley office the first two weeks of August. There was no trouble setting up an interview for that very afternoon. Renada said she had two Saturday classes but was finished by three o'clock and could meet Elizabeth in Arbor Court near Juniper Hall.

Elizabeth found her easily in the nearly empty court. She was sitting near the door sipping a coffee and waved as soon as Elizabeth came in. She was dark-haired, extremely pretty, borderline beautiful, and even though she was sitting down you could see she was tall with a great body.

Elizabeth knew it was stupid and felt a little ashamed that she could think that way, but she was definitely disturbed by her good looks. Actually, this was the first time she'd ever remembered feeling that way.

Renada turned out to be a twenty-year-old junior studying political science and was delighted to talk about Bruce, Mr. Patman, because he was such a great guy. Everybody said so.

"He didn't come into the office often," she said, "but when he did he was like this really friendly, cool, regular guy. It's horrible what's happening. I don't know who that girl is, but I swear she's lying."

She told Elizabeth that Bruce had a reputation for helping people, like getting them scholarships or even jobs after school.

"Do you know anyone he helped?" Elizabeth asked.

"Not personally, but I remember hearing that he like helped get this girl get a scholarship to Stanford University. And he got someone else a job with the *L.A. Times*."

"Did you ever have a conversation with him?"

"One time I was having a problem with this professor who didn't want to give me time off for my intern work. All I needed was for him to excuse me from like the last hour of his class for the two weeks. I'd asked him a couple of times, but he never responded. And then Mr. Patman said to meet him after work and give him the information and he would call."

An unmistakable wave of nausea slid through Elizabeth's stomach. "So you met him . . ."

"I didn't because like that very day the professor sent me this e-mail saying okay I could leave early for the two weeks."

"So you didn't meet Mr. Patman then, but was there another time?" Elizabeth actually held her breath.

"No."

Elizabeth exhaled.

"But there was this other intern," Renada continued. "I think her name was Ella, and she worked with one of his assistants so she probably knew him better than I did."

"Where can I find her?"

"She's not here. She's doing her junior year in like France or maybe Italy, I think."

"Did you know any of the other interns who worked before you in July?"

"Yeah, Mary Ann DiNato. She started the last week of July and went one week into August when I was there."

Renada found her number on her cell and gave it to Elizabeth. There was nothing else Renada could add, so Elizabeth thanked her and left.

She phoned Mary Ann from her car and asked if she could talk to her about the accusations against Mr. Patman.

The girl was more than willing and said she was free right now. She worked at the BCBG on Rodeo Drive and they could meet at the Starbucks on the same street.

Elizabeth drove up to L.A., incredibly found a parking spot on the same street, and went to meet Mary Ann.

There was no missing her. She was even more gorgeous than Renada. Where were the ugly interns when you needed them? How about just plain? And what about some guys?

All Elizabeth could think was that if she'd realized the competition, she would have worried a lot earlier.

She had done other investigations for the paper, but never anything personal like this. She was actually hating every minute of it. But it was Bruce, so she had no choice. No one else could be trusted to do this.

After some small talk about how expensive Starbucks coffee was and how everyone complained but still kept buying it, Mary Ann launched into a paean to the marvelous Bruce Patman.

Elizabeth agreed, but somehow hearing such admiration from this beautiful young woman was unsettling. Was it possible that Elizabeth didn't know Bruce as well as she thought?

Did she have doubts? Jessica didn't. Elizabeth asked her a few questions about what it was like working as an intern.

Mary Ann was very enthusiastic. She said that it was a great atmosphere, everybody was really friendly, and the work was mostly easy and pretty interesting. They spent most of the time researching young people who were eligible for financial help with school. The only thing she didn't like was when they had to file hard copies of records. It's like no one was used to working with hard copies anymore. She thought the foundation really had to get with it.

She couldn't add much about Bruce other than he was awesome. Cool. But she did know an intern who had worked there two weeks before her in July, which, Elizabeth figured, would put her in the same time frame as the accuser.

Mary Ann had the name, Anne Greenberg, but not her number.

After a few wrong numbers, Elizabeth found the right Anne Greenberg, another of Bruce's admirers. She was happy to help in any way she could.

"I'm looking for an intern who worked sometime in the first two or three weeks in July," Elizabeth told her. "All I know about her is that she's blond, petite, and probably Catholic."

"I may know something, but I'm not really comfortable giving out her name."

"I think she could have some information that might help Mr. Patman. You said you wanted to help him."

"I do. But how do I know you're not just one of those gossipmongers."

"I work for the *L.A. Tribune*. You can call the paper and ask them." Elizabeth was hoping she wouldn't take her up on that.

And she didn't. "Okay, so there were a couple of blond girls who were finishing their second week when I got there. One was Heather Horowitz, but I don't think that's the one you want. The other one, I only know her first name. It was Robin. Maybe Heather knows more. I can give you her number."

She gave Elizabeth Heather's cell number.

"Thanks, I really appreciate your help."

This time Elizabeth tried a little subterfuge.

"Hi, Heather?"

"Who's this?"

"Diana, Robin's friend. We worked together at the Patman Foundation."

"Diana? I don't remember you."

"Oh, right. I think I was the week after you. But you knew Robin, right?"

"Yeah, I knew her. What's up?"

"I lost her number and I'm supposed to meet her tonight and I just can't make it. I mean I feel terrible, but these friends came in from Atlanta."

"I don't know if I have it."

"Could you just check? 'Cause I like can't bring them along. They are so like wrong. Hey, weren't those two weeks great? I mean I loved the foundation. And I even liked the work except for the filing. I mean, when are they going to get with it? Hard copies are so done. Did you find her number?"

"One minute."

A few seconds later, Heather gave Elizabeth the number.

With that number, Elizabeth could use the reverse system to find out Robin's last name and her address. But only if it was a landline. A long shot today.

But if she was lucky and it wasn't a cell, she would have to go there. This had to be face-to-face. But she'd need a story. Maybe something with Father Riley, like that he had asked her to help Robin because of what had happened. She could pass herself off as a parishioner who was a therapist.

It was very difficult to get inside information by introducing yourself as a newspaper reporter, so sometimes you had to fudge it a bit. That's what investigative reporters did.

But not like this. Not outright lying.

It was underhanded. It was journalistically despicable. But it was for Bruce. His life, and ultimately hers, too.

You do almost anything for someone you love who you believe is being unfairly and unjustly attacked. It had to be Warner, and this was no time to start thinking about moral boundaries. She had to use the only weapon she had. It might be the only way to save Bruce.

He would do it for her, no matter what the cost.

And if she was wrong, she would resign from the paper and give up all her dreams of being a journalist.

If she was wrong, all her dreams would be gone anyway.

15

With Jessica's help, Bruce was set up to make his announcement tomorrow, Sunday. Right after that, she had arranged for four of his celebrity friends to be interviewed and give their opinions about Bruce and the accusations. Specifically, what easy targets high-profile people like Bruce could be. Especially if the accuser hit and disappeared. The idea, which came right from Bruce, was to make everyone feel his own vulnerability.

The rest of the celebrities would talk on the Web site and YouTube, and she'd set up a nonstop Twitter feed.

She had also used her contacts to get a story on *ET* and *Access Hollywood* and in major newspapers. With help from colleagues, she'd arranged for stories on other cases where the accusations turned out to be groundless and the accused suffered unjustly. Additionally, she'd arranged for people from the Patman Foundation to speak out about their president. All this was done with Jessica magic in only two days.

In forty-eight hours, she had organized a media blitz that knocked everyone out. Her genius was definitely showing

But at the moment, this Saturday night, no genius was showing. And certainly no passion. Her heart wasn't in this starting-a-new-life thing.

She pulled out whatever dress came first, and it happened to be a micromini frilly thing that she shoved right back in the closet. She pulled out four more dresses, and they were all for adorable, delicious Jessica. No way. Not tonight.

Why was she so overpowered with feelings for Todd just when she'd lost him? Even though they'd been separated almost five months, she still felt attached; she really must still love him. And until those last terrible words, she thought he still loved her, too. His problem with her career was serious, but she felt it was mostly about sharing her. His retro attitude was so not like him; she knew they would have worked things out.

In these past months she'd never truly hooked up with anyone else because deep down she didn't really want it to be over. Not to say she was sitting home moaning—those Miu Miu dresses and Manolo shoes had to do some serious moving. But no one, not Mike or Liam or that great-looking nephew of George Fowler, her boss, meant anything important to her. Only Todd.

She didn't want it to be over. Obviously, he felt differently. How did she miss that? It didn't hit until he'd said those killing words. But now she understood that he really had a commitment to Sarah, no fighting that.

Maybe it was just the old Jessica wanting what Jessica couldn't have. And if she had to move on, Liam was the perfect rebound. Except why was she feeling so shaky inside, like she had opening-night jitters without the opening night?

"No jewelry?" Liza, the sitter, looked up from the gigantic Lego fort she and Jake were building in the living room.

"Whoops. I forgot. It's okay, I've got my lavaliere, that's enough."

"And blue shoes with a black dress? You are so not into this." There was nothing shy about Liza who, after two years, had come to know her employer pretty well.

"I totally am. And I like blue with black. It works!"

"Yeah, right. Totally cool."

"Can we not talk about my outfit?"

It was barely forty-five minutes since she had spoken to Liam in L.A., and he was already at the door.

He came in full of smiles and looking incredibly hot in his Hugo Boss jacket and, of course, jeans, and happy to be here.

It definitely registered on Liza.

He did a quick number on how fabulous the Lego fort was, winning Liza over, but then she was an easy win.

Jake was harder, but he didn't waste time beyond a fake punch and a quick "How ya doin', little guy?" before he turned to the real star.

"Hey, babe, you look sensational."

Just what Jessica needed, and oh, that hint of an Irish lilt worked pretty well.

Liam had been hooked on Jessica since that first meeting three years ago at her grandmother's dinner. And he was still nuts about her. Maybe even more so now that she was available.

Over-the-top adoration was exactly her prescription for tonight.

The first fifteen minutes in the car were all about his new movie. A guy movie she would never see, except if he was in it then she'd have to. Probably have to go to the premiere, too. Poor baby, what would she wear? Without question her vintage Valentino.

Only after a complete rundown of the script did he ask about Bruce.

"Innocent," she told him without elaborating.

Liam had the classic actor's interest in the outside world: minuscule. "Yeah, well, I hope it goes away."

"So where are we going?" Jessica asked him, closing off the Bruce subject.

"I thought we'd drive over to San Clemente to that restaurant you love. The one in the Imagine Hotel." Liam said.

"That's far."

"Forty-five minutes is not really a big deal."

"I guess. Maybe I'll let Liza know just in case."

"In case what?"

"I don't know, just in case. I have Jake at home." She rummaged around in her bag for her cell. It wasn't there. She checked the seat and the floor. Not there.

Jake.

Little as he was, he'd figured out that as long as her phone was there, she was. So he always watched out for it. And sometimes, he even hid it. He was so smart.

"I'm so sorry, Liam, but I left my cell at the house. We have to go back."

"So you're out of touch for a couple of hours . . . not really the end of the world," said the nonparent.

"What if Jake needs me? I'm never out of reach for him."

"So I'll text what's her name?"

"Liza."

"I'll text Liza my cell number."

"I hate being without my phone."

"Look, we're practically at the restaurant."

It was true, Liza could always call Liam if she needed Jessica. Maybe she was just looking for excuses to go home. No way. It was time to move on.

16

Not ten minutes after Jessica left the house, the landline rang. It was Todd.

Liza told him Jessica was out. "You okay? You don't sound so good." After two years as Jake's sitter, Jessica's life was Liza's living soap opera, and she was deep into it.

"I'm fine. I just have to talk to her about something." He was not about to confide in the babysitter.

"Can I give her a message?" Liza didn't give up easily.

"That's okay."

The minute Todd hung up he texted Jessica's cell. And waited.

No response.

He texted her again. And again. And each time he told her he had to talk to her about what he said yesterday.

Still no response.

And the last time he texted to tell her that he was so sorry. That he was wrong. There was never anything fake about their love.

WHATEVER HAPPENED HAD TO HAPPEN FOR BOTH OF US. I WANTED IT AS MUCH AS YOU DID. AND WHAT I SAID WASN'T TRUE. THERE'S NOTHING BETWEEN SARAH AND ME. I DON'T WANT HER OR ANYONE ELSE. I ONLY WANT YOU, JESSICA. FORGIVE ME. WE CAN WORK THIS OUT, I KNOW IT. I NEED YOU, JESS.

Still no response.

After twenty more minutes had passed, he called the house again, figuring she just didn't want to talk to him. She was that angry.

"She's not here, Todd. Really," Liza said, burning with curiosity.

A hesitation, and then, "Where is she?"

"She's out . . ."

"Out?"

"Yeah."

An uncomfortable hesitation. "With Liam?" His voice was practically cracking.

"I don't know." Nosy as she was, Liza was loyal to her employer.

Silence. Then, "I get it. Look, do me a favor, will you? Just forget I called."

And he hung up.

Liza loved this episode. The triangle. Todd and Liam were both super awesome-looking. But Liam was a movie star. And Todd was only a writer. Movie star trumps writer anytime.

17

Jessica felt like she was on a mission. A fuck mission.

This way to freedom.

Liam was back into his movie. Now she was getting the whole plot and pretending to listen while she picked at the salmon on her plate. She wasn't pretending to drink her dirty martini.

Every once in awhile she'd get back to Liam and he'd still be on the movie, but it was like she'd missed the first page so she had no idea what he was talking about. And it was too late to ask. Besides, with the three martinis she couldn't even remember what part he was playing.

"Wow!" she said. *Wow* had to be the best word in the world. All you did was add *awesome!* every once in awhile, and you'd covered everything and made someone very happy.

Actually, the evening wasn't so bad except for the story. She was beginning to feel comfy and warm. Even toward Liam.

He was so adorable. And his smile was made for the movies, big and gorgeous like Julia Roberts's, and he was about the best-looking man she knew. A great choice for this mission.

She remembered back in her teens when she made up her mind to have sex for the first time. She just wanted to do it and get it over with. This was kind of like that. It was the first step in getting on with her life. She needed to get past it.

It's not like she was trying to catch up with Todd. She didn't want it to be like that. Even if it kind of was.

God, how did we let this happen? she thought. Todd and me.

"Do you want dessert?" Liam asked. She hadn't even seen them take the salmon away.

"Not really."

Liam took her hand in his and gave her his beautiful Julia Roberts smile. "Me, neither. What I want to do . . ."

"I'm listening."

"Is make love to the woman I love."

She didn't know why she took her hand away.

"I love you, Jessica. Right from the first time I saw you. I think you knew that."

She smiled.

He reached out to her again.

For a moment she didn't move, and then she put her hand out to his and he took it.

Liam stood up, and she stood with him her hand still in his.

When the waiter came over, Liam said, "Put the bill on room two thirteen."

He led her out of the restaurant to the lobby elevator. She followed him almost blindly. She stood there mesmerized, leaning on him for balance and watching the elevator hit the floors on its way down like it was a slot machine, and never once looking in Liam's direction.

In the elevator alone, he took her in his arms and kissed her softly, sweetly. And it felt very good, but still she was uneasy. In the room, he held her tenderly and the alcohol haze relaxed her enough to allow tingles of excitement to pulse through her body.

This man loved her. She knew it and could feel it in his arms and his body, in the way his lips and his hands caressed her face.

She wasn't going to allow herself to pretend it was Todd. That would be too easy. She could simply close her eyes and feel Todd, the man she knew so well and had loved for too many years now. But she wouldn't because Todd was not that lover anymore. That man was gone. Now he was just the angry man who hated her, who blamed her for everything. Who trashed their love with lies and accusations.

"Luv." It was Liam, the man who had pursued her for three years now, who had never accepted defeat because he was so in love with her.

It was that same man who gently eased her dress down over her shoulders until it fell below her breasts and kissed her with such passion she couldn't help responding.

If she wasn't responding to Liam, she was responding to love. He sensed that and was passionate and gentle, and with her eyes closed and her mind only feeling sensations, she got lost in the moment.

Afterward, lying on the bed next to this man who was not her husband, she felt only numbness, no trace of revenge or anger, nothing . . .

But that state of nothingness lasted only moments until the clarity of regret charged in, shouting, "What have you done!" And she leaped up and grabbed her clothes.

"I have to get home."

"Please, come back to bed and let me hold you. I've been waiting so long."

"No, I'm sorry. I have to get home now."

She couldn't even look at Liam as she dressed. She was at the door before he had a chance to get his shoes on. She waited, staring at the closed door and telling herself it was good to be loved and wanted. But that didn't really help.

At last when she felt him behind her, she opened the door, and they walked out into the hallway. Still, she couldn't look at him.

The drive home was almost silent. He tried to hold her hand, but she wouldn't let him.

He kindly didn't insist.

⌣⟶

When she got back to her house, she went in alone. It was after two and everyone was asleep.

The giant Lego fort took up half the living room floor. Jessica sat down on the couch and just stared at nothing. Until she saw the flashing light inside the fort.

Her phone. Jake. Of course. She moved a couple of pieces, reached in, and pulled it out.

There were twelve messages.

All from Todd.

18

Elizabeth found Robin Platt's house with little trouble. It was in L.A. over the hill in the San Fernando Valley, Sherman Oaks to be exact.

Robin's apartment was on the first floor of a two-story town house that had survived the Northridge earthquake of 1994, but its cement hallways were still frozen in uneven mounds and the window frames didn't quite meet the walls perfectly. To keep out the rain, they had been caulked and painted over. After eighteen years, the white caulking was beginning to leak through. The upkeep was shabby to say the least.

She was armed with her story, a therapist parishioner and friend of Father Riley who had come on his suggestion to see if she could help the poor young woman deal with this traumatic event.

Elizabeth rang the doorbell and put on her attempt-at-a-therapist face, serious and concerned with just a hint of a friendly smile.

A young woman who fit Bruce's description—blond, petite, and pretty, anywhere from eighteen to early twenties—opened the door. And then looked sorry that she had. Bruce was right about her physically, but what he missed was a hardness about her face, yesterday's cheerleader. Or was that just Elizabeth's own preconceived judgment?

"It's okay," Elizabeth said. "Father Riley sent me. I'm Laura Christer, one of his parishioners, too."

That seemed to relax Robin a bit.

"Except," Elizabeth continued, "I'm a therapist, and he thought I might be able to help you."

She tightened up again and with a slight movement of her body effectively blocked the doorway.

"Father said that maybe we could sit down and have a cup of tea together."

Elizabeth was still not inside the door. "He's such a nice guy, the father, and always so sensitive about imposing on privacy outside the confessional. I actually offered when I heard you were in our church."

"How did you know that?" Suspicion added to the tightness.

"When I found out that it was Father Riley who spoke to the press, I knew it had to be our church. So I asked him. And since I'm a professional, he thought maybe it would help you to talk to me. He didn't give away any private conversations and I promised that if you said no, I would just walk away."

"I don't really want to talk about it. That's why I wanted to keep it anonymous."

"As a professional, anything you say to me is between us, private information never to be divulged. Robin, I think I can help you."

It was almost nauseating, Elizabeth's pretense. But she believed in the innocence of the man she loved and would do most anything for him. Additionally, she felt a whiff of something off about Robin, not as big as a gut feeling, but there nevertheless. It might have had to do with the picture that she'd had of Robin in her head. It was of someone softer, with an innocence and nervousness. This young woman was not at all nervous. In fact, you could almost hear the heel clicks of her thoughts.

"If you don't want to talk about it, we don't have to. I just want to give you some general support. You were so right to come out with your accusations. Too many times these powerful men think they can have anything they want. It takes a lot of courage to stand up to those kinds of men. I know because something like that happened to me when I was in school."

This seemed to interest the young woman. Without saying anything, she moved slightly to the side, leaving room for Elizabeth to enter.

Robin led the way down a short hall to the living room.

"You can sit if you want, but I don't have any tea."

"That's all right," said Elizabeth. "I would just take a glass of water."

"Sure." Robin left to get Elizabeth the water.

The furnishings were uninviting. A sad, worn couch facing two mis-

matched over-stuffed chairs. One of them like an old-model recliner ripped from overuse where the mechanism was and the other covered in a terrible plaid that didn't go with anything. There were no signs of the owner. Nothing feminine about the room. No pictures on the walls or even personal pictures on the tables. And not a book in sight.

There was an old cabinet-style television and a bunch of faded artificial flowers in a vase. It was hard to believe the girl actually lived here.

In fact, Elizabeth was beginning to feel that something was more than just off, maybe even fishy. Rick Warner fishy?

Robin came back with a glass of water for Elizabeth, who took it and thanked her.

"What happened to you?" Robin was very interested.

And Elizabeth proceeded to create a story not unlike Robin's experience. And the similarity seemed to strike a chord in Robin, and she began to warm up and ask questions that were surprisingly personal.

Elizabeth was a professional, just not a therapist professional, but she did know the right questions to ask to get information because that was, after all, the business of investigative reporting.

After some borderline lurid details that Elizabeth made up on the spot, Robin began asking more questions, wanting details, especially about how Elizabeth had felt after.

Elizabeth managed to shift the questions until it was Robin who was telling about her experience.

"Like your guy," Robin said, "this one had a lot to drink and was looking to unburden himself. Among other things. I could tell he didn't recognize me. Like that I had been an intern or anything."

"How did he unburden himself?"

"Like whining about the woman he was living with. Like how she had got dumped by some guy she was crazy about forever. And he dumped for, get this, her sister."

Elizabeth was stunned.

"And he said he felt like he was some kind of leftover. She was just using him because he was there and rich and she was still crazy about that other guy. He did manage to get in how rich he was a couple of times, which, of course, I already knew. And then he started on the sex. I don't

know whether he was just trying to make it sound lousy so I would feel sorry for him."

"What did he say about the sex?" Elizabeth wasn't the professional anything anymore.

"He said it was really boring. He could tell she was pretending with him."

Elizabeth was so out of breath she couldn't even find enough air to make a sound, no less ask another question.

"I didn't mean to upset you and bring back bad memories," Robin said, reaching out and patting her shoulder. Actually, by now Elizabeth was the one who needed the comforting touch.

"Then what happened that night with you?" Elizabeth managed to ask.

"I went to the ladies' room and he must have followed me. When I got out he was like waiting for me. And then it happened, so fast I didn't even get to scream. He like shoved me into this empty office and started ripping at my blouse. I was fighting him off. But he was too strong. I was like so scared. He went for my skirt and I tried to push him away, and I did because he was so drunk, he tripped, but his ring scratched my hand. See?"

Robin held out her hand, showing a light scar that could have come from a deep scratch.

"I'm so sorry," Elizabeth said, and now she was the one comforting Robin, who was truly upset at the recollection, her eyes brimming with tears. "What about your father?"

"My father?"

"Yes."

"My father's been dead for years."

Elizabeth felt like she had been clubbed in the stomach. Nothing Bruce said matched. No way this girl would lie about her father being dead. It was too easy to check.

Even yesterday, when Bruce was telling her what had happened, she had had one of those inner alerts when something is even slightly out of place. But it was all so bizarre that she didn't stop to ask anything.

"Oh, Laura, it's been such a horrible week. I don't know whether I made the right decision or not. I mean, like, all I read about Mr. Patman

is that he really was a good guy. I know he had too much to drink, and people do things when they're drunk they would never do normally. . . ."

The look on Robin's face was painful. Elizabeth couldn't help reaching out to her, put her hand lightly on the girl's shoulder.

"I'm ruining his life, aren't I? And maybe mine, too."

"Listen, Robin, no one, no matter who, has the right to force himself on a woman. Or anyone."

Elizabeth couldn't believe she was siding with this young woman against the man she loved.

"But maybe I did something that would make him think I was coming on to him or something. Maybe it was my fault. Oh, I wish I could take it all back."

"Don't say that. It wasn't your fault."

The fact that Robin could even try to make excuses for Bruce was so unnerving. All that hardness she thought she had seen in Robin's face was gone. Now there was only this very frightened young woman.

"I'm so scared," Robin said. And Elizabeth could see she was truly afraid, and it was heartbreaking. "What's going to happen to me now? Are all the newspapers and everything going to come after me?"

"No. They'll protect your name, but you might have to testify in front of a grand jury."

"Maybe they won't believe me. After all, Mr. Patman is a very important man and I'm a nobody."

Even hearing her refer to the man who had tried to rape her with such respect made Elizabeth queasy. Before she allowed her natural response— *No one, no matter who he is, has the right to force himself sexually on another person. Never. Under any circumstances*—she stopped and pulled herself together. How could she let one girl, a stranger she knew nothing about, destroy the man she had known all those years as a fair, honest person, a man she loved? One accusation and she was ready to convict him. What happened to all those ideas about Warner setting Bruce up?

"What does your family say?" Elizabeth asked. She was finished. She couldn't do this anymore. Let the girl's family handle it.

"There's really no one. I grew up in like this little town in Kentucky, and when my mom died two years ago, I just like picked up and left. I was always pretty good at sketching and so I thought maybe I could get something in advertising for movies or something."

She reached out and took Elizabeth's hand. Her grip was hard with desperation and need. "This is so horrible. I never should have said anything. I just want to forget it all. Everything."

Elizabeth was silent. She stood there, her hand still locked in Robin's, but her thoughts were in her own world. Was it possible that she could make this whole miserable thing go away? And Bruce would be free. And she would have her life back.

"Please, Laura." Robin's face was broken with misery. Tears ran down her cheeks. "I have no one else. You have to help me."

EPISODE 2

Lies and Omissions

1

Lila Fowler was not used to being ignored and she didn't like it. First there was her husband, Ken, who'd packed a bag, left the house, and wasn't answering his phone or replying to any of her texts, and now there was her best friend, Jessica Wakefield, who seemed to be far more engrossed with her stupid cell phone than with anything Lila had said in the last fifteen minutes.

"Are you even *listening* to me?" Lila asked Jessica, annoyed. The fact that she even had to ask this question at all made her want to storm out. But then she probably ought to save the theatrics for the *True Housewives* cameras. There were no cameras here in Jessica's tastefully decorated town house in Sweet Valley. *Tasteful,* Lila thought, *if you went for bubble-gum pink.*

"What? Oh, sorry." Jessica glanced up—for the first time in ages—from her phone. "It's the Bruce thing." She flipped a perfect strand of blond hair away from her blue eyes and gave Lila one of her trademark Wakefield smiles.

Right. Bruce Patman, reigning Sweet Valley perv, Lila thought. Lila's family, the Fowlers, and the Patman family never did get along, but even she was a little surprised by the news. In fact, after Lila read the headlines about Bruce trying to force himself on an intern, she'd had a brief flashback to high school, when *she'd* been nearly raped by John Pfeifer at Miller's Point. She probably would have been if she hadn't fought free, stabbing the jerk in the neck with his own car keys. She didn't like thinking about that. It was ancient history, but still, without even knowing all (or even some) of the facts, Lila was on the intern's side.

"I can't believe he turned out to be such a creep," Lila said. "He should go to jail."

"He's innocent," Jessica snapped.

"How do you know?"

"Because I know him. Much better than you do. And I know he could prove it if I knew who his accuser was."

"You don't know yet?" Lila asked her, surprised. After all, it was hard to keep secrets from Jessica, especially when she was determined to find out something.

"Lizzie is working on it, but so far she says she hasn't found anything. If I did know, I could start really tearing her story apart."

"What if she's telling the truth?"

"She's not," Jessica said, refusing to back down.

Lila shrugged. "Whatever." It wasn't worth a fight.

"I've got interviews lined up for him on some morning shows," Jessica said, again thumbing through messages on her phone.

The two old friends were sitting in Jessica's living room. Jake, Jessica and Todd's two-year-old son, and his nanny, Liza, were out at the park, but there were still a few telltale signs of the toddler, like a couple of Lego bricks half hidden in the carpet, one of which Lila had nearly stepped on with her stiletto heel. Lila was still surprised Jessica had gone the kid route. Lila didn't plan to have kids—now or maybe ever—not when a baby was likely to be cuter, younger, and more of a spotlight hog than she was. Lila was the star of her own show, thank you very much.

"It's been a crazy few days, but I think I'm starting to make headway for Bruce," Jessica continued.

Jessica was so engrossed with the Bruce Patman business that she had forgotten entirely why Lila was there, and it wasn't to talk about Bruce or to kick Legos under the coffee table.

"I really think I can nail this, but I need that girl's name," Jessica said, still distracted. "There's got to be some reason she's made this whole thing up. I know it."

Lila let out a frustrated sigh.

"That's great and all, but how about my problems? Think you could work your PR genius on *them* for a second?" Lila tapped her Christian Louboutin—clad foot impatiently on the rug, her diamond bracelet catching the light and sparkling like fire. It was bad enough she had to hear all about how talented Jessica was from her father, since she was his favorite rising PR star in his company VertPlus.net. She didn't need to hear it from Jessica, too. "Sorry, Lila, I just—"

"Sorry doesn't cut it, Jessica. I mean, what kind of friend are you anyway?"

Jessica turned to Lila, blue eyes widening in surprise for an instant, and then reality set in. Surely she could not have thought that spoiled bitch personality was just for TV? No way. Jessica had known her best friend too long.

"I'm in a total meltdown mode here," Lila said. "Ken won't even talk to me! And you're blabbing on about Bruce Patman. Like I care!"

"Lila, calm down." Jessica reached out to touch her friend on the shoulder and gave her a patronizing look that Lila couldn't stand. It was the kind of look you gave losers and pathetic women whose husbands had left them for other women. Lila wasn't going to be lumped in with them.

She shrugged the touch away as she set down her mug of coffee on the table. She was beginning to wish she'd asked for wine instead. Not that Jessica had offered. Coffee was what she had brewing when Lila had dropped in unannounced.

Lila looked at the bright burgundy lipstick smudge on the lip of her coffee mug and thought, *Nothing is turning out how I wanted it to. And I really don't like it.*

She'd gone over to Jessica's for a little bit of hand-holding, and she wasn't getting it. This, after all, was supposed to be *her* moment of drama. Ken wasn't talking to her—at *all.* That had never happened before, not even when she'd asked for a divorce three years ago. It had been too long now with no word from Ken, and she was miserable without him.

Since she'd first married him, Lila always thought he was mostly just a well-groomed accessory to her life—the handsome and sweet onetime high school quarterback turned pro who adored her. She always thought of him more like a lap dog—cute and loyal and one hundred percent *hers*. But since he'd finally grown a backbone and left her, she realized she actually did care about him, which for Lila was like the brink of love.

She needed him.

And since he'd moved out, all she could think about was how to get him back.

For one thing, he was the only one who loved her as much as she loved herself, and that was saying a lot. Would anybody else ever be able to match Ken's devotion? She seriously doubted it.

Sure, back in high school he'd dated both the Wakefield twins, but that was only fooling around. When he fell in love, he fell for her. Hard.

How else to explain that when she tried to divorce him three years ago, he simply refused to leave? Okay, maybe not refused, but he hung around until she gave up talking to the lawyers. And then there were the looks he sometimes gave her, the ones that told her she was the goal line and he was coming across it, no matter what. Nobody else made her feel so worth . . . winning.

"I don't think Ken is gone for good," Jessica said. "He loves you."

"He has a funny way of showing it," Lila said. Like not answering any of her e-mails or texts or a dozen voice mails. "He's never ignored me for this long before."

"Maybe he needs a little more time to cool off," Jessica suggested.

Lila knew Ken was angry with her. She'd said some awful things about him for the *True Housewives* show, but none of them was real. It was all pretend. Just like Paris Hilton and all her reality shows. Didn't she say she was just exaggerating everything for good ratings? Well, so was Lila.

"Maybe if you quit the show . . ." Jessica suggested, even as her phone dinged again, drawing her attention.

"Quit? What! Never!" Lila couldn't even conceive of the idea of quitting *True Housewives of Sweet Valley*. She was the show's starring bitch and she happened to be good at it. Lila hadn't done anything with her life so far except drop out of college, marry Ken, and spend her days dumping piles of money on Rodeo Drive. *True Housewives* was the closest that Lila had ever come to a life's calling. She had great instincts for camera angles and drama, and her perfect little body looked fantastic on camera. If she gave that up, then who would she be? An NFL star's wife. That was bad enough. Now she would be his ex-wife. You can't be more nobody than that.

"I'm just saying, maybe that would help soften things with Ken," Jessica said, her attention again on her phone's lighted screen.

"Are you asking me to *give something up*?" Lila asked. "Um, excuse me, have we met?" She threw open her arms, which were heavy with diamonds and platinum. "When was the last time I had to cut back *on anything*?"

Jessica had to laugh. The thing about Lila was, she might be spoiled, but she was the first to admit it. *You could say a lot of things about Lila, but that she was boring certainly isn't one of them,* Jessica thought. "Sorry, I forgot."

Lila pushed her dark hair from her forehead.

"And anyway, I'm not going to quit. Besides, there's a problem: the producers want him on next week's show."

"You really think he's going to do that?" Jessica's phone dinged again, drawing her attention.

"He *has* to," Lila said. "They said get him on the show or . . . else. I don't know what the 'else' is, and I don't want to find out, either. If I could just get him to talk to me, just once, I know I could straighten this out."

Jessica shook her head in sympathy and was about to speak when her phone vibrated again.

"He *has* to come on the show," Lila continued. Of course, technically, he hadn't signed any sell-your-soul reality show contracts.

"Um-hm," Jessica mumbled, eyes cast down on her phone, hardly listening, as she tapped out a response.

"Jessica, would you stop with the messaging already!" Lila grabbed the phone out of Jessica's hand. "Screw Bruce!"

"Hey!" Jessica lunged for her phone but missed.

"I have your attention now," Lila declared as she held the phone aloft. "No sudden moves or I *will* smash this thing."

"No, no!" Jessica cried, hands up in surrender as she eyed her iPhone nervously. "Look, Lila, I'm sorry. It's just you guys have been separated before. It's not like it's never happened before."

"It's never happened *this* way before." Lila waved the phone.

"Okay, I'm sorry. I'll listen. I know what it's like to have your husband leave." Jessica's voice sounded full of sympathy now that Lila had a hostage—her iPhone. "Trust me, I know."

Lila hesitated. It was true that Jessica knew what it was like since Todd had moved out. Never before had Jessica lost something so dear that she hadn't intended to lose.

"At least Ken hasn't slept with a cheap plagiaristic criminal," Jessica said bitterly. Well, Lila had successfully gotten her to change the subject of conversation away from Bruce Patman. Unfortunately, not entirely in the direction Lila would have liked.

"You mean Sarah Miller?" Lila asked. Jessica's phone was heavy in her hand. She stopped dangling it over the edge of the couch.

"You know?"

"Caroline Pearce, remember? Everyone knows." Lila shrugged. Even though Ken wasn't speaking to her, Lila was totally sure he hadn't slept with anyone else, certainly not her main Housewife competition, Ashley Morgan. Not yet, anyway. Even the thought of him kissing her made Lila's blood boil with jealousy. "Is he in love with her?"

Jessica looked sharply at Lila. "I don't think so. He texted me, actually."

"And told you what?"

"Give me my phone back and I'll show you." Jessica opened her palm, and Lila plunked her phone in it.

Jessica pulled up Todd's messages and showed them to Lila, who skimmed them quickly.

"Sounds like he wants you back," Lila said.

"Yes, but . . ." She paused. "It's complicated. He knows I went out with Liam."

"So?" Lila shrugged. "Who cares about drinks and dinner? So what?"

Jessica grew quiet. It was about that time that Lila realized she'd been sidetracked—again. Who cared about Todd? And why was she talking

about Jessica's problems? She could feel herself getting sucked into the Jessica Show, and frankly, she just didn't have the time.

"Back to me: I need a plan," Lila said. "Calling Ken isn't working. I need to do something else."

"I need a plan, too," Jessica said. "I know I could have a chance with Todd, but I don't know how to make it happen."

"Since when do we sit around and wait for the guys to come to us? We have to be proactive."

"You're right, proactive. I like that." Jessica agreed. "We make the first move and they don't stand a chance."

Lila snapped her fingers. "Ken has a game tomorrow night," she said. "I could be waiting for him afterward. I could wear my new Jason Wu micro-mini with the plunging neckline. He's never been able to resist my . . . assets."

"I could ask Todd on a date . . . somewhere special," Jessica mused, in her own world again.

The fact that neither friend was actually talking about the same thing or providing needed advice on either topic didn't seem to matter. The two friends had been talking past each other for years.

And these two had never been losers and weren't about to start now.

2

Ever since she'd slept with Liam O'Connor, Jessica had wanted to forget it ever happened. Even now, as she sat in her living room watching Lila back out of her driveway, she couldn't even remember all the details.

So far, it was the only sticking point in her plan to win Todd back, and her mind kept going back to that night. If Todd ever found out . . . Well, she was pretty sure he'd never want to be with her again.

She could barely remember most of what had happened. She knew that his growing fan base in Los Angeles and elsewhere would be shocked to

hear that she'd barely even registered his lean and muscled camera-ready physique. She had closed her eyes, allowing her body to respond to the sexual sensations, and lost herself in the moment.

She'd lost herself so much that she didn't even really remember what it had felt like. Jessica should've been thrilled to be with Liam, who had just landed on *People*'s Sexiest Men Alive list. His title? Sexiest Import. He'd even sounded ridiculously close-up worthy when he murmured in a hint of an Irish brogue, "I love you, Jessica." But those words hadn't made her heart soar like they should have.

She saw clearly now that she never should have slept with him at all.

But she knew why she had.

Because she had thought about Todd and Sarah fucking like rabbits all night, every night. She thought of them in all the positions of the *Kama Sutra* and then some. Jessica's imagination was relentless and horrible, and then the anger came, and there was really nothing to do but have sex with Liam.

She thought he would cure her of Todd.

Isn't that what rebounds were for? Like sorbet between courses in a Michelin-starred restaurant. Cleanse the palate and move on.

But that's not what had happened. Instead of helping her forget, everything Liam did—from the way he touched her to the faint smell of his strange, so-not-Todd cologne—only served to remind her of all the many, many ways he was *not* Todd and never would be.

And it was Todd she wanted. Forever and always.

Jessica glanced at the phone in her hand, scrolling through Todd's texts for the hundredth time. There in those sentences she saw everything she'd ever wanted to hear from Todd since he'd moved out several months ago. It had been what she had been waiting for this whole time. He was sorry for the awful things he'd said. He loved her. He wanted her back. He didn't think their love was a sham.

THERE'S NOTHING BETWEEN SARAH AND ME. I DON'T WANT HER OR ANYONE ELSE. I ONLY WANT YOU, JESSICA.

Just reading those words made her heart sing—and then sink like a rock. Why hadn't she known this *before* she'd slept with Liam? If only she'd insisted on turning back and getting her phone that night instead of letting Liam talk her out of it.

Her phone dinged. She looked at the face, hoping to see Todd's name, but instead saw Liam's. She exhaled a frustrated sigh. It was yet *another* message from Liam. He seemed to be texting her every hour on the hour. It was getting annoying. She'd gotten two from him while Lila was here. The rest had been related to Bruce's PR, but Liam was moving into a close second for demands on her time.

HAVEN'T HEARD FROM YOU. HOPE EVERYTHING IS OKAY?

She clicked delete and pulled up the messages from Todd again. She had to play this just right. She didn't want to blow it.

He *knew* she'd gone out with Liam. He'd begun with his heartfelt apologies, and then it ended with the phone call to Liza, her nanny.

She knew Todd. There had to be anger, jealousy, and suspicion. With good reason. He knew.

Or did he?

That night, she'd almost texted him immediately and begged his forgiveness. Even though, she reminded herself, they *were* separated and he was screwing that lying, cheating excuse for a journalist. Jessica had been the one to discover Sarah Miller had plagiarized her newspaper stories— basically taking quotes from Jessica word for word and trying to pass them off as her own writing. The fact that she revealed the information to the *Tribune*, which subsequently fired Sarah, happened to be a short-lived victory—mainly because Todd had gone ballistic and accused her of making it all up.

Really, when she thought about it, she had every right to fuck Liam.

She knew that. But she also knew that if Todd ever found out . . . Well, that would be bad. She felt she would be able to forgive him. At least right now that's what she thought because right now, he was the only one she wanted. But would he forgive her? She didn't know and wasn't going to take the risk to find out.

So Jessica hadn't texted Todd back right away. She'd waited. And plotted and planned. After all, Jessica Wakefield didn't leave anything to chance. She couldn't afford just to play it straight and hope everything worked out. That was for perfect and purely blessed and talented people like her twin, Elizabeth.

Some people might have thought she was a manipulator, but Jessica knew the truth: If she didn't have a plan, she would never have anything or anyone. Todd included. She'd learned that a long time ago. She had to be smart about what she wanted and have a plan. And a plan needed a scheme.

Now she had one. The first part was simple: She would quit her job. She would give up her career so Todd would be able to see just how much she loved him.

And in return for that sacrifice—which wasn't a small one—she was going to allow herself the gift of pretending that night with Liam had never happened.

Lila had given her the idea when she'd said, "Who cares about drinks and dinner? So what?"

Exactly. So what? Only she and Liam knew what had happened that night, and there was no reason Todd would ever need to know.

The important thing was that she and Todd get back together. They were *meant* to be together. They were made for each other, and what he didn't know couldn't hurt him.

Or her.

In this case, the end would justify the means. What was a little lie—really just an omission—if it saved true love?

And she knew exactly how she would *not* tell him. She would *not* tell him about Liam over a romantic dinner at their special restaurant, tomorrow night after the huge MeanGreen gala.

Jessica heard her nanny, Liza, and son, Jake, come rumbling in through the front door, back from the park.

"Mommy!" Jake cried, bounding into the room. Jessica scooped him up in her arms and gave him a snuggle. Instantly, he gave her a full report on his time at the playground.

"Fast slide, Mommy! Fast!"

He beamed with excitement and pride. Jessica could imagine Jake wobbling up the stairs to the toddler slide. As he spoke, she saw that expression he got on his face that was pure Todd, the one when he couldn't wait to tell her about something new. It was the same way Todd looked when he talked about covering some fast-break play in the NBA playoffs.

Jessica gave Jake another big squeeze before she handed him back to

Liza. Seeing Jake gave Jessica a renewed determination to reconcile with Todd, whatever it took. She wanted her family back together again.

Jessica pulled up Todd's cell number and dialed it. Butterflies danced in her stomach as she counted the rings.

One . . . two . . .

"Hello?" Todd's voice sounded hurried, or maybe it was just his haste to pick up his phone. "Jessica?"

The way he said her name, with hope and warmth, caught her by surprise. It had been so long since she'd heard him say her name like that. Without anger. Or bitterness. His voice went straight to her heart and warmed it.

"Todd, I got . . ."

"Did you . . ."

They both spoke at the same time.

"I'm sorry, you first," Jessica said.

"No, you." Todd gave a nervous little laugh. They sounded like awkward teenagers out on a first date.

Jessica decided to take charge. Lila was right. Why sit around and wait for the boys to come to them? Girls rule, right, Beyoncé?

"Todd, I got your messages and I think we should talk. Really talk."

"But you and Liam . . ."

"We're nothing," Jessica added quickly.

"But you went out . . . ?"

"For dinner." This was the omission part, leaving out the sex that came after.

"Hey, that's great. I mean, dinner, who cares?"

Just what Lila had said. Jessica tried not to feel guilty about the relief in Todd's voice. She was doing what she had to do.

"Unless it's us having dinner together. Like maybe a late dinner tomorrow night at Le Bouchon?"

There was a pause on the other end of the line, and Jessica wondered if she'd overplayed her hand. Le Bouchon was *their* restaurant. Their life together as a couple officially started there. At least, their open, nonsecret, nonaffair life.

"We haven't been there in a long time," Todd said.

"Is that a yes?" Jessica's heart hammered hard in her chest as she waited for his answer.

"Definitely a yes." Todd couldn't keep the excitement out of his voice.

Jessica laughed. She knew she had him. Everything was going to be all right.

When Elizabeth arrived at Jessica's town house the next day, she found her sister in party-prep mode, gearing up for the big MeanGreen gala, a Bluetooth handless receiver accessorizing one ear and a diamond chandelier earring dangling from the other. Jessica's makeup artist and stylist were just leaving. On big gala days like this one, Jessica left nothing to chance.

Jessica wore a glittering diamond choker necklace on loan from Tiffany and a sleeveless red slinky gown and strappy heels. Her hair was blown dry straight and fell long past her shoulders. Elizabeth felt dreary and dull, the left-at-home sister in her jeans and flats and her hair thrown up in a hasty ponytail. She never knew how her twin could make walking in six-inch stilettos look as easy as meandering around in Keds, but she managed it. *Glamorous* was what she thought when she looked at her twin. *Everything I'm not.*

"The models are used to marathon makeup sessions, or they should be, so I wouldn't worry about that," Jessica said into her hands-free set as she gave Elizabeth a quick hug hello. "I'll be there in twenty, but make sure to put the *Vogue* photographer front and center. He gets to set up first. I know—you have this covered. Thanks, Katy."

Jessica clicked off the phone.

"Is now a bad time?" Elizabeth asked her sister.

"What? No. I've got ten minutes before I have to hit the freeway. I went over there this morning and just came back to change. The models are still in prep mode. They're not getting the body paint until tonight, and Katy has things under control."

The body paint was the kicker for the show. It would look like all the models were wearing was green paint, but the giveaway would be the zippers and buttons that couldn't be hidden. . . . except that the zippers and buttons were trompe l'oeil. The models really were naked.

Jessica's eyes shone as she spoke about the MeanGreen gala, and Elizabeth saw that familiar spark whenever Jessica talked about work. It was like a whole other Jessica. Elizabeth was surprised but happy that her sister loved her work. It hadn't seemed like that would ever happen.

"I'm glad you're here, actually, because I didn't get a chance to tell you I'm having dinner with Todd tonight," Jessica said.

"He's going to the gala?" Elizabeth sounded surprised.

"No, no. I'm meeting him after. At Le Bouchon."

When she heard the name of the restaurant, the darling French bistro known for romantic, candlelit dinners, she felt a little twinge of something close to jealousy. "The bistro where he proposed?" Elizabeth asked. She knew that because Jessica had told her. Sometimes, Elizabeth wanted to believe that she truly was fine with Jessica and Todd as a couple, and yet there were moments like these when she was reminded she might not ever be completely fine.

She could tell herself all she wanted that Jessica taking Todd turned out to be a life changer for her. It had made Bruce possible, but sometimes, she wondered, would she ever, truly forget the way it had happened?

"Yes. Our place." Jessica was beaming, her eyes brimming with excitement. Elizabeth realized it wasn't just the MeanGreen gala that had brought the color back into her sister's face.

"What's your plan?"

"What do you mean?" Jessica tried to sound innocent.

"Don't play coy. I know you have a plan. You always do."

Jessica shrugged. "Well, you know what we've been fighting about. You know how Todd feels about me working. So, I've come to a decision." Jessica took a deep breath. "I'm going to quit my job."

Elizabeth just stared. She couldn't have been more surprised than if Jessica had told her she planned to join NASA's space program to Mars.

"I'm sorry—did you say *quit*?"

"Todd doesn't like me working, and he can support us all, so I'm going to tell him tonight that I'm going to stop working. I'm going to be there for him and Jake—one hundred percent. That way, he will see how much I love him and how much I'm willing to give up for him, and, well, how can he say no to an offer like that? Don't you think it's perfect, Lizzie?"

No, Elizabeth did not think it was perfect. It was about as far from perfect as you could get. Jessica had only just found this career where she was not only a valuable member of a team but was also supremely competent. Elizabeth thought of the magic her sister had worked with Bruce's PR nightmare, and she knew it wasn't just a fluke. Jessica had serious talent. To give that all up for Todd? Was she crazy?

"Have you thought about . . ." Elizabeth began softly, trying to figure out a way to say what she thought needed to be said without upsetting her sister.

"How I'm going to do it?" Jessica cut her off, eager to tell her all about her plans. "I'm going to resign tonight, right after the gala. By the time I meet Todd for dinner, I'll be able to tell him it's already done."

"Are you sure you want to do that today? You could wait."

"Why wait? My mind is made up. I'm doing it tonight."

Elizabeth thought Jessica was making a huge mistake, but as she looked at her sister's face, her twin, and saw the happiness and hope there, she knew she wouldn't be the one to burst that bubble. Besides, when Jessica had a plan it was almost impossible to derail her. And Elizabeth could be wrong.

Not to mention, Elizabeth didn't trust her own motives. She did want Jessica and Todd back together for Jake's sake and for everyone, really, but maybe part of her . . . Well, maybe a very small part of her hoped they wouldn't. The smartest thing would be to stay out of it, she decided.

Jessica failed to notice the doubt on her sister's face. She was busy scooping up a spare lipstick and compact and sliding them into her clutch. "But here I am going on about Todd. Did you find out anything about the lying skank who is accusing Bruce?"

Elizabeth flinched at the harshness with which her sister dismissed Robin Platt's claims. If she knew how scared and sincere the girl really seemed, she doubted Jessica would be so heartless.

Elizabeth remembered the girl's shabby place and the fear in her eyes when she'd talked about Bruce nearly raping her.

Elizabeth didn't know what to think or whom to believe anymore.

And as much as she tried to forget, all she could think of was how Robin seemed to know such private things about Elizabeth that only Bruce could have told her. Plus, there was the little tidbit about him saying that the sex with her was boring. It was hurtful, horrible actually, and it tapped right into Elizabeth's lack of confidence, her fear that she was just the way she looked tonight—dreary and dull, the boring, do-gooder sister, plain old Elizabeth, without any of the sparkle and excitement of her fabulous sister.

Standing in her jeans next to Jessica's sequins and platform stilettos only seemed to underline this point.

"Um . . . No, nothing more . . . but . . ." Elizabeth couldn't meet her sister's gaze. She didn't like lying to her about Robin, but she wasn't ready to tell her or anyone else what she'd found, either.

"But what?" Jessica's radar was up and sharp.

"Well . . . the more I dig, the more I talk to the bartender and . . . everyone else. I don't know, Jess. Some things just don't match. I have doubts."

"Doubts? What do you mean? About Rick Warner being behind this?"

"No. There are inexplicable holes in Bruce's story, Jess. Like the bartender saying he was really trying to pick up this girl. And how he supposedly had had too much to drink and . . ."

"You can't honestly be suggesting that Bruce tried to rape an intern." Jessica's voice was stony. Elizabeth could see her mistake. Jessica was firmly in Bruce Patman's camp and there was no budging her. Of course, she knew only part of the story. "We've known him most of our *lives*. You can't doubt him now. And you *live* with him. Come on, Elizabeth. You can't let some random bartender talk you into something that's just not true. You know Bruce."

"I know." But did she? Did she really? After all, he'd been kind of a jerk—actually worse than a jerk—in high school. What if, after all this time, he still was that guy? Maybe the new Bruce personality was just some kind of put-on for her, a cover story to hide the real Bruce underneath.

"So? Don't let the story get to you," Jessica said. "I know in the end he'll be vindicated. Just you watch."

4

Mme Dechamps placed a bowl of steaming bouillabaisse in front of Elizabeth in Bruce's formal dining room.

Since there was no red meat in it, it was actually something she could eat, and yet ironically, she had no appetite.

"Bon appétit!" Mme Dechamps sang, then retreated to the kitchen.

Elizabeth could feel Bruce's gaze on her as she pushed mussels and bass listlessly around her bowl.

"Did you want to go out?" Bruce asked. "I could ask her to wrap this up for later. We could try."

Elizabeth shook her head.

It wasn't likely that the two of them could make a clean getaway with the paparazzi lining up outside his gate, and they both knew it. Not that Elizabeth minded a quiet night in, but the air was thick with questions she needed to ask Bruce. Yet she was afraid of the answers he'd give.

"Elizabeth. Is something wrong?"

"I interviewed the bartender," Elizabeth said, still staring at the bouillabaisse. "He said you'd had more than one drink."

"I'm pretty sure it was one," Bruce said. He paused as if remembering.

Elizabeth didn't like the uncertainty in Bruce's voice. Why did it seem like his story was shifting? Or was she just imagining that?

"He said you were hitting on this girl," Elizabeth said, and then instantly tried to talk herself out of it. "But then, bartenders see pickups all the time. They probably assume all conversations between strangers are pickups."

"Impossible," Bruce said, sounding firm and certain again. "The girl was obviously frantic. And I suggested she call a shelter. There wasn't anything sexual about it."

"To you, maybe. And you still aren't certain how many drinks you had."

"Okay, I wouldn't swear . . ."

"And you were dizzy."

"From the food poisoning," Bruce said, raising his voice a little.

"Okay, so you weren't feeling quite yourself," Elizabeth said. "And you were just being friendly and she misinterpreted."

"No, it wasn't that way at all. She was upset. I was just trying to help."

Elizabeth opened her mouth to tell him she'd interviewed the girl, but something stopped her. Somehow, she knew, if she told Bruce, he'd insist on talking to Robin or on releasing her name to the public. She wasn't ready to do that to Robin. Not yet. But she still needed to know about some of the things she'd said.

"You were overheard talking about me that night." Elizabeth glanced down at her uneaten dinner.

"You?" Bruce said. "Why on earth would I be talking about you with this girl?"

"You supposedly said I was . . ." Elizabeth swallowed. She couldn't quite get out the words *boring in bed.* "You weren't happy with me."

"Elizabeth." Bruce turned three different shades of red. Was he angry? Or was he just trying to figure out how to lie his way out of being caught? Elizabeth couldn't help remembering the Bruce Patman of high school: the arrogant, entitled Bruce who believed he could get away with anything. "You know me. Do you really think I'd talk about you to a stranger? Where are you getting this stuff?"

Elizabeth glanced up at him, hoping she'd regain her trust and confidence in the new Bruce, the thoughtful and caring man who wasn't an arrogant kid anymore. That was the Bruce who had helped her through the most difficult period in her life, after Todd left her for Jessica.

All she wanted was to believe him. Why was she having such trouble?

"Maybe because of the alcohol and being dizzy you don't remember what you said," Elizabeth said. She wanted an excuse. If he admitted to drinking, maybe this would all make sense.

"No." Bruce shook his head.

"The bartender was sure he'd served you more than one drink."

"Well, he's wrong." Bruce put down his spoon and it landed with a tight *plink* in his bowl. "You don't believe me."

His voice sounded hard like steel and there was a flash of anger in his eyes. For a second, Elizabeth tensed, remembering a flash from the past.

It had been after she'd been in that motorcycle accident in high school. She'd had a concussion so severe it put her into a temporary coma. A few weeks after the accident, she'd been at the Patman's beach house, and Bruce had been plying her with wine. She'd been flirty with him at the time, she remembered, which, in high school, since she didn't like him then, was proof of just how much the concussion had affected her.

At some point, Elizabeth wanted to leave. She remembered that. But then Bruce had grabbed her and forced her to kiss him. His lips had been so rough and his hands tight on her shoulders.

She didn't remember his words, only the fear she felt.

Even now she could feel the chill that had gone down her spine. Was he threatening her then?

She shook her head. No. Was that even right? She couldn't be remembering that right. She'd had the concussion and hadn't felt like herself. Plus, she'd just been a kid—they were both kids then—and she'd been making out with him and they were drinking wine. Too much wine.

Besides, that was the old Bruce. This was the new. The new Bruce had already apologized for being a jerk in high school, blaming it on being shortsighted and immature. The new Bruce was responsible and caring and would never do anything like that. Right?

But now, looking at the simmering anger in his eyes, Elizabeth couldn't be completely sure. Doubt blossomed in her brain, taking root like a stubborn weed, choking out the trust she thought she had with Bruce.

"No, I do, Bruce. I believe you." She tried to meet his eyes, but she couldn't quite. Elizabeth truly wasn't sure she did, after all.

The next day, early in the morning, before Bruce was awake, Elizabeth snuck out. She wanted to talk to Robin before she was due at work. Somehow, she knew she was missing something. If she could just ask Robin the right questions, she could find out the truth.

On the way over, she turned up news radio and heard another report about Bruce. Jessica's PR campaign was working like a charm. Two more celebrities had come out in favor of him, both of them women. He was fast becoming a more popular cause than climate change.

"Frankly, Bruce is the most honest, forthright, and socially responsible person I know," said one of the actresses on the radio. Elizabeth remembered her for being a big fund-raiser for the American Theatre Wing. "I do think that once all the facts come out, he'll be exonerated. It's a shame that some people will do anything for a little fame or money."

Elizabeth leaned forward and switched off the radio. She should've been cheering the woman on, grateful for the support for Bruce, and yet she just felt a little nauseous.

She turned down Robin's street and pulled into a nearby space.

When Elizabeth knocked on the door, it took a few minutes for Robin to answer. She saw movement by the front curtain, as if the girl was peering out. She heard two bolts slide open and then Robin was at the door.

"Thank God it's you, Laura," she said, relief visible on her face. Elizabeth felt a pang of guilt about continuing the lie that she was Laura Christer, a counselor from Robin's church. But if Robin had known Elizabeth's true identity, she would have never opened her door—much less talked. "Hurry. Come inside."

Robin ushered Elizabeth in and then glanced out the door right and left, as if double-checking to see if Elizabeth had been followed. Inside, the lower level of her town house was as shabby as Elizabeth remembered, and yet now it seemed even more in disarray. There were takeout containers littering the table and even an empty pizza box on the floor. Robin herself wore a pair of stained yoga pants and a worn sweatshirt, her hair up in a hasty knot on top of her head. She looked like she hadn't left her place in days. It had the feel of a bunker.

The television was tuned to the news in her living room. Another actress—an Oscar winner—sat talking on some morning show.

"I know the truth will come out," she was saying. "I've known Bruce Patman a long time. I know he's innocent."

Robin looked at the television and then back at Elizabeth.

"Everyone thinks I'm a liar," she said, her eyes wide and bright, tears visible in them. "Even Oscar-winning actresses. Nobody is going to believe me now. They all just think I'm an opportunist. And . . . Laura . . . I'm so scared. I'm starting to get phone calls."

"What kind of calls?"

"Reporters, I think. I'm not sure. They keep hanging up. I think they've found me."

Elizabeth wondered if Andy, her colleague at the *Tribune* who was officially covering Bruce's story, had dug up Robin's name. After all, Elizabeth had found her. Andy could, too. Except a reporter would want to *talk* to her. Still, obviously *someone* had found her. The question was who?

"It's okay, Robin. We'll figure something out."

"I just . . . I don't know what to do, Laura. I haven't left my house in days. I'm just . . . I'm scared. Really scared. If reporters find me, then maybe Mr. Patman, will, too. And after what he did . . ."

Tears brimmed in her eyes and then slid down Robin's cheeks. She buried her face in her hands. Almost without thinking, Elizabeth laid a comforting arm on her shoulders. Instantly, Robin convulsed in sobs.

"It's okay. It will be okay." Elizabeth's heart broke for this young girl who was so clearly frightened. If she was telling the truth, she was victimized not just once with the near rape but again with the public smear campaign. Elizabeth gave herself a mental shake. If she believed this girl, that meant Bruce was guilty.

And yet . . . Robin seemed so sincere. How do you fake tears like that? And the fear in her eyes was real. Elizabeth knew that. And she seemed so shaky.

Standing in the girl's shabby living room, Elizabeth knew she wouldn't be able to decide right now. Seeing Robin only brought up more questions than answers. She needed time to think. But she also knew she had to protect Robin. From everyone. And that meant Bruce, too.

Then she remembered the for-rent sign in front of a house near Robin's church. She had enough money to cover the girl's rent for a few months, and if she used her own name on the lease, no one would find her.

"I have an idea," she told Robin. "How do you feel about moving?"

5

Lila Fowler had been plucked, waxed, and spray-tanned to perfection. Her favorite stylist had worked her usual magic with makeup and hair, and she looked killer in her new Jason Wu micromini, so short that she was pretty sure she couldn't sit down without giving away the show. Her sparkling, platform Jimmy Choo stilettos were sky-high, and everything about her outfit screamed sex.

She looked good enough to eat, and she knew it.

Getting past security at the stadium had been a breeze. Her name was still on the players' private guest list. She took it as a good sign that Ken hadn't yet thought to strike her name. It wasn't exactly an offer of reconciliation, but Lila chose to see it that way.

She waited outside the men's locker room in her dangerously high heels, feeling a bit overdressed in the concrete-encased hallway leading to the showers. She was also starting to feel a tad bit nervous. The longer she stood outside the locker room, the more she started to doubt her plan. What if Ken left by a different door? Was there another door to the locker room? Honestly, she couldn't remember. Lila had only ever gone to two other games before. She'd barely taken an interest in his career before now, much less the layout of the stadium.

Now she began to worry that maybe there was another exit on the other side, closer to the parking lot. Every so often, a coach or player would pass by and give her the eye. Even the married ones couldn't quite keep their eyes off her.

"Can I get you something, Mrs. Matthews?" asked a red-faced intern who was probably in college but looked like he was a freshman in high school. His face burned bright red and he couldn't look Lila in the face. His eyes landed in a fixed position about six inches lower.

"No, I'm fine. . . . Actually, it is drafty out here. Do you think I could go in and look for my husband?"

"Actually, women who don't have press credentials aren't allowed . . ."

extension off her shoulder, and Lila felt a twinge of jealousy. That's how she knew that Ashley might actually be some serious competition.

Not that Lila had ever let a little thing like a rival get in the way of winning before. She stood up a little straighter and walked with purpose across the parking lot, her stilettos clacking with determination against the asphalt.

"Ken," she purred as she squeezed herself in between her husband and Ashley, all but shoving Ashley out of the way. Ashley stumbled backward and let out a small squeal of protest. "We need to talk."

"No, we don't," Ken said, his eyes growing hard again as he looked at her. "We have nothing to talk about, Lila."

"But, Ken . . ." Lila arched her back in a move that she knew put her cleavage in the most mouthwatering light, and pursed her lips in a kissable pout. Lila knew Ken couldn't resist her sexy sad face. At least, he never had before.

Ken waved a hand in front of her, dismissing both her sexy sad face and her sexy . . . everything.

"We're *over,* Lila. I told you that. I'm done trying to make you happy when you don't care about me at all. I'm done bending over backward trying to please you. What do I get for it? Insults on national television. I swear, Lila, you're so selfish, you can't even see the truth right in front of your face. I'm done *with you.*"

The words cut through Lila like a cold wind. Beside her, she could feel Ashley gloating, which made this situation a thousand times worse. Lila's face burned with humiliation and shame for being rejected by Ken, and even worse, having it witnessed by Ashley.

Lila stood, frozen to the spot, speechless. She couldn't figure out why this wasn't working and why Ken didn't seem to want her at all. It was as if someone had changed the locks on her house without telling her. Why didn't her old keys work?

"Come on, Ashley," Ken said, ignoring Lila's flushed face as she stood as still as a statue and watched Ashley curl her arm around Ken's. He led her to the passenger-side door, and she showed most of her leg and nearly everything else as she slid into the front seat.

As Ken came around, Lila found her voice again. This time on a different tack. An unusual one for Lila.

"I don't want this to be over, Ken." It was true enough to take her by surprise. But his answer was even more shocking.

"Well, I do." Ken turned, slipped into the driver's seat, and slammed his car door. Seconds later, he backed out of the parking space, spun the car around, and drove swiftly away from her.

Lila watched his taillights flicker and decided so much for honesty. It never was her style. She needed to shift gears. She needed a strong plan B that would get him back, even if she had to play dirty.

She glanced around the parking lot and saw one of the other players and his wife and kids climbing into a silver Cadillac Escalade. The wife carried a telltale belly bump. Clearly baby number three was on the way.

That was it, Lila thought. Her plan B.

⌒

She waited until the perfect moment later that evening, right in the middle of an on-camera cocktail party at fellow *Housewives* star Devone Waters's house. Lila waited until all the housewives had arrived—all but Ashley, who was most likely with Ken at that very moment—before she announced the news.

As Devone offered her a glass of wine, Lila demurely refused and asked for club soda. Then she positioned herself in the center of the living room, at the best possible camera angle, and turned to Devone, whom she knew had three kids already. Devone would be the first one on her side.

"Devone," she said, her voice quavering just a little. "Marina," she added, glancing at the other Housewife. "I need help." She grasped both their hands and held them. That would look particularly good on camera, she knew. Devone and Marina exchanged surprised glances.

Lila sniffed, letting the perfect tear form on her eyelash before it dropped down her cheek.

"Lila! What's wrong?" gushed Devone, taken aback by Lila Fowler Matthews's tears. Lila usually shouted; she never cried.

"K-Ken left me for Ashley." She waited for the surprised intakes of breath all around. Even some of the camera crew appeared surprised by the dramatic turn of events.

"Oh, Lila, I'm so sorry," said Devone.

"But that's not all." Lila inhaled deeply, building the drama. She released Marina's hand to put her own delicately on her lower belly.

"I'm pregnant," she said. She could feel the camera lenses zoom in on her, and she could also sense across the room a subtle but substantial shift in feeling. It was the same shift that would no doubt happen nationwide as soon as this episode aired.

Lila wasn't going to be Public Enemy/Bitch #1 anymore.

Now it was Ashley's turn.

6

Caroline Pearce was like a vindictive elephant—she never forgot a grudge. The fact that most of the people who knew her would also say she looked like one, too, was something she preferred not to think about. No matter how hard she dieted or exercised or what kind of clothes she wore, she'd always be boxy and thick, and at some level, frumpy.

Some might say it was jealousy more than anything else that motivated her now, as she worked to dig up dirt on the gorgeous Jessica Wakefield. Caroline never found it easy growing up two doors down from the beautiful Wakefield twins, always being compared to them and coming up short.

But Caroline saw it differently.

All she ever wanted was their friendship, or so she had convinced herself. Jessica never had been a good friend, a point that was hammered home not too long ago when Jessica so rudely threw her out of her house. Caroline only wanted to be a *good friend,* so that's why she went to warn Jessica that her nearly-ex-husband was fooling around with Sarah Miller.

Had Jessica been grateful to hear the news? No, she'd started screaming like a maniac and had thrown her out.

The rejection still stung.

And it hadn't been the first time, either.

For more than twenty years, Jessica had acted like she was better than Caroline and treated her like dirt, and Caroline wasn't going to take it anymore. Despite spreading often untrue rumors, Caroline easily convinced herself *she* was the victim, and that's why she'd been pressing her sources for any dirt she could dig up on Jessica.

Up until this morning, the rumors were all good news. She heard that Jessica and Todd might be getting back together, a thought that just made her stew with frustration. So she kept digging.

That morning, she finally hit gold.

It happened at yoga class at the Sweet Valley Gym. She had been doing downward dog next to her friend Amy Dent, who also worked as a clerk at the Imagine Hotel. They'd both bonded in the class, being the only women in there who weren't size sixes.

Amy bragged about seeing Liam O'Connor, *People*'s Sexiest Import, with a mystery woman recently at the hotel. After class, she'd even shown Caroline a picture she'd snapped on her phone.

That's when Caroline saw her prayers had been answered. Liam hadn't been with just anybody. The girl with him was none other than Jessica Wakefield.

There they were, standing together, waiting for the elevator that would take them to his room. She looked a little tipsy, as she leaned against him for support. They were cozy, to say the least.

But the juiciest bits came next.

"I snuck up to the room, which is a big no-no," Amy had confided to Caroline. "But I was going to ask if he might need anything, except that when I got to the room, I didn't even knock because I heard . . ." She leaned forward and continued in a whispered hush. "Some serious sex. These two? Let's just say . . . they weren't shy."

That was the quote Caroline planned to put in bold in her blog entry.

Now, she clacked happily at her keyboard. Outside, darkness fell. Tonight was Jessica's big MeanGreen gala, she'd heard about that, too. Well, here would be a nice little exclamation point on the end of *that* evening, she thought.

Jessica and Todd back together? Not when *this* news hit the blogosphere. Caroline only wished she could actually see Jessica's face when she read this. Maybe then she'd finally be sorry.

She decided then and there that when she was done with the blog entry, she'd e-mail Todd the link. Caroline wasn't going to sit around and hope Todd heard about it. She was going to make sure he did.

After all, that's only what a *good friend* would do.

7

Just as Annie Whitman sat down in the courtroom her phone lit up with a text from Jessica.

CALL ME AS SOON AS YOU CAN. IT'S ABOUT BRUCE. WE NEED YOU.

She'd been waiting for this call ever since word of the scandal broke. The Bruce Patman case was right in her line of expertise. It was a case she was itching to handle. And now that she had moved up from San Diego to Sweet Valley, this was just the front-page trial that could shoot her right up to junior partner.

She glanced over at Doug, one of the three named partners in the firm Leisten, Hartke & White, the biggest defense firm in Southern California, and thought she still should be pinching herself that she was working for the biggest and best firm in Los Angeles. Leisten, Hartke & White always landed the most important cases. Granted, she had been known as the best defense lawyer in San Diego. Doug had practically pleaded with her to join the firm. Still, she couldn't help feeling a little nervous today, her first time in the courtroom in Sweet Valley. Her hometown could do that.

Today Annie was representing the starlet who'd been sued by a member of the paparazzi for running over his foot in her Maserati.

"You'll do great," Doug told Annie, and smiled.

Annie took a deep breath. She tried not to think about the last time she'd stood in a courtroom before a judge. She hadn't been a lawyer at all, but a plaintiff.

That was six months ago, when she divorced Charlie Markus, her husband of seven years.

Charlie had been her high school sweetheart, the boy who helped her turn her life around. Without him in her life, she thought, she never would've finished law school. Or become one of San Diego's best defense attorneys.

He convinced her she knew how to defend people—to find in them what needed defending. She'd done it for herself her whole life, ever since she'd had to defend her reputation in high school. "Easy Annie," they'd called her. But not anymore.

She gave Charlie credit for that.

But something shifted during the course of their marriage, though Annie couldn't say exactly when. At some point, Charlie ceased to be the optimistic and loving boy who believed in her and became a bitter, vindictive man who blamed her for everything wrong in his life.

Charlie used to be the one to tell Annie that things weren't so bad. That was before he'd spent twelve years trying—and failing—to get one of his four novels published.

While his career floundered, hers flourished. She earned promotion after promotion; he got stuck with boring freelance assignments writing about suspension and brake systems for car magazines. Her salary passed his years ago. They weren't even in remotely the same tax bracket anymore.

At some point, Annie came to realize that Charlie's resentment wasn't a passing phase. That happened about the time she read, first page to last, one of his unpublished manuscripts, the one called *Easy Annie*.

Charlie would never have let her read it. He guarded his laptop more closely than his ATM PIN, but she'd stumbled on the manuscript by accident. He'd left a copy he'd planned to send to a prospective agent out on the kitchen counter. She moved it to avoid dripping coffee on it, never intending to read it. The first sentence, however, caught her attention:

Before she met me, Annie was nothing but a cheap, sad girl, the kind all the boys would use, but none of them could ever love. She was nothing but sloppy seconds.

Annie couldn't stop reading after that, and as she read more, she found it didn't get better, only worse. A switch flipped inside her then. She saw clearly for the first time that Charlie only wanted to be with her as long as he was the savior and she was the save-ee, as long as she never got more respect than he did.

During the last year of their marriage, Annie went through her angry phase, but eventually, by the end, after all the mediation and the back-and-forth about custody of their beautiful son, who would soon start kindergarten, and a lot of counseling, she came to forgive him.

Now she knew she'd always be grateful for the kindness Charlie had shown her in high school. A part of her would always love him, too, despite the cruel things he wrote about her. He had saved her back in high school. But now she was going to save herself.

And she did—by cutting the cord and leaving him.

She took a deep breath now and told herself she was a long way from that woman who'd lived under the thumb of a bitter husband in San Diego. After the divorce became final six months ago, she moved back to Sweet Valley, into the house her mother had left her when she died, and now she was going to start a new life here with her son.

A new life that included being a part of Leisten, Hartke & White.

She began her arguments to the judge. Her words flowed smoothly and none of her nerves showed. The more she talked, the more confident she became, until she was completely in control. She felt the judge coming to see her side.

Doug gave her a slight nod and she knew she'd nailed it. The starlet would go free and not have to pay a dime; the photographer would have some explaining to do about why he'd thrown himself onto the hood of her car in the first place.

At that moment, she felt more like herself than she had since she'd filed for divorce.

After the hearing, she texted Jessica. SORRY—JUST GOT OUT OF COURT. WHAT'S GOING ON?

Jessica texted back. WE NEED A LEGAL EXPERT. CAN YOU COME TO BRUCE'S HOUSE TODAY?

Annie answered: ABSOLUTELY.

She slipped her phone back into the front pocket of her briefcase. Bruce hadn't officially hired her as his defense attorney, but she hoped he would eventually. She'd been born to take his case. It would be monumental for her career, and it was one she felt pretty sure she could win.

She had no doubt Bruce was innocent.

Sure, Bruce had been full of himself in high school, but Annie had always had a soft spot for him, and now she was a little gleeful at the thought of helping him.

And she had Jessica to thank for that.

Amazing what a difference a few years makes. Since she'd come back to Sweet Valley, the two had actually become friends. She had always been close with Elizabeth, but since her firm began to handle VertPlus.net, Jessica's company, she had also been spending a lot of time with Jessica. The fact that they both were now single, working moms of little boys (hers now six and Jessica's two) also gave them lots to talk about.

Motherhood had mellowed Jessica, Annie thought. She wasn't quite the same spoiled Jessica from high school, the one who'd set out to keep her from the cheerleading squad. Boy, had she hated that Jessica then.

No, this was a more rational, more professional Jessica. Sure, she would always be a little self-centered, but that was just Jessica.

Now, Jessica had brought her—even unofficially—the most sought-after case in Southern California. Annie felt grateful.

Annie had good instincts. She had a talent for sniffing out something fishy with a victim's account, and in *this* story, something just didn't add up. She couldn't put her finger on it exactly, but she felt something was wrong, and she'd told Jessica so.

Eventually, she was sure, the truth would come out. It almost always did.

8

Steven Wakefield gently put baby Emma into her cradle shortly after two in the morning. He always held his breath when he put her down, praying the handoff to the crib wouldn't send her eyes flying open and unleash cries of protest.

Steven knew if she made even so much as a peep, his partner, Aaron, would be running down the hall and would scoop her up and rock her the rest of the night in his arms. And then she'd spend yet another night out of her crib.

Steven knew Aaron really did *mean* well. They both did. Both of them had instantly fallen for little Emma the day she was born to surrogate mother Linda Carson, whom Steven and Aaron had paid to supply the egg and carry Emma. They had both donated their sperm, and neither one knew who was actually the biological father. Not that it mattered. They were both her dads. So far she didn't look like either of them, really. She looked most like Linda, her mother, who shared her light blond hair and pink bow lips.

The problem was, Aaron spoiled little Emma. Aaron had read somewhere that babies who were held more often were better adjusted or smarter or something, and so now he had it in his head that the crib was evil and Emma should not spend time in it or in a stroller. Aaron went around with Emma strapped to him all day in a BabyBjörn, and at night, more often than not, Emma ended up in bed with them.

So now Emma cried bloody murder when put down—whether in her crib, her swing, or on her play mat—and insisted on being carried or held at all times. It was exhausting. And easily avoided, Steven thought.

All Emma needed was a little bit of tough love, a *tiny* bit of crying it out in her crib, and she'd adjust. That's what babies did.

Steven laid little Emma in her crib without waking her and thought *Victory!* as he edged his way out of the nursery. Near the door, his right foot landed on a stuffed cat with a voice box, and the ensuing *meow* rocked the quiet nursery. Steven cringed, waiting for the high-pitched wail. Emma just let out a soft little cry, almost like a yawn.

A microsecond later, Aaron was at the door.

"What are you *doing*? You know you can't just put her down in that pink prison." Aaron walked straight in and snatched the half-asleep Emma off her pink Land of Nod crib sheet.

Emma, now fully awake from the jostling against Aaron's shoulder, started to cry.

"That pink prison cost us fifteen hundred dollars," Steven pointed out. Aaron had been the one to insist on the top-of-the-line crib, and now he refused to even *put* her in it. The nursery itself was a designer shrine that Emma spent next to no time in at all, since every one of her waking and sleeping hours was spent in somebody's arms.

"You want Emma to grow up to be a sociopath? Because that's what you're doing if you leave her all alone at night in this jail." Aaron patted Emma on the back, and she snuggled into his shoulder and fell asleep.

"Do *you* want her to grow up to be spoiled and entitled like Jessica?" This, of course, was Steven's greatest fear. After all, he had vague memories of Jessica never sleeping in a crib, either, and demanding to be held at all hours. End result? Well . . . Exhibit A: Jessica Wakefield.

"She's not Jessica," Aaron said, his tone implying that even the comparison was an insult. "She comes to sleep with us."

"It's not safe, Aaron. What if I roll over on her? What about SIDS? The crib is the safest place to be."

"The crib is the loneliest place to be," Aaron said, refusing to back down. "What kind of parent abandons their child in a crib? She cries when she's in it."

"That's why you let her cry it out."

Aaron just looked at Steven as if he'd suggested they ought to have Emma's left arm amputated.

"I'm going to pretend I didn't hear that," he said as he walked down the hall to their bedroom.

Steven sighed. This is what happened when Aaron spent too much time with the granola-hippie moms down at the baby yoga classes on the weekends. What's wrong with a baby sleeping in a crib? Steven didn't understand.

When Emma slept in their bed, Steven couldn't sleep. He was petrified he'd fall asleep, roll over, and suffocate her. He didn't know how much longer he could take it. These days Steven was a zombie at work. He held a lucrative but demanding job as a junior partner at Leisten, Hartke & White. That was sixty-plus full hours a week of difficult work on no sleep.

But Aaron, who'd taken an extended leave from his job, was happy to catch up on sleep in the afternoons, when Emma napped.

Steven walked down the hall, dejected. When he got to their bedroom, he saw Emma was now wide-awake and bouncing on Aaron's knee.

"Did that pink prison scare you, little sweetheart?" Aaron was cooing in baby talk.

"You have to be kidding me." Steven sighed as he slumped down on his side of the bed.

"I think my princess needs a little surprise," Aaron said. "How about it, Ems? A surprise?"

The baby cooed a little and clapped her hands. She might have been not quite five months old, but she already knew the word *surprise*. It was something Aaron had been saying since she was born. Aaron never met a baby rattle or toy he could resist buying, especially if it was wildly expensive and would be played with only once or twice. Little Emma had more clothes than both of the men combined. In less than five months, she'd filled all the closets in their house.

"Aaron, doesn't she have enough toys?"

"Nothing's too good for my princess," Aaron declared, handing her a brand-new rattle from the bag of goodies he'd bought yesterday at some designer baby shop.

She promptly put the rattle in her mouth and gummed the edges.

"You can't give her a new toy *every* day." He plucked the little rattle from Emma's hands. Yesterday, Aaron had "surprised" Emma with a plush rocking horse, even though she couldn't even sit up on her own yet.

Emma grabbed at the empty air.

"She wants it back," Aaron said.

"Not until she goes to sleep. *In her crib.*" Someone had to be a disciplinarian around here.

And then Emma's bottom lip started to quiver and the waterworks began. Emma might have been a baby, but she knew already that neither of her papas could stand it when she cried. All she had to do was turn it up a little, and she'd get anything she wanted.

At these times, the Jessica Wakefield gene was strongly suspected.

In seconds, Emma had the new toy back in her hands, and neither of her daddies insisted she sleep at all, in her crib or anywhere else.

That didn't escape Emma's notice, either. She knew for a fact just who was running this show.

And it wasn't either of them.

Jessica had never felt so much like she was flying as she did backstage at the MeanGreen gala. Everything went exactly as planned, actually *better* than planned. The models in their body paint stalked down the runway in breathtaking form; Jessica could already feel the buzz building in the night, and the dramatic makeup only heightened the whole experience.

The audience was filled not only with industry people but also with a few well-placed celebrities who liked to tweet about *it* things.

The show was only half over when the Twitterverse exploded. In fact, by the time the show was over, the models and their all-nude paint was all anyone was talking about. #MeanGreen, in fact, hit the top three trending topics by night's end.

"You nailed this one, boss," whispered Katy Johnson, her assistant, backstage. In that one moment, Jessica knew she really had. For the first time, she didn't feel like an imposter. She'd really done this. It wasn't some fluke or happy accident. This had been her brainchild and it had been a wild success.

Even her boss, Michael Wilson, executive vice president of VertPlus .net's Sweet Valley office, agreed.

"Great work out there tonight," he told her as he gave her elbow a little squeeze. In the background, the indie band Hilt was rocking the stage.

Hilt had been a suggestion from Liam, who knew the band's lead guitarist. Despite his overtexting lately, she had to admit that Liam had really come through with the band. She'd have to thank him tomorrow.

Michael grabbed a flute of champagne from a passing tray and handed it to her. Jessica took it happily. The gala was winding down, and it was now or never. She had to put her plan into motion so she could go meet Todd for their late dinner at Le Bouchon.

She glanced at Michael's face, framed by short, sandy-colored hair, and thought he carried the kind of boyish good looks that she could really go for. That is, if she weren't already in love with Todd.

"Thanks, Michael. Actually, there was something I wanted to talk to you about."

Michael met her eyes, and for a split second, she saw hope there. It was clear to nearly everyone he liked her beyond a professional level. He'd ratcheted up the flirting since Jessica had publically separated from Todd. Of course, Michael never stepped over the line. He kept their relationship friendly and professional, but in recent months, he'd grown slightly warmer. He also found excuses to touch her more. Like his hand on her elbow right now.

In his eyes, she saw a flicker of desire . . . and hope.

Jessica hesitated, but then decided to rip off the Band-Aid quickly. She had never been one to baby anybody.

"Michael, I have loved the opportunities I've had here at VertPlus.net. I've enjoyed working with you so much."

Confusion passed across Michael's face. "Jessica, it sounds like you're leaving."

"I'm sorry, Michael, but I think I need to spend more time with my family." Jessica knew this was the last thing he wanted to hear, but she pressed on. There wasn't any need now to pretend that she put her career first and her family second. Now she could just put her family first. In some ways, that came as a kind of relief. Mostly. Except for the nagging doubt in her mind. Was she doing the right thing? She pushed aside the thought. It was too late now anyway. Todd was waiting for her.

"My son, Jake, needs me, and I'm going to try to spend some time working on my marriage."

She could see those words came as a real shock to Michael. Like the rest of the office, he'd been hearing rumors she might be dating Liam O'Connor. Nobody had ever mentioned she was getting back together with her husband, Todd.

"Jessica, please. Have you thought this through?"

Jessica didn't know if he meant the job or Todd, but in either case, her answer was the same.

"I have, Michael. I've made up my mind." At least, she thought she had. But something about the look on her boss's face, and the fact that she was about to walk away from the one place where she'd proven to everyone just what a winner she really was, made her pause. Was she doing the right thing? Somehow, it didn't quite feel like it.

"If it's the money, we could negotiate something. . . ."

"No, Michael. It's not about money. It's personal. I want to make my marriage work and I have to do this."

Michael's shoulders slumped and he looked at his feet, realizing there really wasn't any way he could force her to stay.

"Well, we'll miss you, Jessica." Michael moved in for a hug, and she let him.

For a horrible second, she even thought she might cry. But she didn't. As hard as this was to do, she knew she'd made her choice. She was giving up her career for Todd. And, as she thought about her husband waiting for her at Le Bouchon, all doubt and sadness disappeared.

She was going to have her family back and this sacrifice would be worth it.

10

Todd was waiting for her in the all-white lobby of Le Bouchon with a bouquet of white roses. He had on a dark suit, which he wore like the former athlete he was. He was tall and broad, and as she walked in, he had flicked the hair off his forehead in that gesture she'd come to know so well.

Instantly, a smile broke out on both their faces; they grinned at each other like teenagers in love.

Jessica hadn't had time to change before heading to Le Bouchon, but her strapless red dress was a stunner, she knew.

"Wow," Todd said, giving a low whistle. "You look . . . beautiful."

A dozen other people had told her that same thing during the gala, but she realized Todd's opinion was the only one that really mattered. Jessica took the flowers he offered and inhaled.

"Madame is here, then," said the maître d', grabbing two leather-bound menus. "Your table is ready. If you will follow me. . . ."

Todd offered her the crook of his arm and she took it. The cozy, up-scale bistro, with its intimate, white-linen-covered tables and candlelight, rose up before Jessica and took her back three years ago, when Todd had proposed.

Theirs had not been an easy relationship. Both of them had resisted the attraction they had felt for each other for years, for Elizabeth's sake. After all, Elizabeth and Todd were the ones everyone thought would get married, not Jessica and Todd. That all changed when Elizabeth found out about them, and then moved to New York. A bitter and heartbreaking eight months passed, but eventually Elizabeth began to forgive them as Bruce came into the picture.

It was three years ago, next month, that Todd got down on one knee in the middle of Le Bouchon and offered her a beautiful diamond solitaire platinum ring. He'd had tears in his eyes when he proposed, and Jessica had, too.

Now here they were again, back in the place their life together really began. If there was a better place to reconcile, she didn't know it.

The maître d' led them to the cozy table in the back where they had sat on their one-year wedding anniversary. The top of their wedding cake hadn't survived the ceremony, but Todd had gone to the same bakery and had commissioned them to re-create just the top with the decorative pink roses.

Sitting across from Todd now, Jessica realized that she was never as happy as she was when she was with Todd. This was where she belonged.

After he'd ordered a bottle of their favorite wine, he took her hand in his and drew her close.

"Jessica, I have to say, I feel so happy tonight. These last few months I have been miserable. And I just want to tell you how sorry I am . . . about Sarah, about . . . accusing you of trying to get her fired . . . for everything. Mostly about the things I said about that first night all those years ago. I knew it wasn't true."

"These last few months have been the hardest for me, too. I'm so sorry." And then, because she had to know: "Are you still seeing Sarah?" Jessica took a deep breath to brace herself for the answer. Her throat went dry and she reached for her water glass.

"No." Todd shook his head. "Jessica, she doesn't mean anything to me, and I'm so glad to hear that nothing happened between you and Liam, because . . . well, nothing happened between Sarah and me, either."

"What?" Jessica nearly choked on her sip of water. "What do you mean nothing?" Could it be possible that Todd had *never* slept with Sarah? "But what you said, and the rumors . . ."

"Were just empty threats and rumors," Todd said. "Look, I'm not going to lie to you. Sarah wanted to take things further, but any time she tried . . . well, I just thought of you. And I couldn't. Because I love you, Jessica. You're the only one I really want."

Jessica felt a rush of relief—Todd really *hadn't* slept with Sarah.

"I love you, too," she said, shaking off the little twinge of guilt she felt, and squeezing his hand. "And that's why, tonight, after the gala, which was completely amazing by the way . . ." Jessica saw the tight look cross Todd's face, and she immediately backed away from any talk of the gala. That's not what this night was about. Who cared if it went well? Her job with VertPlus.net was history. Todd was her future. "What I meant to say was that right afterward, I quit. It's over. I'm not going to work at VertPlus.net anymore. I want to be your wife and the best mother I can be for Jake. That's it."

"Jessica . . . are you sure?"

"I've never been more certain of anything in my whole life," Jessica said, and right at that moment, holding Todd's hand and seeing him gaze at her with love, she meant it.

Todd slipped into the seat next to her, wrapping his arm around her waist, and gave her a kiss that made everything worth it. Jessica didn't care if other patrons were staring, either. This was the man she wanted to spend the rest of her life with.

Todd pulled away first.

"You know, I knew we would be good together, but I had no idea *how* good."

"Me too." Jessica's voice sounded a little husky.

"And I knew we would get back together the moment I found out that there was nothing between you and Liam," Todd continued. "You don't even know how the thought of you and him drove me crazy. I know I shouldn't ask, but I can't help it. How did he take it when you turned him down? I bet he doesn't get turned down very often."

Jessica's stomach tightened a little. It was one thing to omit the truth. It was another thing to fabricate a whole story about how it didn't happen. Was she going to have to do that?

Thankfully, the waiter interrupted them.

"Are you ready to order?" the waiter asked, and Todd and Jessica looked at each other and grinned.

"My wife will start with the beet salad and then have the salmon." Todd knew her favorite meal by heart.

"And my husband will start with the tomato bisque, followed by le steak frites."

"How would you like the steak cooked, monsieur?"

"Medium rare," they both said at the same time, and then laughed a little. The waiter bowed and then retreated, and Todd lifted his wineglass.

"To us," he said. "To true love."

"To true love," Jessica agreed, and they clinked glasses.

There might have been other customers that night, but Jessica didn't notice them. All she saw was Todd. The meal was the best she'd ever eaten, and she just felt warm all over. She knew she'd made the right choice. She was happy for the first time in a long, long time.

"Todd, I only ever wanted to be with you. There's no one else for me. Will you come home?"

Todd smiled. "You don't know how long I've been waiting to hear you say those words. Yes, yes, *yes*. I want to move back home. You and Jake are all I've ever wanted."

Todd leaned in to kiss her just as the waiter arrived with their check. The couple sprang apart but couldn't help giggling a bit. Todd reached for his wallet and Jessica excused herself to go check her makeup in the ladies' room.

Once inside, she gazed at her reflection in the mirror and saw a beautiful girl whose face was flushed with love. Her blue eyes shone, and she knew she was truly happy. Her makeup was flawless as always, but she did reapply a little bit of lipstick. She wanted to look her best for Todd. She imagined the two of them leaving the restaurant hand in hand, and how quickly they'd be home together. Already, she thought of what it would be like to have Todd back in her bed.

Jake and Liza would be asleep by the time she got home, of course. She would have to wait to tell Jake in the morning. Then again, maybe she wouldn't have to. Maybe Todd would be there himself to tell his son they would be a family again. No more Daddy-Wednesday nights and every other weekend. Just Daddy every night. Forever.

Back at the table, Todd signed the credit slip and, out of habit, pulled out his iPhone. That's when he saw a new e-mail waiting for him. Oddly, it was from Caroline Pearce. She was always sending him some new gossip, but Todd usually ignored her.

But this e-mail caught his attention. The subject read: "Jessica and Liam— Friends with Benefits."

Todd clicked open the e-mail. And there, sitting at the table, he read every detail, down to the orgasmic sounds coming from Liam O'Connor's hotel room. But the worst thing of all, the most damning evidence, was the photo of Jessica leaning against Liam, waiting for the elevator that would take her to his room. How much more proof did he need?

Todd felt like someone had ripped up the floor beneath him and he was in a desperate free fall.

Jessica had manipulated and lied to him *again*. He'd temporarily forgotten what a conniving and devious person she could be, but he swore he'd never forget again.

How could he trust her at all? He couldn't. It was just that simple.

He threw down his napkin on the table and left.

Jessica missed him by less than a minute. When she came back to the table, she found the busboy sweeping away the dirty dishes. At first, she didn't understand. Where had he gone? She took her purse and walked out through the lobby of the restaurant and into the parking lot.

That's when she saw his car was gone.

She grabbed her phone from her purse. Surely he'd texted? But, no. No message from Todd.

She did, however, have one new e-mail from Caroline Pearce.

She didn't even have to open it. The title alone told her she'd lost and nothing would ever be the same again.

11

A week later Elizabeth stood in the wings of the local Sweet Valley morning show, watching Bruce talk to Mindy Pete, the perky news anchor with the wavy strawberry blond hair and bright green eyes. In any place other than Southern California, she would've been supermodel material, but here in Sweet Valley, she ranked only barely above average.

Bruce had asked Elizabeth to come this morning and she had, despite the fact that she should've been checking in with Robin. She had moved to her new house yesterday, and Elizabeth had promised to come by and help her unpack.

Instead, Elizabeth was stuck watching Bruce and the perky news anchor slowly dismantle the scared girl's credibility.

"Unfortunately, we've really come to a place where there's no due process anymore," Bruce said in his level, reasonable-sounding voice. "Anyone can accuse anyone of anything, and there's just the assumption of guilt."

"Yes," agreed Christina Black, an actress who had been one of Bruce's most vocal supporters. She was sitting next to him on the little couch on the morning show set. The actress, brunette and tan and leggy, also happened to be in the top spy thriller released just that week.

Jessica had said Bruce shouldn't be alone in any of his interviews. She thought it best if he appeared with a supportive woman by his side, someone credible but not an attorney, because no one went on television with a lawyer unless they were guilty.

Part of Elizabeth felt like she should've been the one sitting beside Bruce on camera. Yet she'd quickly backed away from the idea when Jessica had mentioned it a few days ago. Bad idea. Robin would certainly see her on television next to Bruce and her cover would be blown. But, worse than that, deep down, she wasn't sure she could convince other people that Bruce was innocent. Elizabeth didn't know what she herself believed these days. Bruce's story had so many holes. It just didn't add up. And then there was that nagging memory of the Bruce from high school at his family's beach house that she just couldn't quite forget. Had he just been a dumb, drunk teenager? Or was there something more to it?

"The sad thing about this whole situation," Christina continued, "is that most people think someone like Bruce, who has wealth and power, is invincible. But the fact is, anyone, for *any* reason, can come forward and make a ridiculous claim like this and suddenly all of Bruce's hard work championing the environment and other social causes just goes out the window. It's unfortunate that good men like Bruce have become such easy targets in this accuse-first, ask-questions-later society."

Mindy nodded her head solemnly, agreeing. Mindy would likely agree with whatever Christina said.

"The sad fact is there are a dozen reasons why a scheming person would want to target Bruce," Christina added. "In fact, even people who oppose his environmental policies aren't above these kinds of tactics. Or just someone looking for a bit of fame or money. It's really sad what desperate, selfish people will do."

Mindy nodded again. Elizabeth felt a twinge of anger on Robin's behalf. The actress was so convincing, and beside her Bruce looked like a battered puppy dog. Who really *was* the victim here, anyway?

"Honestly, I just wish I knew who my accuser *was*," Bruce said. "I frankly just feel blindsided."

Yeah, like Robin felt when you tore her clothes . . . The thought jumped into Elizabeth's mind before she could stop it. Is that what she thought? Did she really think Bruce was capable of violently attacking a woman? She thought not, and yet the evidence was stacking up against him. Elizabeth always prided herself on basing her opinions on facts. That's what made her a good reporter.

Of course, on the public front, more people came to Bruce's side every day. Jessica's PR offensive was paying off.

"The woman who did this? She's just despicable," Christina said.

The interview ended there, and Christina gave Bruce a quick hug before she darted offstage. Mindy walked back to her news anchor desk, and Bruce sauntered over to Elizabeth, a look of relief on his face.

"How'd I do?" he asked her.

"Um . . . good." Elizabeth tucked a strand of blond hair behind one ear. She shifted uncomfortably on her feet and tried to look anywhere but at him. She felt he'd be able to read the suspicion on her face.

"What's wrong? Did you think Christina overdid it? I've known her forever and I know she has strong opinions."

"No, she was good. It was all good. Really."

Bruce studied her face a moment. "Well, she was good, but you would've been better."

Elizabeth couldn't quite meet Bruce's eye. "You know I don't like to be on camera. That's why I'm in newspapers, not TV."

The two of them walked together outside the studio to Bruce's waiting car.

"Yes, but you know me better than anyone," he said as he paused by the door.

"I'm sure Christina won you more fans than I ever could." Elizabeth sent him a weak smile.

"Something is still bothering you." It was a statement of fact, not a question. Suspicion lurked in Bruce's eyes.

Elizabeth sighed. "I just don't understand how food poisoning could've made you dizzy."

"*This* again?" Bruce's voice rose a little bit. "Elizabeth. Don't you trust me? I mean, it sounds like you're doubting me."

"No, no—of course not." Elizabeth put her hand on his arm. "I trust you, Bruce. I believe you."

Relief fell across his face, and Elizabeth felt guilty. All he wanted was her support. Why couldn't she just give it to him—no questions asked?

Bruce folded her into his arms for a hug and Elizabeth went, but stiffly. She couldn't quite relax with his arms around her. The reporter in her would never stop asking questions. That's just who she was.

"Elizabeth . . ." Bruce said, and in that moment she knew he could feel her discomfort, too. Elizabeth had never been a good actress. She stepped away from his embrace.

"I'm sorry, Bruce. This whole thing . . . I'm just so upset . . . for you. For both of us. It's just so much to handle and I want to help you, but I feel so powerless about everything."

That part was the truth. She felt powerless to protect Bruce . . . if it turned out he was really guilty.

"If we could only find out *who* this girl is, then I'm sure we could get to the bottom of it," Bruce said. "Have you found any new leads?"

Elizabeth cleared her throat. "No, and that's partly why I'm so frustrated. I'm going to work on it today." The lie came so easily. Since when had she become so good at lying? Elizabeth never used to lie, hardly even white lies. Yet ever since these allegations had surfaced, she'd turned into a habitual liar. Lies, she realized, were more addictive than potato chips. She started with one and had to keep going with another, and another, and another. She wondered if she'd ever be able to stop.

"I'm going to work on it today," Elizabeth promised.

"Okay," Bruce said, but a sliver of doubt remained in his eyes.

During the car ride home, both were silent, lost in their own thoughts.

12

Elizabeth asked Bruce to drop her off at her car, parked at the newspaper's lot. She promised him she would do more digging on his case. That, for a change, wasn't a lie. She needed to find out more about Robin. After speaking with the girl, she'd gotten more details about her work history before she was hired at the Patman Foundation. Pretending to be Laura Christer, the concerned therapist, she'd gotten Robin to talk about when she'd moved to L.A. two years ago.

Born and raised in small-town Kentucky, Robin had moved to Los Angeles in hopes of working in films. She'd been a creative artist-type back home and decided she wanted to use her talents in film. She wasn't sure how, though. Creating PR posters, perhaps, or even working on art direction. She came without a definite plan and just hoped everything would work out—like so many hopeful people who flooded L.A. every year.

Robin's first job had been as a nanny to a family in Malibu with two girls, ages five and three. Elizabeth hadn't had any luck tracking them down yet, since they'd moved to Italy, but she did have a reference letter that Robin showed her, sent via e-mail. It seemed to check out.

After that, Robin got a job working for Filmart as a secretary. Robin said she'd hoped to just get her foot in the door at a production studio, even if it was just answering phones.

Elizabeth drove to Burbank, where Filmart Studios rented their offices. She formed her cover story as she went. The last thing she planned to do was introduce herself as a reporter from the *L.A. Tribune* investigating the Bruce Patman scandal. Instead, she just made up another story: She was thinking about hiring Robin for a freelance job and just happened to be in the neighborhood, so decided to drop in and check her references in person.

Robin's boss, the Filmart office manager, seemed happy enough to chat about her. He was a slightly overweight man in his forties. Even though he worked at a movie studio, it wasn't every day a pretty blonde took the time to ask him such detailed questions.

Elizabeth found with a little smile and nod of encouragement, Larry volunteered Robin's whole story.

"She was great," he said. "Nice girl. Dependable. Always came in on time. Was happy to work overtime, too."

"Did she like being a secretary?"

"Well, I knew she wanted to work on films," he said. "She was a graphic designer or something."

So far, Elizabeth thought, everything Robin had said checked out. She hadn't found a single inconsistency yet.

"Why did she leave?"

"That's personal information I couldn't give you even if I did know, which I don't. I haven't seen her since she had that internship this past summer. After that she quit." He sat down behind his own desk.

Elizabeth leaned forward.

"Last I heard from her was just after she did that internship at the Patman Foundation. She called up crying one morning."

"Crying?"

"Yeah, really upset. She said she couldn't tell me what happened, but she said she was quitting."

"When was this?"

"Oh, July, I think."

That would've been around the same time Robin claimed Bruce had attacked her. Elizabeth swallowed.

"What do you think happened?"

Larry shrugged. "Maybe she broke up with her boyfriend? Who knows. But she said she was really sorry but it was personal and she couldn't go into the details."

Elizabeth felt the knot in her stomach grow. Robin had said she'd felt so victimized after that night with Bruce that she didn't leave her house for a full week and that she'd had to quit her job.

"Don't get me wrong, she's a nice girl," Larry said. "I'd hire her back if she called me. She never missed a single day before that. Whatever happened must have been really bad."

"Thanks, Larry. You've been really helpful."

Elizabeth picked up her purse and walked out the door, hoping her hands weren't shaking. The more she dug into Robin's past, the more impeccable she seemed. The evidence was stacking up against Bruce.

She got into her car just as her phone chirped, announcing an incoming text message. She looked at the phone and saw it was from Bruce.

SORRY I WAS GRUMPY THIS MORNING. LET'S DO SOMETHING SPECIAL FOR DINNER.

The thought of going home to Bruce—and, actually, spending any time with him at all right now—just made Elizabeth feel queasy. How could she keep up the pretense? She'd never been any good at pretending.

Already this morning, he'd seen right through her. She was trying *hard* to be the supportive girlfriend, but even he could tell she was faking it. Now, armed with new information supporting Robin's side of the story, it would just be ten times worse.

Elizabeth texted back. GOT HUNG UP AT WORK WITH A LATE DEADLINE. DON'T THINK I'LL MAKE DINNER TONIGHT. MIGHT EVEN STAY AT JESSICA'S.

Jessica's town house was slightly closer to the newspaper office than Bruce's mansion. This was pure avoidance, but Elizabeth couldn't think of a better idea.

I REALLY NEED YOU RIGHT NOW. PLEASE COME HOME.

Elizabeth's heart ached. She hated not being there for him. He sounded so lost. Maybe she was just being selfish. Then she remembered Robin's tearstained face.

If he was guilty . . . then he'd have to learn to soothe himself. Because Elizabeth couldn't be with him. Nothing could make a near-rape okay, no matter how much he'd had to drink.

She decided to go check on Robin. Basically an orphan with few friends, Robin truly had no one. She texted Bruce. SORRY. I CAN'T.

That much, Elizabeth thought, was true.

13

Bruce looked at his phone and sighed. Elizabeth wasn't coming home. She was avoiding him. He'd been in love with her for years, long before she'd even seen him as anything more than a friend. He knew her better than she knew herself, and it was obvious she doubted him. Every day, it seemed, she moved further and further away from him, and he didn't know why. He asked her all the time what was wrong, and yet she refused to tell him. Or if she did talk, it came out as a veiled accusation that he might be lying about what had really happened that night with the intern. Or was it some veiled reference to high school? Yes, he knew he hadn't always been the nicest guy. Sure, he did stupid things in high school, but didn't every seventeen-year-old? And, besides, he really thought that was ancient history. That short-tempered, spoiled kid wasn't him now. He'd changed. Grown up. Matured.

Of course, none of that seemed to matter these days since he felt like he was fighting against enemies he couldn't see, phantom accusers who popped up to hit him and then disappeared before he could strike back.

Just like the intern. If he only knew who she was, he felt convinced, he could solve this mystery. But he had no idea of her name or where she lived. All his power and connections weren't helping, either. Someone was keeping her hidden someplace where she could say all those terrible things about him and not even give him the chance to defend himself properly.

Rage bubbled up in his throat and for a second, he felt the urge to throw his phone across the room. He thought about how satisfying it would be to watch the phone's screen—and Elizabeth's text—go dark as it cracked to pieces. He almost let the phone fly, but a beep from an incoming text stopped him.

He glanced at the phone's face, hoping Elizabeth had reconsidered. Maybe she would say she was sorry. Maybe she'd come home.

But, no. It wasn't from Elizabeth.

I'VE GOT NEW INFO ON YOUR CASE. MEET AT NEVIN'S BAR TONIGHT?

The text came from Gavin MacKay, the private detective he'd hired to try to find his accuser. Bruce had hired him after it became clear Elizabeth wasn't getting anywhere finding her. And Gavin was the top private detective in the business.

Maybe now he'd finally get some answers. He certainly wasn't getting any from Elizabeth.

Bruce grabbed his jacket and headed out the door.

14

Elizabeth pulled up in front of Robin's new house, a modest but clean one-story bungalow just down the street from Robin's parish. The minute Elizabeth had seen the little house for rent she knew it would be the perfect hideaway. It was close to Father Riley's church and no one would know Robin was there.

With Elizabeth's name on the lease, she'd be safe from reporters or anyone else searching for her.

Elizabeth rang the doorbell, and Robin opened the door seconds later.

"I'm so glad to see you," Robin gushed, truly happy to see her. This girl needed her. "Sorry I'm late," Elizabeth said. "Got hung up at the office with . . ." She nearly said "deadlines" and then stopped short. Elizabeth was supposed to be therapist Laura Christer, not Elizabeth Wakefield, newspaper journalist. ". . . clients."

"I understand." Robin smiled. "Someone like you just wants to help people."

Right, and lie to everyone she knows. Everything she was saying and doing seemed like a lie these days: lying to Bruce, lying to Robin. Elizabeth hated lying. It would be horrendous if either one found out the truth.

"Sorry about the boxes," Robin said as Elizabeth sidestepped a few stacked up in the living room. "Do you want something to drink? I might be able to find some iced tea. Or there's tap water . . ."

Robin dug around in one of the boxes in the kitchen and pulled out a glass only to lose her grip on the tumbler. It fell to the floor with a crash.

"Great." Robin knelt to pick up the broken pieces and began to cry almost immediately. "This is just great."

"Robin, it's okay. Here. Let me help." Elizabeth instinctively went into mother-hen mode, picking up the bigger shards and looking around for something she could use as a broom. She settled on an empty plastic trash bag on top of one of the boxes.

Robin rocked back on her heels and tears dropped down her cheeks. Elizabeth abandoned the cleanup effort and wrapped her arm around Robin's shoulders.

"Don't cry. It'll be okay. Here, let's go sit down." Elizabeth steered Robin to a nearby couch and helped her sit. She reached for a tissue inside her purse and handed it to Robin.

"I'm sorry. I'm such a mess." Robin swiped at her eyes with the tissue. "You've been so kind to me, getting me this house and everything, and here I go and make a mess of it all."

"No," Elizabeth said, shaking her head. "You haven't made a mess of anything, Robin. It's okay. I'm not even thirsty."

Robin smiled weakly at Elizabeth's joke, and then blew her nose loudly in the tissue.

"It's just that I really don't know if I can do this." She glanced around at the stacks of unopened boxes.

"Don't worry. I can help you unpack."

"No, it's not that." Robin sucked in a deep, shaky breath. "I mean these accusations. Against Mr. Patman."

"What do you mean?"

Elizabeth stared at Robin, noticing for the first time just how disheveled the young girl was. She had tossed her hair back in a hasty and uncombed knot at the base of her neck. She carried dark rings under her eyes like she hadn't slept in days. Her face was gaunt and thin, as if she hadn't been eating all that well, either.

"I-I-I don't know, Laura. I'm so scared he'll find me."

"That's why I moved you here," Elizabeth reassured her.

"I have nightmares that he's found me already." Robin looked at Elizabeth with eyes wide with fear. Robin's bottom lip started to quiver and then she dropped her face in her hands. Elizabeth was more convinced than ever before that this girl was telling the truth. You couldn't mistake the real terror in her voice. "What if he found me?"

No way could Elizabeth imagine Bruce coming after this girl. But then, none of this seemed like Bruce, and yet there was no question that Robin's terror was real. She couldn't help thinking about the news story that ran just last week in the *Tribune,* the one about the woman who'd been married to a serial killer for ten years and never knew it. If being a reporter had taught her anything at all, it was that sometimes people were very good at hiding their true selves.

Look how she was hiding her own life now.

"It's okay, Robin." Elizabeth patted the girl's shoulder. "It will be okay."

Robin took a deep breath and lifted her chin. She wiped her tears and shook her head.

"I don't know, Laura," Robin said. "I'm starting to think that this was all a big mistake. Maybe I shouldn't have come forward at all."

"What do you mean?"

"I don't know. I'm more scared now than I've ever been. Maybe I should just walk away from this whole thing."

Elizabeth didn't know what to say. Robin was clearly in a lot of pain and very frightened.

"It's okay. We'll get through this." Elizabeth hoped that wasn't a lie.

"Maybe it's not too late, Laura," Robin said. "Maybe I *could* still do it. I mean, that night that he almost . . ." She swallowed. "It was the worst night of my life. But since then, it's only gotten worse, not better. I'm afraid all the time, terrified he's going to find me. I should just drop the whole thing, go away, and start fresh. I did that once before when I moved here from Kentucky and I can do it again. Maybe then the nightmares will stop."

Elizabeth froze, unsure of what to say and not trusting herself to speak. Robin was so close to offering to end this nightmare—for Bruce and everyone else. It would be a perfect solution.

This could be her chance to save Bruce. A little nudge and Robin *might* just drop these allegations and disappear. All she had to do was say just the right thing, and it would be over. And with this whole scandal gone, maybe she and Bruce could pick up their life again.

But what about the young, frightened girl in front of her? Could Elizabeth—in good conscience—tell her just to give in and call it quits? And what if what she was saying was true? The damage to her life would be devastating. Where was the justice in that?

Not to mention, if what she said was true, Bruce could do it again. Could Elizabeth live with herself if she told Robin to run and some other girl wound up his next victim?

Elizabeth mentally shook herself. She couldn't believe her mind had even gone there. Bruce wasn't a serial rapist. He wasn't a criminal.

Elizabeth had the power to make this all go away for him. She could do it with one word.

Robin clutched at Elizabeth's hand. "Laura," she pleaded. "I trust you completely. Should I stay and fight this or should I just stop cooperating with the police investigation? What should I do?"

15

Bruce Patman looked at the photos and papers Gavin MacKay had brought to Nevin's Pub and shook his head, trying to make sense of it all. Gavin, the big, burly ex-L.A. cop turned private detective, had found his accuser's identity.

"Robin Platt? I don't even know her," Bruce said as he scratched his head. He caught the bartender's attention and signaled for another round of scotch. He'd lost track of how much he'd drunk so far. Three? Four? He didn't know anymore. He'd gone to the bar early and Gavin had been a little late. He'd drunk from pure nerves, but now he'd ordered another because he wanted to dull the harsh reality of his situation. Now that he had his accuser's name, it made everything all the more real to him.

"She didn't work for the foundation very long," Gavin said. "But she was there. Take a look at this photo. Remember her?"

Gavin held up a color picture. In it, Bruce saw a pretty, petite, blond girl standing with a man unloading moving boxes from a rental truck.

"That's the girl from the bar," Bruce said. "But I swear, I never saw her in my office."

"Records show she was there for at least two weeks in July."

Bruce tried to think back to last summer. Had he been out of the office a lot that month on business? It was possible. Otherwise, when he was around, he always made an effort to meet the interns. He just thought it was a nice thing to do. He had gone around and introduced himself in August, he remembered that much. But by then, she would have been gone.

"Robin had been living in Sherman Oaks," Gavin continued. "But I talked to her neighbor, who said she just moved to a house in Sweet Valley. The neighbor didn't know the address, but I found it. That's where I took this picture."

Gavin tapped the photo to show Bruce. In the background, he could just make out the address on the mailbox.

"Did you find anything about why she would do this to me?"

Gavin shrugged. "Still digging. Don't worry, we'll find something."

"I have to believe that. And thanks for finding this girl so quickly. I know it wasn't easy."

"It wasn't—the police made sure she was well hidden—but being a private eye for twenty-five years gives you some advantage. And then a few well-placed bucks doubles it."

"I can only assume the police were protecting her from me. No wonder Elizabeth couldn't find her." Still, he couldn't help thinking she'd been working this case for more than a week. How could she have missed finding the girl no matter how they hid her? She was a good reporter. Scratch that—great reporter.

Something wasn't right. He'd been feeling it since this whole thing started. First Elizabeth was with him one hundred percent, but then she seemed uncertain. Okay, he understood. Even if it wasn't true, it was horrendous to have the guy you've been living with for three years accused of attempted rape. But he couldn't understand how it was possible after all these years of friendship and of loving each other, of planning to spend their lives together, that she could have any doubts about him.

She did love him, didn't she?

God, he didn't know what he believed anymore.

Gavin stood to go. "I'll find out whose name is on that lease tomorrow."

Bruce waved a hand to show he had Gavin's drink covered. The private eye flipped on a dark baseball cap and then hesitated by the bar stool, eyeing the fresh scotch on the rocks the bartender slid in front of Bruce.

"Do you want me to call you a cab? Make sure you get home okay?"

Bruce waved away the offer. "No. I'm going to stay here awhile." He downed half of his drink in one big slug. He motioned for the bartender to bring him another.

Gavin felt a little uncomfortable about leaving him in this condition, but he was Bruce Patman, not a guy you could tell what to do.

"See ya," he said, deciding to leave him.

"Thanks, Gavin," Bruce said.

Bruce didn't know how long he'd stayed at the bar downing scotch, but it was long enough to push Elizabeth into the background and give full concentration to Robin Platt as he stared at the picture Gavin had given him. Who the hell was she anyway? And why was she doing this to him?

He had to find out, and there was only one way. His anger cut through the foggy blur of alcohol, and he began to think about what Jessica had said about Robin being an opportunist—someone just out for fame and money. He looked at the picture again and saw the address on the house showed up clearly. After a couple of clumsy minutes, he managed to pull up the GPS on his phone. Her house was less than five minutes away.

He stared at the picture and at the map, and the fury inside him began to boil over. How dare she do this to him? He was *Bruce Patman*. Yes, he was worth millions, maybe billions, but he always thought of himself as a good guy. Someone who cared about people, someone who wanted to protect the environment, someone who would never come on to a strange girl at a bar. She was in trouble and all he had wanted to do was help her.

How could she smear his name and alienate the woman he loved? In his mind, this Robin person owed him an explanation. And he was damned well going to get it.

He slid off the bar stool and stumbled out to his car in the parking lot. For a bleary second, he couldn't see it, but the remote on his key chain lit the parking lights and made his two-seater beep. He slunk into the driver's side and put the key in the ignition. He had no idea how many drinks he'd had, but the road wasn't spinning, so he thought he was okay to drive.

He swerved out of the parking lot and followed the blinking blue arrow on his phone down the map to Robin's new house.

He made it there in three minutes. It was late, and the house was dark. She was probably sleeping. Not that he cared. He hadn't had a good night's sleep since this whole thing started. Why should she get to sleep?

He stumbled out of his car and slammed the door.

"Robin!" he shouted, his words coming out a tad bit slurred. "Robin Platt! You have things to say about me? Well, I'm here. Why don't you come say them to my face?"

The house remained dark. Bruce shouted louder.

"You afraid, Robin? You should be!"

Down the street, a dog barked. Next door to Robin's house, a light came on.

"I tried to help you, Robin. You asked me for help, and I gave it to you!"

Now a light came on in Robin's house. Bruce staggered down the front porch to her door and tugged at it. The knob wouldn't turn. He banged on the door hard.

"Robin Platt!" He banged on the door some more. After a minute, he left the door and climbed into the shrubs to look in the window. Inside, he saw a living room filled with boxes. He smacked the window so hard it cracked.

Down the street, a siren wailed.

"I've called the police!" shouted a scared voice from inside. Robin's, he assumed.

"Good! Let them come. Then you can tell them what a little liar you are! Is this how you feel good about yourself? By making up lies?"

Bruce banged at the window again and the small square of window broke. He heard a scream from inside. Numbly, he looked down at his hand and saw a trickle of blood where a shard of broken glass had sliced his hand. He knew he should feel some kind of pain, but he didn't feel anything. The alcohol, he guessed.

As he was studying his wounded hand, a black-and-white police car screeched to a halt in front of Robin's house, half in and half out of the driveway. Two uniformed officers jumped out, drawing their guns.

"Step away from the house!" one of them cried.

"Put your hands up where we can see them," demanded the other.

Bruce turned around, blinking against the white searchlight the officers had turned on him and the house, blood dripping from one hand. He was temporarily blinded. One of the officers moved slowly toward him.

"Wha . . . ? I'm not the criminal!" he bellowed at them. "She's the one . . . she's the one who's destroying *my* life!"

He swung his arms wide to make his point, showing off his wounded hand. The officers took one look at his bleeding palm and at the broken window behind him and had nearly all the evidence they needed. This case? Open and shut.

One officer signaled to the other, who began moving slowly around to Bruce's blind side.

"Look, sir, we just want to talk, so come over here, hands up, and we can talk."

"That's just what I want to do! I *want* to talk. That's why I came here!" Bruce waved his arm around furiously. He desperately wanted to make them understand.

But before he could, something big and heavy came down on him. The officer closest to him had lunged and tackled him. His face hit the concrete sidewalk hard, and he tasted blood in his mouth.

"Do yourself a favor and don't struggle," the officer said as he wrenched Bruce's arms behind his back and clicked cold, metal cuffs on his wrists.

For a second, Bruce really didn't understand what was happening. His brain moved in slow motion. Why was he wearing handcuffs?

"You have the right to remain silent. Anything you say can be held against you in a court of law . . ."

"I'm not a criminal!" Bruce shouted, but he only got a knee in the back for his trouble. The officer's knee knocked the breath out of him for a second, and he gasped to recover. Bruce couldn't remember a time when anyone had put their hands on him like this. He commanded hundreds of people at his company and foundation and elsewhere. Nobody treated him like this. As he squirmed under the officer, he glanced up and saw Robin's door open a little. A blond head stared out at him with frightened eyes.

Another officer walked up the stoop and began to ask her questions. Nobody put handcuffs on *her*. Why was nobody arresting her? She was the one who deserved it. The unfairness of it all just shot through Bruce like white-hot lightning.

"There she is! The lying little bitch! I swear . . . I'll . . ." Bruce sputtered.

"That's enough!" the officer on top of him said. He grabbed Bruce by the arms and yanked him to his feet. The officer pushed him roughly toward the police car. In seconds, he'd been dumped in the backseat. The officer slammed the door, and Bruce was left alone, sitting on his handcuffed hands. Both officers were now talking to Robin, who was crying and looking every inch the victim.

As the anger slowly drained out of him, Bruce glanced down the street and saw neighbors standing on stoops and porches in bathrobes and pajamas, whispering and pointing. One even had a camera phone out, and snapped a picture of Bruce in the squad car.

Even through the fog of alcohol, he realized how bad this looked. He'd been arrested on Robin Platt's lawn at two in the morning. His first thought was Elizabeth. How would he ever explain this to her?

Panic rose up in his throat.

Oh, God, he thought. *What have I done?*

EPISODE 3
Too Many Doubts

1

Elizabeth Wakefield woke up to the sound of her phone ringing at three in the morning. Bleary-eyed, she lunged for her iPhone, grabbing it on the third ring. The backlit face glowed in the darkness and Robin's name flashed on the screen.

"Hello?" Elizabeth answered with a puzzled but sleepy croak.

"Laura, you've got to help me! The police are here and—"

"What?" Adrenaline flooded Elizabeth's system, jolting her wide awake. "What are you talking about?"

"Mr. Patman . . . he just tried to attack me again! He came to my house and broke the window and, oh, my God. The police handcuffed him and are taking him away right now. I can't believe this."

Panic shot through Elizabeth. She glanced at the other side of the bed, where Bruce usually slept. Empty. He hadn't come home.

That's because her boyfriend had gone to Robin Platt's house instead to confront the former intern who had accused him of attempted rape.

But how had he found her in the first place? And why hadn't he said he knew? Not to mention, just how much did he know about Elizabeth's involvement in hiding his accuser in the first place?

"Take a deep breath," Elizabeth said, wondering just whom she was trying to calm down—Robin or herself. "Tell me what happened."

"The police are saying they are going to book him at the county jail. They say I should think about pressing charges."

"Oh, God." Elizabeth felt like someone had sucker punched her in the stomach.

"I'm freaking out, Laura. Please come here and help me! Completely and totally *freaking* out."

Robin's fear and panic was horror enough, but hearing the false name Elizabeth had been using to trick this poor, trusting girl so that she could save Bruce—who might not even deserve saving—was almost too much.

Robin needed her, but could she risk going now that Bruce knew who Robin was and where she lived? He might be one step away from finding Elizabeth's name on the lease. She and the landlord were the only ones with copies of the lease. Even Robin didn't have a copy. But that didn't mean the lease couldn't be found.

No matter what, it was too late to stop now. Elizabeth threw off the covers. "I'm on my way."

She put on the first things she could find, jeans and a T-shirt, and dashed to her car and sped away from Bruce's mansion, her home that might never be her home again.

Well, at least this explained why the house had been empty when she got home last night. She figured Bruce had gone out because he'd been angry with her after she'd said she wasn't coming home for dinner and might even spend the night at her sister's. Of course he'd been upset with Elizabeth. He'd have to have been blind not to see that she'd been avoiding him. She couldn't help it; she just didn't feel comfortable pretending to be the supportive partner when she'd begun to doubt she could really trust him.

After Elizabeth had found Robin, heard the girl's frightening story, and made the decision to hide her, she thought she'd been protecting both Bruce and Robin. Now she had a sinking feeling that she might not be able to protect either of them anymore.

She hit the accelerator, dreading what she would find at Robin's house.

Just yesterday afternoon, she'd sat in Robin's living room and heard the frightened plea in her voice.

"I'm so scared. Should I drop the allegation against Mr. Patman and leave town?" Robin had clutched Elizabeth's hands in hers. She had been terrified.

Yes. That's all Elizabeth had needed to say, and with that one simple word, Bruce's name would be cleared of all charges. Life could return to normal. No more spin campaign, no more worrying about whether Bruce had lied about any of it. With just one word, the nightmare would end.

Only to start a new one, she'd thought.

Because if she did say yes and *if* Robin was telling the truth . . . Elizabeth couldn't even think about the repercussions from that nightmare.

There were holes in Bruce's story that disturbed her. Robin swore Bruce had come on to her at the bar, coaxed her inside the manager's office, and tried to force himself on her. Bruce said that had absolutely never happened. Yes, he'd been in the manager's office, but only because he'd gotten dizzy and had to lie down. He remembered being sick to his stomach and woozy, and then he must have passed out, which is why he didn't remember anything. He figured it was food poisoning from something he ate for lunch, but that disturbed Elizabeth; people don't have memory loss from salmonella.

They do from alcohol.

And the bartender said Bruce had had a lot to drink and was coming on to Robin. Then there was Robin herself. Everything she'd told Elizabeth about her past turned out to be true. The deeper Elizabeth dug, the more credible the girl seemed.

Before meeting Robin, Elizabeth had been sure Rick Warner and his natural gas company had set Bruce up. It made sense. Warner had lost the land deal to Bruce and his windmills, and he was not a man to take loss easily. Plus, it was something that Warner was low enough to do.

But the more Elizabeth tried to force Robin into the Warner jigsaw puzzle, the more she simply refused to fit.

No way could she tell this frightened girl to drop everything and run.

"No, Robin," she'd told her, "you can't back down now. If things happened as you said, you have to see this through."

"But my nightmares . . . I really think Mr. Patman will find me."

"You've moved now. There's no way anyone can find you, and running away will not solve anything. I think you have to face it."

Robin had pressed her lips together, as if summoning strength from some inner well of courage, and nodded. "You're right. I've got to see this through. You're so wise. I'm so glad you're here for me, Laura."

Laura Christer, the fake therapist giving fake advice. What was Elizabeth doing? Whatever it was, it was too late to stop it now. Bruce had been arrested, and now things were messy.

For a brief second, Elizabeth wondered if she should just come clean, admit who she really was, and be done with the charade. But she couldn't. That would close her door to Robin and then she might never find out the truth.

Elizabeth had no choice. She needed to keep walking the tightrope she teetered on, with Robin dangling from one end of her balancing pole, Bruce hanging from the other, and absolutely no net underneath.

Except she felt like any second she might fall. Now that Bruce had shown up at Robin's house and *broken her window.* God, how Elizabeth hoped that wasn't true. If Bruce had done that, maybe he was guilty. Breaking in wasn't the act of an innocent man.

Elizabeth turned down Robin's street and saw a police car pulling out of her drive. She didn't stick around to see if Bruce was in the backseat. In a startled panic, Elizabeth turned her car down a side street and steered into an alley that ran behind the house.

She parked, jumped out, and ran up to the back screen door. She saw the curtains flutter and Robin's scared eyes peering through, then heard the rush of bolts being unlocked.

"Thank goodness," Robin said, pulling Elizabeth inside. "They say I need to come down to the station and file a report. Oh . . . this is insane!"

Robin bear-hugged Elizabeth.

"It's okay," Elizabeth said, trying to be calm. "Tell me everything."

Robin began to pace. She wore a faded blue sleep shirt and a battered terrycloth robe that at one time might have been white but was now just a grungy, dull gray. Her blond hair lay stringy and flat against her head, as if she'd just rolled out of bed. She ran her hands through it and exhaled. Her eyes had a frantic look to them and the pupils were constricted to pinpricks.

"God, I can't believe . . . I really need a—" Robin stopped short, suddenly glancing guiltily at Elizabeth. For the briefest of seconds, Elizabeth thought she had been about to say "a drink." And why wouldn't she? Elizabeth wanted one herself, to be honest. It was the middle of the night, but who cared? But before she could follow that thought, Robin's bottom lip began to quiver.

"This is all such a mess," Robin sobbed, changing tack as she slumped into her worn couch. Clearly, Robin was just upset and scared. Nothing more. If Elizabeth had been in her shoes, she might not have been able to complete sentences, either.

"Just start at the beginning."

"I was asleep, *fast* asleep, and I heard this hard knocking on my door. I woke up, thinking it's my neighbor, you know? Maybe he'd lost his dog or something. Or there's a house fire. I mean, it was *two* in the morning!"

Elizabeth nodded and took a seat next to Robin.

"But then Mr. Patman . . . he started shouting at me. He started shouting awful things."

Elizabeth's stomach tightened.

"Like what?"

"Like, 'Are you afraid, Robin? You should be!'"

Elizabeth swallowed hard.

"And then, next thing I knew, he was trying to get in my house. He smashed the window. Oh, God, Laura. It was awful."

Robin pointed toward the front door. Bits of broken glass glinted on the floor. A fist-sized hole gaped in the window closest to the door handle, irrefutable proof of Robin's claims.

"I can't even imagine," Elizabeth said, stunned, and she couldn't. How could Bruce do this? Yet he had. That broken window couldn't be explained away.

"I-I called 911, and the police came practically in seconds," Robin continued. "They got here just in time. I knew he would find me, and he did!" She swallowed. "He called me a lying bitch!" Robin buried her face in her hands and started to cry.

Elizabeth's heart broke for this girl, and her maternal instinct took over. She wrapped Robin in her arms and gave her a fierce hug.

"Don't worry, I'm here to help. We'll get through this together." She hoped that much was true.

Elizabeth's phone chirped in her pocket. She pulled it out and saw Bruce's name pop up on the screen. He was texting!

ELIZABETH—ARE YOU THERE?

Robin glanced up and stared at Elizabeth's phone. Quickly, Elizabeth dropped the phone back in her pocket and prayed Robin hadn't seen Bruce's name on the screen.

"Who's that?" Robin asked Elizabeth, suspicion in her voice. For a second, a hardened look came into Robin's eyes. For just the briefest of moments, Elizabeth was certain she *knew*.

"My roommate. She was concerned that I left the house in such a rush," Elizabeth lied quickly. Her fingers touched the screen of the phone in her pocket. How she wanted to respond to Bruce, but she didn't dare. Not with Robin in the room. "Do you have any idea how Mr. Patman found you?"

"None at all," Robin said. "I thought you said I'd be safe here, Laura!"

The accusation stung. Elizabeth felt a surge of guilt. Maybe it *was* her fault. Had she not done enough to cover her tracks? She thought she had, but what if she was wrong?

Headlights swept in through the front window, and Robin jumped.

"Who's out there?" Robin's whole body tensed and her voice dropped to the level of a terrified whisper.

Elizabeth went to the window. The headlights belonged to a news truck, which rolled to a stop in front of the house. Newspapers and news stations regularly tuned in to police scanners, and they must have picked up Bruce's arrest. It would be news when police arrested one of Sweet Valley's richest residents for trying to attack the woman who had accused him of attempted rape.

"More bad news," Elizabeth said. "Reporters are here."

"What?" Robin stood, her face going as pale as her grayish white robe. She scurried close to Elizabeth in time to see another satellite news truck roll up to her house. Another car arrived, too, and a man with three cameras slung around his neck popped out. She clutched Elizabeth's arm.

"Oh, God. Everybody will know who I am! This was supposed to be confidential! Oh, no, no, no!" Robin turned to look at Elizabeth, panic and desperation in her eyes.

"Don't worry, Robin. It's highly unethical for the media to report your real name. They keep rape victims' names confidential." Elizabeth inwardly cringed as she used the word "rape." Was Bruce really capable of that?

"But won't they still want to ask me questions?"

"Probably. But you don't have to answer them. Don't answer the door or the phone."

"This is all insane! I can't believe this. What am I going to do?"

Inside the county jail, Bruce sat with his head buried in his hands. Six cement benches were arranged in rows across the pale cement floor. Bruce sat on one, and two college kids were passed out on two more. He overheard the officer say they'd driven their car through the front of a rival frat house. Luckily, no one was hurt. In the far corner, another man lay sprawled on the floor in the corner. Bruce didn't know his story, but it looked like he was sleeping off a bender.

Bruce had never felt so humiliated. His fingers still bore the ink of being fingerprinted and his lip felt swollen and tender from connecting too hard with the pavement outside of Robin Platt's home when the police officer threw him to the ground and cuffed him.

He still remembered the fury he'd felt when he'd banged on the girl's door at two in the morning, demanding answers.

Stupid. It was stupid to try to confront her like that. He knew he must have looked like some kind of crazed stalker, showing up at her house at that hour. But he hadn't been thinking rationally. He'd had a lot to drink. And he was feeling it now. Along with the throbbing cut on his hand from the broken window, his head was pounding with a plain old hangover.

Where was Ben?

He'd called his lawyer thirty minutes ago with the one phone call they'd given him. Before they'd confiscated his iPhone, he'd managed one text to Elizabeth. He never found out if she responded.

He looked up and rubbed the stubble on his chin.

"Hey," said one of the college kids, who was now sitting and staring at him. "Hey . . . I know you."

Bruce ignored him.

"Hey, you're that rich dude who raped that girl." The kid nudged his friend, but the friend just groaned and rolled over on his side. "Bruce, right? Bruce . . . Postman. No. Something else. I saw you on TV with all those celebrities."

Just when Bruce thought the day couldn't get worse, a frat guy from Sweet Valley U had managed to kick it up a notch.

"Dude, can I get my picture with you? My bros will not believe . . ." Distantly, Bruce heard a steel door creak open and footsteps in the hall.

"Bruce Patman." An officer appeared at the cell door.

"Bruce Patman! That's it!" The college kid snapped his fingers.

Wearily, Bruce glanced up at the guard, who pushed a key in the lock.

"Patman, you've been bailed out. Time to get up." The guard turned the key and then swung open the door.

Finally! Bruce thought.

In the lobby of the police station, Bruce saw Ben Bookman waiting for him, wearing jeans and a sweatshirt instead of his usual suit and tie. Obviously, he'd run out of the house in a hurry. But then, it was after four in the morning and his most important client had just been arrested.

"I came as soon as I could," Ben said, looking apologetic.

"How bad is it?" Bruce asked Ben.

Ben glanced down, as if not wanting to meet his friend's eyes. "So far, I've talked them down to just drunk and disorderly conduct—a misdemeanor. They're holding off on the other charges until they talk to the D.A. But there is an emergency restraining order in place, so you can't go within one hundred feet of Robin Platt's house."

Bruce groaned.

"I don't think I should tell you just how lucky you are. What were you thinking, driving drunk and then showing up at this girl's house? Just *what* did you plan to do if you did get inside?"

The words hung in the air between the old friends.

"I know it was stupid," Bruce said. "I wasn't thinking."

"You'd better start," Ben said. "This isn't the end of it. And intimidating the accuser sure doesn't help you."

"Shit." Bruce ran a hand through his already tangled hair.

"This is serious, Bruce."

Bruce nodded. None of this was good; he knew that much.

The police officer at the processing desk handed Bruce a plastic bag containing his wallet and cell phone and keys. Bruce dug out his phone. It had only a sliver of battery life left. He saw Elizabeth hadn't answered his text. He decided to try again.

He *needed* her. He called her number. He knew she slept with her phone on the bedside table.

The phone rang only one time before going straight to voice mail.

"Damn it," he cursed, switching off the phone without leaving a message.

"Uh-oh," Ben said as he walked with Bruce to the front door.

Outside in the early dawn, news cameras and paparazzi lined the walkway from the jail to the parking lot.

"You're probably going to be the lead story this morning."

Bruce's headache just got worse. He put a hand to his temple. "Where are you parked?"

"Not close enough," Ben admitted.

Just then, a limited-edition white Bentley with gold trim glided through the sea of cameras. It pulled to a stop in the middle of the drive and the orange hazard lights began blinking. Bruce saw Missy LeGrange hop out, wearing solid white from head to toe, as if she'd planned to coordinate with her car.

"Don't touch the car. None of you can afford to fix it," she proclaimed to the news crews as she shoved her way past them. She pushed open the door to the police station and instantly fell upon Bruce.

"Oh, Bruce, I am *so* sorry. I came as soon as Daddy told me the news."

Bruce glanced at Ben, confused, and Ben shrugged. "I called Thomas LeGrange right after I got your message. I figured since he's executor of the Patman Estate . . ."

Bruce waved a hand to show it was fine. Actually, more than fine.

Bruce felt happy to see another supportive face. For a brief second, he wished it were Elizabeth's. He glanced down at his phone and wondered where she was.

"I know this will all get cleared up just as soon as we get the right attorney on this case," Missy said. "Honestly, when *nobodies* try to mess with *somebodies* the *nobodies* never win." Missy thought anybody who didn't have substantial wealth was a nobody. Normally Bruce was amused by Missy's snobbery. Elizabeth was not, but right now, snob or not, Missy had shown up when he needed her. She was a good friend. Which made him ask himself, Where *was* Elizabeth?

As if Missy had heard his thoughts, she asked, "Where's Elizabeth?"

"Um . . . I wish I knew," Bruce grumbled.

"Don't tell me she's abandoned you," Missy said, shaking her head in happy disapproval. "*Where* is her loyalty? A little bit of trouble and she runs and hides? Honestly."

Missy's assessment felt a bit too close to the truth for Bruce's comfort.

"No, no, it's not that," he said quickly. He felt the need to defend Elizabeth. "She's probably just got her phone off."

"Well, isn't she a reporter?" Missy said the word as if it tasted bitter on her tongue. "She should *know* already, and she should be here. I mean aren't those *her* people out there?" Missy waved her hand at the gathering reporters outside.

"And why wasn't she with you last night? If she'd been there to drive you home from that bar, none of this would've happened."

The truth of Missy's words hit Bruce like a slap. She was one hundred percent right. Bruce never would've showed up drunk at Robin's house if Elizabeth had been there. Not that Bruce would blame Elizabeth for his mistakes, but facts were facts.

Bruce couldn't help feeling that Elizabeth had managed to abandon him when he needed her most—again.

"Oh, Bruce, I am so sorry." Missy put her hand on Bruce's forearm. "And those animals out there just have no right to be badgering you like this. Whatever happened to innocent until proven guilty? Not on TMZ, anyway."

"Maybe I should try to get my car and bring it closer?" Ben offered.

"Nonsense," Missy said, waving her hand. "I can drive Bruce. My car's right here."

Her Bentley was as close to the door as a car could get, but there were still half a dozen cameras between it and Bruce.

"Okay, remember, we have no comment," Ben said. "Just move as quickly as you can to the car."

Ben swung open the door and almost immediately Bruce felt blinded by the white-hot lights of the cameras as reporters shouted questions.

"Is it true you attacked the same Jane Doe who accused you of attempted rape?"

"What do you have to say to the allegation you broke her window and tried to force your way in?"

"Are you a rapist, Bruce?"

Missy shoved one camera out of Bruce's face. "Would you animals leave him alone?" she yelled as they moved quickly past.

Bruce sent her a grateful glance.

"No comment," Ben said. "My client has no comment!"

The questions kept flying at him, each new one more awful than the last. Bruce forged ahead with Missy holding his arm, helping to clear the way. Even with only a few feet separating him from the Bentley, the trip seemed to take forever. By the time he'd slid safely into the front passenger seat, Missy had the car in drive and roared out, whipping one of the cameras into the air with her side-view mirror.

"Reporters are animals—all of them," Missy exclaimed with disgust. "I honestly don't know how Elizabeth does what she does."

On any other day, Bruce would have felt the need to point out that Elizabeth was a print journalist and not one of the opportunistic paparazzi like the TMZ photographers they'd just run past, but he didn't have the energy to defend her or her chosen profession at the moment.

Not when she wasn't there to defend him.

Missy glanced over at Bruce and laid a sympathetic hand on his arm. "Why don't you let me drive you to my family's vineyard? It's only about two hours away. The paparazzi will never find you there."

3

Elizabeth picked up her phone, frantically scrolling through her messages from Bruce as she sat in her car at a red light. She'd calmed down Robin with a Tylenol PM and comforting words and promises to come back as soon as she could. She'd also managed to convince the girl not to talk to the police again—at least not right now. In the meantime, she told her not to let anyone in. Luckily, Elizabeth had been able to slip out the back door unseen.

Bruce's texts were growing desperate. He needed her. He said he could explain. The journalist in Elizabeth told her there were two sides to every story. No question that Bruce had done a crazy thing, but she wouldn't be an objective reporter unless she gave him the chance to explain.

Plus, the man she loved was in *jail,* and no matter what Elizabeth suspected, she did still love Bruce. She wanted to help him if she could.

But she also worried. Did he know she'd been the one to pay Robin Platt's rent?

I CAN EXPLAIN, Bruce had texted.

So can I, Elizabeth thought. Or, at least, she hoped she could.

The light turned green and she tossed the phone to her passenger seat and stomped her foot on the accelerator. As a reporter, she knew where the jail was, of course, and with hardly anyone on the street at almost five in the morning, she could easily make it in less than ten minutes. *Please God, don't let me be too late,* she thought.

By the time she sped into the parking lot, she saw a news crew cameraman climbing into a satellite truck in the parking lot. A hard pit formed in her stomach. She'd missed him.

She recognized Daniel Scott, a local news anchor for Channel Five, from seeing him on the local morning show.

"Daniel!" Elizabeth called. The reporter paused, his hand on the truck's door handle, and glanced over in her direction. "Hey, I'm a reporter from the *Tribune*."

"Oh, right. I think I saw you at the mayor's press conference last month."

"That's right. Did I miss Bruce Patman?" Elizabeth asked.

"Yep." Daniel laughed a little. "You *Tribune* guys are always sooooo slow. You missed the money shot. Patman's been bailed out. He left already."

"Do you know where he went?"

"We're not TMZ. We don't give chase," Daniel said, and shrugged. "But he was with some woman who drove a white Bentley. A flashy one with gold trim." Daniel rolled his eyes.

Elizabeth knew exactly who was driving a white Bentley with gold trim. How did Missy get there so fast? Just in case missing Bruce wasn't bad enough.

"How long ago?" she asked Daniel.

"Just a few minutes."

"Damn," Elizabeth breathed.

"Oh, trust me, no need to be that upset. He didn't say anything. It seems he's lawyered up. You didn't miss much."

Elizabeth thought of Bruce, alone in his time of need in jail, only to be saved by Missy LeGrange, and she couldn't stop the thought, petty though it was: Why did it have to be her?

4

Bruce let Missy drive for a few minutes in silence. Did he want to go to her family's vineyard? Should he be going somewhere else? His head throbbed, and the thought of even trying to make a decision only made it hurt more. Part of him didn't even trust himself to make the decision at all. Clearly, after last night, his judgment was off.

The sunrise bathed the street in a grayish pink glow. *A new day, a new headache,* Bruce thought.

His iPhone dinged, announcing an incoming message. He looked at the screen, hoping to see Elizabeth's name there. Instead, he saw Gavin MacKay, the private investigator he'd hired to find Robin in the first place.

JUST FOUND MORE NEWS ON YOUR CASE. CALL ME.

He didn't ask why his private eye was working so early. He didn't care. Desperate for any news, Bruce dialed Gavin's number.

"Are you sitting down?" Gavin said, not even bothering with a hello.

"Yes." Bruce glanced over at Missy, who sent him a concerned look.

"I've got a copy of Robin Platt's new lease. You're not going to believe who signed it and put up the deposit."

"Please tell me it's Rick Warner," Bruce said.

"No, I'm afraid not," Gavin said, his voice somber. "Bruce . . . it's Elizabeth Wakefield."

"What?" Bruce sat up straight, straining against his seatbelt. "Elizabeth! That's not possible!"

"I'm afraid it is," Gavin said. "I just sent you a picture of the lease with her signature."

"But . . ." Bruce felt like he couldn't breathe. Somehow, this all had to be a big mistake.

"Take a look at the lease I sent and call me back later. I'm headed into the office to check on a few more things."

"Thanks, Gavin," Bruce said, and clicked off. He scrambled to scroll through his text messages. Gavin's popped up, and the picture was there, crisp and clear.

Elizabeth's loopy *E* jumped off the page. It was Elizabeth's handwriting, all right. And all of her personal information: her phone number and work address—everything.

Feverishly, Bruce clung to the pathetic hope that somehow this might have a logical explanation. Yet the sinking feeling in his stomach told him nothing could explain why his girlfriend seemed to be in bed with the enemy. All this time he'd thought Rick Warner or someone else might be playing him. He never suspected Elizabeth.

He texted her.

WE NEED TO TALK.

"What's Elizabeth done now?" Missy asked Bruce. She'd heard every word of his conversation and hadn't even pretended otherwise.

"Take me home," Bruce said.

"But . . ."

"I need to go home, Missy." Bruce's tone left no room for argument.

When Elizabeth pulled up to her home—Bruce's mansion—she found a crowd of paparazzi and two news trucks already waiting outside his gate. She clicked the remote and the gate opened even as reporters shouted questions at her rolled-up windows. She inched her car through and closed the gate behind her. She pulled up the drive but soon found her normal parking spot taken—by Missy LeGrange's white Bentley.

Elizabeth swung her car into the circular drive, where florists and deliverymen usually parked, and hopped out of her car. All she wanted was to see Bruce.

She slipped her key in the lock and felt her heart rate speed up. Elizabeth hurried inside and found Bruce and Missy sitting together on the large, coffee-colored leather couch. Despite the fact that it was not even seven in the morning, both held cocktails in their hands. Bruce drank scotch, and it looked like Missy had opted for a wine spritzer, as if this were a garden party and not the morning after Bruce had been arrested for trying to break into a woman's house.

They looked up, surprised.

"Well, *look* who's finally showed up," Missy said. Elizabeth took the hit and flinched. She ignored Missy and searched Bruce's face for clues about how he felt, but he wouldn't look her in the eye. She felt the knots in her stomach tighten. Missy put down her wine spritzer. "*Where* were you?"

Elizabeth opened her mouth to tell Missy it wasn't her business, but before she could get out an answer, Bruce interrupted.

"Missy, I need to talk to Elizabeth."

"I should say you do," Missy agreed, but she didn't budge from the sofa.

"Alone," Bruce clarified, his voice hard as he stared into his glass.

"Oh," Missy said, rising.

"I mean, thank you, Missy, for everything." Bruce's voice softened as he looked up at her. Missy smiled.

"You know I'll always be there for you." Missy squeezed his shoulder before moving away from the couch. She strut past Elizabeth in her platform Christian Louboutins without another word, her expression saying it all and none of it nice.

Elizabeth stood there in front of the sofa, feeling guilty and angry at the same time. She couldn't think of a worse person to rub her guilt in her face than Missy. But none of that mattered as she watched the painful expressions cross Bruce's face. He exhaled slowly, still staring at his glass. Elizabeth listened as the click of Missy's heels on the marble floor retreated, punctuated by the soft thud of the front door shutting behind her.

Elizabeth took a deep breath. "Bruce, I am so sorry I wasn't there for you this morning. I—"

"No," Bruce held up his hand, stopping her midsentence. "I don't want to hear about that. I don't even care that you weren't at the jail, Elizabeth." He lifted his eyes to meet hers. She saw pain and it broke her heart. "I know what you did and I want to know . . . why?"

His words rolled over Elizabeth like a tsunami; they felt unnaturally loud, a roar in her ears. He *knew*. He knew about Robin Platt.

"I don't know what you mean," she began, even though she knew exactly what he was talking about. She only prayed she was wrong.

"Don't lie to me," Bruce shouted, his voice a bellow that nearly knocked her down. "I know you signed Robin Platt's lease. I *know* you've been hiding her from me. But what I want to know is . . . why? Why would you do this to me?"

Elizabeth's knees buckled and she sank into the oversized leather chair nearest her. She began to cry as she told Bruce everything—how she'd found Robin weeks ago, how desperate the girl was, and how all she wanted to do was protect Bruce *and* the girl.

"You've got to believe me, Bruce. I only wanted to find out the truth."

"I *told* you the truth, Elizabeth. I *told* you what happened. But you never believed me, did you?"

"I wanted to, but——"

"God, Elizabeth, I've known you for years. *Years*. I've been in love with you for God knows how long, and you've been living with me for three years, and all this time you thought I was a *monster*?"

"No, you don't understand."

"I understand that the woman I thought I loved never really loved me at all. Never even knew me. Did you ever really love me? Or were you just using me to get back at Todd? Is that what I am? Some kind of rebound for you?"

"No, never! Please, Bruce, I *love* you."

"This is what you call love?"

Elizabeth could hear the pain in his voice. And at the same time she felt it in her chest, too. All she wanted to do was go to him, put her arms around him, hold him, and tell him how sorry she was and that it wasn't too late to fix things.

Except she couldn't. Because it was too late, far too late, to make all of this right. Yet she couldn't stop herself from trying.

"I just thought maybe there was some other explanation. Like maybe you had a seizure or something and you blacked out. I mean, what if there's something going on—some emotional issue, you know, like your mother."

Bruce leaped to his feet and hurled his glass across the room. It hit the wall on the opposite side of Elizabeth with an explosive pop, shattering into tiny pieces that rained down on the floor.

Elizabeth jumped back.

"Goddamn it, Elizabeth. I am not my mother!" Bruce's face flushed red. Every nerve ending in his body was alive and angry, and he looked like he wanted to kill her. "I told you about my mother's condition *in confidence*. And now you throw it back in my face? How dare you?"

"S-s-sorry, I . . ." Elizabeth actually had her hands up, as if to protect her face. "Please don't . . ."

He took two steps and grabbed her by the arms and pulled her up to her feet as if he wanted to shake sense into her. Their faces were so close, almost touching. She could feel his angry breath on her cheek.

Elizabeth feared what would come next. A slap? A shove? Was this what had happened to Robin Platt? When she looked into Bruce's rage-fueled eyes, she didn't see any trace of the man she loved. His hands dug into her arms, pinching her.

"Bruce, please, you're hurting me." Her voice was hardly a whisper, the fear in it unmistakable.

Then, just as suddenly, the anger drained from his face and confusion took its place. Bruce looked down at his hands around her arms as if he couldn't remember how they'd gotten there. He seemed as shocked as Elizabeth that his temper had gotten so far away from him. He released her instantly, as if her arms were the handles of a hot pan.

"Elizabeth, I'm sorry. I . . ."

But Elizabeth wasn't going to stay. She couldn't stay. Not anymore. She just wanted to get away. From Bruce, from everything. With tears streaming down her face, she turned and ran to the front door, down the steps, and to her car, all the while hearing Bruce's voice calling behind her. But she didn't stop.

Elizabeth roared away from Bruce's mansion and before she'd had time to think about it found herself on the road to the only safe place in the world for her: Jessica's house.

Jessica, of course, had her own problems. It had already been a week since Todd had left her at Le Bouchon, dashing any hope she held of reconciliation. Jessica had been devastated; there simply wasn't any other way to describe it. The only thing that saved her had been Liam, who called the day after Todd had walked out on her and asked her out again. Jessica should've said no, but she didn't. She needed the attention and no one was more attentive and adoring than Liam.

And that's how she ended up out with him on a swanky dinner date just two days after Todd left.

When they walked into the jammed bar of Blu, Sweet Valley's new it-restaurant and she took one look at the sea of Stella McCartney dresses, she immediately wanted to go home. She was in no mood to rub elbows with twenty-two-year-olds squeezed into designer microminis and carrying around oversized martini glasses as if they were the latest must-have accessory. Normally, she'd be more than up for the challenge, but tonight her heart just wasn't in it.

"Maybe we should go somewhere else," she told Liam, who had his arm draped protectively around her shoulders. Jessica had noticed that he liked to keep his hands on her, as if he thought she might bolt when he wasn't looking. And maybe there was some truth to that.

But Jessica wasn't out with Liam for fun; she was out to prove to herself that she was strong—that Todd hadn't broken her, that no one could break her.

It also helped that Liam was gorgeous and just Jessica's type. Even she noticed the micromini brigade at the bar who scoped out Liam's lean, muscled figure, his stark blue eyes, and floppy, close-up–ready jet-black hair. Not to mention, she already saw that a few of them recognized him. He was a certifiable star now, and they knew it. The whispers intensified as they passed by. They'd be whispering even more if they knew Jessica had already slept with him.

The old Jessica would've been proud to be with Liam, would've loved all the cold looks of envy from the girls at the bar. But the new Jessica couldn't enjoy it because she was pining for Todd. No matter how hard she ordered herself to forget Todd, she couldn't seem to manage it.

Now that Todd knew she'd slept with Liam and had lied about it, there'd be no reconciliation. He'd made that much clear the night he'd left her at Le Bouchon.

Just thinking about Todd at all made her want to cry.

"Come on, luv," Liam purred in his lilting, faint-but-there Irish accent. "I admit, I was a little worried when I didn't hear from you after our amazing evening together. It was for me anyway."

"And me, too; it's just that I've been busy, but now I'm free." Jessica beamed at him. She didn't want to tell him the reason she'd been avoiding his calls before now was that she thought she could reconcile with Todd. The less Liam knew about that, the better.

Jessica glanced at Liam and, as usual, nearly drowned in the pool of devotion in his eyes. It was scary sometimes how deeply and completely Liam had come to love her in such a very short time, but Jessica didn't like to dwell on that. Because Liam was all she had.

She'd just quit her job at VertPlus.net for Todd, and then Todd had left. She felt bereft. Jessica might not have loved Liam, but she needed him. Jessica did feel a little guilty about using him, but decided she shouldn't. The old Jessica wouldn't have. The scheming, manipulative Jessica wouldn't have cared all that much about Liam's feelings. The new Jessica had become soft, weakened by love—by *Todd*—and now she'd lost almost everything she'd cared about. Her job. Todd.

Now her little boy, Jake, would grow up without a father. Or at least, with only a part-time father. And Todd would probably go on to marry that awful Sarah Miller, the plagiarizing, lying bitch.

Jessica pushed the unwanted thoughts from her head. She was supposed to be out tonight with Liam, trying to put the past behind her and attempting to have a good time.

Liam moved easily through the crowd in the lobby of Blu, taking care to pull Jessica along with him. He stopped in front of the restaurant's hostess, a tall, leggy redhead with dazzling green eyes. She took one look at Liam and lit up like a slot machine.

"Liam O'Connor, we're honored," the hostess said, recognizing him instantly. She used a voice that implied she would be more than happy to take him home and show him something decidedly naughty in the confines of her own bedroom. It should've bothered Jessica, but the fact was she honestly didn't care. This made it obvious that while Jessica liked Liam, she just wasn't in love with him.

"We don't have a reservation, but . . ." Liam said, flashing his Crest-ad ready smile. The hostess melted.

"Oh, no worries at all. We will find you the perfect table." She beamed at him. Her eyes slid very briefly to Jessica, but then wiggled eagerly back to Liam. Clearly, she didn't see Jessica as competition. Now *that* irked Jessica. Did she have "my husband left me for a two-bit skank" tattooed on her forehead? Just because Todd had dumped her didn't mean that Jessica had lost all her juice. She cozied up to Liam, wrapping her arm around his back. Liam responded like a puppet on a string, stepping closer to her and affectionately nuzzling her neck.

"Thank you *so* much for the table." Jessica addressed the hostess in her sweetest voice and flashed her brightest smile, all the while showing her just how much Liam was hers. For a second, Jessica felt like her old self as she soaked in the discomfort and envy radiating from the hostess's pinched face. *That's right,* Jessica thought, *I win.*

This time, at least.

The hostess grabbed two menus from the hostess stand and nodded at Liam.

"This way," she said tightly.

The feeling of triumph quickly faded. What had she won, really? A date with a man she wasn't in love with? She'd trade a million of them for just one more chance with Todd.

At some point, her life had become like a clichéd country song about heartbreak. She hated it.

The hostess led them to a table front and center in the restaurant, right by the window. Jessica slowed her gait. The table faced the outside. It couldn't get more public.

"Something wrong?" Liam whispered in her ear.

Sure, something was wrong. Jessica's heart was broken and she wasn't sure she could really fake it anymore. Her confidence fled and she felt like going to hide in the bathroom. All she really wanted to do was go home and drown her sorrows in a bottle of wine and cry. But she knew she couldn't do that. She *wouldn't* do that.

"It's fine," Jessica said, thinking she needed to stop being such a wimp. She slid into the chair Liam pulled out for her. Reluctantly, she took the menu the hostess held out for her.

"My agent told me the crab cakes here are amazing," Liam said.

"Oh?" Jessica tried to muster some enthusiasm but failed miserably.

The waiter came by and Jessica hardly even acknowledged him. Liam took over easily, ordering drinks and appetizers for them both—without consulting her. Under different circumstances, this controlling part of

Liam's personality might grate, but tonight Jessica honestly couldn't pull together enough energy to care.

Liam gently took her hand across the table as if he planned to single-handedly lift her out of her funk. Jessica let him.

"Have I told you how gorgeous you look tonight?" Liam asked her.

The compliment got Jessica's attention.

"Maybe—once or twice." She managed a wan smile. He'd told her at least five times in the car alone. So far, it hadn't gotten old.

"I was hoping after dinner tonight, you'd come home with me." Liam's eyes rested on hers steadily.

"To your house in Los Angeles?" Jessica shook her head. "Liza's not staying over. It's just me and Jake tonight."

"Maybe I could come to your place then?" Liam offered.

"I just think it's too soon, Liam. Jake would be confused if you stayed over. He's only two."

In truth, Jake might not mind. But Jessica would. Despite the fact she'd slept with Liam hastily at his hotel room not that long ago, she wasn't ready to repeat the experience. She'd lied to Todd, claiming nothing had happened between them, but thanks to Caroline Pearce and her vicious blog, the truth had come out.

Technically, Jessica was single now, and there wasn't anything to stop her from sleeping with Liam again. Except that she just couldn't manage to really *want* to do it.

Liam wasn't good at acting patient. Even now, Jessica could see he wanted nothing more than to take her home and rip off her clothes. She could see the desire in his eyes, like an addict with a fix in reach.

"Another night. Soon." She smiled at him and squeezed his hand, his unspoken reward for being patient and understanding.

He wrapped her hand inside both of his. "I know it's not easy being a single mom. I just wish you'd let me help."

It was at times like these that Jessica thought she really should try to like Liam more. Maybe even love him. He was a nice guy, really. He leaned over the table, and Jessica knew where this was headed. She decided to let him kiss her.

A bright flash of light from outside brushed across her eyelids. Her first thought was *Lightning?* but then she opened her eyes and saw three paparazzi staked out on the sidewalk, their large round lenses of their cameras pointed straight at her.

Jessica grabbed the menu and held it up to the side of her head, but it was too late. They'd gotten her and Liam *kissing* of all things. The thought of that picture all over the Web made her feel queasy. *But, why should it?* she thought. *Todd doesn't want me, and Liam does.*

Still, Jessica couldn't shake the feeling that the walls were closing in. This night was not turning out at all as she'd hoped. More flashes exploded in the dark. Liam, Jessica noticed, didn't bother trying to hide behind a menu. He even waved and smiled at one of the cameras. But he was an actor, and no actor she ever knew could turn down a little attention.

Liam turned back to Jessica.

"Sorry," he said, and shrugged. "It's just part of my job. If they're bothering you, I could tell them to leave."

Jessica could see the headline now: *Liam O'Connor Caught in Altercation with Paparazzi over Girlfriend.*

No, she thought, that would just make things worse.

Her small silver clutch vibrated in her lap. Someone was calling. She slid out her phone and saw it was Michael Wilson, her old boss at VertPlus .net.

"Excuse me," she said, relieved to have a good reason to flee the paparazzi ambush. She answered the call as she walked away from the table. "Hello?"

"Jessica? Am I catching you at a bad time?"

"No, Michael, not at all." If he were here right now, Jessica would've hugged him.

"Well, good, because I would really hate to reschedule my daily groveling session for another day. I'm all ready to beg. And plead."

Jessica laughed. She couldn't help it. Michael had been hounding her since she'd quit, hoping she'd come back to work for him. Just hearing Michael's voice reminded Jessica how much she missed working for him and everyone else at VertPlus.net.

"You're laughing, so that means I'm wearing down your resistance."

"Do you call every one of your ex-employees on a daily basis?"

"Only the good ones *or* the pretty ones," Michael said.

"Which one am I?"

"Both," he said. "That's why I'm calling every day *and* texting."

The flirty tone was new to their relationship. Jessica knew Michael probably had a crush on her, but so far he'd never actually acted on it.

"Michael, you know I miss work, but—"

"Before you say another word, I want to tell you that we landed Bobbi Brown this week. Thought you might be interested."

He knew that was one of Jessica's favorite makeup companies. Already, her mind started spinning about how to package a new environmentally sound line for them. But as soon as the wheels started to turn, she put on the brakes. As much as she would love to go back to work at VertPlus.net, she'd given up her job for Todd. And while Todd wasn't speaking to her at the moment, she still held on to a small sliver of hope that he would change his mind. If she went back to work, Todd would assume she was just using leaving her job as a lure.

Eventually, she felt she could prove to Todd that she could handle being a mother, a wife, and an amazingly brilliant PR woman, but she needed to get him to talk to her first. That would likely never happen if Jessica went back to work so soon.

Even if Todd *was* truly done with her, Jessica wasn't done with him.

"You know I would love to, Michael but—"

"No, don't say 'no.' My fragile ego cannot take another refusal. So, do me a favor and say 'I'll think about it.'"

"There's nothing about your ego that's fragile, Michael."

"Four little words, Jessica."

She sighed.

"All right. I'll *think* about it."

"That's what I like to hear."

Jessica ended the call and nearly collided with Liam's broad chest. She craned her neck to look up at his face and saw he was frowning.

"Who was that?" He sounded suspicious and more than a little bit annoyed.

"What? No one." Jessica paused. Something about the set of Liam's mouth made her feel a little uneasy. "Just Michael Wilson. My old boss."

"What did he want?"

"The usual—to offer me my old job back."

"I don't think you should take it." There came that controlling Liam again. Why did he care if she took the job or not? Except that then she wouldn't be available for spur-of-the-moment brunch dates or late-afternoon lunches. Since he was currently between movies, he had a lot of time on his hands, and he seemed to want to spend every minute with her.

Liam, sensing Jessica's disapproval, softened his own expression and tried a different approach.

"I mean, Jessica, things are tough at home right now, and the last thing you need is more stress with a job that has you working all kinds of hours. And if money is an issue, you know I'm happy to help. You and Jake could even move in with me."

Jessica suddenly wasn't angry anymore. Liam was just trying to help, wasn't he? Besides, she didn't want to alienate one of the few people who still loved her.

"Thanks, Liam, I really appreciate that." She touched his arm gently. "I'm fine for now, though, really."

Liam looked at her for a long second. Then, deciding to drop it, he broke into one of his genuinely warm smiles, the disarming one that currently graced the cover of *Entertainment Weekly*.

"Come on, luv, let's get out of here. We can sneak out the back and ditch the paparazzi."

Grateful, Jessica smiled back at him and looped her arm through his.

Not too long after Jessica and Liam's big night out, Todd Wilkins stopped at his local 7-Eleven to pick up some disposable razors. He glanced up at the tabloid magazines lining the checkout counter, and that's when he saw them: Jessica and Liam, *kissing*.

He felt the shock like a bucket of cold water. What the—?

He grabbed the tabloid so hard it ripped.

"Sir, you'll have to pay for that." The clerk glared at him from behind the register. Todd didn't answer. He was too busy thumbing through the tabloid, trying to find the article that went with the cover photo.

He saw the headline: *Liam O'Connor Gets Cozy with Mystery Girl.* There on the page were two more pictures of them at some swanky restaurant, laughing, and one of Liam with his hand on the small of her back, leading them outside to his waiting car.

His blood began to boil. He wanted to hit somebody. Preferably Liam O'Connor.

Todd knew Jessica had slept with him, but he still hoped they were just a casual thing—maybe a one-night stand. But this tabloid dispelled any hope of that. The two of them having a romantic dinner didn't *look* casual. They looked like they were a full-blown couple.

Damn it. He felt like a fool. Here was more proof that Jessica had played him. She didn't look like she was missing him at all. She certainly didn't seem sad or the least bit heartbroken. On the contrary, she was having the time of her life.

Maybe she'd never really loved him at all. Maybe she didn't even care about anybody. Or maybe she just couldn't get enough people to love her. Some people were like that. No matter how much love you poured into them, it was never enough.

"Sir? You'll need to buy that." The cashier nodded at the tabloid.

Insult on top of injury, he thought. "Whatever." Todd threw down his money on the counter and marched out of the store. On the way out, he almost tossed the tabloid in the trash. But then he decided he couldn't quite let it go. He knew he'd go home and read every word about Jessica and Liam, no matter how much torture it was. He knew he wouldn't be able to help himself.

He barely remembered driving home, his thoughts entirely on the tabloid that sat next to him in the front seat.

He pulled into the driveway of the town house where he lived and saw a familiar car parked in front—Sarah's battered old red Volvo. Sarah herself sat on his stoop, a large duffel bag next to her.

"Sarah? Everything okay?" Of course, he knew it wasn't. Sarah looked like she wanted to cry.

"I couldn't pay rent and my landlord changed my locks," she declared, and threw herself into Todd's arms. A sob caught in her throat. "Oh, God. I have nowhere to go. I have no money. What am I going to do?"

Todd wrapped his arms around her. Immediately, he felt a surge of guilt. Sarah wouldn't have been in this mess if she hadn't lost her job. And she would never have been fired if Jessica hadn't twisted the truth because she'd been jealous of her.

Jessica had been jealous they were dating and had dug up something about Sarah plagiarizing Jessica's old quotes. Todd was convinced it had been purely accidental, but their editor sided with Jessica and now Sarah was blacklisted—probably forever—in the news business.

"Don't worry about anything," Todd said. "We'll figure something out. For now you're going to stay with me."

"You mean it?" Sarah looked up at his face, eyes hopeful.

"Absolutely," he said, even though he did have a tiny flicker of doubt. Was having Sarah move in the *right* thing? Maybe not, but he knew he had to help her. Quickly, he pushed his misgivings away. He owed her this much. "Let me get your bag."

Liam called Jessica's phone and she let it go to voice mail—again. She had bigger problems now that she was trying to help Bruce swim out of the publicity swamp he'd made for himself when he got arrested. Jessica was sitting in Bruce's living room, hastily typing an e-mail to another one of her contacts at yet another news show. She didn't have time for Liam right now. All her energy was focused on helping one of her oldest friends.

"Eliz——" Bruce began as he walked in the room and then stopped short. "I mean, Jessica. Sorry." His shoulders slumped in defeat.

"It's okay, Bruce," Jessica said. He'd never mistaken the twins before, but these days, Bruce just wasn't himself.

It was almost as if all the fight had gone out of him. He'd been a wreck

Having come through her own bitter divorce, she knew firsthand about loss. "Annie," Bruce said, and gave her a big hug. Even looking tired and run-down, Bruce still carried a bit of that old charisma. Suddenly, instead of the big-time successful defense lawyer, Annie was right back in high school, feeling like a giggly girl again. He'd always had that effect on her.

"It's time you hired Annie," Jessica said without preamble.

"Are you sure?" He glanced at Jessica, and Annie could read the doubt on his face.

She'd seen it before. Not everyone believed she could really be as good as people said. She'd gone to more than one deposition when a prosecutor had made the devastating mistake of thinking she looked harmless. Annie knew her business very well.

"Bruce, I've run a few scenarios of what we can expect from the D.A.'s office. Here are some of the charges they might decide to file." In a no-nonsense way she presented Bruce with some papers. "I've had my paralegal do some research, and I think, given what I know about your case, whatever route the prosecutor chooses to go, their case is weak and circumstantial at best. There's no DNA. No eyewitness accounts of an actual attack, aside from Robin's, no hospital report or rape kit, and additionally, cross-examination is a specialty of mine in any case."

Instantly, a change came over Bruce's face. He glanced at Jessica, who nodded as if to say, *I told you so.*

"Wow, Annie . . . you've changed." Bruce managed not to sound too surprised, which Annie appreciated. "I mean, I knew, even back in high school, you had a lot of potential."

Annie glowed under the praise. There would always be a part of her that would be that insecure high school girl who just wanted the popular kids to like her.

Now, here she was, helping two of the most popular kids ever in Sweet Valley. She felt the warmth of pride.

"Annie is the best there is," Jessica said. "If she's on our side, the prosecutor's screwed."

Annie and Jessica exchanged smiles. And for the first time in many long, miserable days, Bruce Patman smiled. The three of them felt pretty good. At least, for the moment.

9

Elizabeth had been staring out the office windows of the third floor of the newsroom at the *Tribune* for who knew how long. Seconds? Minutes? An hour?

No matter how hard she tried to focus on the school board story in front of her, she just couldn't do it. Every time she looked at the blinking cursor on her screen, she just thought about Bruce.

Jessica had offered her the guest bedroom, but she had turned it down, deciding to stay at the Wakefields while they were on another one of their endless cruises.

She knew Jessica had been spending a lot of time at Bruce's house and she was truly glad of that. She desperately wanted Bruce to beat the charges *if* he really was innocent. But another part of her just wanted the truth to come out—whatever it was.

Elizabeth sighed as she sat at her desk. It was all so awful. If Robin was telling the truth, Bruce was destroyed. If Robin was lying, Elizabeth had betrayed Bruce and lost him forever. Both scenarios were so painful she couldn't bear to think either one was true. Yet it had to be one or the other. Her mind spun in circles, trying to digest it all.

"Elizabeth! My office—now!" shouted Tim White, the assistant managing editor, from the door of his glassed-in office. He sounded furious. Tim wasn't the gruff newspaper editor stereotype you see in all the movies. Tim always had a smile and a joke at the ready, which is why Elizabeth knew she was in serious trouble.

Reluctantly, she pushed back her rolling chair from her computer. She felt the eyes of the newsroom on her as she walked toward his office. The problem with working with a bunch of reporters was that they never missed anything.

"What's up?" she asked once she got to his door. She glanced over at the other chair in Tim's office and saw Andy Marker sitting there, looking grim. Andy was the *Tribune* reporter assigned to Bruce's story.

"Andy just told me that you not only *know* where Jane Doe lives, but *you* signed her lease. Is this true?"

Elizabeth glanced at Andy, who avoided her eyes.

"How did you find that lease?" she demanded.

"I'm not revealing my source," Andy said. "It's confidential."

Elizabeth was impressed with Andy's sleuthing. He was even better than she thought. She wondered if he'd been following her around to get leads in the case. Still, it annoyed her, too. She didn't blame him for seeking the information. It was his job. She only wished Andy had come to her first before he'd gone to Tim.

"It doesn't matter how he knows," Tim said.

"Sorry, Tim. I was going to tell you . . ."

"You're becoming part of the story. You know that's not what we do here."

"I know. I'm sorry. I . . ." Elizabeth felt like the world was coming down on her head. First she'd lost Bruce, and now it seemed like she was going to lose her job, too. She didn't know if she could stand it.

"You've got to give me something to tell Walt," Tim said, rocking back in his chair behind his desk. Walt was the managing editor and Tim's boss. He was hard-nosed and gruff and never, ever smiled. "He's going to go crazy when he hears this. Walt's fired people for less."

"I know."

"You know I hate to be the bad guy, but I really have no choice here."

"Tim, I'm really sorry. I just . . ."

"You fell for the poor kid's pitiful story. I know. But now the thing is, Elizabeth, you and I have jobs to do. We don't always *like* our jobs, but that's what they pay us for. You understand what I'm telling you?" Elizabeth shook her head. Tim rubbed his temples. "We need an exclusive interview with Jane Doe. Tell her we absolutely will keep her name confidential, but we need the exclusive. You have to interview her."

"Hey—wait, this is *my* story," Andy protested.

"Not anymore. You two have to work together. Elizabeth, give me the interview with Jane Doe and then all is forgiven."

"But . . ." Elizabeth couldn't even begin to imagine telling Robin the truth, much less getting her to agree to being quoted in the newspaper, even if they kept her name out of it. "This girl is skittish and scared and there's no way she would agree to be quoted."

"Tell Jane Doe her name won't run," Tim said. "Since you two are such good buddies, I know you can convince her to give you the story."

"I don't know . . ."

"Well, find a way, or *you* get to tell Walt why you're neck-deep in this story."

Elizabeth knew she had no choice. Not if she wanted to keep her job. "Okay, Tim."

"That's what I like to hear," Tim said.

10

While Elizabeth reluctantly grabbed her jacket and keys from her desk, Lila Fowler was busy across town filming the next installment of *The True Housewives of Sweet Valley*. Lila and two of the other Housewives sat in Lila's elaborately decorated living room.

It was supposed to be a wine and cheese afternoon party, but Lila had filled her glass with seltzer and had pointedly skipped the cheese for a snack of pickles and peanut butter. Lila wasn't actually pregnant, but she'd seen enough movies to know how she ought to act.

"I thought food cravings didn't start until the second trimester," said Marina Delgardo, sipping from her glass of wine.

"Lay off, Marina," Devone Waters said, putting down her own wine-glass. "It's not easy being pregnant. Give the woman a break."

Marina stared at Lila's still-flat abdomen. "She's been pregnant two seconds, and already she's got cravings? Please."

Lila sent Marina a *back off or you'll regret teasing a pregnant woman* look. Ever since Lila had announced she was expecting her estranged husband Ken's baby, Devone had been her true friend and supporter. Marina, however, wasn't nearly so warm, and sat stubbornly on the fence, hedging her bets and ensuring she would be on the side of whichever Housewife won the standoff: Lila or Ashley Morgan.

Right now, Lila was the clear favorite in terms of fan support. Online and elsewhere, Ashley was called a backstabbing home wrecker who should be ashamed of herself.

Lila glanced down at her plate and the gooey peanut-butter glob on the end of the dill pickle and felt like retching. The combination smelled awful. How could any woman—pregnant or otherwise—ever eat this? Luckily, she had a way out.

"I don't feel so good," Lila said, and dropped the peanut butter–clad pickle onto her plate. "Excuse me."

She ran to the nearest bathroom, slammed the door behind her, flipped on the fan, and leaned against the marble countertop. She took the opportunity to muss her hair strategically, so that it looked at once like she'd been sick, but also managed to be close-up ready at the same time. It was an art, much like perfecting the deliberately rumpled bed-head look.

She had to admit, since dyeing her hair a few shades darker, she looked a lot like a younger Demi Moore. The darker hair suited her. Her cheeks, however, didn't seem rosy enough for pregnancy, so she applied some extra bronzer, hoping to get that perfect expectant-mother glow. She sighed. Faking pregnancy was a lot of work.

A text came in from Jessica.

GIVEN UP ON THE PLAN YET?

Lila grabbed the phone. NO AND IT'S WORKING, SO THERE, she typed.

Jessica might have been one of Lila's oldest and dearest friends, but sometimes the girl simply had no faith. Jessica had made it clear from the start she didn't support Lila's fake-pregnancy plan.

"What happens when you do get him back and then he finds out you're *not* pregnant?" Jessica had asked.

"Miscarriage, obviously. But not until I've got Ashley out of the picture. Way out."

"Lila, we're not in high school anymore," said Jessica suddenly, sounding just like Elizabeth.

But Lila wasn't buying. "Are you kidding? All of life is high school."

She wasn't about to listen to Jessica for love-life advice—not given the state of her estranged marriage. Lila thought her friend might be jealous. After all, Jessica's big ditch-her-career-for-Todd plan hadn't worked out. Lila was on the verge of really winning Ken back, and she knew firsthand just what a sore loser Jessica could be.

Like that time the two of them were nearly at each other's throats when they both went after that gorgeous Jack in high school. Of course, Jack turned out to be a pitiful thief and druggie, so maybe that was a memory best left forgotten.

"And what if he doesn't come back to you before you're supposed to start to show?"

"I'll think of something," Lila said, glancing down at her still-flat belly. She made a mental note to eat something salty. That would give her just the little bit of bloat she might need to look pregnant. After all, it worked for the starlets on TMZ. If any one of them went to In-N-Out Burger, the next day there'd be "baby bump" rumors.

Lila hadn't seen Ken since last week's *True Housewives* show aired. In it, they showed Ken and Ashley on a romantic date. The two of them even *kissed*. If Lila closed her eyes, she could still see that scene as it had played out on her television.

"You know, you're so pretty." The minute he said that, he had blushed bright pink. He might have been six foot three and able to throw a fifty-yard touchdown against a blitz, but the guy just had no defenses against pretty women. At his core, he was just kind of shy.

Even when Ashley had thrown herself on him in the limo ride home, he still seemed reluctant to take advantage. Ken was just too sweet. No wonder Ashley had sunk her talons into him so deeply. He never stood a chance.

After that show aired, Ken's Twitter page and even his NFL team received tons of hate mail. Nobody liked it that Ken was messing around with Ashley while he had a pregnant wife at home. Nobody cared if they were separated or not. The scandal even led ESPN news.

For that, Lila might have felt a little twinge of guilt. Ken was *not* the asshole they were making him out to be. He was actually sweet to a fault. But then, she didn't really feel bad. All was fair in love and war.

Just like some of the rumors Lila may have started online about Ashley Morgan—that, for instance, she might have once been a stripper and, briefly, an escort. No truth to it, of course. That's why they were called *rumors*.

Lila heard a commotion outside the bathroom door. She heard Devone shouting, and another voice, too.

After a quick check in the mirror, she went to investigate and found Devone nose-to-nose with Ashley in Lila's living room. All the *Housewives* cameras focused intently on the train wreck.

"You need to leave this house right now," Devone shouted at Ashley Morgan, who had just arrived bedecked in too much jewelry and makeup, per usual. Her long, straight blond hair gleamed shiny and thick with new extensions.

"This is *my* show, too, and the producer invited me, so you can't tell me *not to be here*." Ashley wasn't about to back down. "And I'm here to talk to Lila."

"Devone," Lila said, trying to appear like the mature one. After all, she was pretending she was going to be a mother. "It's okay. Let's hear what she has to say. Maybe she wants to apologize."

"Apologize?" Ashley spat. "I am *not* going to apologize to you. *You* need to apologize to me about all those vicious rumors you started about me. I've never been a stripper—or a call girl."

"No? Well, I don't know what you're talking about. I never started any rumors, but I could see why someone would."

"Exactly what does that mean?" Ashley threw down her clutch on the couch.

Marina jumped up, her eyes bouncing back and forth between Ashley and Lila, trying to decide whom she should support. Marina only backed winners.

Devone, however, came down decidedly on Lila's side.

"You need to calm down, Ashley," Devone said. "Lila's pregnant. Don't go upsetting her. Remember the baby."

"Right. Like anybody is believing that!"

"Are you calling me a liar?" Lila's voice was low and dangerously calm.

"So what if I am?"

"Take it back, you bitch," Lila hissed.

"Who are you calling 'bitch,' you stupid slut?" And then Ashley just lunged.

Lila couldn't have orchestrated a more perfect scene.

Lila put her hands protectively over her stomach. "Don't hurt the baby!" she cried, frantic. She met Ashley's furious gaze, and thought *check-mate,* even as Devone grabbed Ashley from behind, stopping her midstride, and all Ashley managed to do was swipe at Lila's arm, leaving barely a scratch. Lila wasn't really hurt, but the damage to Ashley's reputation would be permanent.

Ashley had just tried to hit a pregnant woman on national television.

"Back away from my wife!" Ken's voice thundered in the living room. All the women turned to look.

"Thank God!" Lila stood, her palm still resting on her lower belly.

Ken's anger drained away as he looked at Lila. He looked at her holding her stomach. "She's having my baby, and I'm the father. I want to be with her—if she'll have me."

Tears sprang to Lila's eyes. In that moment, she knew she'd won him back. She nodded. A huge smile broke out on Ken's face, like he'd just been handed a Vince Lombardi trophy.

He crossed the room in four big steps and swept her up in his arms.

"I love you, Lila and I love our baby," he declared, covering her with kisses. "You should have called me. I found out from the TV!"

"I know, Ken. I'm sorry. I didn't know how to tell you."

"Well, I'm here now, and I want us to be a family."

He didn't care that the room was full of *Housewives* costars and a whole camera crew. Neither did Lila. She returned every one of his kisses. Lila did manage a triumphant glance thrown at Ashley, who was busy turning five different shades of furious.

"Let's go somewhere a bit more private," Lila suggested, glancing around at the cameras.

In true form, Ken's face lit up. He cradled her carefully in his arms, lifting her up off her feet, and then jogged with her up the stairs.

They fell on the bed together, outside of camera reach, with a laugh, and proceeded to shrug off their clothes. Neither one cared that they'd left the rest of the crew downstairs.

"I'm so glad you're back," Lila said, wrapping her arms around him.

"You've made me the happiest man alive."

"You mean it?" Lila asked, a guilty twitch working its way up her spine. She quickly squashed it. *Love and war,* she reminded herself. And her feelings for Ken were as close as she ever got to love.

"I've never meant anything more," Ken said, a sweet grin on his face. "Wait," he said, struck by a sudden and urgent concern. "I'm not going to hurt . . . the baby, am I?" He blinked innocently at her.

Poor, sweet Ken, Lila thought. "No, of course not, silly."

But by then there wasn't any more time for talking.

11

About a week later, Bruce shaved and showered and put on a suit. Annie was the first to notice.

"Wow, Bruce, you really look great."

"You think so?"

"I second that," Jessica said, looking up from her laptop. She and Annie sat in his living room, which had seen better days. The makeshift PR war room for Bruce's case just couldn't seem to stay neat, no matter how much Mme Dechamps fussed with it.

Extension cords ran in all directions, feeding power to a small army of laptops, a fax machine, and a paper shredder. Despite all the clutter, little progress had been made in Bruce's case. They all still waited to hear what other charges the D.A. might throw at him in the Robin Platt case. Meanwhile, Jessica kept plugging away at the PR campaign, even though it seemed more and more avenues for positive PR dried up every day. Morning shows weren't interested in promoting innocent Bruce anymore. Most of them were desperate to get a Jane Doe exclusive. They were offering to shadow her face, disguise her voice, anything to get the accuser on television, but so far Jane Doe remained elusive.

"I thought it was about time I stopped sulking," Bruce said, and straightened his tie. "Besides, I want to look good when I get fired today."

"Bruce, you own the company. They can't fire you," Annie said. This much was true. He was the chairman of the board of directors at Patman Social Impact Group. The company had already invested in projects that built waste-product renewing plants and experimental methods of cleaning water.

Before the scandal broke, Bruce and Patman Social Impact had acquired prime real estate for a wind-powered plant to clean water, beating out Rick Warner of Warner Natural Gas for the same stretch of land. But yesterday, word came in that the EPA planned to deny them the permits they needed to develop the land.

Skittish members on the board had called an emergency meeting for that afternoon to deal with the news. Bruce couldn't blame them, even when he'd heard a rumor they might want to take a vote of no confidence in him.

"Don't let them bully you," Jessica told him.

"It's okay, I can handle it." And for the first time in weeks, he felt like he could. Yes, he was heartbroken over Elizabeth's leaving, but he'd never been the kind of guy to sit around and wallow in self-pity. At least, not for long. The company needed him, and so did Sweet Valley. The land deal wasn't just some other business deal that fell through. If Rick Warner got ahold of that land, he'd mine it for natural gas, and with Warner's controversial fracking methods, Bruce really believed the drinking water of the entire county could be at risk. He had seen the documentaries of people lighting their tap water on fire. He wasn't going to let that happen in his hometown.

And despite what Elizabeth or anyone else thought, he was a good guy, and he was going to show them all.

He climbed into his Porsche, tearing through the gate just as it slid open. He didn't stop to offer quotes to the paparazzi still hanging around the sidewalk. And he didn't bother slowing down.

Patman Social Impact Group took up the entire top floor of a glassed-in office building near the freeway. Bruce parked in his usual spot, front and center, and walked past the security guard in the lobby, who gave him a respectful nod as he passed.

Most of the board was already there when Bruce arrived. He grabbed a few notes and files from his assistant, Jill, on the way in.

"What's the mood like in there?" Bruce asked her.

"Bad," she said. "There are rumors they're going to ask you to step down. Is that true?"

"It might be."

"But you can't let them do it," Jill pressed. "You're the heart and soul of this company. And . . . and . . . it's just not right."

"Sometimes things just aren't fair," Bruce said. "But whatever happens, it'll be okay."

"I hope so."

Bruce took a deep breath and stepped into the boardroom. Conversations stopped midsentence as he walked briskly to the head of the glass conference room table. At least no one had taken his seat yet.

He glanced at the members of the board, some of whom he'd known for years. Few of them would actually look him in the eye. These were the men and women he'd golfed with, strategized with, and trusted with his company. They were like family. And now they were planning a mutiny.

"I call this meeting to order," Bruce said.

"I ask for a no-confidence vote," called Don Edgewater. Of all the board members, Don was the one Bruce knew least well. He'd come on board late, after the initial start-up, and they'd never really clicked. Not that it mattered now.

"Ladies and gentleman, a no-confidence vote won't be necessary," Bruce began.

A few, including Don, protested loudly.

"Let the man finish!" declared Thomas LeGrange, Missy's father and trustee of the Patman Estate. Bruce was grateful to Thomas for at least allowing him the opportunity to speak.

"As I was saying," Bruce continued. "A vote won't be necessary because, effective today, I am voluntarily stepping down from my position as president of the board of directors of Patman Social Impact."

Shocked gasps met the news. Even Don Edgewater was speechless. Bruce barreled on, determined to see this through.

"I realize that my personal life has become a distraction to the business of this company, and I do not want anything to interfere with the mission of Patman Social Impact." Bruce took a deep breath and continued. "What we're doing here is far more important than one person. I ask the board to continue the fight to win approval for our project. I think we all know the stakes if Warner Natural Gas manages to get that land. Potentially, it could affect the groundwater from San Diego to Los Angeles. Should that water become polluted, millions of people will be affected, including our own families. I ask the board to appeal the EPA's ruling and seek another way to keep this project viable. We owe it to ourselves, to our communities, and to our families to see this project through."

Several board members nodded their heads in agreement.

"I know every one of you personally," Bruce continued as he met the gaze of each man and woman sitting around the table. "And I know that all of you believe in the importance of leaving the world in a better place than when we found it. I ask you to continue on in that spirit. That means I'm asking you to continue this fight. Our future and our neighborhoods depend on it."

As Bruce finished, enthusiastic applause met his words, and every one of the board members gave him a standing ovation, even a reluctant Don Edgewater.

He nodded a thank-you in response, certain that he had done the right thing. Too bad Elizabeth wasn't here to see this, he thought. Maybe then she wouldn't be so quick to doubt him. Then, maybe she wouldn't see him as a monster. As soon as he had the thought, he hated that he was still trying to prove himself to her.

When would he stop caring what she thought?

12

Elizabeth had spent the last week desperately trying to find a link between Robin Platt and Rick Warner. But no matter how hard she investigated, she couldn't find anything. Her gut still told her Rick Warner might be at the bottom of this, but so far she could find no proof.

She desperately wanted to discover holes in Robin's story, anything that might shed doubt on her version of events. Then she could hand her editors a story that would help Bruce instead of hurting him.

While she hadn't given up on the Rick Warner link, she also knew she'd run out of time. She would have to run with the Robin Platt exclusive interview or she'd lose her job.

Now came the even harder part: admitting to Robin Platt she wasn't Laura Christer, supportive therapist, at all, but Elizabeth Wakefield, investigative journalist.

Robin sat in front of her now, blinking.

"You *lied* to me?" she said, after Elizabeth had rushed through the story. "And now you want to run my story in the *newspaper*? But you can't run my name! You said you wouldn't." Robin jumped up and began frantically pacing the room. "No one can know my name!"

Elizabeth felt a little nudge of suspicion. Robin seemed completely panicked at the thought of her name getting out there. But then, she *was* a victim, and unfortunately, there was still something of a taint and certainly an embarrassment to having your intimate life exposed. Elizabeth could understand that. That was the reason the media protected victims' names—to give them the privacy they needed to bring their story forward.

"It will be anonymous, of course," Elizabeth said. "You'll be known only as Jane Doe."

"Oh." Robin visibly relaxed.

Elizabeth couldn't put her finger on it, but something wasn't quite right. In fact, Robin even seemed a little glassy-eyed. But maybe that was just her imagination. Or her own guilt at work. Elizabeth couldn't trust herself to see anything clearly these days.

"I'll do it," Robin said after a minute, shocking Elizabeth. "I'll give you the interview."

"You will?"

"No, I think it's the best thing. It's about time my story got out there," Robin said. "And I've already told you so much already. It might as well be you. As long as my name is kept out of it, I'll do it."

"I promise you it will be. Are you sure you want to do this?"

"I'm sure," Robin said, and her voice sounded a little bit too hard.

Elizabeth clicked "record" on her tape recorder to start the official interview before Robin changed her mind. She knew that even after the interview, she wasn't done with this story yet. Something felt wrong, and Elizabeth was going to find out what it was. No matter how long it took.

13

In a bungalow not too far away, Steven Wakefield stood in his kitchen, squared his shoulders, and met Baby Emma's stubborn gaze.

"Come on, Emma, it's time to sit in your high chair," he told her as she squirmed against him, violently kicking her legs out as he tried to put her in the chair. He put her in and she promptly began screaming her head off.

"What are you putting her in that thing for?" Aaron declared as he walked briskly into the kitchen and plucked Emma out of her designer high chair. "You know she prefers to sit in my lap."

"She's almost six months old," Steven said. "She needs to learn how to survive one second without being held."

This was an old argument. Aaron was in the parent camp that said you never put your child down, even if that meant wearing them strapped to your body at all times. Steven felt like Aaron was just spoiling Emma. If it were up to Aaron and Emma, she'd be held 24/7.

But Aaron would do anything to avoid Emma's dreaded five-alarm wail, which was actually so ear-piercing it could make dogs a street over howl. Admittedly, Steven hated the five-alarm wail, too, but sometimes, he thought, they needed to risk it.

"Besides," Steven continued, "how else are we supposed to feed her this?" Steven held up a bowl of freshly made rice cereal, which held all the watery appeal of gruel. But it was what the pediatrician had said they should start feeding her, and Steven was going to do it, high chair or not.

"I can feed her while I hold her," Aaron said, overconfident as usual.

"It's not a bottle," warned Steven, but a beat too late. Aaron spooned a mouthful of the watery gruel into Emma's mouth, only to have her spit the whole thing out down the front of Aaron's newly ironed Oxford.

"Great," Aaron said, and stood, handing a pouting Emma over to Steven so he could go change. Steven was about to set Emma back in her high chair when the doorbell rang.

"Our savior," Steven whispered to Emma, and he took her to the door. He opened it and Emma's new nanny, Agneta, came in. Emma smiled instantly when she saw Agneta, who had started only a couple of weeks ago, and reached her pudgy little arms out to be held.

Agneta, a petite, young woman with dark hair and warm brown eyes, scooped up Emma and immediately started cooing at her.

"There's my beautiful baby girl," Agneta said. "All the other babies must be jealous of you—you've taken all the adorable just for yourself."

Emma broke out her single-toothed smile as if she understood the compliment word for word.

"We were in the middle of breakfast, but she hasn't eaten much," Steven explained to Agneta, nodding to the small baby bowl on the counter.

"No problem, Mr. Wakefield," she said. "We'll fix that, won't we, my perfect little rose?"

Emma giggled and clapped her hands in approval. Steven breathed a sigh of relief as she watched Agneta glide into the kitchen with Emma. She had been the only nanny candidate—out of twenty they'd interviewed—that Emma actually liked. Most of the women—and the two men who had interviewed for the job—couldn't even hold Emma without her screaming bloody murder.

And what Emma didn't want, nobody was going to force c
could try, but he was almost always undercut by Aaron,
whatever Emma wanted, Emma should get. And Emma der
Somewhere in the back of his head, she reminded Steven of c
ters. And it wasn't Elizabeth.

Sometimes, he suspected she really had the Jessica Wake
even kept him up nights, worrying if Emma might be as s
younger sister. Despite that unpleasant thought, he couldn't
smile—he liked the idea that she might be a true Wakefield.

Still, the fact was, he couldn't fight Emma *and* Aaron at
tried and failed before, which was nearly every night, when E
up in their bed instead of her crib.

Plus, it wasn't just Emma rejecting nanny candidates. A
seem to like any of them, either. He dismissed most of them i
judgments like "too mean" or "too hippie" or "too old-school" or

Steven was starting to get the impression that Aaron might
sabotaging the whole process. Steven sometimes wondered if
Emma, had the greater separation anxiety.

But with Aaron's extended paternity leave running out and
ing decided he would go back to work, they'd had to find some
didn't like the idea of day care, but it wasn't like that was an c
way, since all the best ones had six-month-long waiting lists.
on the verge of simply quitting his job and staying home when
Agneta, the last candidate they interviewed.

Against all odds, both Aaron *and* Emma loved her. Steven
hire her on the spot, agreeing to whatever she asked in pay. A
out, she asked for a reasonable sum, and she was willing to star
day.

As Steven watched, Agneta masterfully balanced Emma o
while stirring a little bit of formula into the rice cereal to make
sweeter. Why hadn't Steven thought of that? As he watched, A
only got Emma to open her mouth, she managed to get the baby
swallow a full bite without spilling a drop.

Steven shook his head. Agneta just had the magic touch and
right away—don't put this baby down. As Aaron came boundin

kitchen, clad in a fresh shirt, he broke into a grin when he saw the nanny. Agneta could do no wrong in Aaron's eyes (not since she introduced them to a new organic line of baby ointment that cleared up Emma's nagging diaper rash in a single day).

"Time to run. Love you, pumpkin," Aaron said, and gave Emma a kiss on the forehead.

"Bye, bye, Ems," Steven said, waving to little Emma, who gamely waved back, a big pink spoon clutched in one chubby fist.

After the dads left, Agneta fed and changed Emma and then got her ready for their morning trip to the park. Agneta had babysat dozens of babies, and she knew that little Emma was a girl who wanted to be on the move, as long as she was carried there.

Agneta had never met another baby who so stubbornly refused to sit in a stroller, a high chair or even be put down for one minute. Some would call this baby high-maintenance, but Agneta didn't mind carrying little Emma. Most nannies would've insisted the baby sit strapped in a stroller, but Agneta was happiest when Emma was happy, which was probably why the two got along so well.

Agneta just loved babies. One day, she wanted to have two or three babies of her own, but that was later, after she got married. For now, Agneta walked with Emma on her hip the block and a half to the park with the small playground.

As she drew closer, she saw her friend Melissa, the pretty flaxen-haired woman who sometimes came to sit on the bench with her Starbucks cup in hand. Melissa had been at the park nearly every day for the last week or so, maybe longer, and the two had started to chat. Agneta felt sorry for Melissa, the woman with bright blue eyes who had told her the story of how she'd lost her baby girl recently—a stillborn, Melissa had said.

Agneta couldn't think of a more tragic story—to be pregnant and then go into labor, only to deliver a baby that wasn't breathing and couldn't be revived.

Melissa saw Agneta—and little Emma—and her face brightened instantly.

"Good morning," she said.

"Good morning," Agneta said, and smiled, glad to see her friend. She loved Emma, but she also wouldn't pass up a bit of adult conversation. Agneta sat down next to Melissa on the bench and put Emma in her lap.

"How's little Emma this morning?" Melissa said, rubbing Emma's rosy cheek. "Such a beautiful baby."

"Loving the compliments," Agneta said. And it was true. There was nothing Emma loved more than being at the center of attention. Shades of her aunt Jessica.

Emma cooed and gamely took in Melissa's praise, but then, fickle in her ways, quickly tired of it and squirmed in Agneta's lap as she reached toward the park. Agneta knew what she wanted: a trip to the baby swings, her favorite. The swings were on the other side of the park, a little bit of a walk, but Agneta was happy to carry her over there.

Melissa followed, coffee cup in hand.

Agneta sat Emma in the little bucket swing—which as far as Agneta knew was the only time Emma was happy outside of someone's arms— and gave the baby a little push. Emma's curly blond locks blew up in the wind, and she clapped her hands in glee.

"She's adorable," Melissa said, a wistful look on her face.

"She is the cutest," Agneta agreed. "And her dads are just the nicest. They fawn over her, both of them."

"Sounds like they might be spoiling her."

"Spoil?" Agneta laughed. "You can't spoil a baby. Whatever Emma wants, Emma gets! Isn't that right?"

Emma clapped her hands to show she agreed with the sentiment.

"Dadas!" Emma cried suddenly.

"Did you just say 'Daddies'?" Agneta cried.

"Dadas!" Emma said again.

"Oh, wait. I've got to send Aaron and Steven a text. They won't believe this." Agneta reached into her pocket to grab her phone but found nothing but the house keys there. "My phone!" She glanced around the ground in dismay. "I know I had it."

"I think I saw one on the bench we were sitting on. Maybe that was yours?"

Agneta squinted, trying to see the bench on the other side of the park, but the trees hid it. It was a brand-new phone and she couldn't afford to replace it. Plus, Aaron and Steven had been adamant: She needed to carry her cell phone at all times, in case of emergency. She was just a couple of weeks into this new job and she still wanted to impress them.

Agneta reached to pick Emma up, but Emma let out a cry of protest. Emma wasn't done with the swing. Agneta sighed, defeated. She knew what was coming next: Emma's patented five-alarm wail.

"I'll watch her," Melissa offered. "You run and get the phone."

"Are you sure?"

"It won't take you but a minute." Melissa gave Emma a little push in the swing. "We'll be fine here."

Agneta took a quick look at Emma, and saw Emma coo and smile in the swing and thought: *What's the harm? Why upset her? It's just across the park.* Fleetingly, she thought, *I don't know Melissa that well,* but then just as soon as the thought popped into her head, she dismissed it. Melissa was very nice, and all she would do was watch Emma in the swing for a couple of minutes. No big deal, right?

"Okay, I'll be right back." Agneta hurried over to the bench. It was a longer walk than she'd remembered, and there were large trees between her and the baby swing. But when she got there, she saw her phone sitting right in the middle of the bench, as if it had slipped out of her pocket. As she stood there, her phone dinged, a message from her boyfriend. She read it and replied as she walked slowly back. She became engrossed for a few minutes in her phone, and looked up again only once she got closer to the swing.

She stopped abruptly in her tracks.

The swing was empty, swaying back and forth. No sign of Melissa or Emma anywhere.

"Emma?" called Agneta. "Melissa?" She whirled, her eyes scanning the park. Cold, dreadful panic set in as she frantically searched the park.

But all she saw was an empty playground. Even the jogging trail was deserted.

"Emma!" she shouted, but it was too late. Emma and Melissa were gone. With trembling fingers, she dialed 911.

14

Pandemonium reigned at Steven and Aaron's home. Two police cruisers sat outside while inside, Agneta was beside herself with panic, barely able to speak to the police officers through her sobs. If Steven had any thoughts of being angry at the nanny, they all evaporated at seeing the pain and heartbreak on her face. Nothing he could say or do would be worse than what she was already saying to herself.

"Oh, Mr. Wakefield, I-I-I am so sorry. It was only a second. It's all my fault. Oh, I just won't be able to live with this. I won't be able to bear it. If . . . If . . ." and then she dissolved into more sobs. Steven met Aaron's gaze over her head. They'd have to decide what to do about Agneta later. Right now, they needed to find Emma.

"It's okay, Agneta, we'll find her."

"But beautiful Emma. Oh, God. It's my fault . . ." Agneta couldn't finish her sentence.

"Ma'am, let's sit down and go over what happened one more time." One of the police officers led Agneta to the living room. Outside, police combed the nearby park for evidence. It had been just two hours since Melissa had left the park with Emma. Everyone working the case knew that every minute that ticked by lessened their chances of finding the baby. The officers were grim and silent, working quickly.

The doorbell rang and Steven opened it to find his younger sister, Elizabeth, in obvious distress.

"Oh, God, poor Emma! I can't believe this. Who is this Melissa person? How did she take Emma?"

"We're still trying to figure that out," Steven said, taking his trembling sister in his arms.

Not two minutes later, Jessica, his youngest sister, was at the door.

"I came as soon as I got your voice mail." Steven gave Jessica a big hug, too, and found he was grateful she was here. They'd come a long way in their relationship since Jessica had first discovered he'd been living most of his life in the closet. Now they were closer than they'd ever been. And at a time like this, Steven was just glad to have both his sisters close to him.

"Have the police sent out an Amber Alert?" Elizabeth asked.

"Yes," Steven said, and nodded. "But we don't know what car Melissa might have been driving, or if she was just on foot."

"Steven! I need you in here," called Aaron from the kitchen.

"Back in a minute," Steven said to his sisters. The doorbell rang, and Steven paused.

"I'll get it," Elizabeth said. "You go on."

She walked to the foyer and swung open the door. Bruce stood on the doorstep. He wore one of his best suits, looking handsome and in charge with his dark hair perfectly combed and his stark blue eyes clear and determined, reminding her of the Bruce she loved so well. For a second, she was so grateful to see him that her eyes lit up and she almost threw her arms around his neck. But as his eyes slid uneasily to the side, she remembered the painful truth: They weren't a couple anymore.

The reality hit Elizabeth hard as she awkwardly tucked her arms down by her sides. All she wanted during this awful time was to feel his strong, reassuring arms around her.

But she knew that was not possible. Not now, not ever. Painfully, Bruce wouldn't even meet her gaze.

"Elizabeth," said Annie Whitman, who appeared by Bruce's elbow. "We came as soon as Jessica told us." Annie wrapped her in a hug and Elizabeth felt hot tears prick her eyes, partly because of Emma, but also because Bruce had slunk past her without a word. Elizabeth swallowed a sob.

"We'll get through this," Annie said, and squeezed.

"Thanks for coming." Elizabeth wiped her eyes. "I know you're busy working on Bruce's case."

"All that matters is we get Emma home safe," Annie said. "Bruce was the first one to say we needed to come over here. We're still waiting to hear about the D.A.'s decision, but he didn't care. He said we needed to be here."

Elizabeth should have been grateful, but instead she just felt a searing pain. This was the Bruce she had fallen in love with, the man who would do anything for the people he cared about. Right in the middle of his own problems, he'd shown up to help. That only made her feel worse about the horrible doubts she harbored about him. How could she think he was capable of attempted rape when he was here, doing what he could for her family in a time of crisis?

"I just can't believe someone would do this," exclaimed Aaron, walking into the foyer and breaking up the conversation. "Thank you so much for coming."

"Aaron, I'm so sorry," Elizabeth said, and Aaron hugged her.

"I'm sorry, too." Annie said. "If there's anything I can do, say the word."

"Thanks, Annie." Aaron gave her a wan smile. The three of them moved into the kitchen, where Bruce and Jessica and Steven were talking in low tones.

Elizabeth glanced at Bruce quickly, then away. To anyone paying attention, their heartbreak was obviously still new and raw.

Steven's phone rang. He glanced at it and said, "Oh, it's Mom and Dad. They must've gotten my message on the cruise ship. They were docking on one of the Greek Isles today. Hello? Mom? Yeah, I'm here. Yes, it's true . . ." He walked away, explaining the situation into the phone. Jessica trailed after him. Aaron's shoulders slumped under the weight of worry. "Why don't we go sit down?" Annie said to Aaron, moving him into the living room.

For the briefest of moments, that left Bruce and Elizabeth alone in the kitchen. Stricken, Bruce looked at his shoes. For a man who had recently given a rousing speech to his board of directors, he could think of absolutely nothing to say to the one woman he once wanted to spend the rest of his life with. Bruce could never have imagined a time when seeing Elizabeth would be so painful. He had always thought, no matter what, they'd be friends. But he couldn't be friends with her. Not now. Maybe not ever. That new revelation hit him hard. He didn't know which was worse: losing the love of his life or losing his best friend.

As they stood there not looking at each other, Bruce felt a surge of anger, too. Why had she thrown away everything they had? For what? For some stranger who had to be lying. But even as the resentment surged, it quickly faded. Bruce could never hate Elizabeth. She was his love. Even now, standing there, so beautiful, just the way he always saw her, dressed simply in her own classic style like she'd just walked off the set of a Ralph Lauren ad. Part of him wanted never to be in her company for another second; another part never wanted to leave her. Either way, he simply couldn't bear it.

She glanced up at him, but the pain in her eyes was something he couldn't stand to see, so he looked away. Eventually, she left, moving into the living room. He should've felt relief, but instead he missed her. How long would he live like this? he wondered. Would every time he saw her rip him apart?

Steven and Jessica walked through the kitchen as Steven wrapped up his phone call.

"Thanks, Dad," Steven said into his phone. "Listen, I've got to go. I'll call you when we know something, okay? Listen, let me put Jessica on the line. I have to go talk to the police." Steven handed the phone to Jessica, who took it readily. Steven figured nobody would be better than Jessica at calming down the near-hysterical grandparents. After all, Steven felt like he was only barely fighting off hysteria himself, and he, above all people, needed to remain calm.

He glanced over at Aaron, who was sobbing into Annie's sleeve, and tried to focus. He was an attorney, and when things got stressful, he just got more analytical. That worked except when it was his own baby. Steven moved into the living room, where two police detectives were questioning a still distraught Agneta.

"Tell us again what she looked like," said Detective Lopez, a dark-haired woman in her mid-thirties wearing a smart black suit and holding a notepad.

"Like I said before, she was a pretty girl, probably in her twenties. Average height, blue eyes, very fair skin, and blond—"

"Wait, what kind of blond? Light blond?" Steven asked, suddenly starting to put the pieces together. "Shoulder-length hair? Almost white-blond?"

Agneta nodded.

Suddenly, Steven knew exactly who had taken Emma: Linda Carson.

"The surrogate!" Steven shouted, smacking one fist into his open palm. Quickly, he ran to get his phone from Jessica.

"Sorry, Mom and Dad. We'll call you back." He hung up the phone and pulled up his photo album. Steven had taken a picture of a very pregnant Linda a week before she was due, when they'd all gotten together for lunch.

"Is this Melissa?" Steven held up his phone with the picture on the screen in front of the nanny.

Amazed, Agneta nodded. "That's her! But how did you—"

"That's the woman we paid to carry Emma," Steven declared. "Linda took her."

"Linda Carson? Are you serious?" Aaron echoed, lifting his head from Annie's shoulder.

"I *told* you there was something wrong with that woman." Jessica couldn't quite keep the superiority out of her voice. After all, she'd had doubts about Linda from the start. "I *knew* it! You should have listened to me!"

"We're going to need her full name and anything else you can give us," the police detective said, holding her notepad ready.

15

Steven, Aaron, and their family and friends waited a heartbreaking seven hours while police scoured Sweet Valley and San Diego, where Linda Carson lived, for any trace of Linda and Emma.

It was an especially painful seven hours for Bruce and Elizabeth, who sat on opposite sides of the living room, looking anywhere but at each other. Jessica sat close to her sister and put her arm around her. She was probably the only one in the room who knew exactly how much her sister was hurting. No one could comfort Elizabeth like her sister.

"It's taking too long," Aaron declared.

"The police are doing what they can," Steven said.

"We should be out there looking for her," Aaron said.

"They sent police cars to her house and her work; they've got her license plate. They'll find her." Steven actually felt confident they would find her. Now that they knew it was Linda, the odds were in their favor.

"But what if it's too late?" Aaron said. "I should never have agreed to a nanny. If I'd stayed home and held her like I wanted to . . ."

"It's not your fault," Steven told Aaron, sternly. "And we're not going to even think about something bad happening to Emma. Linda would never hurt Emma. Believe me, she only wants money."

"She's such a stupid woman. She wouldn't even know how to take care of a baby." Aaron ran a frustrated hand through his hair. "Nobody can care for her like we can! Nobody! If we get her back—"

"*When* we get her back, we're going to figure something out." Steve crossed his arms. He was determined to remain optimistic until it killed him.

Just at that moment, a strange sirenlike wail cut through the conversation. Everyone stopped talking and looked around, confused, except for Steven and Aaron, who leaped to their feet and charged through the room to the front door and flung it open.

Emma!

And there she was, their baby, in an oversized basket, wrapped in a flannel blanket, red-faced and screaming the five-alarm wail that only Emma could do.

Aaron bent down and swooped her up in his arms, and Steven wrapped his arms around Aaron and Emma and they hugged for a long, long time.

"Oh, thank God," Elizabeth said behind them.

"Is that Emma? Oh, thank heaven," Jessica said.

Steven glanced down and saw a note pinned to the flannel blanket. He read Linda's scratchy handwriting:

CAN'T STAND THAT WAIL ANYMORE! SHE'S ALL YOURS! THANK GOD!

Greedy as she was, it was obvious that Linda was undone by the wail that only the fathers could love.

"And you said it was bad that I was spoiling her," Aaron said, holding up the note for the others to see as he hugged little Emma, who quickly calmed down now that she was back among the people who adored her.

And in her father's arms. Which father didn't matter as long as she was being held.

"She's not spoiled, she's perfect," Jessica said. Steven hugged Jessica, never before so grateful they were related.

The Jessica gene had saved Emma's life.

After that, Steven and Aaron decided to let Agneta go. Actually, she insisted on going. After the whole ordeal her nerves were shot. Police kept searching for Linda but seemed to have trouble finding her. But Aaron and Steven weren't too bothered. They were happy little Emma was back with them, safe and sound. If the police found Linda, great. If not, they weren't going to stay up nights worrying. In their hearts they felt she would leave them alone. Emma's five-alarm wail ensured that.

The bigger problem was figuring out day care for Emma.

For a while, Aaron insisted on being a stay-at-home dad, but then Steven found a solution that worked for everybody.

All it took were a few calls around at his office building. He found five other couples who had also recently had babies, and then it just took a few more calls, and the renting out of the empty office on the third floor. Some people at Leisten, Hartke & White had been clamoring for on-premises day care for years. Even Annie was glad to join in. In a few weeks, Steven had made it real.

And somehow, being with other children was more interesting to Emma than being held by adults. As for the wail, she saved that for her fathers.

Additionally, Aaron would be close enough to swing in at lunchtime to visit with Emma, and Steven could sneak down in between meetings. And the best part? Everyone who entered the day care had to have a special swipe card, ID tag, and background check. Steven wasn't taking any more chances.

Now, in the mornings, Steven, Aaron, *and* Emma got ready for work. From now on, there wasn't going to be a stay-at-home anybody.

16

Seeing Baby Emma doing so well with her doting dads in the weeks that followed made Jessica sentimental. Back at her stylish townhome, she watched as Jake built a new Lego tower with his aunt Elizabeth, and thought: Jake needs his dad.

Not that Todd was returning her texts or phone calls. She'd tried earlier in the week, but she'd gotten nothing in response. She couldn't blame him, if she was honest with herself. She'd lied about sleeping with Liam and he'd found out from Caroline Pearce's blog—the worst way to get bad news.

"Mommy?" Jake asked as he plunked a red brick on top of a blue one. "Emma has *two* dads?"

Jessica glanced at Elizabeth.

Jake didn't wait to hear the answer. "Not fair!" Jake cried. "She has two, I have no dads!"

"You do so have a daddy, Jake," Elizabeth cried, surprised. "Your daddy loves you very much."

Jessica sighed. Todd had missed his last two scheduled visits—the last Wednesday and the weekend before—because he'd been out of town for work, covering the basketball team, which had back-to-back away games in Phoenix and then in Dallas. He wasn't due to see Jake until the weekend. And a week in the mind of a toddler might as well be a year.

"I know you miss Daddy, but he'll be here soon," Jessica said. In fact, Jessica knew he was back in town. The team had a home game tonight.

"Want Daddy now! Want Daddy here!" Jake stood, stomped his Lego tower to bits, and ran off to his room. Elizabeth stood to follow him, and Jessica put up her hand.

"Give him a minute," Jessica said. "Trust me on that one." If you got in Jake's face during a tantrum, it wasn't a pretty scene. After a minute or two, he was much calmer. Jake took the terrible twos to a new level sometimes. But who could blame him? Sometimes when Jessica thought about

Todd, she, too, felt like having a full-on meltdown in the middle of the living room.

Jessica sighed and glanced over at Elizabeth. "I don't know what to do."

Elizabeth nodded. "I know this is hard, but Jake is young. He'll adjust."

"I don't know if I want him to adjust," Jessica said. What she wanted—as much as Jake did—was for Todd to come back home.

Jessica's phone dinged—another text from her former boss, Michael. He'd been relentless in trying to recruit her back to VertPlus.net. She scrolled down through her messages, hoping against hope she'd see one from Todd. What she saw instead was two more new messages from Liam.

Liam had been away the last few weeks shooting a cameo for some new film. He'd missed the entire Emma drama, but some part of Jessica had been glad. She didn't like the idea of Liam and her family getting too close. She wanted to keep Liam in the "casual fun" category.

Not that Liam was in the mood to keep things light. Every one of his messages to her phone read like a dying love declaration.

I MISS YOU MORE THAN ANYTHING! WISH YOU WERE HERE. LOVE YOU SO MUCH.

Jessica tried to walk the fine line between encouraging him too much and hurting his feelings. And there were few things Jessica liked less than worrying about *other* people's feelings all the time. It just went against her nature.

MISS, YOU, TOO, LIAM! she wrote, wondering if it was a lie. Did she miss him? Or was she glad to have some breathing room?

She pushed aside thoughts of Liam and tried to figure out the more pressing problem of Todd.

"Maybe you should take up Michael's offer and go back to work," Elizabeth suggested.

Jessica glanced at her sister. She was tempted to take her old job. She'd been a genius there. She missed all the excitement of the work, and more frankly, she missed all the praise. VertPlus.net had been the one place where she really felt like she belonged.

"No." She shook her head. "I can't do it. If Todd found out, he'd think I was just using my job as some kind of bargaining chip."

"But aren't you?" Elizabeth pointed out.

"No," Jessica said, and meant it. *Sort of.*

Elizabeth let out a long sigh. "The last thing you want to do is take love-life advice from me. Look at the mess I'm in now."

"Well, I know how to fix that," Jessica said. "Just tell Bruce you think he's innocent."

"Even if I think I'm lying?"

"Whatever you think, you have to help him. And what if you're wrong and he is innocent?"

Elizabeth wished she could believe in Bruce as completely as her sister did. Truth was, she didn't.

"I am helping him. I'm still trying to get to the truth—whatever that is."

"Good."

"But you can't tell Bruce or anyone that I'm working on it, okay?"

Jessica shrugged. "Whatever you want, just don't give up." And then it hit her: Don't give up!

"That's it!" She snapped her fingers. "I know what I'm going to do. I'm going to go over to Todd's house right now."

"You think that's a good idea?"

"I've got to try. For both of us, Jake and me."

"Are you going to go get Daddy?" Jake peeked into the living room, obviously having been lurking near enough to have heard the entire conversation.

"You bet I am," Jessica said, scooping up Jake for a big hug. The little boy beamed. "Do you mind watching him?"

"Not at all. Come on babe, let's go."

Jake squirmed down from his mother's arms and ran to his aunt.

Jessica ran upstairs to change, putting on a formfitting dress and sky-high heels. In the car, on the way over to Todd's, she practiced her speech, glancing at herself in the rearview mirror.

"Todd, I know you don't have any reason to trust me, but I'm here hoping you . . ." Jessica stopped. "No . . . *begging* you to listen to me." Yes, *begging* sounded better. That's what Jessica planned to do, after all.

Begging was something she never imagined she'd have to do her whole life. But if there was anything worth putting aside her pride for, it had to be Todd and Jake. At last she had her priorities straight. If only Todd could see that, too.

Butterflies whirled frantically in her stomach as she pulled up in front of Todd's house. Luck was with her; he was home. His car was parked out front. Fear trickled through her brain. *What if he slams the door in my face? What if this is all too late and he hates me forever?*

Jessica shook herself. She'd promised Jake she was coming to get his father back, hadn't she? She wasn't about to break a promise to her son. Being a mother was hard right from the start. Jessica thought back to her labor and delivery, and remembered all that searing, mind-numbing pain of labor before the epidural had kicked in. She'd gotten through that. She would survive this.

She opened her car door and just sat there, mustering the courage. She took some deep breaths, stood, and slammed the car door behind her. No place to go but forward. Her sleek and sexy heels clacked on the concrete sidewalk as she walked up to the door. She looked good; the formfitting, short mini showed off her mile-long legs and her perfectly rounded hips. She knew it was one of Todd's favorite outfits. He couldn't keep his hands off her when she wore it.

She hoped it still worked the same old magic.

Taking another deep breath, Jessica reached out and rang the doorbell. She exhaled slowly, feeling the nerves tingling along her arms and down the backs of her legs. She never thought she'd be this nervous.

This was the man she loved, she reminded herself. This was the father of her baby, and she was going to get him back—whatever it took. A little groveling was a small price to pay.

She thought about her practiced speech as she watched the doorknob turn. She opened her mouth to begin, but when she glanced up all the words dried up on her tongue.

It wasn't Todd at the door.

Instead, leaning casually against the doorjamb, stood Sarah Miller, her dark hair cropped short, her long legs naked, her feet bare, wearing nothing more than a black, nearly see-through lace teddy.

A triumphant little smirk played across her lips.

"Jessica Wakefield," she purred, as if soaking in the moment. "Can I help you?"

17

Across town, District Attorney Tom Colton sat on the other side of the mirrored glass at the Sweet Valley police station and watched as detectives interviewed Jane Doe—again. This was the fourth or maybe fifth time they'd gone over the details of the night Bruce Patman had allegedly attacked her.

Colton hated this case already. If he just looked at the facts, given the lack of hard evidence and Jane Doe's sometimes shaky testimony (even now the girl seemed to get flustered when pressed too hard by the detectives), Colton would probably lean toward charging Bruce with forcible touching and third-degree sexual abuse, both misdemeanors.

The bartender, whom Colton had also watched being interviewed, was a better witness. And he could testify to the fact that Bruce had had too much to drink that night and had been hitting on the girl. Bruce himself had also come in to be interviewed by police, and all Colton could tell was the guy couldn't remember much of what had happened that night, which probably meant he'd drunk too much.

Colton's gut told him this was a misdemeanor case. While attempted rape was a terrible crime, this one just didn't rise to the level of a felony. He also knew that if he brought it before a jury, he'd have a hard time making a felony stick. The defense could easily argue that Bruce Patman had simply had too much to drink and that the girl had, too; that it had been a simple misunderstanding, nothing more. These kinds of cases were a prosecutor's nightmare.

But there was something that stopped Colton from following his gut: Rick Warner.

Warner was one of Colton's best campaign supporters. Colton was up for reelection in the fall, and he had tough competition in newcomer Jill Gray. Warner had already lined up at least two big fund-raisers among his district's wealthiest contributors, and Colton needed Warner's help to fund his campaign.

Colton knew that Warner and Patman had been fighti[...] piece of land. Warner had hinted that, should Patman be [...] gal proceedings, Warner might have the time then to thr[...] more fund-raiser dinners for Colton. Hinted, of course [...] Promising would be illegal. Hinting was perfectly fine.

Colton knew he couldn't let Warner influence him. F[...] ried if he went too soft on Patman, he wouldn't lose just a f[...] dinners. He'd also hand Jill Gray the fodder she'd use to l[...] vember. She was already saying he didn't pursue charges [...] ties like he should. This could be a problem.

Colton sat behind the mirrored glass and listened, ho[...] would give him something more to use. Either way, he k[...] decide soon. He also knew that whatever he went with, he [...]

18

Bruce Patman paced the empty study of his mansion, wai[...] from Annie Whitman about whether he'd officially be cha[...] tempted rape. Annie told him she'd call as soon as she heard. [...] time, she had a couple of court appearances to make and [...] she'd come over as soon as she finished.

He was so grateful for her support, but it was times like th[...] was all alone in his enormous mansion, that the loneliness o[...] out Elizabeth felt like it might choke him.

He glanced at the small business card he kept in his desk, w[...] ber of his therapist on it. He considered calling, but hesitate[...] been to see him for almost three years.

He knew most of the kids he went to school with would b[...] hear that *the* Bruce Patman needed a therapist. But he'd been [...] end when his parents died. Their tragic deaths when he was st[...] had turned his world upside down.

He began therapy to get over the grief, and he had stayed [...]

nself. But it was falling in love Elizabeth that had really changed his life.
 understood for the first time how careless he'd been with people—his
nds and girlfriends—throughout most of high school and college. Some
the things he'd done and said in high school he simply couldn't imagine
ng now.

He'd been going—on and off—to the same therapist for years, stopping
ly once Elizabeth had moved in with him. He was so happy, so perfectly
ntent, he just didn't see the need for counseling anymore. His life was as
rfect as it could get. He was a new person and he'd won Elizabeth. That
s all that mattered.

He thought Elizabeth was one of the few people who understood just
w he'd fundamentally changed. How he had clarity for the first time
er. Bruce had shared details of his life with her that he'd never shared
th anyone.

Like his mother's condition.

After his parents died, he discovered his mother had been bipolar. Ap-
rently, she'd been on medication for years and had never told him. It ex-
ained a lot: why sometimes she'd seem upbeat, with nearly unstoppable
ergy to do almost anything, and then other days, she'd have trouble get-
ng out of bed. It also explained her sometimes unprovoked fits of anger.
he could fly into a rage over the smallest things. It was only later he learned
at she had been emotionally unstable.

And now, he had to ask himself, was he, too?

Was Elizabeth right? Was he suffering from the same illness as his
nother?

The very comparison made him furious, and yet maybe it made him so
ngry because he was really afraid it was true.

Bruce walked to the minibar built into the wall across the room and
oured himself a glass of scotch. He took a swig and then ran a hand through
is dark hair in frustration.

Bruce thought back again to that night he'd seen Robin Platt at the bar.
He could've sworn she'd been the one upset; he'd been *comforting* her.
He'd had only one drink . . . that he remembered.

Then he'd gotten dizzy. But what if he didn't remember because he'd
ad more to drink? What if he was just as crazy as his mother?

Bruce clutched his cocktail tightly. No, he couldn't be like her. He always thought he was more like his father, anyway. After all, it had been his father, Henry, who also spent half his life in love with a Wakefield who didn't love him back. Henry Patman had been engaged to Jessica and Elizabeth's mother until she left him for Ned Wakefield. Now Bruce finally understood the hell his father must've gone through all those years ago.

Bruce desperately wished his father were here now. Maybe he would have some good advice for him.

But no advice could change the fact that Elizabeth didn't believe in him. And strangely, of all people, Jessica did.

"There's nothing wrong with you, Bruce," Jessica had said yesterday when he'd confessed he was starting to doubt his own innocence; that he wondered if he was going crazy. "You did *not* do this. Don't imagine for one second that you did." Nothing seemed to shake her confidence in him.

Bruce glanced at the glass of scotch in his hand. He wasn't so sure anymore that it mattered if he had or hadn't done it. Already, public opinion had turned against him. All he had to do was read the screaming headlines of the morning paper.

More Damning Allegations in Billionaire Rape Case.

They weren't even bothering putting in "attempted" anymore.

Bruce walked over to cabinet that hid the wall safe, flipped the door open, and dialed the combination. He pulled the handle and the metal door swung open, revealing a stack of documents, a jewelry box, his passport, and about twenty thousand dollars in cash. He always kept cash around. You couldn't be too careful.

Bruce knew all he needed to do was make one call to the pilot he kept on staff to fly his jet. Within an hour, he could probably be in the air, ready to fly to any number of foreign countries that didn't have extradition treaties to the United States. Then there were the half a dozen Swiss bank accounts in the Patman family name. They could seize all of his American funds, and he'd still have plenty to live on, thanks to the Patman fortune.

He picked up his leather-covered passport, held it in his hand, and wondered, again, what his father would say. Would he think it cowardly that his son was thinking about running? Or would he encourage him to get out while he could?

Bruce dropped his passport back into the safe. Running is what the old Bruce would've done: the conceited, selfish Bruce of high school, the one who always thought about himself first and everyone else second. He closed his eyes and thought for a second about the mess he'd leave behind for his friends . . . for Jessica and Annie. And Elizabeth. They'd have to clean up for him. Could he do that to them?

Or, could he prove to himself that he really had changed, that he wasn't that egocentric, entitled boy from high school?

He was afraid of what was coming. Yet maybe he still had a choice.

19

After she finished up her hearing at the courthouse, Annie Whitman walked to the lobby, checking her phone, hoping to hear news from the D.A.'s office about Bruce's case. As she'd told Bruce, they had to hope he didn't go with felony charges, but given that it was an election year, they had to be prepared for anything. Prosecutors were always particularly tough on crime when their jobs were up for a vote.

Annie's phone lit up. She got the official word: Tom Colton planned to file felony aggravated assault and attempted sexual assault charges.

"Damn it," Annie cursed under her breath as she scrolled through the message. "Felony sexual assault!"

A few lawyers huddled together in the lobby of the courthouse, looked up, startled. She shrugged and then went back to her phone.

She took a deep breath. *Calm down,* she thought. *Maybe this is a good thing.* Because Tom Colton was crazy if he thought he could prove felony sexual assault beyond a reasonable doubt. No jury would convict, especially after she got through with them.

"Colton, you just overplayed your hand," she murmured under her breath.

She walked past the metal detectors and out the courthouse door. There could be another way to play it: If they laid low, and Bruce didn't do anything crazy between now and election day, they might even get a plea deal together well before trial. If she worked it just so, Bruce would probably get a slap on the wrist, no more than community service.

She tried to call Bruce's number, but got no answer. She dialed Jessica, but that also went straight to voice mail. Where *was* everyone?

Annie got into her car and decided to drive to Bruce's house. She needed to talk to him and calm him down. Plus, at a time like this, he'd need a friend.

She was glad he called her one.

On the way over, she decided she'd have to tell him how important it was that he keep a low profile. If he kept a stellar record—not getting even so much as a speeding ticket—this could all still work out. They just had to play it smart and wait. Nothing crazy between now and trial time— nothing that would make headlines that could push Colton into a corner— and Bruce would walk.

The more she thought about it, the more upbeat things seemed. Annie grinned to herself. She loved that she could really help Bruce.

Annie arrived at Bruce's front gate and slid through the paparazzi bunched up at the property line. She was sure it would jam up even more when word got out that the D.A. was pursuing sexual assault charges.

Annie buzzed Bruce's gate and waited to be let in. As she drove up the drive, she noticed his black Porsche was gone.

She parked her car and walked up to his driveway, ringing the bell.

Mme Dechamps answered, looking surprised.

"Where's Bruce?" Annie asked the cook.

"So sorry, *madame*," Mme Dechamps muttered in her broken English and then paused, searching for the right words. "He . . ." She trailed off and then gave up, making a motion with her hands like a plane taking off.

Annie wasn't sure she understood. *Bruce in a plane?* Her stomach dropped.

Just at that moment, Annie's phone lit up with a message from Bruce:

SORRY TO LEAVE YOU WITH A MESS, ANNIE. I JUST COULDN'T TAKE THE RISK. TELL JESSICA I'M SORRY, TOO.

"He left *the country*?" Annie muttered, the enormity of what he'd just done only beginning to sink in. That would mean . . . Oh, no. No, no, no. Please. Not that. Her hopes of a plea deal vanished before her eyes.

"Country . . . yes," Mme Dechamps nodded. "On his plane, yes? Far, far away!"

All the air went straight out of Annie's sails. *Oh, God, Bruce, you don't know what you've done,* Annie thought. He'd committed the worst mistake a criminal defendant could possibly make.

Because everyone knew this simple fact: Only guilty men run.

EPISODE 4
Secrets and Seductions

1

Lila Fowler Matthews thought she'd died and gone to heaven. She sat in the middle of her enormous, expensively furnished living room while her husband, Ken, gently rubbed her feet. Her stylist rolled in another full rack of designer maternity wear for her to try on. *True Housewives* cameras sat strategically in all the corners, filming her every move, and #lilasbaby and #lilafowler had been trending on Twitter all day. Lila was officially a star.

"I love this," Lila murmured. She didn't know what she loved more: her husband at her feet or the four cameras in her living room that would beam her face out to all her adoring fans. Ever since Ashley, her rival on the show, had tried to punch her on television, everyone—even Marina, who'd been hedging her bets—was fully on Lila's side. Ashley Morgan had become the most hated housewife in America.

And Lila loved every second of it. Her inner neglected fourteen-year-old, desperate for attention from her rich but always distant daddy, was finally getting the love she so badly needed.

"I love you, too, sweetheart," Ken said, mishearing her. He gave her a goofy, love-struck smile. "Does this help with the morning sickness?"

"Sure does, honey." Lila smiled at him and he grinned back. God, but he was sweet. Too sweet for his own good. Lila patted his head gently, like she would a good lap dog.

"How about this dress?" asked the stylist as she held up an original Jen Kao. The bright colors popped, and so did the flattering A-line. "It's not technically maternity, but it will grow with you."

Lila nodded. One almost-maternity dress was as good as the next. She had no intention of actually growing into anything. Her belly was going to stay nice and flat, thank you. She had three more weeks before she officially hit twelve weeks. She had it all planned: She would tragically miscarry her fictional baby before she hit the safety of the second trimester.

In some ways, she was looking forward to that day. Granted, she'd lose some things, like the couture maternity wear and the foot rubs. But she also wouldn't have to stick her finger down her throat every day to fake morning sickness. That would be a relief.

"I still think it's a terrible idea," Jessica had said just that morning on the phone before the camera crew had arrived.

"You're just jealous because *my* idea is actually working." Lila could hear the envy in Jessica's voice. Lila had known Jessica most of her life, and she knew just how much she hated to lose. "Ken and I are like newlyweds— better than newlyweds. He can't keep his hands off me!"

And Jessica knew that Lila never could pass up an opportunity to gloat. Things had fallen apart with Todd and Jessica when Jessica had found Sarah Miller wearing her barely there lingerie at his place.

"Right." Jessica sighed. "I just think maybe this whole plan is going to end badly. Remember when you tried shoplifting in high school?"

Lila did recall her shoplifting phase. It had been a desperate attempt to get her father's attention.

"But it worked," Lila said. "Dad started hanging out with me more."

"For maybe a week," Jessica said. "Then he went right back to all those business trips he was always taking."

"Whatever. You're just upset because you got blamed for my shoplifting at first." It was true. Lila, who didn't really need any of the things she'd stolen, had generously "given" them to Jessica, which led the police to think she was suspect number one. Eventually, Lila had been the one who'd had to face police charges, though.

"No, I'm just telling you this plan of yours won't work. You can't trick Ken into loving you."

"This from the person who tried to trick Todd into coming back."

"I didn't trick him!"

"No, you just let him think you *didn't* sleep with Liam. And that you were giving up your job."

"I did give up my job."

"And you slept with Liam." Lila couldn't quite keep the smugness from her voice. "And you're already back at your job. You went back to work practically right after Todd left. So who's the scammer now?"

"Thanks for rubbing it in."

In any other friendship, this would have been enough to do big damage, but Jessica and Lila had been doing this kind of one-upmanship since grade school and were still best friends. They were so much alike they didn't even notice each other's faults. "Look," Jessica said, "I'm just trying to help you. This is going to backfire. Trust me, I know."

"Please. What do you know, anyway?" After all, Lila had her husband. Jessica didn't. Who was the expert?

Jessica sighed. She wanted to tell her friend that this was no way to get love. Jessica knew Lila well. Her dad had always thrown money her way instead of love and now, as an adult, Lila didn't understand how love really worked. Jessica had been a lot like her—before she'd fallen for Todd. Now she knew what love was. True love wasn't something you could buy or manipulate or fake.

"I know you're going to do this anyway, but don't say I didn't warn you," Jessica said.

⁓

Lila spent the next two weeks as the blissful, pregnant star everyone adored. She waded through dozens of presents fans had sent in. She had enough onesies to stock a baby boutique. Of course, none of them were remotely close to her style. Yet on some level it was sweet.

Still, Lila was secretly glad her fake baby would never have to wear them.

Lila planned out the exact moment when she'd have her miscarriage. She would do it on television, at Ashley Morgan's formal dinner party.

The party was Ashley's way of offering an olive branch to Lila. Not that Ashley wanted to be friends, but she really had no choice. For weeks,

"Ken, I just . . . I don't think I can handle it. How could you have even thought of leaving me for her? You know how much pain that caused me!"

"She doesn't mean anything to me," Ken said quickly. "It was all a terrible mistake, Lila. I love you. We're going to have a family together and that makes me the happiest man in the world."

Lila smiled at him through her tears. "I don't blame you at all, honey. I blame her. It was her plan from the beginning. She schemed and lied to get you."

Ken nodded in agreement and pulled her into a hug again.

The cameraman followed them inside the house. This, of course, was too good to miss. Ken kept murmuring, "It's okay, honey. It'll be okay," over and over into her hair.

He was so tender, so caring, that Lila almost felt bad about what she was about to do. *Almost.*

After Ken had gotten her a cup of warm herbal tea and made her comfortable on the couch, shrouding her in an expensive cashmere afghan, Lila knew it was her time.

"Oh," she began, a little peep, as she put down her cup. She shrugged off the blanket, and put a little hand over her stomach. "Ow."

"Honey?" Ken asked. "You okay?"

"Um . . . I think so." Lila put on her best game face. Then she faked another cramp. "Oh . . ." She groaned, holding her stomach. "Oh, that one hurt."

"What is it?"

"I don't know." She could feel the camera lens focus on her face, catching every expression. She made sure to show them all: pain, concern, confusion and then . . . fear. "Ohhhh!" she cried again, doubling over this time. "Oh, no. What . . . what is happening?"

"Honey?" Ken rushed over.

"No . . . No . . . Can't be . . ." Lila stood and ran to the bathroom. She slammed the door behind her, locking it. This part, Ken didn't need to see.

"Honey! Honey, let me in!" Ken cried, banging at the door.

"Oh, God!" Lila shouted through the door, loud enough for the microphones to hear.

After this, Lila thought, Ashley wouldn't be able to show her face anywhere. Lila knew how the Twitterverse worked, and she'd just given *True Housewives of Sweet Valley* fans the chance to argue conspiracy around the miscarriage. Was it the ceviche? Maybe that was too farfetched. But Ashley's insult and the stress of everything, including Ashley scheming to steal Ken, easily could have pushed poor, delicate Lila to the brink.

In any case, all theories pointed right back to Ashley.

It was almost too perfect.

2

Caroline Pearce, Sweet Valley's reigning gossip, loved nothing better than to be the bearer of bad news. Preferably bad, *juicy* news.

Unfortunately, she'd not found any big scoops lately. In recent days, her blog had been decidedly boring. No great scandals, nobody calling her in tears. Readership had been steadily dropping since her last big coup: the bombshell news of Jessica Wakefield and Liam O'Connor's steamy hotel tryst. She'd heard the blog entry, which she'd kindly forwarded to Todd because that's what friends do, had stopped cold any hope of reconciliation between the unhappy couple.

Some people might have felt bad about that, but not Caroline. The truth will set you free, right? She was only doing her duty as a friend. Reporting the truth—give or take a few white lies here and there for the sake of spicing up a good story—was her reason for getting up in the morning.

Caroline knew of one surefire place to get some dirt on the residents of Sweet Valley: her OB-GYN's office.

Everyone Caroline knew who had been anybody at Sweet Valley High used Enid Rollins. She was considered the area's top OB-GYN, and she wouldn't let you forget it, either. Everyone went to see her: Lila Fowler, Jessica, even Elizabeth, who was not an Enid fan at the moment. Enid used to be Elizabeth's best friend, before she became the self-involved snob no one could stand.

Even if I were a hundred percent sure, I could never be part of that betrayal. It was hubris that involved me from the beginning. I thought I was going to save him, but I didn't. I only made it worse."

It was one thing to help the girl, and she had, but writing a story that pronounced to the world that Bruce was a rapist, guilty or not, would never come from Elizabeth.

Tim sighed and put his head in his hands.

"Elizabeth, you're a journalist. You're not supposed to take sides, and you write the story, no matter what."

"I'm not going to talk about it anymore."

"You leave me no choice."

"I know. Whatever I've done up till now, I would never do again. I regret it so deeply. I got involved to help Bruce and I turned out to be the one who destroyed him."

"You did what you had to do, Elizabeth. Plus, it's obvious he's guilty. He ran! We know he's in France. We just don't know where. But you do, don't you?"

Of course she knew. He had houses all over the world, but she suspected he had gone to his villa in the south of France. She'd told Annie Whitman about his house there and she was recently able to confirm that's where he was. But there was no way she was going to tell Tim.

"Clearly, you've lost all objectivity—if you had any to begin with," Tim said. "What was I thinking, putting his girlfriend on this story? My mistake."

Girlfriend? Hardly. Ex-girlfriend, more like it. But Elizabeth didn't correct him.

Tim's tone softened a little. "I like you. You know I do. You're a very good writer, but . . ."

"I know, and you're a very good boss, too."

Tim genuinely liked Elizabeth. She was a smart, idealistic young reporter, the kind who got into the business because she thought she could make a difference. He hated to see her go.

"Don't make me fire you, Elizabeth. It won't look good on your résumé. And of course, then I can't give you a recommendation."

"Okay. I quit, then." The words were out of her mouth before she could stop them. It was the only way out. "Thanks, Tim, for everything."

Even though it was her choice, Elizabeth felt a sharp stab of disappoint-ment. She loved her job. The idea of quitting after she'd worked so hard to get here felt like she was giving up on a lifelong dream.

She realized she'd been holding on to the naïve hope that despite every-thing, she could keep her job. Okay, Tim might move her back to beginner stuff like suburban city councils or restaurant openings, a kind of Siberia of reporting, but she could see that wasn't possible.

He was a good guy, but he wasn't going to budge, and neither could she.

"Maybe I should give you a couple of days to think about it." Tim made one last offer.

"No, but thanks anyway." Elizabeth had made up her mind. There was no going back.

Elizabeth left Tim's office and went straight to her desk. She could feel everyone's eyes on her. Without looking up, she began packing her things.

"You okay?" That came from Andy, the only one brave enough to ask.

"I'm not going to do the Jane Doe story." Elizabeth felt a rough ball of tears forming in her throat. She swallowed hard.

"I get it," he said.

And she knew he did and felt, in the middle of all this shit, she was do-ing the right thing.

It felt funny to be on the other side. How many times had she been cavalier with other people's lives? How often had she thought, "Hey, I'm a reporter and it's my job," when she'd run with a story that was sure to destroy people's lives? Now she knew how those people felt: very human and vulnerable. Bleeding.

Elizabeth grabbed her purse, her office plant, and her family pictures: those of her sister, brother, nephew, and niece. She looked at their smiling faces and felt like crying.

Andy gave her a pat on the shoulder as she walked by. He'd had the Bruce story first, and he'd no doubt get it back now. He'd be after the Jane Doe/ Robin Platt interview the minute she left. Maybe he would get it, too. Maybe Elizabeth couldn't really protect Bruce, no matter how hard she tried.

But at least the story wouldn't have her name on it. That was some-thing. And maybe he would see how toxic the story really was now that she'd given it up. Maybe it would make a difference.

Elizabeth climbed into her car and drove aimlessly. A black Porsche zipped across the intersection and she instantly thought of Bruce. Her eyes went to the license plate, but of course, it wasn't him. He was long gone.

The tears slid down her cheeks and a sob broke free. Now she'd lost everything.

Over the next few weeks, Elizabeth hung out at her parents' house, the house where she'd grown up, and wondered what she was going to do. As she walked the rooms of her childhood home, she thought, *It used to be so easy.* Sure, high school seemed like a killer—each new day brought some new drama—but in hindsight, all of her problems that had seemed so big then were really pretty small.

As she moped around the house, she made a decision. She wasn't just going to sit and wait for the Robin interview to come out. Andy was a good investigator. He would take his time getting the story. She could count on at least two weeks before it hit the paper. In that time, she was going to do what she could to help Bruce. Just because she'd lost her job didn't mean she'd lost her skills as a reporter.

Maybe it wouldn't make a difference to their relationship, but still she desperately wanted somehow to save him. If his name could be cleared, she was the one who had to do it. And she wouldn't stop trying until she knew for sure it was impossible.

Elizabeth decided that no matter what, she was going to keep digging until she found the truth. And she just prayed it would be Bruce's innocence.

Either way, she wasn't going to give up.

She went back to her first suspicions that Rick Warner, owner of Warner Gas, must somehow be behind Robin and the allegations against Bruce. Ever since Bruce had outfoxed Warner, snagging some of the valuable drilling land right from under his nose in order to turn it into an eco-friendly wind farm, Rick had been his sworn enemy. Elizabeth toyed with the idea of trying to go undercover at Warner Gas headquarters in San Diego to see if she could dig up a link between Robin Platt and Rick Warner, but she knew it would never work. Rick knew who she was, and so did much of his staff. She'd thought about sending someone else from the *Tribune,* but she wasn't sure she could trust anyone else. She needed someone who could blend in and someone she could trust to do what really needed to be done.

Then it hit her. She knew the perfect person she could trust and he was family now: her new brother-in-law, Aaron Dallas. He and her brother, Steven, with Emma in tow, had snuck off to New York the week before to exchange their vows officially. Even if California wouldn't recognize them, the couple had decided, spontaneously, to make the vows to each other, hoping that one day California would change the law.

The rest of the family was a little put out about not being there for the wedding, but both Steven and Aaron said it was just a spontaneous decision they'd made when they were visiting New York.

Elizabeth called Aaron and arranged to meet in an hour at Zee, the new brick-oven pizza place downtown.

Elizabeth parked her car in front of the restaurant and found Aaron waiting for her.

"Hey, brother-in-law, congratulations," she said, hugging him, since it was the first time she'd seen him since the wedding. He returned the hug. "You took us all by surprise."

"It was completely spur-of-the-moment," Aaron admitted. "I'm not sure we even really thought about it. But I had to fly there to visit a client who wanted me to design a hotel for him, and then Steven said he wanted to come along and bring Emma, and then, next thing I knew, we're all at the courthouse saying 'I do's.'" Aaron took a sip of his water. "You know, since Emma was kidnapped, it just sort of put things in perspective. We've been talking about getting married forever, but Steven didn't want another year to drag on while we planned a ceremony or waited for California to sort out the politics. He just wanted it done. Like he said, why wait?"

"So you don't incur Alice Wakefield's wrath, that's why." Elizabeth chuckled. "She *will* get her reception, anyway, one way or another."

"I know, I know." Aaron held up his hands in surrender. "I hear there are already plans in the works. So . . . I hate to be nosy, but why all the secrecy with the lunch?"

Elizabeth took a deep breath. "I have a favor to ask you. It's kind of a big one."

"For you? Anything."

"How do you feel about going undercover?"

Aaron couldn't help thinking the *Mission Impossible* theme should've been playing in the background when he went to the Warner Gas headquarters in San Diego. He felt a little like a secret agent armed with the cover story Elizabeth gave him: He was an architecture student from UCLA doing research for his thesis. Warner Gas, after all, was housed in one of the most distinctive new glass high-rises in San Diego.

His mission, as undercover spy, was to find out if Robin Platt was working for Rick Warner.

Aaron wasn't sure if he could do it, and he felt a cold sweat trickle down his back as he told the lie to the receptionist sitting behind the front desk. Spying looked much easier on TV.

But to his surprise, she bought it easily. Apparently, he hadn't been the only graduate student interested in touring the offices and looking at the plans.

Nola the receptionist was stylishly dressed and older than he was. He put her age somewhere near forty. She wore a Missoni scarf around her neck. "I love that scarf," Aaron said. "Missoni, right?"

"Missoni, yes!"

"Looks good on you."

"Thanks." The receptionist beamed under the praise.

"I'm Aaron, by the way," he said.

"I'm Nola," she said. "Nice to meet you."

Aaron knew he was making a necessary friend.

"You, too. So I'm not the only graduate student who's asked about the building?"

"Definitely not. Would you like a tour?"

"I'd love one."

"Mr. Warner commissioned the building himself," Nola said as she led him back through the offices. Aaron looked out of the impressive, top-floor view. "He wanted to make an impression on the skyline."

And apparently on all the rivers and lakes, too, Aaron thought. Warner's controversial drilling techniques had environmentalists in an uproar. It was one of the main reasons Bruce's company, Patman Social Impact, had bought the land Warner had wanted to use for more fracking.

Aaron himself was a green architect, and he appreciated what Bruce's company was trying to do. Rick Warner's building, he noticed, wasn't green in any way. Made of no recycled materials and with a pretty big carbon footprint, it paid a steep price for being pretty, he thought.

Nola finished the tour quickly. "And if you want to look at blueprints, they're in this file," she said, nodding toward a nearby cube filled with file cabinets.

"That would be great."

Aaron sat down and began looking through the designs. He had to play this slowly. Too soon to ask about Robin, so for now he just had to do some digging on his own. After the first day all he could find were copies of design plans. He had to be patient, to keep digging. And to stay very friendly with Nola, compliment by compliment.

The next day, he got a break.

"I'm off to lunch," Nola said. "Need anything?"

Aaron looked up from the plans and glanced over at the receptionist's computer in her nearby cube. "Actually, could I use your computer to send a quick e-mail? It won't take long."

"No problem," Nola said, and then with a wink: "Are we talking girlfriend?"

"You got me." Aaron smiled.

Nola typed in her password, unlocking the PC, stood up, and grabbed her purse. "You can tell me all about it for dessert."

Nola headed toward the elevators, happy with her new friend.

As Aaron slid into Nola's chair he gave a quick look around the office and saw that it had emptied out for lunch almost entirely. Now was his chance.

He felt a little like Tom Cruise hanging from the ceiling as he looked through the company directory, searching for anybody whose description fit Robin Platt. Some, not all the employees, had photos.

Aaron had a picture of Robin on his phone that Elizabeth had sent. She was somewhat pretty with blond hair and fair skin.

A quick search of the employee records brought up no Robin Platt, but he did find a Rose Pally who would be the right age and seemed like she might be a fit. She would've been working for Warner Gas right before the allegations against Bruce had surfaced. And the initials, R.P., were the same as Robin Platt's. Aaron searched every company newsletter and internal Web page for a picture of Rose Pally, but he couldn't find one.

He did quick Facebook and Google searches, too, but came up empty. None of the Rose Pallys he found lived in San Diego.

After a quick search of her employment records, he found that Rose Pally was on an extended paid leave that had started a week before Bruce had allegedly attacked Robin Platt at that bar. That fit, too.

Aaron wasn't sure it was anything, but he thought there was enough of something to make copies of the records and e-mail them to Elizabeth.

BINGO! Elizabeth wrote back almost instantly. THIS IS WHAT I'VE BEEN LOOKING FOR!

⌒

With the Wakefield seniors still away, Elizabeth had the house to herself. What Aaron had sent her was a bonanza. She sped through the files, feeling a little giddy with excitement. This was it, the break in the case she was dreaming of. Except for the missing picture.

Aaron couldn't find one, but that didn't mean there wasn't one to be found. Elizabeth's reporter's instincts told her she was on to something big.

It was a double-edged sword. If Robin had lied and Bruce really was innocent, she'd betrayed him. How could she not have trusted him? He'd loved her as no one else ever had, and she thought she loved him as well, but when push came to shove, she'd let go. Too easily.

No matter what it looked like, no matter how it seemed, truth was on

Robin's side. She should have closed her eyes and gone with Bruce. That's what people who love do. Screw the facts.

Now she would.

And pray it wasn't too late.

Elizabeth grabbed her phone and speed-dialed her sister.

"Tell me you have something for Bruce," Jessica said.

"Maybe."

She filled Jessica in on the details and waited.

"Yes! It's got to be her," Jessica said, excitement in her voice. "It's too much of a coincidence. Robin Platt must actually be Rose Pally. Don't you see this is exactly how Warner would work? Lizzie, this is Bruce's big break. I gotta tell him."

"You can't! And you have to promise me that when you can, you won't tell him I was the one who found her. He can't know I'm involved."

"But Elizabeth . . ."

"Promise me, Jess. I don't want him to know I'm working on this."

"Why? Liz, you know he still loves you. He'd want to know you were doing this for him. He'd also want to know you gave up your job for him. That's a big deal."

"No! Don't." Elizabeth thought about the look of hurt and betrayal in Bruce's eyes the last time she'd seen him. "No, I don't think he would want to know," she said softly. "I don't think he wants to know anything about me anymore."

Jessica let out a long, frustrated sigh. "I think you're wrong, but I'll do whatever you want. If it turns out that she really is connected to Warner, she could be dangerous."

"Right now it's nothing until I can get Rose Pally's picture."

"Still, you have to be careful."

"I will be," Elizabeth promised, but she really didn't care how dangerous Robin could be. All she cared about was finding out what had really happened. She needed the truth, whatever the cost. And maybe she'd already paid the price by losing Bruce forever.

"Oh, no," Jessica said suddenly, sounding distracted.

"What is it?"

"Sorry, it's Lila," Jessica said. "There's a story that just broke on TMZ, and *E! News* is running it now. Oh, boy. This is what I was afraid of. I *told* her this would happen."

"What is it?"

"It's trouble," Jessica said.

All morning, Lila felt sick to her stomach, and she didn't know why until she turned on her television.

Her shriek could be heard throughout her nine-bedroom mansion and probably down the street.

"An anonymous source sold her story to TMZ with what she says is proof that Lila Fowler, *True Housewives* star, *faked* her pregnancy and her miscarriage on the popular reality show." The news anchor on E! swept back her long blond hair and delivered the devastating news with just the hint of a smile.

Lila felt her bedroom spin. Suddenly, she felt dizzy. Her hairstylist and makeup artist sat frozen next to her, their eyes glued to the TV set. Lila slunk out of her chair and ran to the bathroom, where she locked the door behind her.

Think, she told herself in a panic. *Think.*

Downstairs, the *True Housewives* cameramen were setting up in her kitchen. She heard the hustle and bustle of giant light fixtures and sound booms moving in and out.

Think of something! She silently screamed at herself. She glanced up at her reflection in the mirror, a pale, wan version of her face glaring back. She looked a little green, and she felt worse. She had that panicky, clammy feeling that she hated so much. Being caught red-handed made her want to throw up. Her heart pounded in her rib cage. When Ken found out . . . She felt sick just thinking about it. But maybe she could tell him it was all a mistake! *He's not a neurosurgeon, he's a quarterback,* Lila told herself. *You can fool him. He'll believe anything you say.*

In the mirror, her dark, normally shrewd eyes looked back at her with fear in them. Even she couldn't convince herself she'd get off that easily.

Maybe she could tell the cameras to go. The idea of facing them made the room spin. She already knew she wouldn't be able to convince the producers to leave. They were like sharks, and they'd smell blood in the water.

God, what a mess! Lila dropped her head in her hands.

"*Lila!*"

She heard Ken's roar right before she heard the front door slam so hard it rattled the windows. Fear shook her. She wanted to hide in the bathroom forever, but she also knew she had to face him. There was still hope she could turn this all around. Wasn't there?

"Deny everything," Lila told her reflection in the mirror. She nodded at herself, but the pale face with too much makeup blinked back at her, unconvinced.

"Lila! Get down here or I swear to God . . ." Ken shouted up the staircase. TV cameramen scrambled to get mobile cameras on their shoulders for the impromptu shot. Two cameras hovered around Ken, but he was too furious even to notice.

Lila appeared on the stairs looking pale, but she held her chin high. Haughty had always been her best look.

"What's wrong?" she asked, playing dumb.

"You damn well know what's wrong!" Ken held up a printout of the TMZ report. "You played me *again!*"

"Ken . . . it's not true. It's just not true! You can't believe TMZ over me!"

Lila flew down the stairs and got close enough to Ken to try to hug him. He shrugged her away. The cameras around them pivoted and turned, but Lila didn't even care that they were there. For once, she forgot completely about the story she was trying to play, about the angles of her face that looked best on television. She just desperately wanted Ken to understand he had to stay with her. He was the only one who would!

"Please, baby . . ."

"Don't 'baby' me!" He ground out the words between clenched teeth.

His face turned beet red splotched with white. He stomped right up to Lila and grabbed her arm—hard. "You are a liar, Lila."

"I'm not. You can't believe TMZ!"

"If you're not lying, then prove it. Let's call Enid. She can confirm your pregnancy, right? And the miscarriage."

When Lila hesitated, Ken pulled out his cell phone. Lila saw Enid Rollins's office number flash on the face of it.

Oh, God. Her stomach roiled in protest; she felt bile in her throat. She knew the truth: There was no pregnancy test. She'd never gone to her OB-GYN for anything other than a routine exam.

"What? Speechless?" Ken hit the "call" button. He put it on speaker, and Lila heard the phone ringing.

"Hello, Dr. Rollins's office," a woman's chirpy voice answered.

Ken shoved the phone in Lila's face, but she put up her hands, unable to hide the guilty panic in her eyes.

Ken ended the call.

"I knew it," he said, disgust on his face, and something more heart-breaking—pain.

"Ken—please. I can explain." She'd had her reasons for doing it. She had to make him understand that all she ever wanted was to be loved. Why was that so wrong?

"No, Lila. I know you think I'm stupid. But I'm not. Everyone always warned me to stay away from you, that you were a first-class bitch. I always told them they were wrong about you. But you know what? They were right!"

His words rained down on Lila's head like oversized chunks of hard, icy hail. Ken let her arm go as a look of disgust passed across his face.

"I want you to look at me when I say this. I'm going to tell you this one time, in front of the whole world, Lila. Do not call me. Do not even *look* at me. I don't want to hear about you. I don't ever want to see you again, do you hear me? I am going to file for divorce, and *this* time I mean to see it through."

A sob broke from her throat and tears streamed down Lila's cheeks before she could stop them. She didn't even have to pretend, like she usually did. These were real tears—she was slobbering and blubbering in a way that would look terrible on camera. She *knew* it but she couldn't stop.

Even the thought of Ashley Morgan triumphantly watching this show when it aired didn't stop the flow.

"Ken, please don't! Please don't do this!" She swiped furiously at her nose with her sleeve, but it was no good. She couldn't control herself—tears and snot went everywhere.

Ken shook his head, a horrible sadness clouding his features.

"Do you know how cruel it is? What you've done?" His voice sounded small as he shook his head, his heartbreak heavy in the room. "I loved that baby. He was real to me. When I found out we were going to start a family, I was on top of the world, Lila. I really couldn't have been happier."

"Ken . . ." Lila felt an ache in her chest. His pain was so real, so heartfelt. He really had loved that baby. She realized in that moment how she had completely miscalculated, how terrible her mistake was. "Ken, we could try for a real baby. We could try. We can be a family!"

Ken's head snapped up and his eyes turned cold. "Get away from me," he growled, shrugging off her touch. "You think you can *fake* a pregnancy and then make it all okay? Are you *insane*?"

"Let me try. I'll do anything."

"No." Ken shook his head. "This is actually a blessing, Lila, because now I see that I don't want you. You're not worth having. Not now. Not ever. You're pathetic, Lila, a sad scheming bitch, and God help anybody who thinks you're worth a damn. They'll soon know all you have is on the outside—money, nice things, whatever—but inside, Lila, at your core, you're not worth a goddamn cent."

With that, Ken turned and stormed off, slamming the door behind him. The sobs racked Lila, and all she could think was that now the whole world knew what she had always feared: She wasn't worth loving.

In mid-sob, her whole body convulsed, her stomach rebelled, and then it was all over. She only just made it to a potted plant before she retched, throwing up what was left of her breakfast.

She swiped at her mouth and ran up the stairs to her bedroom, mortified and heartbroken. She wasn't ever going to come out; she would stay there long after the last camera had left. She retched two more times, hanging over the toilet, wondering what was wrong as she cried and cried and cried. She was heartbroken, yes, but it was more than that. Something was wrong with her body. It didn't just act like this.

She felt like a woman who'd lost control of everything. Like her hormones had taken over and . . .

Hormones.

Crying.

Sickness.

Oh, God.

Quickly, Lila did a calculation. *Oh, no, no, no.* She'd been so busy faking a pregnancy she hadn't even bothered to notice that she'd missed her last period. She was more than a month late.

Her mind instantly went back to all those nights of celebratory sex, all those times Ken couldn't keep his hands off her. And the fact that with all the cameras around and everything, maybe she'd missed a pill or two. Or three. She hadn't even bothered to worry about it at the time. She had other things on her mind. But now . . . Oh, God, now . . . !

Lila scrambled on her knees to the cabinet next to the sink. She threw it open and tossed out boxes of Q-tips and Kleenex and reached far, far into the back. She had a pregnancy test back there, she knew, one of a two-pack she'd used the year before when she'd been a couple of days late. It had turned up negative at the time. She grabbed the box and tore open what was left of the package. Lila scrambled to take the test and then waited the painstaking three minutes.

One line means I'm not pregnant, and two blue lines means I am.

One line. Please, God, I will do anything. Just let there be one line!

Lila stared at the stick, watching as the blue line materialized.

Yes! One line!

Relief flooded through her. Food poisoning then. Must be, right?

But, no. As she watched, horrified, the second line came into view. She blinked, speechless, as she stared at the two unmistakably clear blue lines.

This time, there wasn't anything fake about it. No matter how long she stared at the stick, the result never changed: Lila Fowler, who had just faked a miscarriage, was eight weeks pregnant.

6

Jessica kept trying Lila's number, but it always went straight to voice mail. Lila had hidden in her house for more than a week since the news had broken about her fake pregnancy. Jessica felt bad for her friend, but she'd seen this coming from miles away. She was beginning to think this scheming stuff never got you anything but heartbreak.

Ironic sentiment, she realized, coming from Jessica Wakefield. But nonetheless true. She put down her phone and leaned back in her office chair, glancing at her desk. It felt strange being back at VertPlus.net, especially since it hadn't exactly been the homecoming she'd hoped for.

It wasn't the same job—or the same office—that she'd left. Since her departure, Tracy Courtright had swooped in and taken her place, moving right into the director of marketing role and her coveted corner office. Tracy had fifteen years of experience. She also hated Jessica with a passion.

"We had to do it," Michael Wilson, the VP of the Sweet Valley office, had told her almost apologetically. "But I promise you that if you work the magic you did before, you'll be in that office again in no time."

Until then, Jessica had the humiliation of sitting in a cubicle in the middle of the office space with the interns and the low-level sales staff, and basically, the nobodies. She sat right outside Tracy's office, so that Tracy could shout her name without even getting out of her chair, which she did often and for no good reason. Tracy seemed to be under the mistaken impression Jessica was her own personal indentured servant.

The old Jessica would have schemed and manipulated and beaten Tracy at her own game. It would've taken her less than a week to wiggle back into her old office. The old Jessica didn't bring anybody coffee.

But these days, Jessica couldn't quite muster enough energy to care. Ever since she'd come face-to-face with Sarah wearing next to nothing at Todd's door, she'd known it was truly, finally, over between them.

She shut her eyes, remembering the humiliation of standing there on

Now Jessica was adrift and alone, except for too-bubbly Emily. Emily, who was straight out of college, wasn't as much interested in work as she was in telling Jessica about her sexcapades from the weekend before. The girl shared *too* much for Jessica's taste, and she wasn't in the mood to hear about her *Jersey Shore*–like adventures. Honestly, Jessica was surprised Emily had any, given her lackluster looks.

"You won't believe what happened Saturday night," Emily gushed, launching into one of her stories. Jessica tried very hard not to listen. She hated to hear about all the great sex Emily was having and how fun it was being single when Jessica felt there was literally nothing at all good about her own single life, not even the movie star she was dating.

She glanced over her tiny, crammed desk and saw the small color picture of Jake, her beautiful baby boy, and smiled. These days, he was about the only one who ever made her smile, and even then, not always.

". . . can you believe that?" Emily finished her latest tale.

"Wow, no. I can't," Jessica said, even though she had no idea what Emily had just said. "Actually, Emily, if you could do a little bit more research on Maybelline for me that would be great. I'd like to know more about their fall line."

"Oh, uh . . . sure." Emily nodded. "Big meeting with Tracy and Michael tomorrow where Tracy will probably take all the credit for the work we do."

"Right." Jessica said, barely listening.

Jessica's phone dinged with a text from Liam.

HI, BABY.

Nonchalantly, Jessica flipped her phone facedown.

"Are you going to answer him?" Emily asked, surprised. "If I was dating one of Hollywood's sexiest men alive, I would certainly answer his texts."

"That's a little personal, Emily." Jessica was surprised that the girl had read her phone *and* copped to it.

"I'm just stating the obvious." Emily rolled her eyes.

"Excuse me?" God, Emily was mouthy, Jessica thought.

"Whatever." Emily shrugged and walked away before Jessica could put her in her place. The old Jessica would've stridden over to her desk and dressed down Emily right there, but the new Jessica . . . she just couldn't quite muster the energy. *Emily is just jealous,* Jessica thought. Nobody who looked like her could date someone like Liam.

Jessica's phone dinged again, and she flipped it faceup. BABY? YOU THERE? Liam again. Jessica's phone dinged two more times with more incoming texts. She sighed and put the phone on mute.

Jessica really thought sometimes that Liam used texting as a kind of GPS tracking system, trying to get her current position at all times. But that probably wasn't fair. Liam loved her. And he was so kind to her.

Just the other day, Jessica had been the one defending him to Elizabeth.

"Why does he want to know what you are doing *every minute* of the day?"

"I know it sounds annoying . . ."

"More like stalkerish."

"To you, maybe, but for me it's just what I need right now, okay, Liz? Unconditional love. Some guy who will just be there for me. I mean, at least he *cares* where I am. Who else does?"

"I do. Your friends do. Jake does." Elizabeth was relentless in pointing out the good things in Jessica's life. And it was true that her family was her lifeline, but right now Jessica just didn't want to see it. She couldn't seem to leave the pity party she'd been throwing for herself.

"Mom and Dad are worried," Elizabeth had said.

Jessica shrugged. "I didn't even know they were home from their latest trip."

"They just got in last night."

"Jake is going to be thrilled. I'll take him over when Liza and Jake get back from the park."

"Look, I don't want you to be angry at me, but I had to tell them a little about what's going on with you."

"Lizzie." Jessica rolled her eyes. The last thing she needed was pity from Ned and Alice. "So what did they say about you and Bruce?"

"I didn't exactly spell it out."

"But you had no trouble telling them about me and Todd, right?"

"I didn't tell them everything."

"Gee, thanks. Hey, look at us, Lizzie. The Loser Twins."

"I love it. It would make a great article, 'Advice for Failure.'"

"Very original. Everyone is always giving advice for success. This will be a nice change, and we're so good at it."

And probably for the first time in a lot of days, even weeks, the twins were smiling and enjoying themselves. No one could make them laugh more than each other. They had been doing it for thirty years now.

Jessica turned her attention back to her computer, smiling as she remembered her conversations with her sister.

A new message from Annie Whitman popped up, and she clicked on it eagerly.

With Elizabeth's help, Annie had found Bruce's hideaway in the south of France. Annie had told Jessica she planned to go there but had to do so carefully, given Bruce's fugitive charges. Jessica thought this was above and beyond what an average defense attorney would do, and she was grateful.

Jessica might not have been able to go to bat for herself right now, but she would swing for the bleachers for Bruce.

This e-mail was Annie's reply to Jessica's message that Robin Platt might not have been who she said she was.

Annie sounded cautiously optimistic, and said Jessica should keep digging. Jessica found herself feeling slightly guilty for taking credit for the news, but she had promised to keep Elizabeth's name out of it.

She understood why Elizabeth had to be behind the scenes now. Bruce had been devastated when he'd found out Elizabeth had been renting an apartment for Robin, and the betrayal was at the heart of their recent breakup.

The most heart-wrenching part was that Jessica absolutely knew that they were both still deeply in love. But as she had learned so painfully, sometimes love wasn't enough. It should have been, but sometimes it just wasn't.

Jessica glanced back down at the e-mail from Annie.

WE STILL NEED PROOF, she'd written. CAN YOU GET MORE?

Jessica forwarded Annie's message to Elizabeth and Aaron. They had to find more evidence because Bruce was innocent. She just knew it. He had to be innocent, for Elizabeth's sake. There was no other way Jessica could see the two of them getting back together. That's why Jessica would work so hard to exonerate Bruce. She had to because she knew how much her sister loved Bruce. She'd clear his name. For Lizzie.

Aaron got the message from Jessica just as he was walking into Warner Gas that morning around ten. He put his phone in his pocket. He hadn't been back to Warner Gas in weeks. He'd been too busy with his real job, but it just so happened he had a client meeting in San Diego that afternoon, so he'd driven down early, having decided to spend the morning at Warner Gas getting to the bottom of the Rose Pally/Robin Platt mystery.

He clutched a little bag with a chocolate-stuffed croissant that he hoped would work its magic on Nola, even though he hadn't seen her in weeks.

"Hey, Aaron," Nola said, beaming at him as he walked in. "Long time no see!"

"I was in the neighborhood and decided to drop in," Aaron said. "I brought your favorite." He set the white bakery bag on her desk.

"You're a godsend. I'm starved!"

"Breakfast is the most important meal of the day."

Aaron glanced at Nola's computer screen. It looked like she was sorting through a company photo album. He saw a girl in one photo who looked a tad bit like Robin Platt but clearly wasn't, and that gave him an idea.

"Hey, that's not Rose Pally, is it?" Aaron asked, pointing to the picture on her screen.

"What?" Nola looked at her computer. "Oh, no. That's not Rose. That's Beth Kinsella. Wait—do you know Rose?"

"I used to know her, years ago," Aaron said. "She lived in my neighborhood. Haven't seen or spoken to her in a long while, but I really liked her. But wait a minute. You know Rose Pally?"

"You're not going to believe this: She works here."

"Come on. Can't be the same one."

"I'll bet it is."

"No way. You got a picture of her?"

"I don't think so, but I can do you one better. You could go see her. She works on the second floor."

"Wait, she's here *now?*" Aaron could've sworn according to the records she was out on leave. She had to be out on leave. That was the only way she could be Robin Platt.

"She was gone for a while, on maternity leave or something, but she's back now. Just take the elevator to two. She works in Accounting."

While Elizabeth waited to hear whether Aaron could get a picture of Rose Pally—potentially Robin Platt—she decided to take matters into her own hands. Even though she didn't have proof, she decided to show up at Robin's house unannounced, just to see what she might find.

Elizabeth stood on the porch and rang the doorbell. She waited a bit longer than usual before the curtains parted for a quick look. Then the door opened.

"Uh . . . Elizabeth," Robin said, "I wasn't expecting you."

"May I come in?"

Robin hesitated for an instant, hovering behind the door as if not quite sure she wanted to open it. But then it was Elizabeth, and she had to.

"Uh, okay, just a minute." Robin ducked back behind the door and Elizabeth heard rustling and clinking and obvious cleaning up. Immediately, Elizabeth felt her suspicions rise: Was it just tidying up or something more? After a few moments, Robin opened the door.

"Sorry," she said, apologizing. "The place was a little messy."

Elizabeth frowned. Robin had never cared about the state of her place before. Elizabeth stepped over the threshold, glancing around sharply for any clues about Robin's strange behavior. But the room inside looked normal, except for the scattered newspaper across the coffee table and the couch.

"Uh, what brings you by?" Robin's eyes settled on Elizabeth and, for the first time, Elizabeth saw hardness and suspicion in her usually unguarded face. Actually, to Elizabeth, she seemed wired—as if she'd downed one too many lattes. Her eyes, the pupils dark pinpricks, darted back and forth, and her hands shook a little. She was nervous, like she was hiding something.

"I just wanted to see how you were doing." Elizabeth's voice was harder than she'd intended. Robin shifted her feet, uncomfortable. She could feel antagonism, unusual from Elizabeth.

"Uh, fine." Robin studied Elizabeth warily, her stance defensive.

"Did you give your deposition to the D.A.?"

"You know I did." Robin's eyes darted away from Elizabeth's. "I went yesterday. I texted you."

"So how'd it go?"

"Fine."

"What did you say?" Elizabeth pressed.

"The same thing I told you already." Robin's eyes narrowed. Elizabeth hadn't imagined it. The girl had an edge to her. "What's with the third degree?" Robin folded her arms across her chest.

"I just want to know."

"Well, I told them the same thing we'd already gone over. The thing we talked about for the paper. You know . . . for the story you're writing?"

Was writing, Elizabeth thought. Her phone dinged, indicating an incoming message. Holding the phone close to her chest, she saw the text was from Aaron.

JUST SAW ROSE PALLY IN ACCOUNTING. IT'S NO GOOD. NOT THE SAME WOMAN.

"Damn it," Elizabeth cursed. She flipped her phone back in her pocket. She glanced up at Robin.

"Something wrong?" Robin asked, and the meanness and suspicion had disappeared from her voice. Now there was only worry.

Instantly, Elizabeth felt flooded with shame. She'd doubted Robin based on something less than a hunch. She wondered for a fleeting second if she was trying too hard to make Robin a fraud. Maybe this all boiled down to her own guilt about Bruce clouding her judgment.

"I'm sorry," Elizabeth said, feeling contrite. "I'm just having a bad week. I'm taking it out on you and it's not fair."

Immediately, Robin brightened. "It's okay," she said, giving Elizabeth a small smile. "I understand."

Annie Whitman had been to plenty of luxury hotels and homes while representing some of her more high-profile defense clients, but never in her life had she seen anything as gorgeous as Bruce's six-bedroom villa in the south of France. She'd flown there to try to convince him to return home.

"It's so beautiful here," said Annie as she stepped into the exquisite interior of La Bergerie, a white stuccoed villa carved into a hillside overlooking the Mediterranean just outside of Cannes. The entire first floor was done in a soft cream with taupe accents that created a quiet background for the bold colors of the antique painted screens and magnificent paintings. The kitchen, by contrast, was all dark glass, stainless steel, and ebony granite.

All the rooms on the ground floor opened out onto a terrace that ran the entire length of the villa with views of the sea. Down below the terrace was a horizon pool with a cascade on the far side that appeared to empty into the crystal blue Mediterranean, a sight that nearly took Annie's breath away.

"Look at this view—amazing." Annie didn't know what she'd been expecting, but nothing quite so majestic.

Bruce barely glanced up from his laptop. He shrugged. His family had owned the villa for years. The villa could bring in up to $5,000 a night from a wealthy tourist, if he chose to rent it out, which he didn't. He had a marvelous Philippine couple, Frank and Lynne, who ran it impeccably when he wasn't there and even more perfectly when he was.

It was the place he went when he needed to regroup. This was where he'd come shortly after his parents had died. He'd spent nearly a month here in solitude after their funeral, staring out into the blue water and wondering how he was supposed to carry on alone. The view never quite looked the same after that.

And now he had other painful memories to add, the many times he and Elizabeth had come here over the three years they were together.

He wasn't going to allow himself to think of the past.

"Yeah, it's nice." Bruce cut the conversation short and went back to his computer to finish the e-mail he was sending to his company, Patman Social Impact. He might not have been on the board of directors anymore, but he still had influence, and he planned on using it. He felt more strongly than ever before that Rick Warner and his gas-mining project needed to be stopped. He still thought Social Impact should keep the land, even if they couldn't get the permits they needed for their wind farm. But most of the board was in favor of selling if the permits didn't come through. And, right now, the only buyer would be Rick Warner. Just because the EPA was throwing up some roadblocks for their project didn't mean there weren't workarounds. He sent that message and immediately moved on to another.

"Bruce, maybe we should talk about the case . . ." Annie began. That was another thing he didn't want to think about, no matter how often she tried to bring it up.

"Hold on a minute. I'm writing to the congressman who so gladly took my campaign contribution last fall." Bruce tapped angrily at the keyboard. "He owes me, and now's his chance to pay me back by getting the EPA to see reason."

Annie fell silent watching Bruce. As he typed at the computer, determination in his stark blue eyes, she remembered the Bruce from high school—the one who never took no for an answer. This was the Bruce she remembered: cocky, a little bit entitled maybe, but always sexy. He went straight for what he wanted and he never made excuses. Annie had loved that about him. Nothing seemed out of Bruce's reach.

"There," Bruce said as he clicked send and shut the laptop. "Done."

Annie, who'd been waiting patiently with her legal pad and her iPhone in hand, readied herself to bring up the more difficult points about the pending attempted rape charge against Bruce. Somehow, Annie needed to convince him he had to return to the United States to face the charges, and yet part of her wondered if he was going to take that risk. After seeing his stunning villa and the safety it offered, she wasn't so sure.

Before she could speak, Bruce looked up and said, "Are you hungry? I'm starved. Maybe we should do this over lunch."

⟶

Bruce took her to his favorite restaurant, Plage L'Ondine on the Croisette, the broad avenue in Cannes that runs along the sea.

Most of the tables were set up with umbrella protection from the sun, but others, for the sun worshipers, were out in full sun with tables dug into the sand.

It was easy to tell that most of the other patrons were French simply by the dogs they'd brought with them. There seemed to be one to nearly every table. Some were under the tables, where pets belonged, and others were seated on chairs like small, furry guests. All were remarkably well behaved.

Bruce suggested Les Trois Demi Homards. Each half lobster came covered in a difference sauce. He ordered the Salade Folle Ondine, a specialty with house-cured salmon and homemade fois gras.

Bruce had been coming to Cannes since he was a child, and his French was flawless.

For the wine he found his favorite Sancerre.

The waiter poured them both glasses of the pale white wine and then retreated.

Annie took a sip and thought she'd never before tasted anything so good in her whole life. The wine was icy, crisp, and perfect.

"You really should have let me in on your plan," Annie said, swallowing and trying to steer the conversation to Bruce's case. "I think if you'd stayed in Sweet Valley we could've beaten the charges."

"I just wasn't ready to take that chance," Bruce said.

"Well, even with you here, as long as you go back for the trial, we can still win. The D.A. really overplayed his hand this time. There's no way Tom Colton can get a jury to convict you. He's got circumstantial evidence at best, and no prosecutor likes to go to a jury with a case like this. There's too much of a he-said, she-said element."

Bruce took a long swallow of wine and looked at Annie with grudging admiration. "I really think it's true what they say: You are the best defense attorney in Sweet Valley."

"I try." Annie smiled. "So, should we go over the facts of the case one more time? Maybe we missed something."

"Maybe."

The waiter came back and set the food down in front of them. Her lobsters' three sauces looked rich and delicious: one was a curry, another *Armoricaine,* and the third was a delicate champagne. All were divine. After the first scrumptious bite, she knew it was perfection. The tail meat melted in her mouth.

Annie Whitman was a California girl who had done little traveling. She quickly found herself taken in by everything Cannes had to offer: the fabulous villa, the glorious food, and the decadence of the ambience. She marveled at all these people with their four-hour lunches in the middle of a workweek. Add to that the wine and the devastatingly charming man sitting across from her—a man she'd maybe always liked, ever since high school—and she felt herself being seduced to this new life.

He had, after all, made love to her so many years ago. Except the making-love part was largely in her head. For him, it had been just getting laid. Just like all the other guys who had dated Easy Annie.

"This is delicious," she said. "Oh, my God. So good."

Bruce smiled. "This place never disappoints." He took a bite. They finished the lunch along with another Sancerre. All the while Annie was trying to hold on to whatever legal credibility she had left by doggedly going back to her notes. There was no danger that the D.A. could extradite Bruce since France had no extradition treaty with the United States, not as long as America allowed capital punishment. He already knew that, so Annie gave him a tutorial on international extradition laws with the other European countries in case Bruce decided to travel. Then she went into the workings of the D.A.'s office in an election year.

That was her last line of defense. After that she just let herself slide into the haze of the wine. She wanted badly to reach out and take Bruce's hand in hers, but discipline kept her hand still. Her willpower, however, didn't stop the longing.

Lunch lingered leisurely. Soon the restaurant emptied and they, along with one other table, a young couple, obviously lovers, were left. Annie wished they'd never have to leave. Bruce paid the bill and they walked back to the car. As they crossed the street, Bruce put his hand on the small of her back, and Annie tingled from head to toe.

Back at the villa, Bruce opened another bottle of wine, this time a light Pommard, and the two of them sat on the upstairs balcony that, because of its height, overlooked the sea and the maritime Alps as far east as Italy. The view was open to everything but people. It was just the two of them.

The extravagance of the glorious lunch and the view and the wine brought a sensual aching that Annie tried hard not to feel. They watched the day slide into the softness of late afternoon.

They were out of legal talk, both of them. Just from the way Bruce looked at her, the unmistakable intimacy in his eyes, she could feel some of his old confidence coming back. Enough to make her a little uneasy.

Annie hadn't slept with anyone since divorcing Charlie. She had been heartbroken, but more than that, she'd been worried about what casual sex might do. It had undone her once before in high school, and she wasn't about to go there so readily again. But now, sitting here with Bruce on the balcony of this fantasy villa, which was very real, she didn't know how she would stop herself.

She tried to remember the awkward fumbling they'd shared in the backseat of his Porsche in high school, but all she could come up with was that he'd been surprisingly tender afterward. He'd even held her a moment. Most boys back then just pulled up their jeans and wanted her out of the car. Bruce had been different.

Annie gave herself a mental shake. She shouldn't go there. She couldn't get involved with a client. Plus, this was Elizabeth's ex. She knew her friend still had feelings for him. She tried to keep her thoughts anchored there even as undeniable desire tried to blur them. She couldn't let it.

"Bruce, I need everything you can remember that might have any bearing on the incident." Annie asked, trying to wrench the conversation back to work.

Bruce glanced up. "There is something." He paused, staring at his wine-glass. "But you have to promise me not to tell anyone."

"Of course," Annie said. "I'm your attorney. Anything you tell me is covered under client privilege. You can be completely honest with me."

Bruce took a deep breath. "Okay. Well, we've known each other a long time, right? You knew me back in high school when I was . . . well, you know. I wasn't very nice."

"I liked you in high school." Annie blushed a little as she said this. It felt like she was revealing too much. She was still struggling against the wine.

Bruce studied Annie's face a moment. He hadn't expected that. He thought most people considered him obnoxious. It was one of the reasons he'd avoided the Sweet Valley High reunion a couple of years earlier.

He continued. "But you know after my parents died in college, well, I did a lot of thinking and self-appraisal and it didn't come out so well. I made some good decisions then, with Elizabeth's help. But about that time, I found out that my mom . . ." Bruce sighed. "She had some emotional problems. She was bipolar."

"Oh, Bruce. I'm sorry."

"It's just that she was on medication her whole life. And I know it's something that can be passed down in the genes. And given that night at the bar with Robin—that I can't really remember what happened—it makes me wonder if maybe I just blacked out. Maybe there is something wrong with me."

"Have you ever been diagnosed?"

"No, but I've gone over that night a thousand times in my mind and, logically, I can't figure it out. Unless it's some kind of, I don't know, sickness. I remember I'm at the bar, and that Robin is this very pretty girl, but she is upset."

"Small thing, but I thought you told Elizabeth she wasn't that pretty."

"Well, I just didn't want to make a big deal about it at the time. But she was very young and very pretty."

"I see."

"But, I swear, Annie, I only had one drink and there was that thing with the spilled drink and then I got dizzy, and next thing I know, I'm asleep in the office of the bar. That's all I remember. But what if . . . I mean, what if I just had some kind of psychotic episode?"

Annie had never seen Bruce look so vulnerable before. He desperately wanted her help. She reached out and took his hand. It's what she had wanted to do all afternoon but for entirely different reasons. This was to console, pure succor.

"Bruce, I know you. There's nothing wrong with you. I've never heard of anyone who wasn't drinking heavily blacking out like that, and you said you weren't and you are certain, right?"

"Absolutely."

"So there's got to be another answer, and it's not that you're unstable. You're the most stable guy I know and that kind of thing just doesn't come out of the blue."

"Right, but what if . . . I mean, what if . . . there's something wrong with me. Okay, maybe not bipolar, but what if that not-so-nice guy from high school is who I really am? What if that girl at the bar, if she brought it out in me? What if this nice-guy routine I've been doing since the accident is fake? Maybe I'm just a bad guy."

"No, Bruce. You've turned into a really good guy. The things you've done with Patman Social Impact and the foundation are great. Everyone says so."

Annie had defended enough clients to understand that morality in this world was decidedly a gray area. Rarely was something black or white.

"Hey, look, Bruce, you're beginning to fight back, that's all, and sometimes, fighting back doesn't look so good. But it doesn't mean you're wrong to do it. We're all complicated. Good, bad, whatever. It's the combination that makes who we are. And being yourself—your real self—is nothing to be ashamed of."

What Annie was saying was so simple but so true. He was like everybody else: a mixture of good and bad. He had to stop focusing on what used to be and stop blaming himself. Maybe all this time he'd been trying to bury his past and smother that tougher part of his personality had been a mistake. Maybe he was actually suppressing an essential part of himself.

He felt a surge of freedom. All this time he'd been trying to stay buttoned-up, and maybe that's why he was in such trouble. He'd spent so much time fearing the old Bruce that he'd forgotten how powerful the old Bruce was. No one dared mess with him in high school, and it wasn't because he was a nice guy. If he was going to fight the good fight, he needed some of the cockiness of that old Bruce. Nobody would push him around— not Robin Platt, not Rick Warner. Not even Elizabeth.

He was done being the nice guy who finished last. He was innocent and he had to believe in himself. That very simple thought came straight from Annie.

He looked at her, surprised to realize how much he desired this beautiful, smart woman sitting right next to him.

He'd seen the way she'd been looking at him all afternoon. He knew she felt the same way.

The new, nice-guy Bruce would never have taken advantage, but the nice guy was a wimp, hiding and letting other people take over his life. Bruce was done being that guy. If he was going to win this case, he needed the power of the old Bruce back, and there was one way he knew he could get it.

He needed to remember what it was to be a real man, and there wasn't any better way to do that than by being with a woman.

He reached out and pulled Annie toward him. She came willingly, her eyes never leaving his. Then their lips touched. Hers went soft and parted, and he knew she was all his. With that kiss, a spark popped that surprised them both. This was no ordinary kiss. Not at all.

After an intense moment, she pulled away.

But Bruce wasn't going to let her get away so easily. He was angry, angry at everything that had happened to him, at everyone who didn't believe him. Angry at Elizabeth. Furious at her betrayal.

"Bruce, I don't know . . ." Annie stood, but Bruce was right there in front of her.

"Annie, tell me you didn't feel that, too. Tell me, and I'll walk away right now."

Annie glanced down. "No, I felt it, too." She'd felt it all the way down to her toes.

Bruce went forward into the guest bedroom. Annie followed, drawn by his magnetism, by the promise of what that bed offered. She walked right to him, and he took her into his arms.

"Bruce . . ." His lips were on hers again, just as she wanted them to be. Her head was a whirl of confusion: Did she even want this?

Yes! Without a doubt, she did.

Annie's heart beat fast, and her body came alive. Suddenly they were standing in front of the bed, and then they toppled down onto it.

Annie's head felt dizzy with wine and buzzed with Bruce's fierce kisses. The distant, logical part of her brain told her she needed to stop this. He was her client and the man her best friend loved. But all of that seemed so distant and so irrelevant, and so far away from the south of France and the need that rushed through her body.

It had been so long since she'd had sex with anyone, and she realized she wanted to make love to Bruce. It was that simple. But it wasn't.

What about Elizabeth?

If she did this, could she ever face her again? And what about the career she'd worked so hard to build? She'd be risking everything if she did this.

"Annie . . ." growled Bruce, his face flush with desire, his hands wrapped tightly in her hair. He tugged a little.

Annie, lying there, panting, looked up at him. His blue eyes met hers, fierce and demanding and full of power. Her heart pounded and her mind raced. Somehow, she felt, this was the moment that could define everything.

Would she do this? *Could* she do this?

He pulled her to him; her lips went soft and wet.

"Wait," she murmured as she pulled back.

"What?" Confusion flickered across Bruce's face.

"I don't want to get carried away," Annie whispered, her voice low. This was a lie. Part of her *did* want to be carried away. Far, far away, with Bruce.

"Annie, come on. Look at what you did to me." Bruce grabbed Annie's hand and put it on the front of his pants. Annie could feel exactly what she'd done to him and the thought excited her; she couldn't deny it.

"I know, but . . ." There were so many buts. So much of the real world got in the way. "I don't want to regret this."

"If you tell me to go away I will."

She was silent. He moved his hand up along her thigh, under her skirt, and beneath her thong. He found her more than ready for him. She realized how weak her words sounded when her body told him the unflinching truth.

"Why fight it, Annie?" he said, moving his fingers against her, making her moan. "I know you want me as much as I want you."

"Wait . . ." Annie murmured, trying to focus her thoughts. Everything was moving so fast, and the room seemed like it was spinning. "Wait, Bruce, I'm not sure about this. . . ." And she wasn't. Not at all. Yes, she wanted to do this, but should she? Could she risk her career—and Elizabeth's friendship—over a tryst with Bruce?

As Bruce's hands roamed up her thigh, sending tingling sensations up her spine, she knew she had to make the decision now. Another moment, an instant more, and it would be too late.

10

It might have been just a couple of months since Jessica had been back to work at VertPlus.net, but it seemed like an eternity. No matter how many ideas she pitched, her hostile new boss, Tracy, shot down every one of them.

"I don't know why she doesn't like *anything*." Jessica sighed and glanced over at her assistant, Emily. The plain, freckled redhead, wearing too much makeup as usual, shrugged.

"Well, Tracy just has very high standards."

"Excuse me? Are you implying I don't?" Jessica's temper flared. Emily needed to learn how to respect her boss.

"*Sorry,*" Emily said in a tone just touched with sarcasm. Jessica could never quite tell whether Emily was being sincere.

"Just watch it," Jessica warned.

Every day Jessica worked with Emily, she liked her less. She talked back, had no respect, and as far as Jessica could see, didn't really do her job. Jessica always had to ask her two or three times to do the simplest things.

Jessica had brought up the issue with Tracy but had gotten nowhere. "Emily knows her stuff," Tracy had said flatly. It figured that Tracy would love her, since Emily made it her purpose in life to annoy Jessica.

Jessica sat back and glanced at the latest thing to hit the reject pile: an "occupy fashion week" promotion where models wearing eco-friendly makeup would pop up with impromptu catwalk struts carrying placards in the middle of fashion week. Jessica thought it was a dynamic, original idea, but Tracy had turned it down flat. In fact, it almost seemed like Tracy had known what Jessica was going to say before she'd even said it, but the only other person Jessica had even talked to about the idea was Emily.

For a fleeting second, Jessica wondered if that was just coincidence.

"What's your next strategy?"

"I don't know."

A new e-mail arrived in her in-box on her computer screen.

She glanced up at the notice and groaned. It was from Caroline Pearce. The subject line read: "Thought you'd be interested in this . . ."

Jessica had a sinking feeling she wouldn't like it.

She opened the e-mail and then clicked the link Caroline had provided. It sent her straight to TMZ, where she saw the headline *Liam's New Flame, Jessica Wakefield, in Bitter Divorce Battle*.

"But I didn't file!" Jessica leaned forward, trying to devour the news.

"What is it?" Emily asked, reading over her shoulder. Emily knew no personal boundaries, and Jessica was too shocked to shoo her away.

The two-paragraph story named her and said she was in the middle of a bitter divorce from her estranged husband, Todd Wilkins. Except that Jessica had never filed for divorce. She swallowed. That must mean . . .

"Excuse me," Jessica said as she clicked the article closed and ran to the bathroom. She didn't see that Emily slid straight into her desk chair and clicked open the e-mail.

Jessica stood in front of the mirror in the ladies' room, breathing hard.

Her own stark blue eyes stared back at her, looking as shell-shocked as she felt.

Todd must have filed for divorce. It was the only explanation. While part of her knew this would be coming, the harsh reality of it still hit her hard. How could he have done this without telling her? They were officially separated, yes, but given all they'd been through in the last three years and that they had a child together . . . how could he let her find out he'd filed for divorce from Caroline Pearce and TMZ?

Her heart felt like it was breaking all over again, and the sadness threatened to swallow her whole.

The unfairness of it ripped through her. He couldn't call her and let her know he planned to do this?

The heartache and sadness soon were drowned out with a righteous anger. How could he have done it like this? He must never have really loved her at all if he planned to end things like this.

She smoothed her hair and lifted her chin. Fine, if this is how he wanted it, she thought. She thought about walking straight to her desk and calling Liam, but realized that he was out of town for a movie shoot. He wouldn't be back for another week. And she needed someone right now.

She strode out of the bathroom and immediately spotted Michael Wilson across the office. He was standing near a file cabinet talking to his assistant, and he had his bag slung over one shoulder, like he was headed out the door. It was nearly six, after all.

Michael glanced up and gave Jessica a tentative, almost shy smile. Something inside Jessica clicked. She knew Michael liked her. So far, he'd been entirely professional, but Jessica knew it wouldn't take much encouragement to goad him into something more.

She walked over to him like a woman on a mission.

"Michael," she said, touching his arm, "can I talk to you a minute?" Her tone and the way she let her hand linger on his arm had the desired effect. His face lit up like a boy who'd just found a toy at the bottom of his cereal box.

"Uh, sure, Jessica."

"Walk me back to my desk?" Jessica offered.

"Sure," Michael said.

Michael fell into step beside her.

"I was hoping I could pitch you a couple of ideas before the meeting tomorrow."

"Oh." Michael's face fell a little as he realized it was business related.

"I was thinking, though, maybe we could grab a bite to eat?" Jessica stood very close to him and touched his arm again. He'd have to not have a pulse to miss the clear change in vibe as she amped up her flirting.

"What about your boyfriend?"

"What boyfriend?" Jessica deliberately played dumb.

"Oh, I mean, I heard . . ."

"Don't believe all that you hear."

"Good point." Michael glanced at Jessica, looking like a man who'd stumbled upon a winning lotto ticket.

"So, dinner?"

"Oh, y-y-yeah, sure. I'd love that." Michael grinned.

"Me, too," Jessica said.

11

Todd sent in his final story from the Lakers game, snapped shut his laptop in the press room, and stood.

"Hey, Todd, a few of the guys are grabbing a drink. You in?" asked Stuart, the AP wire reporter and one of Todd's friends.

Todd shrugged. "Thanks, man, but no, I'm going to pass."

"Getting out would do you good." Stuart nodded toward the newspaper sitting on the table. It was open to yet another picture of Jessica and Liam.

Todd felt his stomach tighten just looking at it.

"No, I just don't feel like it."

His colleague nodded and slapped his shoulder.

He tried not to wear his broken heart on his sleeve, but everyone seemed to know about it anyway. It was getting pathetic. Todd knew it, but he couldn't quite shake himself of the gloom.

It had been months now since he'd found out Jessica had lied to him about Liam O'Connor.

But despite it all, Todd still loved Jessica. He thought he would always love Jessica. There would always be a part of him that would want to be with her. That was why he'd left Le Bouchon that night without a word, why he couldn't face her once he'd found out the truth. It just hurt too much. He didn't want her to see him so vulnerable, so raw.

And part of him had hoped she'd come after him. He knew Jessica Wakefield and understood that she never begged for anything. But he had hoped that she loved him enough to come after him. To explain.

She hadn't. More than three months later, she still hadn't made any move to apologize. She didn't have to apologize, really. She just needed to show up one day at the door. With the way he felt about her, that probably would have done it.

Sometimes he fantasized that she would come to him out of the blue, but she never did.

Todd wanted to be with Jessica; he would do anything to be with her, but she had to give him a sign that's what she wanted, too. He wasn't going to grovel, not after the way she'd treated him.

Todd pulled into the driveway of his house, parked his car, and hopped out. He unlocked the back door and instantly could smell Sarah's cooking.

Ever since Sarah had shown up on Todd's doorstep, upset about losing her apartment, Todd had let her stay with him. He couldn't imagine turning her away, not after Jessica had had her fired. Jessica insisted Sarah was a plagiarist, and the *Tribune* editors had believed her, but Todd didn't think Sarah would do anything like that on purpose. It was just careless reporting.

Since moving in with him, she'd become a good friend and confidant. Nothing physical had happened between them. If Todd was honest with himself, it wasn't for Sarah's lack of trying. It was because Todd wasn't ready. He was still hung up on Jessica.

He inhaled the smell of hearty lasagna and sighed. This is what home should smell like. Todd couldn't help it. He was an old-fashioned guy. Jessica had accused him of being last-century old-fashioned, but he couldn't help who he was.

And now there was no point to even trying.

"Oh, hey, Todd, you're home." Sarah turned around, and he saw she was wearing skimpy cutoff shorts, a clingy tank top, and no bra. The effect was dizzying for a moment. Todd might have been in love with Jessica, but she was the woman who wasn't there. Sarah was right here. Close. Hot.

"I was just whipping up some dinner. Want some?"

"Sure." Todd felt grateful. "That would be great."

Sarah wiggled past him to get a pot holder, brushing him with her chest as she went. Under different circumstances, that would've been a huge turn-on, but Todd couldn't quite focus entirely on Sarah.

"How's it going?"

"Good."

"Anybody been by today?" Stupid as it seemed, he had to ask. Actually, he always ended up asking.

"No, why? You expecting someone?"

"No," Todd said. *Just hoping.*

"Are we talking about Jessica again?" Sarah asked, wagging a spoon in his direction. "I know you're still hurting, Todd, but I really think you can do better."

"I know, but . . ." Todd loved this Sarah, the good friend and listener, the one who kept stubbornly but gently trying to help him heal. Todd spent hours talking to her about how much he missed Jessica. It had been such a relief to admit that to someone. Sarah also didn't seem to mind that he'd pulled back romantically. He just couldn't jump into a new relationship now. It didn't seem right.

"No, buts. I promised to help you through this, and I will." Sarah gave him a warm smile and immediately Todd felt better. He hated being so wrapped up in Jessica that he couldn't think straight. While he knew part of him would never get over her, he liked to think that one day he'd be able to get through a day without thinking about her every minute. "Here, have a taste," Sarah offered, holding up a wooden spoon with the lasagna sauce on it.

Eagerly, he went forward and she dipped the spoon into his mouth. A bit dribbled down his chin and she wiped up the sauce with her forefinger. Then she popped the finger in her mouth.

"Yummy, right?" she purred. Even Todd was having a hard time avoiding the sexual tension now. And Sarah was pretty . . . and perky in all the right places.

Suddenly, the evening seemed to take on a new dimension of possibility.

"You want a beer?" Sarah asked him, dipping into the refrigerator. She made sure to bend down low, revealing just how high the shredded cuffs of her cutoffs could rise.

"Yes," he said, and swallowed. She fished out a bottle and twisted off the top. "Here you go. Now go sit down while I finish up in here."

Todd sank into his favorite recliner and clicked on the TV, beer in hand. He had to admit, it felt good.

Then he saw the channel in front of him. He'd landed on E! and the entertainment news was on. He stopped abruptly as he heard the report.

"*Star* is reporting that Jessica Wakefield, Liam O'Connor's hot and heavy, is getting divorced. It looks like Liam's love is leaving her husband for him. But who wouldn't? Have you seen Liam's abs?"

In shock, Todd dropped his beer.

"Damn it," he cursed as he scrambled to pick up the bottle and beer foamed all over the carpet.

"What's wrong?" Sarah asked. She stood in front of him now, and when he straightened, he found himself at eye level with her chest.

"It's just . . ."

Sarah glanced over at the screen and saw the picture of Liam and Jessica. "Oh, Todd."

"She's filed for divorce, Sarah," Todd said now, his voice sounding distant and numb.

Sarah plucked the beer deftly out of Todd's hand and put it on the coffee table, and then she sank into his lap, wrapping her arms around his neck.

"Oh, Todd, I'm so sorry."

"I don't know what I expected . . ." Todd rested his forehead against her shoulder and she hugged him tight. "I thought . . ."

He realized he really had been naïvely holding on to the hope that Jessica would show up at his door. That they would somehow get back together. Now, with divorce papers in the works, that dream disappeared.

"That's why she never made any move at reconciliation. Liam. How dumb I was."

Sarah stroked Todd's hair. "Obviously, she's in love with him. Nothing you can do about that."

Of course, Sarah knew Jessica had been by. There was that afternoon the bitch had come by wearing those killer heels and a snug-fitting dress, ready to beg to get Todd back. But as luck would have it, Sarah had answered the door wearing one of her best teddies and had quickly gotten rid of her. Of course, she'd never told Todd.

Why would she? Sarah wanted him for herself. She'd been trying for months to seduce him. She wasn't going to give up now.

"How could she do this to me?" Todd shook his head.

"I'm not surprised," Sarah said. "This is the same woman who left her job supposedly because she loved you and then went running back to it the next day."

"Shit. You're right." Todd closed his eyes.

"It's all just a big game to her," Sarah said gently. "You deserve someone better." She rubbed her hand against his shirtfront.

"Sarah . . ."

"Todd, I'm going to say this because I care about you, okay? Jessica is moving on," Sarah said. "Maybe you should, too."

Sarah rubbed herself against Todd, wiggling in his lap. "Maybe what you need is someone who really knows how to take care of you," she said, and then she dipped her lips to his and started kissing him.

At first, Todd froze. His heart was broken and he felt a well of despair bubbling up inside him. But another part of him, a deeper, instinctual part, couldn't resist the comfort Sarah offered.

As he hesitated, he found himself getting lost in Sarah's softness, in the wetness of her mouth and her eagerness to please him.

In that kiss, he realized that she'd been here in front of him for months, eagerly waiting for him to come to his senses. His hands roamed her body and slid under her shirt, caressing her bare breasts.

She moaned.

She was offering herself up to him and he would be foolish to turn her down. Besides, he liked Sarah. Maybe more than liked her. She'd been there for him these last few months when no one else had. Certainly not Jessica.

His body responded to her. The truth was he was a man who'd gone without sex for too long, and as he kissed her, his need turned more urgent. He suddenly wanted to have her in every way possible, to show Jessica Wakefield that he was not broken.

Desire soared in his blood, and he shifted, scooping up Sarah in his arms as he kissed her again. She giggled in surprise as he marched her to her bedroom. They tumbled down on the bed together, and her clothes were off.

Todd looked at her appreciatively. She was nothing like Jessica. Her dark hair was cropped short; her skin was darker than Jessica's, and her body not quite as lean. He relished the differences.

Maybe she would help him put Jessica in the past. Who knew? Maybe she was the right kind of woman for him. Maybe he could love her.

"Are you sure you want to . . . ?" Todd's voice trailed off. He couldn't help asking. He always asked first.

"More than anything."

Todd bent down and caressed her gently, exploring her body, relishing the unfamiliar details, like the crescent-shaped birthmark on her upper thigh. She dug around in the drawer next to her bed and fished out a condom. Once the wrapper was off, she gently tugged it on him.

He moaned as she guided him straight inside her. He moved slowly, deliberately, as he met her gaze. This wasn't just sex, he realized with a start. They were making love.

She had been such a good friend to him, but now she was much more than that. He found himself thinking, *This feels so right.*

She responded to him, coming again and again, and with each new climax, Todd felt his own power growing. Sarah would be his way out of the Jessica Wakefield nightmare. She would be his savior. Sarah was his future.

At the end, he came with a guttural shout, then crumpled on top of her, exhausted and spent. He cradled her gently in his arms, caressing her hair, murmuring, "Sarah . . . Oh, God, Sarah. You saved me. That was so good . . ." as he drifted off into a peaceful sleep.

Sarah lay by his side, eyes wide-open and calculating. After a few minutes, she slipped out of his bed, grabbed her shirt, and tiptoed to her cell phone on the kitchen table.

She listened to Todd's snores, waiting for any change in the sound before she clicked open her text messages. There was a long line of communication with Caroline Pearce.

Todd might not have known it, but in the last few weeks Sarah and Caroline Pearce had become close pals. Sarah had been the one feeding Caroline Pearce information, like that Todd had filed for divorce. Sarah told herself it was only a matter of time; eventually she would convince him to file. Just as she'd finally convinced him to come to her bed.

Men were simple creatures, she thought. They could be easily led. Like the fact that Todd still thought Sarah had plagiarized Jessica by accident. She hadn't. She'd copied Jessica's quotes word for word, just the way she'd been plagiarizing for years. She was still picking up freelance money the same way.

She would've gotten away with the Jessica thing if the bitch hadn't been so nosy. But she would get her back now by taking away Todd. Sarah knew how much Jessica wanted to be with Todd. She'd seen it in her face when she'd come to Todd's house.

Jessica might have gotten her fired, but Sarah was going to make sure Todd never went back to Jessica again. Not now, not ever.

Sarah texted Caroline. IT'S OFFICIAL—TODD AND I ARE A COUPLE.

Sarah thought about this a moment and then added: HE SAYS HE'S GETTING A DIVORCE BECAUSE HE WANTS TO BE WITH ME. HE WANTS TO BE A FREE MAN FOR ME. . . . SO YOU CAN DRAW YOUR OWN CONCLUSIONS.

Let Jessica chew on *that* awhile, Sarah thought. She could almost imagine the bitch's face when she read it.

Sarah hoped she suffered. She heard Todd stir in the next room, so she locked her phone and got up.

Time for round two, she thought as she wiggled out of her shirt.

EPISODE 5
Cutting the Ties

1

Still in the moment, Annie Whitman felt dizzy with desire, lost in the warm and wet deliciousness of Bruce's kisses, in the raw passion it offered. Wasn't this exactly what was supposed to happen in a beautiful bedroom like this in the south of France?

She could feel the moment of decision slipping by as he tightened his grip, sending shivers through her. Annie loved a man who took control, a man who knew what he wanted and wasn't afraid to take it. That was Bruce.

"Come on, Annie. I know you want this, too," he said, a growl in her ear. She knew she excited him; she could feel just how much as he ground himself against her.

She could see the old gleam of the confident Bruce in his eyes, the boy who got what he wanted, no matter what the cost. He wanted her at that moment, and the invitation sent her head spinning. She realized, maybe for the first time, just how much she liked him. Maybe she'd always been fostering a crush on him, ever since high school and that quickie they'd had in his Porsche.

Bruce kissed her again, his hands roaming under her shirt and cupping her breasts. She moaned, beyond tempted to give in to his hands. Her body came alive under his touch: she was hot and cold all at once, burning with a hungry need. Distantly, she couldn't believe how readily her body responded, how much she wanted him. She hadn't had sex since she'd left her husband, Charlie Markus. She'd almost convinced herself she didn't need sex; that maybe it was just heartbreak waiting to happen.

But now, with Bruce's insistent hands roaming under her clothes, she knew that had all been a lie. She needed this. She wanted this.

But you can't always have what you want. No matter how much you want it.

Back in high school, she'd gone with any boy who'd have her, not only because she liked sex, but because she liked the attention. She looked for approval in the arms of more boys than she could count. All she wanted to do was make them happy so they would like her, but instead, she'd just felt cheap, and that was the way they treated her.

Would she let that happen again? Now, with so much at stake?

She was a respected lawyer and he was her client, the ex-boyfriend of her best friend, Elizabeth, who made no great secret of the fact she still had feelings for him.

No, she wouldn't. She couldn't. He might be the old Bruce again, but she wasn't the old Annie. She had grown far beyond the girl who craved approval from any boy who looked her way. She'd worked hard to build her career—and her self-esteem. She no longer needed a man to feel good about herself.

"Stop, Bruce," Annie said, pushing a little against his chest and pulling herself back. He loosened his grip in surprise. She took the opportunity to twist out from under him and stand up.

Confusion flickered across his face for only a second. But then the old Bruce returned.

"Are you sure?" he asked. He stood, too, and pulled her to him again, kissing her hard. She felt herself melting into him again. The passion was real, and the intensity of it surprised them both. She realized in that moment, she did feel something for Bruce. Something more than just lust.

If he pushed her even harder, she knew she'd give in. She wouldn't be able to hold out much longer. Annie mustered her strength for one more denial. If he didn't go now, she would wind up sleeping with him.

Her body ached for him. She wanted him as much as he wanted her.

"No," she said again, and put her hands on his chest, pushing him away.

"No, Bruce. We're not going to do this." She pulled back from him, but it took every ounce of her self-control to do so.

Bruce searched Annie's eyes. For a fraction of a second, she thought she saw a flicker of hurt there, the pain of rejection, but then it was swallowed up with anger.

Bruce's eyes burned. She understood suddenly this was not just the anger of sexual frustration, but the fury over how pathetic his life had become. This man of power, who prided himself on being a good man, had suddenly been brought to his knees by false accusations from some cowardly mendacious nobody out to destroy him. And for all intents and purposes, Robin Platt had succeeded. She'd sent him into hiding, taken away his dignity, his reputation, and perhaps, most painfully, the woman he had spent the better part of his life loving.

After weeks, months now, of flimsy, inadequate responses, Bruce Patman exploded.

He ripped himself away from Annie, and with his hands clenched into fists, turned and stormed out of the room and onto the patio. There, she heard him kick a chair with such force that it flew against the balustrade, bounced off, and smashed onto the stone tiles with a reverberating clang.

Annie's whole body tensed. She'd never seen Bruce so angry, and she knew it wasn't all her fault, but she had been the trigger for pent-up rage at what had happened to his life. She sat very still on the bed. Would he control it? Or was she in danger?

No. Bruce wouldn't hurt me. Would he?

For the first time, Annie felt a stab of doubt. Bruce's worries came back to her then, the worry about inheriting the emotional troubles of his mother and her bipolar diagnosis. Could this temper be part of that? She leaned over to where she could see the chair lying on its side in the patio, its sides crushed and bent.

Her lawyer's mind took over then. She pushed aside emotion and thought about what a jury would think if they saw an outburst like that. Would they presume guilt?

She knew that his temper was something they would have to deal with sooner rather than later. Annie made a mental note to talk to Bruce's therapist. She'd need to get permission, of course, but she'd do that later. In the meantime, she slid the glass door closed on her room and locked the patio door.

She looked at the door and wondered if she was locking Bruce out, or locking herself in. Annie knew she'd done the right thing turning him away, but a part of her couldn't help feeling an ache of disappointment.

Now she knew she wanted him more than she'd ever allowed herself to believe before. It would be hard to pretend now that she didn't know what it was like to kiss him, to have his hands on her.

Would he come for her again? And if he did, would she be strong enough to resist her own desire?

2

Lila couldn't get her favorite skinny jeans to fasten. No matter how hard she tugged at the fabric, she couldn't get the zipper all the way up.

"Come on," she whined. She lay down flat on her bed and tugged hard on the zipper. After several hard pulls, she finally zipped them. But, when she sat up, she felt like a one-pound bag of Play-Doh crammed into a two-ounce bag. This time, it had nothing to do with eating In-N-Out Burgers. She had to face the very real fact she was pregnant, and eventually she wouldn't be able to fit into jeans with buttons and zippers at all.

Another wave of nausea hit. She bolted up from bed and ran to the bathroom, barely making it in time before she threw up—again.

Someone—probably a *True Housewives of Sweet Valley* PA—knocked on the door. "Mrs. Fowler Matthews?" asked the PA in a hesitant voice. "We're ready for you."

"One minute!" Lila shouted, sweeping back her darkly dyed hair from her face. She looked up at herself in the mirror. A green, ghastly face stared back. How was she going to do this?

It figured that now that she was really pregnant she had all the worst symptoms: fatigue, nausea, bloating, violent mood swings, all the symptoms she'd pretended to suffer for her make-believe pregnancy were now real. And in spades.

She glanced at her watch. It was four in the afternoon. *Morning sickness, my ass,* she thought. *Morning, noon, and night sickness is what they should call it.*

Another wave of nausea hit, and she doubled over, retching again.

"Mrs . . . ?"

"*Excuse* me," came a voice that Lila knew well. "I need to get in there." Lila threw open the bathroom door.

Jessica Wakefield stood on the other side, purse slung over one shoulder, her blond hair immaculate, shiny, and flat-ironed straight. Lila grabbed her friend's arm and pulled her into the bathroom.

"Give us a minute," Jessica told the confused PA with the headset and the clipboard as she shut the bathroom door behind her and locked it. Lila reached over and flipped on the fan, too, just to make sure that if the PA decided to hang around and eavesdrop, she wouldn't hear much.

This was Lila's master bathroom, and it was larger than most people's living rooms. In one corner lay a massive, Jacuzzi-style tub, along with a huge his and hers vanity covered entirely in marble. The pristine granite tile floor gleamed under soft lighting.

Lila pulled Jessica over to the far corner of the room, away from the door.

"Thank God you're here," Lila breathed, and hugged her friend like she was a life preserver. "Did you get it?"

"I did," Jessica said, pulling out the little prescription baggie from the outer pocket of her purse. Enid Rollins, her OB-GYN, had called in some special prescription medicine for Lila's morning sickness, since Lila couldn't manage to hold down a single meal. "How are you feeling?"

"How does it look like I'm feeling?" Lila pointed at her too-pale, greenish face.

"It'll get better," Jessica said, giving Lila's hand a sympathetic pat. "The first trimester is the worst. I felt like hell with Jake."

"I'm not sure if I'm going to make it to the second trimester." Lila met Jessica's gaze. A look passed between the two women. Jessica knew exactly what Lila was talking about. She was thinking about terminating the pregnancy.

"Before you do anything, Ken should know," Jessica said.

"No way." Lila shook her head fiercely. Jessica was the only person alive—aside from Enid Rollins—who knew Lila was pregnant, and for now that's exactly how it would stay. Ken had humiliated Lila on national television for faking her pregnancy. She knew he would never believe she was really pregnant now.

She was the girl who cried wolf one too many times.

"I don't know what to do," Lila said, and tears filled her eyes.

"Hey, it's okay," Jessica said, and wrapped her old friend in a hug. "One way or another it will be okay."

"I don't know if I'm coming or going."

"Hormones," Jessica said. "They're killer."

"I should just end this." Lila slumped down on the edge of the tub and put her head in her hands. Then, she promptly started to cry again.

"Hey, it's going to be okay." Jessica sat down next to her and put her arm around Lila's slight shoulders.

"Will it? I'm the most hated woman in America. Have you seen the blogs? Or Twitter? #LiarLila is all over the place."

"Who cares what those morons think?" Jessica shrugged. "And look on the bright side. You're famous. Jimmy Fallon did a joke about you last night."

"Great." Lila grabbed a Kleenex from the counter and dabbed at her eyes with it. "This is not what I wanted to be famous for."

"Well, don't worry. It will all blow over. And don't worry about all the negative press. Those people don't know you."

Maybe they do know me and that's the problem, Lila thought. She remembered Ken saying that eventually everyone would be able to see the truth: that she was worthless on the inside. Lila sobbed some more.

"I hate this," she moaned. "I hate that people hate me. And I hate that I delivered Ken on a platter to that obnoxious bitch Ashley. It's like salt in the wound."

"You saw last night's episode then?" Jessica had watched her TV last night with dread about what Lila would think about it. The entire episode showed Ken and Ashley happily reunited, and talking no end of trash about Lila and how pathetically two-faced and desperate she was to make up her pregnancy. *Mostly Ashley talking.* The show made sure to show Ken and Ashley kissing and touching as much as possible.

"Yes, I watched it—when I wasn't vomiting. Hard to say if it was the pregnancy or Ashley."

"Maybe he'll change his mind. You know Ken is crazy about you."

"No, not this time." Lila shook her head. All the times she'd thought Ken had been so easy to manipulate, but now she'd found herself dealing with a completely different person. It seemed that once he'd truly and finally made up his mind, there was no convincing him otherwise.

He refused to answer her calls or texts and he was even more furious now with her than he'd been the last time he'd packed up his things and left. Only, this time, Lila knew, there was no real hope of getting him back. Not after what he'd told her. And, besides, she didn't have any more tricks to play. He hated her.

"Men change their minds," Jessica said.

"Not Ken. Not this time." Lila said. "Ken has officially filed for divorce."

"Oh, Lila." Jessica hugged her friend harder. "I'm so sorry. I know how that feels. Todd filed, too."

"He did?"

Jessica nodded. "Well, look at us, two almost divorcées. What the hell happened to us? This would never have happened in high school."

"No," Lila sighed, an almost wistful look in her eye. "Never."

The two former cheerleaders spent a moment commiserating in silence.

"You know, you're going to have to figure out what to do about the baby." Jessica handed Lila another tissue.

"I know. I'm running out of time." She had to get something decided before she hit her second trimester. "I just don't know what to do."

"Think carefully about this," Jessica said. "A baby is a lot of work, but a baby is also a wonderful gift." Jessica thought of Jake. She couldn't imagine her life without him. Since Todd left, he was one of the only good reasons to get out of bed in the morning.

"I am thinking about it. It's all I think about." Lila felt the tears start to crowd her eyes again. Just when she thought she'd made up her mind to go one way, a flood of doubts washed away her resolve. She hated feeling this out of control. Is this what pregnancy was like?

"I still think you should talk to Ken."

"Absolutely not." Lila couldn't be more certain of anything.

Jessica said nothing. She knew the look on Lila's face. It would be hopeless to argue at this point.

"Whatever you say. Your secret is safe with me."

"I've only got a couple of weeks to decide, otherwise, it gets more complicated health-wise. That's what Enid Rollins said. I'm running out of time." Lila couldn't help but feel like the weight of the world was crushing her. "What do I do?"

Elizabeth sat in the kitchen of her parents' house and poured herself another glass of wine. Was it her second? Third? She'd lost count. She knew she'd started with a full bottle. She tilted it now and through the darkened glass saw she had a third left.

Technically, it was afternoon, but just barely.

She knew she was getting a little bit drunk, but what did it matter? She didn't have a job to go to anymore, didn't have a boyfriend or an apartment of her own; in fact, you could say she didn't have a life.

She stared at her iPhone, at a picture of her and Bruce from months back. They looked so good together, so happy. She took another drink of wine.

The Malbec was supposed to help her forget, but the more she drank, the more she remembered. Like how good she and Bruce were together, how very much in love, how much she missed him.

She took another gulp of wine and had a sudden urge to call him. Not for the first time, but this time she actually pulled up the number for his villa in France. It would be late, nine hours ahead, which would make it after dinner there.

But even if she did call, what would she tell him? *I know I betrayed you in the worst possible way, but I still love you? Give me another chance? Sorry I believed you were a rapist?*

She dropped her phone on the counter and put her head in her hands. The room spun from too much wine.

She ought to stop drinking. Eat something. Forget about Bruce. Instead, she picked up her phone and hit "call."

She pressed the phone against her ear. Her heart thudded as she heard the odd, foreign-sounding ring. *Why was she doing this?* She didn't know. She didn't care. She just wanted to hear his voice again, she reasoned. That's all. That would be enough.

Or maybe not. Maybe she would just tell him she was wrong and she was very sorry. She'd tell him she needed him.

But, as the phone rang again and again, no voice mail picked up. She waited for three more rings and then, dejected, hung up.

Bruce was probably just out to dinner or taking an evening walk on the Croisette. It was what they used to do together. She hoped he was finding a way to relax and have some peace.

Then she was suddenly struck by the vision of Bruce sitting in one of the many outdoor cafés, chatting up a beautiful brunette French woman. *How long before he moved on?* she wondered. *Maybe he already has.*

She threw back another glass of wine.

He was free to be with whomever he wanted, she knew. She knew she'd let him down when he needed her the most, but if she could only tell him how sorry she was, maybe she could get him to understand. She felt a sudden urge to make things right with Bruce before it was too late.

Desperate to apologize, Elizabeth dialed Bruce's number again. This time, after the third ring, a woman answered.

It wasn't Lynne, Bruce's housekeeper. Even in her wine haze, Elizabeth knew that. She had a sudden vision of a beautiful woman—her replacement—in a bikini top and sarong. In a panic, she hung up, her heart thumping hard in her chest.

Who was that?

She didn't have a French accent. It wasn't the siren Elizabeth had imagined was seducing Bruce at the moment.

No. She sounded American and vaguely familiar.

And then it came to her: Annie. Of course. Annie was in France to help Bruce with his case. Elizabeth felt a rush of relief.

She was quickly glad she hadn't said anything. She didn't want Annie to know she'd drunk-dialed Bruce. It was too embarrassing.

In fact, even trying to call Bruce back would be humiliating now. Annie would be there to hear the whole conversation. Elizabeth didn't want that. She didn't want her friend to know she'd gotten drunk at one in the afternoon and called Bruce.

But she had to do something.

As she stared at her phone, she realized just how much she wanted Bruce back. She needed him in her life. She was desperate to get him back. She'd do anything.

Yes, she'd had too much wine, but it was still the truth.

In vino veritas.

Elizabeth sat with an empty wine glass in front of her, imagining what it would have been like if she could go back in time and do everything over again.

She remembered finding out for the first time about Bruce being accused of attempted rape. She was just out of the shower, getting ready for a dreaded night at Missy LeGrange's house—a dinner they never made—when Bruce got the call.

At the time, Elizabeth had been stunned. She thought it was surreal; that it couldn't really be happening. But at the time, she never had a doubt about Bruce's innocence. She knew Rick Warner had to be behind it, and she'd vowed to prove it.

It was only later, after she'd found Robin and heard the girl's heart-wrenching story, that she began to have doubts. When she hadn't immediately found the link to Rick Warner, she'd started to doubt Bruce. Robin had been so scared and vulnerable. She'd brought out Elizabeth's maternal instincts. She'd thought hiding her away from the press had been the right thing to do.

But now, she kicked herself. Why did she give up on the Warner-Robin connection so soon? Rick Warner was a careful man. The connection wouldn't be obvious. It would be hard to find. You don't become as power-ful and as rich as Rick Warner by having your dirty laundry easy to find.

What if she'd never let Robin influence her? What if she'd been like Jessica, determined to believe, no matter what, that Bruce was innocent?

What if she'd kept digging into Robin, no holds barred? If she'd gone after Robin and ripped her life apart until she found just what *really* moti-vated her to accuse Bruce of attacking her. What if she'd never really lost sight of the possibility that Robin worked for Warner?

Maybe I would've found something.

Maybe I still can.

She'd abandoned Bruce too soon. She'd lost her trust in him, so fast, so completely, that maybe she'd been blind to Robin's involvement.

But it wasn't too late. Bruce hadn't gone to trial yet. She could still help. If only she could prove his innocence.

Yet the last promising lead linking Robin Platt to Rick Warner had fallen through. When Steve told her Warner's employee Rose Pally wasn't Robin Platt, it had taken her straight back to square one.

Think, she told herself. *There has to be something I overlooked. Go back to the beginning.*

"Wait, that's it." Elizabeth sat up straight. "The beginning! Of course."

Elizabeth leaned forward and pulled up a map of Kentucky on her phone. Robin Platt grew up there in Richmond, and that's where Eliza-beth needed to go. That's where Elizabeth could interview her old friends and track down whatever family might still be alive. If there was any hope of finding out once and for all if Robin Platt was telling the truth, she'd have to go deeper. She'd have to go back to the beginning.

She knew she had to go to Richmond, but first she needed to do as much research as she could in Sweet Valley. She had to question every-thing and start from scratch. She'd need to re-interview Robin and get all her ducks in a row before she went to Kentucky. She needed to go armed with all the information she could gather.

Let's see if you really are who you say you are, Elizabeth thought. *Your home-town is small, and nobody forgets or forgives you there. Just like Sweet Valley.*

4

Jessica sat at the elegant table at Nine and glanced over at her boss, Michael Wilson. He gazed at her with unabashed admiration, his blue eyes bright with excitement as he told her a story about an infamous business trip to Miami.

"It was a disaster from start to finish," he said, with that smile he always used when he recounted a story. Michael knew how to keep a person interested. It was the same way he managed to captivate a boardroom. "The airline lost my luggage, so I had to go straight into the pitch room wearing a day-old wrinkled suit. But it gets worse . . ."

Jessica liked listening to Michael. He didn't take himself so seriously, unlike Liam. With Liam, it was always about what project he was working on, and what the tabloids were saying about him. Most of the time, Jessica had to fake interest.

Not with Michael. They were both in the same business; they would never run out of things to talk about. Of course, she never ran out of things to discuss with Todd, either.

She shook herself. She wasn't going to think about Todd tonight, she resolved. Todd was off-limits.

"And then, right in the middle of the presentation, a fire alarm sounded, and the sprinklers completely malfunctioned."

"No!"

"So, not only am I in a wrinkled suit, but now it's a wrinkled, wet suit."

Jessica couldn't help but laugh a little imagining Michael, who was always immaculately dressed, in such a state trying to impress the board of CoverGirl.

Michael loved to hear Jessica laugh. He'd been shocked when Jessica had asked him out to dinner. For years, he'd felt like there was an invisible wall that Jessica deliberately put up between them. But now, the wall seemed to be showing cracks. More than that. Jessica had taken a sledge-hammer to it.

Michael had been crazy about Jessica almost since the moment he'd laid eyes on her. And who wouldn't love her? She was gorgeous and smart. But never before had he thought he would be this close to having a chance with her. Something had changed with Jessica, and the air between them held the electric charge of possibility.

She laughed and touched his sleeve. Michael took note.

If there was one thing Jessica knew how to do, it was get a man to sit up and take notice. She'd had the instincts since age fifteen. Some people are just born with them. For Jessica, it was as easy as breathing.

She wanted to draw in Michael at that moment because she knew she could. Todd had left her and taken her heart with him, and Liam was off shooting a movie, and right now, all she wanted was to feel a little bit like her old self again.

"So, there I am in the middle of the pitch meeting, and the computer just dies," Michael continued. "Completely. Flooded."

"Oh, my God, what did you do?"

"Only thing I could do: laugh."

Jessica took a big drink of wine. She couldn't help but compare Michael to Liam. Liam had zero sense of humor about himself. If something like this had happened to him or somebody on TMZ said something bad about him, he'd stew about it for days.

Michael wasn't like that at all. Self-effacing and funny, he carried his responsibility as vice president of VertPlus.net with ease.

"By the end, the guy had to laugh, too. But that didn't stop him from signing on the dotted line."

Michael grinned and Jessica smiled back.

"So . . . mind if I ask you a personal question?" Michael's eyes gleamed a little.

"Okay." Jessica hoped it wasn't about Todd. She took another drink of wine to steel herself in case it was.

"You and Liam, you've been in the tabloids a lot. So, there's really nothing between you?" Michael looked as if he was bracing for an answer, as if he almost hadn't want to ask the question at all.

"Liam! Oh, no . . . They play it up much more than it really is. I mean, we see each other, but it's no big deal. At least it isn't on my side."

And, technically, of course, we've slept together. But Jessica wasn't about to tell Michael that. Or the fact that just a few days ago, before Liam had left to shoot more scenes for his movie in Vancouver, he'd pressed her to be exclusive.

He had asked Jessica to promise him she wouldn't date anyone else. No way was she going to make that commitment to Liam. Not when they hadn't even slept together again since that first time. Since that one night, she'd found a million reasons to avoid going back there. She'd been as delicate as she could to explain how she wasn't ready for such an important relationship now. Liam left frustrated, but promised to give her more time.

Now, Jessica saw Michael's shoulders literally sag with relief. He beamed at her.

"I'm glad to hear that," he said, the corners of his mouth pulling upward in a contagious smile.

The check came and Michael paid with his credit card. Soon, they were walking together in the parking lot toward his new black BMW. Michael walked to her side to open the door, but then he hesitated, raising his eyes to meet hers.

"Jessica . . ." His voice came out low and a little husky. "You know . . . You really are so beautiful."

She turned, feigning surprise. But she wasn't. She knew what Michael planned, and she had already decided she would let him do it.

She shifted a little, putting her back against the car door, effectively blocking it. Standing close to him now, she put her hand on his chest and looked up at his face. Michael wore the expression of a man who couldn't believe his luck. She parted her lips just a little, and that's all the encouragement Michael needed. He was drawn in, like a marlin on a line. His mouth covered hers, a gentle, hesitant kiss at first, as if he were asking her lips for permission.

He pulled away, briefly, and their eyes locked. Michael was giving her the opportunity to stop and turn back, but Jessica had no intention of doing either. Her expression gave him all the information he needed. The kiss grew deeper, and Michael's hands more urgent, as they settled on her small waist. Jessica wrapped her arms around his neck and returned his kiss, fully pushing herself against him. Her hands roamed through his hair as his moved down to her hips and explored the delicious curve of her lower back.

Just as things were really beginning to heat up, Jessica pulled away.

"No, stop. We can't!"

"Why?"

"Office romance."

"I don't care. Do you know how long I've wanted to do that?" Michael was out of breath and dazed and by the grateful look on his face, Jessica knew she might have made his whole year with a single kiss. "I just didn't think you liked me like that . . . What changed?"

"Everything," Jessica breathed, and it wasn't a lie. Everything in her life *had* changed.

Jessica remembered the day Sarah Miller—nearly naked—opened Todd's door. She thought about Todd filing for divorce and moving on, and about how she needed to do the same thing. No matter how hard it was, or how much heartbreak she was suffering, she had to find a way to move on. If that meant using Liam and Michael like crutches until she could walk on her own two feet, that's exactly what she planned to do.

Given how excited Michael looked under the fluorescent lights of the parking lot, he wouldn't mind being used.

Michael moved to kiss her again and she let him. As he trailed kisses down her neck, she thought, *This is exactly what I need.*

"I feel like the luckiest man on earth right now," he whispered in her ear. And he brought his mouth up to hers again, pressing her against the hard door of his BMW, and Jessica let him.

5

With Liam away, Jessica went out with Michael for the next two weekends. Despite the heat between them, she was taking it slowly. Meaning she wasn't sleeping with him yet and they were keeping it a secret at work. It was an office romance, always dangerous.

Liam continued to check in on a daily basis by phone or text, but Jessica conveniently omitted mention of all of her plans with Michael. She knew they'd just drive Liam mad with jealousy, and there was no need to do that. Besides, she and Liam weren't exclusive. She could see whom she pleased.

And Michael was fun. He didn't ask too much or press too hard and he wasn't controlling like Liam, who had annoying habits like ordering her dinner and telling her whether or not she should have another drink.

And, Michael didn't come laden with a crew of paparazzi following his every move. Going out with Michael felt reassuringly normal. But she still wasn't ready to move it up a notch and into bed. Michael didn't seem to mind too much. Besides, it was still early in their relationship.

But then, without warning, Michael abruptly stopped returning her texts.

Maybe he's sick, Jessica thought. *Or maybe he lost his phone.* And then, an uncharacteristically insecure thought popped up: *Did I say or do something wrong?*

Her instincts told her he should be hers for the taking. Those instincts had never failed her before, and yet . . . something was wrong.

There had to be some explanation. She called, but only got his voice mail.

At work the following Monday, Jessica planned to get to the bottom of the Michael mystery, but she was sidetracked by the shit storm that engulfed her the moment she walked in the door.

"You picked a lousy day to be late," charged Emily, Jessica's redheaded assistant, who always wore a bit too much makeup.

"I'm not late." And even if she was, this was not a fact an assistant should dare point out to her boss. Emily needed to learn a little respect. "What's going on?"

"There's a big dust-up because we may be losing Maybelline."

"What do you mean we're losing Maybelline? It's not possible." That was Jessica's account. She'd been working with them for weeks about planning a launch of a new green, all-organic cosmetic line. "Let me call the VP there I've been working with."

"No good. Tracy already has the president on the phone." Emily nodded toward Tracy Courtright's office—the office that once belonged to

Jessica. Tracy looked serious, her face lined with concentration as she spoke into the phone.

"But that's my client! I've been working with them for weeks."

Jessica didn't like this. *Why is Tracy going around me? What is she telling them?*

Jessica didn't trust for a minute that Tracy had her back. If anything, she'd look for any opportunity to sell Jessica out. Tracy couldn't stand her and made that clear at every turn. By the end of a phone call with Tracy, the entire Maybelline board would believe Jessica was an incompetent dilettante.

Jessica glanced over across the room and saw Michael with his laptop bag heading into his office.

"You'd better just let Tracy handle this," Emily offered.

"Emily, when I need your advice, I'll ask for it." Jessica glared at her assistant with a cold stare frigid enough to make the twenty-something freeze in her tracks.

Jessica stood and strode over to Michael's office. Michael had always been her advocate, even before they started to date. She had no doubt she'd find a friendly ear with him.

But he didn't answer your texts, a nagging little voice said. *Must be some explanation,* she thought, brushing aside the doubt as she knocked on his office door.

Michael glanced up and met her eyes. Usually when Michael saw her, he lit up like a light parade at Disney World. But, today, oddly, a shadow of annoyance passed across his face. Jessica didn't know what to make of it.

"What is it?" Michael's voice was brisk and distant.

In an instant, Jessica realized that Michael's radio silence over the weekend was no mistake. He was out of sorts about something. But what? Jessica didn't understand. They'd gone out last weekend and everything had been fine. More than fine: electric.

"Uh . . ." Jessica felt unsure all of a sudden. And since when did Jessica feel tentative in the presence of any man? "I'm sorry to bother you, Michael. I just wanted to talk to you about Tracy. I think she's trying to hijack my account . . ."

"Stop right there." Michael put up a hand like a conversation crossing guard. "If you're talking about Maybelline, we're going to have a meeting in two minutes."

"Meeting? What meeting?"

"Emily didn't tell you?"

"No." *Emily doesn't tell me anything,* Jessica thought. "Is this all Tracy's doing? Because whatever she told you . . ."

Michael cut her off. "She's just doing her job. I suggest you do yours and we'll all get along just fine."

"Excuse me?" *Where did that come from?* "Since when do I *not* do my job?"

"We'll talk about it at the meeting." Michael met her eyes. She saw clearly he was angry, but she had no idea about what.

"Michael . . . come on . . ."

"I'm sorry, Jessica, but we're late already. It's time to go to the conference room." He stood and walked past her out of his office. Jessica trailed after.

"Michael . . . I don't understand. What's wrong?"

"You know what's wrong."

"I don't. Enlighten me."

Michael sighed and shook his head. "You're a real piece of work, Jessica."

By now, they'd made it to the conference room. The entire staff and Tracy were waiting inside. Michael stalked past her, ending their conversation, and took the seat at the head of the conference room. Jessica was left with the only empty seat, the one opposite Emily.

"Thanks for coming, all," Michael said. "I called this meeting because we have to do some spin control. Somebody leaked the particulars of Maybelline's big new eco-line on Facebook before the board had even approved it, and now we've had to do some damage control."

Leaked details? This was news to Jessica. *What is going on?*

"A quick thank-you to Emily for alerting Tracy and the rest of us to this problem."

Jessica's head snapped up and she glared at Emily, who ignored Jessica completely and instead nodded sagely at Michael. Emily hadn't mentioned a *single* word to Jessica. This was becoming a bad habit. Inwardly, Jessica fumed. Instantly, she knew Emily had done this on purpose.

"Michael, if I may, Maybelline is my client and . . ." Jessica was about to propose some kind of solution, but Michael cut her off before she could finish.

"No, Jessica, Maybelline isn't your client anymore. Tracy is going to take the lead on this one. Your team will shift to her, now."

"What?" Jessica didn't understand. She glanced around the room at the people who'd been working with her on Maybelline, but nobody looked her in the eye.

"Michael, please, can we just talk about this?"

"Nothing to talk about." Michael shook his head firmly. "The decision is made. Only you and your team knew the particulars of the line. And as the leader of the team, you need to take responsibility. You dropped the ball on this one, Jessica." He met her gaze from across the conference room table and the hardened look he gave her told Jessica he was talking about more than just the Maybelline account.

Jessica's face burned with the humiliation of being publically dressed down in front of the entire office for something she was a hundred percent sure she didn't do.

She felt anger rush through her veins, and she knew where to direct it. As she glanced at her assistant, Emily, she knew she'd been betrayed. And Jessica planned to find out why.

Jessica bolted from the meeting and ran to her desk. She pulled up Maybelline's Facebook page, and right there on the wall, were comments outlining the entire launch of the new line.

"I can't believe this," Jessica muttered, scrolling down the line.

The comments were made by someone simply named Spoiler Alert, who clearly wasn't a real person at all. When Jessica clicked on the profile, she found it locked.

She glanced up and saw Emily striding from the conference room. Doug, a graphic designer who worked on Maybelline, saw Jessica eyeing Emily and swept by Jessica's desk.

"I'd watch that one if I were you," he said, slowing down.

"Hey, wait!"

Doug came back to her desk.

"Emily," Jessica said, "why?"

"Connections."

"She's Tracy's relative?"

"Not exactly, just the daughter of her best friend from college."

"Thanks, Doug." The pieces were falling together. That explained a lot.

How could she have been so blind all this time? Emily and Tracy. Of course. Tracy wanted Jessica fired from the moment she came back to work at VertPlus.net. Emily was her spy.

⁓

"It's all so unbelievable," Jessica ranted to her sister, Elizabeth, on her hands-free set as she drove home from work. "Emily did this on purpose, and while I can't prove it, I think she's also the one who leaked the details of the makeup line."

"Why do you think she did it?" Elizabeth asked.

"She's Tracy's best friend's daughter, that's why."

"That would do it."

"Neither of them can stand me. You know how everyone loves a winner? Well, I'm certainly not one anymore."

"They're both insane if they don't see how talented and great you are. And Michael, too."

"Thanks, Lizzie." Jessica sighed. What would she do without her sister?

"I think you should try to talk to Michael. You guys were getting along so well."

"I have tried, but Michael's not having it. He avoided me all afternoon. I walked into the kitchen to grab some coffee and he was there. He literally turned right around and walked out, without even making eye contact. He took away my team, Lizzie! And now he seems to hate me as much as Tracy does. I don't understand."

"You not understanding a man? That's a first!"

"Ha. Ha."

"I really liked Michael, so much more than Liam."

"I know. Me, too." Jessica pulled over to the curb and stopped. This conversation needed all her attention. "But Liam is always there for me. He calls me every day!"

"Because he's a stalker."

"Because he loves me! And he's been so supportive about the trouble at work even before today's drama."

"Fine, he's a nice guy."

"Don't sound so skeptical! Anyway, you should be happy because I've got a date with a new guy tonight: Cal Ross. He's a lawyer at Steven's firm. Met him last week, and he asked me for a drink."

"Good!" Elizabeth sounded a little too excited for Jessica's liking.

"You really don't like Liam, do you?"

"I just think it's good for you to keep your options open," said Elizabeth diplomatically. "And I do think he has stalker tendencies." Elizabeth sighed. "Speaking of stalker tendencies, I think I may have been stalking Bruce lately."

"What? How?"

"I drunk-dialed him a few times this week."

"No! What did you say?"

"Nothing! I hung up anytime someone answered the phone. God, Jess, I feel like an idiot."

"Forget about it," Jessica said. "Everybody's done it."

"Have you?"

"No, but that's not that point. You didn't say anything, right? For all Bruce knows, you could've been butt-dialing him."

"To his villa in France?"

"Okay, not so likely, but still. It's not so bad," Jessica said, pulling back into traffic. A few minutes later, she was in her driveway.

"So how are you holding up this week?" Jessica asked Elizabeth, who told her about what a funk she was in since losing her job at the *Trib*.

"But I'm starting over again, interviewing everyone, and seeing if I missed anything," Elizabeth said. "Then I'm going to go to Robin's hometown in Kentucky. If there are cracks in her story, I'm going to find them."

"I know there are," Jessica said. "And if anyone can find it, you can."

Her phone beeped with an incoming call. She glanced at the face and saw Liam's number. "Liam's calling. Got to go."

"You going to tell him about Cal?"

"Yeah, right, he'd love that." Jessica laughed before she clicked over to answer Liam's call.

⌣⟶

It had taken much longer than usual for Jessica to get Liam off the phone. He seemed unusually interested in what she was doing for the night, almost as if he knew she might be headed out on a date. He had a sixth sense that Jessica called "mantuition." He had also given her a hard time on all of the nights she went out with Michael. Liam's mantuition was strong. And no matter how many times she told him she had no plans, she could tell he didn't believe her.

There was always more than a hint of suspicion behind his questions. And there were always a lot of questions.

Eventually, Jessica did get Liam off the phone. She double-checked the e-mail Cal had sent earlier in the day. They were going out to a new Cuban restaurant, and he said he'd pick her up at eight, which was right after Jake's bedtime. Liza, her nanny, was staying late tonight.

Jessica liked to be the one to tuck him in, read him one of his favorite bedtime stories (usually something featuring Thomas the Train).

Jessica went to the kitchen and pulled out her laptop. She was still trying to figure out how to fix the damage with Maybelline. They might not be her client anymore, but she still felt responsible. She tried reaching out to a few of her contacts there.

At dinnertime, Liza and Jake came to the kitchen, where Jake happily ate his mac and cheese dinner before heading upstairs for a bath and his bedtime routine. He came bounding down the stairs in his pajamas with a Thomas the Train book and pulled Jessica off the kitchen stool, his eyes bright with excitement that his mom was going to read his favorite book.

At least Jake still thinks I'm a rock star, Jessica thought.

Jessica read the story with Jake hanging on her every word, and afterward, her toddler sat up in bed and gave her a big hug.

"Love you, Mommy. Love you too much."

Jessica grinned. Jake was still getting the hang of phrases like "so much" and "too much." Sometimes the wrong combination was even more heartwarming.

"I love you, too, sweetheart." Jessica glanced at his beautiful face—and his floppy hair that reminded her so much of Todd—and sighed. It was hard to put Todd in her past when she lived with their son. Still, she reminded herself how lucky she was to have Jake. Even if she didn't have Todd, she'd always have a small piece of him in their boy.

"Good night, sweetie. Love you." She tickled him until he giggled.

Tucking the covers around him, she kissed him on the forehead and left him to sleep. In her own room she changed into a coral-colored sheath and heels and was ready when Cal rang the doorbell at eight on the nose. Jessica tugged open the front door and saw a smiling Cal standing there. He was the tall, athletic lawyer with the light brown hair and warm brown eyes she'd met the week before.

This was going to be fun, she thought as she stepped out. After one of the worst weeks, Jessica felt like things might be finally starting to turn around.

Or so she thought.

But then, after a fantastic date with Cal, he never called her. She even broke her own rule about playing hard to get and texted *him* first.

But heard nothing back.

Jessica had started to suspect something was wrong with her phone. Or that Cal had gotten hit by a bus. At that point, she was annoyed enough so that she didn't know which she wished for.

When had a guy *never* called back after one of her patented wow-factor first dates? She'd worn a short hemline and her legs went on for miles.

She didn't understand it. *What is happening? First, Michael stops calling me and then he sidelines me at work. Now, Cal doesn't bother calling me back either?*

What in the world was happening? Was it her?

Was Jessica Wakefield losing her . . . Jessica?

Jessica picked up her coffee mug and walked to the window seat in her living room. She listened to the sounds of Jake playing in the next room, and as she stared out the window, she found she didn't know what to make of her life. How did she get here, back on that same window seat that seemed to have played such an important part in her life? The place where she had waited for her angry first husband, Regan, the place she had waited for Todd to come back. Now, here she was again.

Had losing Todd meant she'd lost herself?

As she agonized over these questions, she saw Liam pull up in his new Maserati. With his new, super-sized star status, he could afford to buy more and more toys.

She jumped up. He wasn't supposed to be back in town until next week.

She threw open the door, and there he was, walking up the steps, carrying flowers and a Thomas the Train toy for Jake.

"Surprise!" he said, wrapping her in his arms and giving her a long kiss. "We wrapped up filming early!"

For once, she was truly glad to see him. Liam never failed her, she thought. Liam never abandoned her. He would always call. She clung to him a little tighter than usual.

"Everything okay?" he asked her in his lilting Irish accent. Concern passed across his handsome face. She knew why he was Hollywood's hottest leading man at the moment. His jet-black hair and stark blue eyes were made for the big screen.

"Just a bad week," she said. "Work," she added quickly. "It's bad!"

"I'm sorry, luv. I'm here now, and I'll take care of you."

Jessica smiled at him. She was glad someone offered.

"Mommy . . . ! Who dere?" Jake said, abandoning his Legos and train set. He came to a full stop when he saw Liam standing in the door. Jake promptly hid behind the living room doorway, suddenly very shy. Jake was always shy around Liam.

"Hey, buddy. Look what I brought you." Liam held out the Thomas the Train box. Jake studied it and then Liam with caution.

"It's okay, sweetie," Jessica said. Reluctantly, Jake came forward and took the box. "What do we say?" Jessica prompted.

"Tank you," Jake muttered, having not quite mastered the *th* sound. He then bolted from the room, new toy in hand.

"That was sweet of you," Jessica told Liam.

"Anything for my little guy," he said. "And you. If he's happy you're happy. And you know I'll do whatever it takes to make you happy."

Liam grew serious, almost too serious, as he did sometimes. Jessica didn't know why every sentence needed to be a love declaration. Why didn't he see that she just wasn't quite there yet?

"Get Liza to watch Jake tonight and come spend the night at my place." He grabbed her and pulled her close.

Suddenly Jessica felt suffocated.

"Liam . . ." Jessica sighed. "I don't think that's a good idea."

"I haven't seen you in weeks!" His tone went harsh and demanding. Jessica sent him a sharp look and he quickly softened his voice. "I just miss you, that's all. I want to spend time with you."

"Soon, I promise." Jessica said. "You just have to be patient with me."

"Jessica, it's hard to be patient around you." Liam's eyes smoldered. He wanted her, he'd made that clear. And Jessica liked being wanted, especially since Michael and Cal had so callously thrown her aside. Still, something made her hesitate.

"Soon," Jessica said, firmly. "Good things come to those who wait."

"I'll wait for you, Jessica," Liam promised. "I'll wait for you as long as it takes."

6

Annie stood on the balcony of Bruce's villa in Cannes and stared out to the sea, watching the beautiful sunset over the crystal-blue water. She breathed in the smell of the salty air and sighed. Beside her, her phone chirped with another email from her firm, Leisten, Hartke & White. It was morning there, and people were just getting into work.

She'd been away two weeks and they were starting to miss her. Case files were piling up, but she kept making excuses to her boss about needing a little more time. So far, they'd given it to her. After all, Bruce Patman was one of the most high-profile clients the firm was handling at the moment. But even Annie was having a hard time explaining why she had to stay here. The case, such as it was, was nearly all back in Sweet Valley.

Yet she stubbornly refused to go home. And it wasn't the view or gorgeous weather that made her want to stay.

"Annie?" At the sound of Bruce's voice, she jumped a little. She'd been purposefully keeping her distance from Bruce ever since the night they'd almost slept together.

Bruce, for his part, had been the perfect gentleman since that night. Hadn't even touched her. In fact, she suspected that saying no to him actually earned her more respect. She loved having the respect, but she hated the distance.

Annie's heart raced whenever he said her name, or when he happened to walk by. When she heard his voice on the phone in a separate room, the sound made her feel happy. And despite how often she told herself she couldn't possibly think of him as anything other than a client, she knew, despite all her best efforts, that she was falling in love with him.

"Yes?" Annie was amazed her nerves didn't show in her voice. Must have been the years of practice presenting cases in the courtroom.

"You wanted this," Bruce said. He handed her a piece of paper with his therapist's name and number on it. "I called him and told him to expect your call. He said he's happy to speak with you."

"Thanks, Bruce." Annie smiled at him, and Bruce's blue eyes softened a little.

They had never spoken about that night. Yet it was a current between them, a secret that seemed—at least for Annie—just beneath the surface of every other conversation they had.

Every time Annie saw Bruce, all she could think about was the way his strong hands had felt running down the small of her back. She wondered if he remembered, too. Or if he chose to forget.

"I'm going to head out for dinner," Bruce said. "Would you care to join me?"

Annie wanted to, more than anything, but she knew it was a bad idea. Dinner would mean wine . . . and wine would weaken her will . . . and then . . . No, she couldn't risk it. She shook her head. "I should stay and work. This is really my only window to make calls."

"Oh, right," Bruce said, as if suddenly remembering the nine-hour time difference. "Of course."

Despite the fact that Annie was trying so hard to keep a wall between them, she still felt a stab of disappointment as Bruce left the room. She had wanted him to try harder to convince her to go. Silly of her, she knew.

These days, she felt like she was at constant war with herself, her brain in one corner and her heart in another.

Her brain told her she couldn't risk her professional reputation by having a fling with her client in the south of France—no matter how good the wine was or how irresistible Bruce seemed. But her heart didn't care what was sensible. Her heart wanted Bruce, plain and simple. Had wanted him for a long time.

In fact, in the war between her heart and her head, right now, her heart was winning.

As hard as she tried to keep her distance, she found herself coming up with excuses to be with him, to follow him throughout the day. The simple fact was that if she really wanted to get away with him, she'd have headed home on the nearest plane.

There really wasn't any more work to be done in Cannes. All of her work needed to be done back in Sweet Valley, and the time difference made that difficult. Yet she stayed on anyway. Her heart stubbornly refused to let her go home.

Alone now in the villa, Annie decided she should get some work done. She called the number on the paper Bruce gave her.

"Dr. Lewis," answered the therapist on the other end of the line.

"Hi, Dr. Lewis. It's Annie Whitman. I believe Bruce Patman told you to expect my call?"

"Of course. Thanks for calling, Annie. I have to say I was shocked to hear about the charges against Bruce!"

"Do you think he's capable of committing the crimes he's charged with?"

"Well, we're all capable of anything. But if you had asked me last year, I would've said Bruce would absolutely not do this."

Annie perked up at hearing this as she furiously scribbled notes on her yellow notepad. This was good news. She was already imagining bringing Dr. Lewis to the witness stand.

"I understand there's a history of bipolar disorder in Bruce's family. Is there a possibility Bruce has this condition?"

"I treated Bruce for several years and I never saw any indication he was bipolar. Usually, we start to see signs in late adolescence or early adulthood, and Bruce simply had none."

"Are you willing to testify to that?"

"Well, I can say what I've seen, but there's no definitive test for being bipolar. There's no way to prove absolutely that he isn't. But I've been treating him long enough to say that in my professional opinion, he's not."

"Thanks, doctor. That helps."

Suddenly, Annie heard the front door slam and Bruce's murmured curses coming from the living room. She hung up the phone quickly and went to see what was wrong. When she got there, she found Bruce pacing in front of the couch, his face a bundle of rage.

"Those sons of bitches," he hissed. "They were waiting for me!"

"Who was waiting for you?" Annie struggled to catch up.

"The fucking paparazzi! I guess they've found me somehow. They had my restaurant staked out."

"Sorry, Bruce. That is a blow."

"Don't worry. I got one of them back, the leeches."

Annie went stock-still. She glanced down at his hands and saw a cut on the top of one knuckle. For a second, she imagined the worst. Had he assaulted one of them? Suddenly Annie remembered Dr. Lewis saying there was *no definitive test for being bipolar*. Just because Dr. Lewis thought Bruce wasn't, didn't make it a fact. Dr. Lewis could be flat wrong about Bruce.

"What did you do, Bruce?" Annie couldn't quite keep the dread out of her voice.

"I broke a camera. I took the camera in my face and ripped it out of his hands and threw it. Cut myself on the lens, too."

"That's it?"

"That's it."

Annie released the breath she'd been holding. A broken camera was property damage, hardly anything. If he'd punched someone in the face, they could claim assault. A new camera would be easy enough to fix. Except, she thought, what it would do to his already fragile reputation. That wouldn't be something easily fixed. Not at all. Annie's mind whirled as she thought about the fallout and how it would affect their case.

Bruce abruptly stopped pacing. "Why? What did you think I'd done?"

"I don't know." Annie shrugged, but didn't meet his eyes.

"You think I attacked somebody? Just like I was supposed to have attacked Robin Platt? Is that where this is going? You're doubting me now, too!"

Annie felt at a loss for words. Part of her did wonder if Bruce was capable of assaulting that girl. Lately, his mood swings had been erratic. He'd be chatty and upbeat one minute, gloomy and downcast the next. His temper flared over any little thing, like the other night when his personal chef delivered his salmon to the dinner table a shade too cold.

So far, she explained it away as simple stress. Bruce was a fugitive and he'd been charged with serious crimes. Even an innocent man might crack under that kind of pressure.

"Bruce, it's not that I doubt you," Annie said firmly. "It's that I'm your attorney, and I have to think about what this means for your image."

"Who cares about my image? That's almost the least of it. It's ruined anyway! Look at me. Far as anyone is concerned, I'm a rapist. That's what Elizabeth thinks. I know it. And it's destroyed everything between us. I've loved that woman for years and no one knows me better and she thinks I'm guilty."

"I don't think she does, she just . . ."

"Don't even bother, Annie. You know how long it's been since I've seen her or even spoken to her? Not since Steven's baby was found. And then she couldn't even look at me."

Bruce looked stricken. Annie felt torn. She wanted to say something in Elizabeth's defense, but at the same time, a small part of her felt jealous of Bruce's feelings for Elizabeth. So she stayed silent, uncomfortable, but silent.

"There's nothing left for us. I can't believe it's over. I've lost her."

The anger was gone, and now there was only heartbreak. And then Bruce pulled himself together, a little embarrassed at showing his true weakness and back on the solid ground of his legal situation and his anger.

"You think I can ever recover from this? Even if I'm acquitted, it will be the little footnote that follows me for the rest of my life. Any time there's a story about me in the paper it will say, 'Bruce Patman, billionaire and the man who was charged with attempted rape'!" Bruce threw up his hands in disgust and walked into the living room, where he sank into his white couch.

Annie followed him.

"I care about your image and what the idea of a man angry enough to break a photographer's camera does to a jury pool back home."

Bruce sighed and put his head in his hands, his shoulders crumpling in defeat.

"I'm sorry, Annie. I don't mean to yell at you. I know you're trying to help me." He looked up, running both hands through his thick, dark hair. "I don't know what's come over me. I just feel like I'm on an emotional roller coaster and I can't get off. I saw that guy with the camera and I just . . . lost it."

Annie crossed the room and took a seat next to Bruce. Violating her own resolve to keep her demeanor strictly professional, she wrapped an arm around his shoulders.

"It will be okay, Bruce."

"Will it?" he challenged, looking up at her with desperation in his eyes. "This nightmare just keeps going. I keep thinking I'll wake up from it one day, but every day it's the same thing. Nothing changes."

"It might change if you go back home and face the charges."

"I can't, Annie. Even *I'm* not sure I believe myself anymore. I think back about that night and there are large chunks of it I don't remember. What if I *did* do those things? What if I *did* and I just can't remember?"

"You really think you could have?"

"God, Annie, I don't know anymore. That's what's so frightening. I honest-to-God don't know."

Bruce let his head fall into his hands, clearly a man at the end of his rope. When he looked up and his eyes were cold and the slice of his mouth was sharp and hard. "But Elizabeth does."

It was obvious to Annie that this was a man whose world was falling apart and he had no idea how to put the pieces back together.

Just at that moment, the phone rang. It seemed to ring a lot lately. But anytime Annie answered it, no one was there.

Still, you could almost see Bruce's heart leap. So few people knew he was here and fewer knew the unlisted phone number. Elizabeth knew.

He stood up, but before he could get to the phone, Annie answered it. "Hello . . . Hello?"

As usual, no one answered. She glanced at Bruce and shook her head. *No one.*

Without saying a word, just his dismissive facial movements said, *Jerk. Of course, it's not her.*

He sank down on the couch. Annie sat down next to him, putting her arm firmly around his shoulders, almost hoping to hold him together by her own force of will.

Her heart broke for him, but she wasn't just his friend, she was also his attorney, and she couldn't help but think about what this meant for his case. With Bruce emanating such doubt, she wondered if she needed a back-up defense. Should he turn out to be guilty, maybe she could run with some kind of insanity defense, possibly. Maybe Dr. Lewis might have some ideas.

Looking at the defeated and crumpled-looking Bruce, Annie knew she needed to prepare for the worst-case scenario. Like all defense attorneys, she wanted to believe her client was innocent, but she'd be prepared to defend him even if he was guilty.

7

Elizabeth knocked on Robin Platt's door the next morning, sober and determined. She hadn't called before she came by. She intended to catch Robin off guard. Elizabeth couldn't shake the feeling that Robin was hiding something. She'd been by Robin's house a few times before, but no one had answered. She wanted one last time to talk to Bruce's accuser before she flew to Kentucky.

This time, the pretty, slim girl opened the door and blinked suspiciously at Elizabeth. She looked the worse for wear, as if she'd spent a hard night drinking. Her hair was a matted mess; her mascara smudged.

"I just need a minute," Elizabeth said.

"Well, I know you're not working for the *Tribune* anymore, so I don't know why you're here." Robin's voice was flat and cold as she folded her arms and stood in the doorway, not letting Elizabeth in.

"Did Andy call you?" Elizabeth tried to sound calm and ordinary. She knew Andy would try to get the interview Elizabeth refused to run.

"He did. I ignored his calls at first, but eventually, he caught me taking out the trash. He's pretty persistent. He said you wouldn't run my story. Want to tell me why? Also, I thought you said my name would be a secret? If it's so secret, then why does this guy Andy know it?"

"Andy's an upstanding journalist. He's not going to put your name in the paper." Elizabeth felt suddenly very uncomfortable. "And, I didn't run your story because I didn't think the paper was being very fair."

"Fair to me or to Bruce Patman?" Robin's eyes missed nothing. And it wasn't anger or betrayal that Elizabeth saw there, but cool calculation. "I know he's your boyfriend."

"How long have you known that?"

"A while." Robin's face grew cold and distant. "But, whatever. It doesn't matter now."

"No, it doesn't, Robin. I'm not with Bruce anymore because he knows I've helped you."

"Really?" Robin didn't sound very convinced.

"Yes. Robin, all I want is the truth. It's all I've ever wanted. That's what I'm trying to find out here." As Elizabeth spoke the words, she realized they were absolutely true. In her sober state, she had to allow that Robin could be telling the truth.

"You're not working for Mr. Patman, are you?" Skepticism came through in Robin's voice.

"No, I swear. He won't even speak to me right now." Again, one hundred percent true. He wouldn't so much as look her in the eye the last time they were in the same room together. "I just want to know what really happened."

Robin glared at Elizabeth, the calculations spinning. She seemed to be weighing the pros and cons of allowing Elizabeth in, and somehow Elizabeth couldn't shake the feeling that Robin was looking for an angle, a way to play Elizabeth. It fanned the flame of her inner doubt about Robin's credibility. Something here just wasn't right.

Elizabeth noticed Robin's right hand shook a little, like she'd had a bit too much caffeine. It wasn't the first time, either. Over Robin's shoulder she noticed a few empty mugs on the counter. Her place, as usual, was a mess. Robin glanced down and then shoved her hand in her pocket.

"Come in," Robin said, reluctantly, letting Elizabeth in.

While there, Elizabeth asked her detailed questions about her past. Where she had lived, where she had gone to school, and the names of her old friends. Robin told it convincingly. She grew up in Richmond, Kentucky, population 33,000, a town big enough to have a Walmart, but small enough that most people did know each other. Both parents were dead, but she had a few friends who might still live in Richmond. Most of them had moved away. With little family left in Richmond, Robin had decided to come to Los Angeles and try to break into the movies—behind the camera. She'd always had artistic talent, and wanted to see if she could work on special effects for the film industry.

"Why so curious about where I came from?" Robin asked.

"I just want to have the whole story." Elizabeth didn't tell Robin that she had a bag packed and stowed in the trunk of her car and a flight to Kentucky to catch in two hours.

So far, everything Robin had told her matched with what she'd said before. Elizabeth could find no inconsistencies in the story, and as she rose to go, she wondered if the trip to Kentucky was just an idea born of too much wine and being too lonely. Would it be a waste of time?

But she knew she had to do something more than just drink wine, mope, and drunk-dial Bruce. She had to find out if Robin was telling the truth. If she dug deep enough, she'd know for sure.

It was the only possible chance she had to put her life back together. She'd do anything to do that.

Her phone dinged as she was walking back out to her car. She glanced at the face of it and saw a text from Caroline Pearce.

Instantly, her stomach tightened. She was tempted to delete it without reading it, but she knew she wouldn't. Like everyone else in Sweet Valley, try as she might, she couldn't completely ignore Caroline Pearce.

CHECK OUT MY TWITTER FEED TODAY! NEWS IN THE BRUCE CASE! Caroline wrote.

Elizabeth sighed. She knew before she clicked on the link Caroline provided that she would regret whatever she found on the other end. Caroline might like to pretend she was an amateur reporter, just keeping her friends updated on the Bruce Patman case, but she was nothing more than a mean-spirited gossip.

Sometimes, Elizabeth thought Caroline was just a miserable person who wasn't happy unless everyone else was miserable, too.

As much as she wanted to, Elizabeth couldn't stop herself from clicking on Caroline's link. Caroline always knew her weakness, and in this case, it was Bruce. She might be able to ignore news about anyone else, but not Bruce. She had to know. No matter how much she knew it would hurt.

She pulled up a series of tweets about Annie and Bruce.

What's this? Elizabeth felt her stomach sink. It was as bad as she thought. Caroline wrote: *Annie and Bruce sizzle in Cannes! Rumor has it the two are up to more than legal posturing in the south of France!*

Elizabeth blinked fast. *Annie and Bruce? Surely not.*

But then she clicked on a link that pulled up a photo, one showing them looking cozy and intimate at a small table on a patio in Cannes sipping wine. Annie was laughing at something Bruce said, and nothing about either one's posture screamed tense legal business meeting. They looked like lovers out having a good time.

No, couldn't be.

Annie was one of her best friends, and Bruce had known Annie forever. He'd never even mentioned finding her attractive, despite having a brief fling with her in high school. And Annie always treated Bruce strictly as an old friend, nothing more.

And Annie knew just how upset Elizabeth was about her breakup with Bruce. She had sat with Elizabeth at their favorite tapas restaurant, shortly after the breakup, listening to Elizabeth go over every painstaking detail about her feelings for Bruce. They'd gone through a pitcher of sangria. Annie knew how devastated Elizabeth was about losing Bruce. There was no way Annie would betray her like that.

Would she?

But she was there. Alone with Bruce. Drinking wine outside a cozy, romantic little bistro.

How long had she been there now? And did she really have to stay? The work was here.

Elizabeth felt jealousy begin to gnaw at the pit of her stomach. Annie was a young, attractive single woman, after all.

And she'd answered the phone at his villa. More than once. Did that mean something?

Elizabeth read more.

Annie and Bruce the fugitive are getting a bit too cozy in his villa. Maybe Easy Annie is back to her old ways!

Inwardly, Elizabeth sprung to her friend's defense. Caroline Pearce was unbelievable. Elizabeth knew how hard Annie had worked to put her less than pristine reputation from high school behind her. She felt angry that Caroline even brought it up. *How dare she?* Elizabeth thought, livid on her friend's behalf.

And . . . yet, Caroline's post planted a small, stubborn seed of doubt in Elizabeth's mind. She didn't want to admit it, but what if what Caroline said *was* true? What if Annie was seducing Bruce? What if she did revert back to her old self, the one who threw herself on any boy who would have her?

And Annie could say, well, he's not in a relationship anymore. And she would be technically right.

If she were the old Annie, then the old Bruce wouldn't be able to resist. Besides, Bruce was just angry enough at her to want to hurt Elizabeth as she had hurt him. It was painful to admit, but this was one way he could get her back.

No. Couldn't be. Bruce wouldn't do that. And even if he tried, surely Annie wouldn't let him. Annie had changed. So had Bruce. There was no way they would fall into bed together.

So why is she staying so long at his villa? A nagging voice in her mind wouldn't let it go.

Elizabeth had remembered the last time she stayed in Bruce's villa. She recalled the gorgeous views and amazing food and wine. The place was designed for seduction. She blinked the memories away.

For now, she wouldn't allow her thoughts to go there. She couldn't. She had to focus on her trip to Kentucky and finding the truth about Robin.

She had to trust that the new Bruce and the new Annie were above cheap sex and mindless flings. Not when so much was at stake, and not when they'd both come so far and matured so much.

9

"Garbage," Jessica muttered as she read through Caroline's Twitter feed on her iPhone. "I hope Annie sues her for libel."

"Sues who?" Liam asked, taking his seat opposite Jessica in the dining room of one of the swankiest new restaurants in Beverly Hills. Liam had insisted they go. It was a testament to his growing popularity that he was even in this dining room on a Saturday night, which had already seen the likes of Angelina Jolie and Brad Pitt earlier that week.

The waiters and busboys had taken note of him, as had a few other patrons in the restaurant. The sleek, modern dining room was filled with Hollywood types: producers, directors, and agents. Only a few of the other patrons were bold enough to stare right at Liam. Others sent more covert glances in their direction. Everyone, however, knew he was there.

"Caroline Pearce," Jessica muttered, and rolled her eyes. "She's telling lies about Bruce and Annie." At least, she hoped they were lies. Jessica had her own suspicions about Annie and Bruce. Annie did seem to be spending a lot of time there, but maybe it was just the case.

"Well, at least she's not talking about you." Liam glanced over at their waiter, who was hovering nearby, and gave him a quick nod. Jessica assumed Liam was going to order drinks.

"Right, but I know the gossip will hurt Lizzie."

"Jessica, I was hoping we could talk about us." Liam reached across the table and took the phone out of Jessica's hands and laid it on the table. Then he grabbed both of her hands and leaned over. His blue eyes bore intently into hers. He was handsome, strikingly so. It was no mystery why the camera loved him so much.

Jessica put aside her annoyance that he'd taken the phone away. She let herself live in the moment a little. After all, since Michael and Cal had dropped out of her life without even an explanation, she was glad she still had Liam. He loved her, even if no other man did.

"You know I love you," Liam began. "I've loved you almost since the moment I saw you. Do you remember?"

"How could I forget? You nearly ruined my grandmother's birthday!" Jessica was only partly joking. That was three years ago, when news of Todd and Jessica's relationship was still new. Elizabeth, heartbroken, fled to New York. She returned—with Liam on her arm—to Sweet Valley for her grandmother's birthday.

Liam, instantly smitten with Jessica, had drawn Todd's ire and jealousy, which in turn, started an argument that somehow ended with the entire table of Wakefields shouting at one another at Sweet Valley's posh country club.

"I did no such thing!" Liam exclaimed. "Back then, I was just a lowly bartender from New York, hoping to get my big acting break."

"You got it," Jessica said.

"And then some," Liam said, growing more serious. "Jessica, I've been successful beyond my wildest dreams. But it doesn't mean anything to me if I can't share it with the woman I love."

Suddenly, Liam let go of her hand and was kneeling in front of her in the restaurant, a small black velvet box in hand. It all happened so quickly that Jessica barely had time to react. The conversational buzz of the other diners at the restaurant abruptly died. Everyone took note of the famous movie star down on one knee.

All eyes turned to Jessica. Her face flamed with heat and her throat went dry as she felt a surge of panic.

She wasn't ready. Not for this, not with Liam. *Why is he always pushing so hard for what I'm not ready to give him?*

He opened the box, and a giant emerald-cut diamond in a platinum setting blazed under the restaurant's lights. It was more diamond than Jessica had ever seen up close. Easily worth half a million dollars.

"Liam . . ." She put up her hands. "Liam . . . the divorce isn't final. I don't even have the papers yet. I *can't* marry you."

"I know, but you can be engaged. This ring is just a promise that you *will* be with me."

"Liam . . . I can't accept that . . . I just . . ." Jessica felt like the walls of the restaurant were closing in. Suddenly, she couldn't breathe.

"Jessica, you can. Just try it on." Liam pulled the ring out of the box and slid it on her finger without waiting for an answer. The enormous diamond glittered under the lights. Beside her, she heard the pop of a champagne bottle and suddenly the waiter was beside them with overflowing glasses. Even though she hadn't said yes, the restaurant exploded with applause anyway. It reverberated loudly in her ears.

Jessica felt trapped, like she was riding a high-speed express train with no stops.

Liam stood and waved to the other patrons, and then he sat back in his seat, while Jessica stewed. She didn't like being boxed in like this; she didn't like being told what to do.

She slipped the heavy platinum ring off her finger.

"Liam, I can't take this," she said, her voice soft but firm. The rest of the dining room had already turned their attention back to their meals.

"You don't like the ring?" His voice was almost plaintive.

"It's beautiful, but I can't accept it." She put the ring back into Liam's palm.

"Jessica." Anger flashed in Liam's eyes.

"Liam, I'm not ready. You said you'd wait for me. Waiting doesn't mean giving me a ring to wear."

"It's a promise *to wait*. That I'll wait for you and you'll wait for me."

"No. It's a commitment I'm not ready to give."

Liam's face turned to stone, unreadable and hard. "I don't understand you." He got up from the table and tossed his napkin in his chair in disgust. "I don't understand you at all." Then he stalked away from the table.

Jessica felt a stab of panic. What if Liam decided he'd had enough of her, too? Could she survive losing her biggest fan? She ran after him and caught him at the valet stand.

"Liam, wait." She put her arm on his elbow. He turned, and she could see the pain in his face.

"I'm not saying no," she said. "I'm saying just not right now. Let the divorce go through, okay? Let things get settled between Todd and me."

"I hate Todd," Liam grumbled with a menace that took Jessica by surprise. "I hate the sound of his name. I hate everything about him. I hate that he ever had you."

"Liam. This isn't about Todd." Even as Jessica said the words, she wasn't quite sure. Didn't everything come back to Todd? "I have to get through this divorce before I can even think about getting married again. Jake is going through a lot, too, and he doesn't get to see his father as much as he'd like and I don't know about introducing a stepfather so soon." Jessica moved closer to him and wrapped her arm in his, cozying up to his side. "Liam, you know how much you mean to me. You're my . . . everything right now."

That got Liam's attention. Now, he seemed all ears. "You have to give me something," he said. "If you won't wear this ring, then you have to give me something."

Jessica thought he might mean sex. He'd been pressing her since that night at the Imagine Hotel.

"I don't know what I can give you," she said. She still wasn't ready to jump back into a physical relationship. He seemed to sense that and changed tactics.

"Tell me you love me," Liam said. "Tell me you love me and that will be enough."

"Liam . . ." She felt a little helpless. She couldn't do that, either.

"Fine." Liam's mouth drew into a thin line. He turned away, but Jessica grabbed his arm.

"Wait, Liam . . . I need you," Jessica whispered. The truth slipped out without her even intending it to.

"You do?" He turned and looked at her, his blue eyes hopeful. She hated feeling this vulnerable, this pathetic, but maybe this was just the new reality of her life right now.

She swallowed what was left of her pride.

"Yes, I do. I need you." Nobody else was as steadfast and loyal as Liam. He was her bedrock. Jessica stood on her tiptoes and planted a small kiss on Liam's mouth.

The little gesture awakened a deeper need in Liam. He pulled her closer, deepening the kiss, showing her how much he wanted her. They kissed so long that by the time he pulled away, the valet was standing awkwardly in front of them holding open the car's passenger door.

"You'll change your mind," Liam growled to her as he stalked to the car. He added something under his breath that Jessica couldn't quite hear.

She wondered if she'd done the right thing running after him. Would it have been better to just let him go?

But now, he was flashing her one of his brilliant smiles. He was placated, but Jessica couldn't help wondering how long the peace would last.

⌒

The next day, Liam came to her house bearing gifts—for Jake. While Jessica and Jake were having a lazy Sunday morning eating cereal in their pajamas, the doorbell rang. Jessica answered it to find Liam standing beside a giant motorized toy Hummer.

"Surprise!" Liam shouted in his Irish accent. Jake stood beside her, peeking out through the door. "Hey, sport! Look what Uncle Liam bought you! Come on, you can drive *this* toy. Take it for a spin."

The black plastic Hummer was wider than the sidewalk and had big wheels and a streak of red and orange flames painted along the side. Jake had never seen a toy truck that big. Liam laid on the horn inside and scared the toddler. He jumped back and hid behind Jessica.

"It's okay, Jake." Jessica patted Jake's head. "Do you want to go see the truck?"

Jake looked up at his mommy, a pleading look on his face. He shook his head silently. Jessica frowned. It wasn't like Jake to be so shy, especially when it came to trucks or trains. Jake never met one he didn't like.

After a little more coaxing than should've been necessary, Jessica eventually got Jake to agree to sit inside the truck. He hit the accelerator once, drove about halfway down the driveway, and then stopped and got out.

He frowned. The truck was big and unwieldy, and made for a four-year-old, not a two-year-old. Jake could barely reach the pedals, and he didn't quite have a handle on steering it. Soon he got frustrated. Jake didn't like the truck.

And he didn't like any of the other extravagant gifts Liam brought over the next two days. The huge, overstuffed bear sat in his room, unnoticed.

Even the giant ride-on train with the indoor track that Liam bought got used only once. The huge backyard slide sat neglected in back.

In fact, any time Liam came to the door at all, Jake would run and hide. Each big, new gift just seemed to scare him. Jessica saw that Jake wasn't thrilled with the presents, but didn't really know why.

Until the afternoon she got a call from Todd. Jessica was at work, and she ducked down in her cubicle a little so that her assistant, Emily, the spy, couldn't overhear.

"Jessica? We need to talk."

"Sure. I have a few minutes." She had more than a few minutes since Michael had all but reassigned every last one of her clients. Jessica's team was down to two people: herself and Emily. And Emily was hers only part-time, not that Jessica could even trust Emily to do anything at this point since Emily reported everything back to Tracy.

"I'm worried about Jake," Todd said.

Jessica sighed. This would be yet another Jake call. Jessica couldn't help but feel disappointed. She always hoped that Todd would want to talk about *them,* about being a family again. But he never did. It was always about Jake having a runny nose or Jake not eating his vegetables.

"What about Jake?" Jessica braced herself for the argument soon to come.

"He's afraid of Liam. And I don't think he should spend any time with your"—Todd coughed—"boyfriend."

"What are you talking about?"

"Jake told me that Liam scares him and that he doesn't like him."

"You can't be serious." Jessica sat up a little straighter in her desk. "You expect me to believe that?"

"Why *wouldn't* you believe it? Jake doesn't like Liam."

"Liam gives him presents all the time."

"That doesn't mean Jake likes them."

The kernel of truth in this made Jessica even more defensive. "Jake is just shy," Jessica said, trying to convince herself as much as Todd. She knew Jake wasn't always that excited to see Liam, but she wouldn't say he was *scared* of Liam. And Jake had never told her a thing. "If he was really scared, he would've told me."

"Maybe he just thought you would be mad."

"Or maybe this is just *you* not liking Liam and has nothing at all to do with Jake."

"Ha! That's rich. You think I'm jealous? Get over yourself."

That hurt a little more than Jessica would've liked to admit.

"You can't tell me what to do anymore."

"Oh, yes I can. Jake's my son, and I say Jake doesn't see Liam."

"You can't decide who Jake sees when he's with me."

"Jessica . . ."

"No, it's my life, Todd. And you're not in it anymore." The words were out, and she couldn't take them back. The silence hung over them, like a thick, itchy blanket that both wanted to get rid of, but neither one knew how to throw off. For a second, Jessica thought about trying to apologize. Had she gone too far?

"That's right, I'm not," Todd eventually said in a toneless voice. The next thing Jessica heard was a dial tone.

Jessica sat there, phone in hand, blood pressure soaring. She hated that her life had become a constant battle with the one person she really loved.

When had Todd become so unreasonable? And why couldn't he see how much his words still hurt her?

10

By the time Elizabeth's plane touched down in Lexington, Kentucky, she'd already spent the day traveling. There had been the flight from Los Angeles to Chicago, where she'd had a two-hour layover, and then the flight to Lexington. Having packed a light carry-on, she went straight to pick up her rental car. Ahead of her was the forty-minute drive to Richmond, where Robin Platt had grown up.

By the time she arrived, it was late already, so she checked into a Days Inn and decided to begin her investigation first thing in the morning.

The next day, Elizabeth drove straight to Richmond's city hall, located on Main Street, sandwiched between two-story row houses that gave the street an Old West feel. City Hall was a plain squat brown building with CITY HALL in blocky brown letters.

Elizabeth walked in and the soft tangy lilt of the southern accent all Richmond residents used washed over her. She found the people warm and friendly and eager to help. She quickly found the records she was looking for: Robin Platt's birth certificate, which confirmed that her mother was Ethel Platt and father, George. Elizabeth also found proof that, just like Robin had said, her father died twelve years ago from colon cancer and her mother died just two years ago.

Her parents left Robin the house she grew up in, an address Robin had given her, and Elizabeth also tracked down in the court records. She decided her next stop was there. She hoped there might be a neighbor who remembered her.

She found Robin's old house not too far from Main Street. The old white two-story farmhouse bore a large wraparound porch, complete with a creaky porch swing. When Elizabeth drove up, she saw a couple of small ride-on toddler toys on the porch, including a Thomas the Train scooter that her nephew Jake had. She figured young children lived there.

She parked and walked up to the front door where she rang the doorbell. A pretty young mother with her dark hair swept back in a ponytail answered, carrying a boy a little older than Jake on her hip.

"Yes?" she asked.

"Hi, sorry to bother you," Elizabeth began. "I'm . . ." Elizabeth stopped for a second. She was so used to saying "a reporter for the *Tribune*" that it almost popped out without her even thinking about it. But she didn't work for the *Tribune* anymore, not since she'd refused to run Robin's interview and her editor, Tim, had fired her. Elizabeth swallowed and tried again.

"A freelance writer," she said. This was true. She was freelance. Nobody was paying her at the moment, but it didn't change the fact she *was* a writer. "I'm doing some research on a story I'm working on involving Robin Platt."

"Robin Platt . . . why does that name sound so familiar?" the woman asked.

"She owned this house," Elizabeth prompted.

Recognition dawned on the woman's face. "Oh, right. She did. I never actually met her. We bought this house two years ago, when we moved here from Lexington. But she'd already moved out somewhere west, I think. The sale was all taken care of through her lawyer."

"Do you happen to have that lawyer's name?"

The woman paused. "Hold on a second. I can get it for you." She put down her son, who toddled after her. She ducked back in the house and returned with a big legal-sized manila envelope with her mortgage papers in it. Her youngest boy, probably no more than two, peeked out from between her legs.

"She left her card in here . . ." She dug around in the folder and retrieved it. "Christina Parr. Here's her number."

Elizabeth looked at the card and jotted it down. "Thanks so much. This helps," she said.

The young mother shut the door and Elizabeth decided to knock on some neighbors' doors.

At the house next door, Elizabeth found an older woman sitting in a rocking chair on her porch with a steaming cup of tea.

She approached and introduced herself. "Did you happen to know the Platt family?" she asked the woman with the gray-white hair in a bun. Elizabeth put her age in the mid-eighties.

"Oh, yes, I did. They were a nice family," the woman said. "Very sweet. Shame the father died of cancer, and the mother, she died not so long ago. Heart attack, I think."

"Did you know their daughter, Robin?"

"Yes, I did. She was a sweet little thing. Great artist, too. She made Halloween signs for the whole neighborhood. Had quite a talent, that girl. She also painted Christmas decorations. I even have one of her plywood Santas."

"Really?" So it was true what Robin said about being an artist.

"Oh, yes. I'm sure she is a successful artist by now. Is that why you're doing a story on her? Talented girl."

Elizabeth was starting to feel dejected. So far, everything Robin had said was panning out. There were no inconsistences. Her worry that the trip might have been a waste of time grew.

"Right. Thanks for the help," Elizabeth said before retreating back to her car and driving back to Main Street. She stopped in a little coffee shop and brought in her laptop. Amazingly, she found a place with WiFi. As she ate a sandwich for lunch, she went over the other information she had on Robin.

Elizabeth had pressed Robin to give her the names of a couple of high school friends: Hillary Park and Shannon Kent. She knew the two would probably be married. She booted up her computer and did a quick Facebook search. Hillary had left town and now lived in Chicago, but Shannon still lived in the area.

After lunch, Elizabeth swung by her house. She found no one home, but did find a sign on the street with Shannon's picture on it. She was a real estate agent in Lexington. Elizabeth dialed the number.

"Hello?" a hurried voice asked.

"Hi, my name is Elizabeth. You don't know me, but I'm calling about Robin Platt."

"Robin? I haven't heard that name in years!" Elizabeth heard background noise, like Shannon might have the phone on speaker while driving in a car.

"I'm doing some research on her for a story I'm working on and just wanted to know how you knew her."

"She was a sweet girl. Really sweet. We went to high school together. We were both on the swim team."

"Can you tell me what she was like?"

"Sweet." Shannon offered nothing else.

"Did she have any boyfriends or anything? Anyone I could talk to?"

There was a long pause on the other end of the phone. "Uh . . . look, now is not really a good time . . ."

"If you could just give me a quick name. Someone to talk to, then . . ."

"Try Josh Elliott. He's in Lexington now."

"Oh, great. Thanks. Do you know how long they dated?"

"Look, I'm actually showing a house now. I've got to go. Sorry. Bye." And then she'd hung up.

Strange.

Why had the topic of boyfriends caused her to want to end the call?

Elizabeth scribbled down "Josh Elliott" and then made a note to look him up. As she sat in her car, she pulled up Facebook on her phone and did a quick search for the name. She found several dozen Josh Elliotts on Facebook, but only two who lived in Kentucky. She messaged them both and hoped to hear back.

In the meantime, she decided her next stop was the Richmond police station. She went to the clerk's office and ran Robin's name, just to make sure she'd never been arrested. Her name never came up.

That was the sum of day one. Day two began with her taking a drive through Richmond, where she happened upon St. Mark's Catholic Church, a white stone building with a small steeple in front and decorated with three pretty stained-glass windows. On a whim, she pulled into the little circular drive in front, parking her car near the double red doors.

Robin said she'd attended mass regularly at a Catholic church in Sweet Valley, and it had been her priest who had first come forward at her request about the allegations, so Elizabeth figured the girl probably also had a hometown church.

She walked around to the office building, and in through the open doors. She found a receptionist up front with her brown hair up in a bun. She gave Elizabeth a smile.

"May I help you?"

"I was looking for a friend of mine, Robin Platt. I thought she might be a member of this church."

"Robin Platt? I don't think I've heard that name. Let me ask Father Robert." She turned and walked toward the back. In a few minutes, she'd returned with a middle-aged priest with a receding hairline and wire-frame glasses.

"I'm sorry. Robin Platt, did you say? I don't think she's a member of our church."

"It might have been a few years ago," Elizabeth said.

"I've been here fourteen years and I've never known a Robin Platt. We don't even have a Platt family in our congregation."

"Thanks, anyway," Elizabeth said, and made her way back to the car. A quick search on her phone found just one other Catholic church in Richmond. She drove there, but found Robin hadn't been a member there, either.

Strange, she thought as she climbed back into her rental sedan; Robin had said she regularly went to mass in Sweet Valley. But neither of the two Catholic churches here had ever heard of her. She could have converted or decided to join a church later in life. But it just seemed a strange choice for a woman in her twenties who'd just moved to California.

It was odd, but it certainly wasn't enough to prove Robin had lied about the attempted rape charges.

Elizabeth glanced through her notes. She still had Robin's lawyer to talk to, but she wasn't sure she'd get anywhere, since there was attorney-client privilege even on real estate transactions. She called Christina's office, but soon discovered Robin's attorney had retired and now lived somewhere in Florida.

Another dead end.

By day three, she was almost out of leads.

Wandering through downtown Richmond, she headed into a diner, hoping for some good, old-fashioned luck. She asked a friendly waitress whether she knew Robin, but found she didn't. The waitress asked the manager, who admitted he had a vague recollection of her, but not much else.

Elizabeth's phone binged. She glanced down at the face and saw an alert from Facebook. She pulled up the app and saw a message waiting for her from Josh Elliott. His profile picture had him wearing aviator sunglasses and pressing oversized headphones to one ear. He was a guy in his twenties, obviously DJing somewhere, probably a club in Lexington. His message read:

YEAH, I KNEW ROBIN. I "DATED" HER FOR THREE MONTHS BEFORE I FINALLY FIGURED OUT SHE PLAYS FOR THE WRONG TEAM. EVERY-BODY AT SCHOOL KNEW BUT ME!

Surprised, Elizabeth messaged him back:

ARE YOU SAYING THAT ROBIN PLATT IS A LESBIAN?

Josh must've been on Facebook, because he instantly replied:

YOU CATCH ON QUICK.

Robin never mentioned that before. Elizabeth wondered why. But it also explained why her friend had been cagey when Elizabeth had asked about boyfriends. Elizabeth wondered if Robin was still in the closet. Surely it would've been hard for her to grow up gay in a small, conservative town. Elizabeth knew some of the pain and fear her own brother, Steven, had experienced spending most of his life in the closet. He'd feared rejection and ridicule from everyone he knew. He'd even married, only to come to terms with his true identity later in life.

She could only imagine what it had been like for Robin.

Maybe that's why Robin didn't respond to Bruce when he tried to pick her up that night at the bar.

Instantly, Elizabeth shook herself. Why was she assuming Bruce *had* hit on her at all? Why did she keep yo-yoing back and forth between Robin and Bruce, blowing whichever way the wind took her?

Bruce was right to leave.

She had no loyalty.

And now he might be moving on . . . with Annie. The thought was so painful, she couldn't really allow herself to consider it for very long. It was much easier just to focus on Robin Platt.

Elizabeth drove back to her motel room, feeling down. She'd found nothing that definitely proved Robin's case either way, but most of what she said had checked out. The reason for her moving to California, her parents, and where she'd lived. All of that was true. The inconsistencies about her churchgoing habits and sexual preference really had no bearing at all as far as she could tell. Elizabeth texted Jessica with the news that she wasn't finding anything.

Elizabeth had spent three days in Richmond, but had found nothing except that Robin seemed to be telling the truth.

She found it impossible not to feel disappointed.

Elizabeth's melancholy came through in her text messages, and Jessica felt like the wind had been taken out of her sails, too. She had been hoping Elizabeth would quickly prove Robin a fraud, and that this nightmare would be over, and that maybe Bruce and Elizabeth could find their way back to each other.

Of course, that might never happen if Caroline Pearce's rumors were true and Bruce was moving on to Annie. Jessica hoped Caroline was dead wrong, but it was hard to shake the feeling that it was weird Annie was staying in Cannes so long. Maybe there was something to Caroline's gossip.

Jessica sighed. She missed her sister and wished Elizabeth were home. She'd only told her the shortened version of Liam's proposal and her big argument with Todd about Jake, and she badly wanted to rehash all the details with *someone*.

Jessica dialed Lila's number. Instantly, it went to voice mail—again. Either Lila had lost her phone, or she was avoiding Jessica's calls. This was the third time she'd gotten voice mail this week and Lila hadn't returned a single call.

Jessica knew Lila was going through a lot and had gone into hiding since the *True Housewives* scandal broke, but she'd never gone this long without calling Jessica before. Jessica wondered if it was because Lila worried she'd gloat and say *I told you so* about the fake pregnancy. Lila had always hated it when she was forced to admit Jessica had been right about something.

Still, something felt off. But all she could do was keep calling and texting and hope Lila returned one of her calls sometime.

Jessica glanced at her watch. It was nearly six and she didn't have any important clients to stay late for these days, so she shut off her computer and packed up her bag. As she walked out of the office, Michael deliberately avoided eye contact and Tracy did, too. Sometimes she felt like Dead Woman Walking at work. Michael had taken away her team; Tracy hated

sister's love for a chance with Todd. They'd risked everything to be together, to take a chance at what both of them knew felt so right, of what
should be. And now, all too quickly, after a few short years, they'd come
apart, and neither one could understand quite how they'd gotten here, with
so many obstacles between them.

Jake, normally bubbly and loud, went silent, watching both parents
carefully, like a scientist in the field. He didn't miss a single pained look.
While he didn't understand what it all meant, he could feel the weight
of unspoken emotion between the two people he loved most in the
world.

Jessica looked away first, and then the spell was broken. Todd ruffled
his son's floppy hair and turned away, walking to his Jeep without another
backward glance.

Jake watched him go, his floppy hair falling into his face, as his bottom
lip started to quiver.

Jessica knew that look. Todd climbed in his Jeep and started the engine. He hadn't even backed down out of the driveway before Jake started
to cry.

Jessica felt a catch in her own throat. For the last several times after
Todd left, Jake cried. She gently scooped her son into her arms and carried him inside. She felt like crying herself, but she had to put on a brave
face for Jake.

"I want Daddy!" Jake wailed, now safely inside.

"I know you do. You'll see him soon." Jessica rubbed Jake's back, but
the little boy was nearly inconsolable as big, wet tears splashed down his
smooth cheeks.

"But I want him! I miss Daddy!" And then he burst into another wail.
Each one cut straight through Jessica, like an ice-cold wind. She felt like
crying, too. The tears burned the back of her throat.

"It's not fair! Not fair!" he wailed, and Jessica couldn't agree more.

Nothing about her life right now was fair. Todd was the man she truly
loved—maybe the only man she'd ever truly loved. Why wasn't she with
him?

Because of Sarah. Because of Liam. Because of all kinds of other complications.

On the coffee table, Jessica's phone dinged and the face lit up. Another text from Liam.

Jessica rocked Jake in her lap, and he began to calm down a little, even as Jessica thought how unfair it all was. She and Todd had caused pain to poor Elizabeth three years ago because they couldn't help it—they'd fallen in love. Neither one had wanted it, but it had happened anyway; the magnetic force pulling them together was not to be denied. They'd gotten married, had a son, and now they were getting a divorce just like that. Not because they didn't love each other, not because the attraction wasn't as strong as ever, but because of lifestyles, philosophies, careers, complications that now seemed hard to even quantify. And without foolish pride, even solvable, when she thought about it.

How could Jessica sit here and let Liam or Sarah come in the way of her and Todd?

Three years ago, she hadn't let Elizabeth get in the way, she realized. This was her best friend, her twin sister, her life, the person she least wanted to hurt in the world. And the only way she could ever have justified doing it was for a love so strong, so compelling, so irresistible, she couldn't help herself.

And yet, now, she was letting something as small as Liam and Sarah stand in the way?

For the briefest of moments, Jessica wondered if she was sabotaging herself. Did she feel guilty for taking Todd from Elizabeth? Was this somehow a self-punishment for the pain she'd caused Elizabeth?

And maybe she deserved it.

But Elizabeth had forgiven her. She'd said so. Jessica should forgive herself, too. Now, there was more than just her involved: there was Jake to think about. She grabbed a tissue from the box on the coffee table and dabbed at his eyes. Jake took deep, shaky breaths as he calmed down from his cry and looked up at her with pain and heartbreak in his blue eyes. He wanted her to fix this.

And she would.

And the first step was breaking things off with Liam. It wouldn't guarantee that Todd would come back to her. It might already be too late. But Jessica had to try.

Her phone began to ring on the coffee table. Now Liam was calling. He couldn't leave well enough alone. She felt a prickle of anger and annoyance. Could he really care for her so much if he didn't respect her wishes? It was always what he wanted on his terms.

She realized in that moment what she had to do. She needed to stop pretending that Liam was any kind of substitute for Todd.

And the first step would be ending her relationship with Liam.

For good this time. And right now.

She had to try again with Todd. She owed it to Jake and herself.

12

The next morning, Aaron was sitting in a business meeting in San Diego, listening to a new client discuss the pros and cons of installing geothermal heating in a new office building they wanted him to design, but his mind was a few blocks away.

He was thinking about Robin Platt, and about Elizabeth's plea for him to keep looking for any connection between her and Rick Warner. He'd been to Warner Natural Gas headquarters half a dozen times so far, posing as an architecture graduate student wanting to know more about Warner and his impressive skyscraper that had altered the city's skyline.

He'd pored through employee records while there, doing his own undercover spy mission, but the best he came up with was a woman who matched Robin's description—a Rose Pally—but it turned out they weren't the same person at all.

While coming and going from Warner Natural Gas, he'd managed to compile a list of all Warner female employees in their twenties. The list contained more than thirty names, and slowly but surely Aaron had Googled all of them. Through Facebook, Twitter, and LinkedIn, he'd been able to confirm that all but one of them were definitely not Robin Platt.

The last one—Mona Thomas—he couldn't find anywhere. It was like she was a ghost. No Facebook page. No LinkedIn. No blog. Nothing. He had nothing to prove she was Robin Platt, but he had nothing to prove she wasn't, either.

He needed to get back to Warner Gas.

"What do you think, Aaron?" asked his client at the end of the long conference room table.

I think I need to get there before lunch hour is over, Aaron thought, glancing up at the clock. Lunchtime on Thursdays was the perfect time to do research, he'd found. Nola, the receptionist who'd taken a liking to him over the last few weeks, was on desk duty, so she was there to answer questions, and few other people were around to ask why he was spending so much time in the office.

⌒

Aaron arrived at Warner Gas a little after noon. Nola's face lit up when she saw him.

"Back again?" she sang, happy to have a little diversion from her front desk duties. "You must be the hardest working graduate student in your class."

"I try." Aaron smiled. "By the way, I didn't know if you brought your lunch, but I've got an extra panini if you want one."

"You're a lifesaver!" Nola declared, snatching up the little white bag Aaron offered. "All I've got in the kitchen is a Lean Cuisine I do *not* want to eat."

Aaron smiled. He knew the way to Nola's heart. Croissants and panini. "Mind if I use my usual cube?"

"Go on," Nola said, and smiled. Since Aaron made regular trips back to Warner Gas and had become quick friends with Nola, she'd not only let him use an empty cube, but had given him her password to use to log in to the computer, where many of the blueprints of the building were kept in large PDFs.

Of course, Aaron wasn't looking for blueprints. He was looking for anything he could find on Mona Thomas.

He glanced quickly around to see if anyone was watching him. As usual, most Warner employees had gone to lunch already, and Nola was busy with a phone call.

He searched quickly through the HR database and pulled up Mona Thomas's file.

He scanned it quickly. There was no picture, just her birthday (making her twenty-three). She had been let go after only just a year. The official reason? "Undependable."

In the document, it looked like large segments were deleted, including her address and phone number, and a separate file, one that was only marked *Mona Thomas* was locked, requiring a special password he didn't have.

Interesting.

Aaron did another Google search, just to see if anything new popped up, but couldn't find a single entry that seemed to match the Mona Thomas he was looking for.

This girl was a ghost online and appeared to be a ghost at Warner Gas, too. He glanced up and saw Nola getting off the phone. Maybe she knew something about Mona Thomas. Nola knew a little bit about everyone at Warner Gas.

13

As Elizabeth checked out of her motel room and packed up her rental car, she couldn't help but feel like she was wasting her time in Kentucky. She hadn't found anything that contradicted what Robin had told her. Everything so far checked out.

The only thing slightly different was the ex-boyfriend who claimed Robin was a lesbian. But, then again, he could've just been bitter or lying. And that new information wasn't even really relevant to Bruce's case. She had nothing left to do but head to the airport, even though her flight wasn't until much later that afternoon, and it wasn't yet lunchtime.

On the road out to the airport, on the forty-minute drive to Lexington, she passed by the Lexington Center for Recovery.

It was a drug and alcohol rehab center. She hadn't seen the sign on the drive to Richmond, but it had been nighttime then and she'd been in a hurry.

Elizabeth slowed down as she glanced at the rehab center in her rearview mirror. No one had hinted that Robin had ever gone to rehab. There'd been nothing to suggest there was a link at all. Yet it was the one place Elizabeth hadn't been to. And if being a journalist had taught Elizabeth anything, it was that everybody had dirty little secrets. This could've been Robin's. If she was a lesbian, growing up gay in a small town like Richmond couldn't have been easy. Maybe she had turned to drugs or alcohol as an escape. It wouldn't be the first time a troubled teen found solace in self-medication.

And she had hours until her flight. What was she going to do, just sit at the airport?

On a whim, she pulled over off the next exit ramp and made a U-turn, crossing under the freeway and headed back the way she came. *Might as well check it out,* she thought.

14

Aaron sat for a second in his cube, trying to think of a good reason to ask Nola about Mona Thomas. He knew he had to find a way to get the information without it seeming too weird or suspicious. He thought—not for the first time—he'd make a lousy Tom Cruise. This whole spy business wasn't for him. He was an architect, not an undercover agent!

He pulled up the picture Elizabeth had sent him of Robin Platt on his phone. He gazed at the blond twenty-something, as if the mute picture could offer him a good plan.

He had to come up with something. Why would he be asking around about a twenty-three-year-old former employee?

He could say they dated, although he was happily married to a man. Not that Nola knew that.

In fact, Nola assumed Aaron had a girlfriend and he'd let her believe it. It seemed easiest. *But how do I ask about Mona Thomas?*

Aaron watched as a couple of clerks filed past him, gossiping about someone who worked at Warner Gas. He didn't hear the particulars, but given that he already knew Nola loved gossip, maybe he should just pretend he overheard them talking about Mona Thomas. She'd been fired and her file was heavily edited. There had to be a story there. And Nola would probably be happy to tell him if she knew it.

Aaron glanced at the picture of Robin Platt once more and then dropped his phone into his shirt pocket. As he approached Nola's cube, she smiled.

"Find everything you need?"

"On the thesis front, yes," Aaron said. "But I've got a different question for you. I heard someone back there talk about something that sounded like good gossip. You've been holding out on me!"

"What gossip?" Nola perked up instantly. The forty-something receptionist loved office scandal almost as much as she loved a free panini.

"You have to tell me: who *is* Mona Thomas anyway?" Aaron asked.

"Mona Thomas! They were talking about her?" Nola glanced around to see if anyone was looking. Then she motioned him back around the side of the desk, which he did.

"Mona is nothing but trouble. She was hired as an accountant's assistant, but I hardly ever saw her when she did work here. Rumor has it she was sleeping with somebody in upper management. But she was fired for embezzlement. Apparently, she diverted some company funds straight into her own account."

"Seriously?"

"Oh, and it gets worse. She was also a drug addict, apparently. That's why she stole money—to support her habit. She was fired at least six months or so ago, I think."

"Wow. Any charges filed against her?"

"No, that's the strange thing. But I guess the company just didn't want to pursue it. I think Warner was just glad to be rid of her!" Nola shifted her elbow on her desk and accidentally knocked a pen to the ground.

Ever the gentleman, Aaron bent down to get it, but as he did so, the cell phone he carried in his shirt pocket clattered to the carpet. It fell right at Nola's feet and the screen lit up, with a brilliant picture of Robin

Platt—the last thing he'd been looking at on his phone before he'd sauntered over to Nola's desk.

Shit, Aaron thought. *This is why I don't work for the CIA!*

"Hey . . . that's her!" Nola exclaimed, glancing at the phone.

"Who?"

"Mona Thomas!"

Aaron couldn't believe his luck. He'd just found the link he'd been looking for. He needed to tell Elizabeth!

But suddenly, Nola's expression changed, and the naïve, trusting, easily flattered, maybe even foolish woman turned hard and cold with suspicion. "Hold on. Why do you have a picture of Mona Thomas on your phone? Just what's this all about?"

EPISODE 6

Bittersweet

1

Elizabeth pulled into the circular drive for the Lexington Center for Recovery in Kentucky, not too far from the Lexington airport, and parked her rental car in a visitor's space near the front door. She was still not sure what she hoped to find there. Whatever it was, it had to be a long shot. She'd been all over Robin Platt's hometown, Richmond, with no luck, and now she was almost done with her trip. In a few hours she'd catch a flight back to California.

She'd come up with nothing. Everything Robin had ever said about herself, down to her childhood friends, had checked out. And if everything she'd said was true, then maybe it was also true that Bruce Patman had attacked her that night. And yet she felt in her heart that wasn't the truth.

No, Elizabeth couldn't concede defeat. She wouldn't. She was here to help Bruce, and she wouldn't stop until she was satisfied that there was no other possibility.

She'd only pulled into the drug addiction treatment center on a whim. She knew she was reaching, but she was early for her flight and she had time. What if Robin had been a patient there? It was beyond a long shot; it was desperation. She knew the treatment center wouldn't tell her about its patients. But she couldn't shake the feeling that she should check it out anyway.

Maybe it was Robin's sometimes shaky hands. When Elizabeth had surprised her once, she had seemed a bit frantic, a little too jumpy, and not just with coffee jitters. There was something weird about Robin and her tremors. And she was often secretive about her apartment, rarely letting Elizabeth in on the first knock. She was always picking up—or hiding something—before opening the door. Suppose she was into drugs. Or alcohol. It would explain a lot.

Not to mention the rumor Elizabeth heard from one of her old boyfriends that Robin might have been a lesbian. The stress of staying in the closet in a small town could've driven her to drugs.

Elizabeth knew she was exaggerating the possibilities, but it was her last chance here. She didn't want to go home empty-handed. She couldn't.

She walked through the sliding glass doors of the recovery center and headed to the front desk, making up her story in her head as she went.

"Hi," she said, smiling at the man behind the counter. He was wearing a white jacket, like an orderly. "Is there someone here who can tell me a little about this place? I'm here for my sister. I think she could use . . . help."

The tall guy blinked. "I'll get the director for you," he said, nodding. A few seconds later, a trim woman with jet-black hair and bronzed skin, wearing a slate-gray suit, came to the front desk.

"I'm Stacey Walter," she said. "May I help you?"

"Hi, Stacey. I'm here to look at your facility and ask a few questions. I think my sister needs help from a place like this."

"Certainly. Of course. Here, let me give you a visitor's pass and then I can take you on a tour."

"Thank you." Elizabeth glanced around at the cream-colored walls and mint-green tiled floor. Behind the receptionist's desk two hallways stretched in opposite directions. The doors Elizabeth could see were closed. She wondered just what she was looking for. A picture of Robin? Someone who knew her? She'd take anything at this point.

"And what was your name?"

Elizabeth met the director's eyes. "Rachel Platt."

The director stopped writing. Elizabeth's heart leaped . . .

"Is that two *ts*?"

. . . and dropped. "Yes, two *ts*."

The director finished writing the name tag and handed it to Elizabeth.

"Rachel, come right this way," the director said, punching in the code to unlock the door behind her. "First, you should know that we pride ourselves on a very impressive success rate for our patients. We believe in a very holistic approach to treating drug and alcohol dependency."

Elizabeth nodded and pretended to listen while she scanned the hallway, trying to get a glimpse into patient rooms, not really knowing what she was looking for. They walked past several group-therapy rooms, and then out the back door and into a small garden where some patients congregated, smoking cigarettes.

Elizabeth noticed that they seemed older, maybe in their forties.

"My sister is only twenty-three," Elizabeth said. "Would she fit in here? Do you even take patients that young?"

"Oh, yes, we do." The director nodded. "We even have a small wing dedicated to teen addiction."

"Oh, good. Well, that makes sense."

They were ending the tour, and Elizabeth hadn't found out anything more about Robin Platt or if she'd even been here at all. She was beginning to feel like this was a fool's errand, a long shot hardly worth pursuing. What did Elizabeth think she'd find anyway? As they approached the front doors of the treatment center, she was prepared to call it a wash.

"Well, if you need anything else, let me know." Stacey gave Elizabeth her business card and opened the front door for her. "If you'd like to talk to some of our therapists, I'd be happy to arrange a meeting. Just let me know."

Elizabeth walked back to her car, dejected. Her last-ditch effort had turned up nothing. Now there was nothing to do but head to the airport and admit the truth: She'd failed.

2

"Just who are you?" Nola, the receptionist at Warner's gas company, asked Aaron, the pretend architecture student. "And what are you doing with a picture of Mona Thomas on your phone?"

Aaron Dallas looked at his phone and tried to think of an answer. He had been tricking Nola for weeks now in order to dig up information that might prove Rick Warner, the company's owner and Bruce Patman's sworn enemy, had something to do with the attempted rape charges against Bruce.

And now he might have found it: Bruce's accuser, the once-unassailable, perfect victim Robin Platt was actually Mona Thomas, an embezzler and former Warner employee. He'd pulled off a *Columbo*-level detective job, but he'd blown his cover in the process. Nola was seconds away from calling security, probably to have him arrested.

"Nola, I can explain." Cold sweat trickled down Aaron's back as he frantically searched for a believable lie. *Think, Aaron,* he screamed in his head. *Think of something!* He had another rash thought: *Could I really go to jail? Is this corporate espionage? Could I, Emma's dad, husband of Steven Wakefield, the respected lawyer, a successful architect in my own right, end up a convicted criminal? I can't go to jail!*

This had all happened because Elizabeth Wakefield, his sister-in-law, had asked him to help Bruce. He loved Liz and would do most anything for her.

Nola frowned. "You sneak around asking about people and then you have a picture of Mona Thomas. It doesn't add up. Just who *are* you? You're not an architecture graduate student."

That had been his cover, despite the fact that he hadn't been a student for years.

"No, you got me, I'm not."

"I'm calling security." She picked up her phone.

"No, wait! Nola!" Aaron put up his hand like a school crossing guard.

"Okay, I'm not a graduate student." Aaron grasped at any story to explain himself—anything but the truth.

There were those rumors swirling around that Mona Thomas was fired for stealing and drug use. Aaron remembered Steven talking about lawyers at his firm who handled just that kind of case. In an instant, he had his story.

"I'm working for Mona Thomas."

"What?"

"She's suing for discrimination and termination of employment without cause. I'm an investigator for the law firm."

"That little bitch!" Nola exclaimed. "She was a thief. She deserved to be fired."

Aaron shrugged. Nola's face clouded with suspicion. "Wait," she said, "if you're working for her, why did you look so surprised just now about her picture on your phone?"

"What?" Aaron's heart thumped.

"It looked like you had no idea that was Mona on your phone."

"No. I mean, yes, I knew it was her. Of course, I did, I just . . ." Again, Aaron scrambled for an excuse. "I just didn't want to blow my cover. But now the jig is up."

"Well, Mona has no case. You're working for the losing side."

"Yeah, that's the way it's looking to me," he said. "I can almost guarantee my firm will drop her."

"They should," Nola said, picking up the phone. She narrowed her eyes at him, suspicion still simmering there. "I still think I should call security."

Aaron squared his shoulders.

"And tell them what? You let a discrimination attorney's investigator in here to look through the company files?"

Nola's mouth dropped open in shock. Aaron hated to play hardball, but he didn't see that he had a choice.

"You wouldn't." Nola put the phone down slowly.

"Look, Mona doesn't have a case," Aaron said, softening his tone. "You don't have to be involved. Why risk it? None of this is going to come out. You won't see me again."

"I think it was very underhanded what you did." Nola glared at him.

"I'm sorry, but what can I do? It's my job." Aaron began backing away from Nola's desk and toward the exit.

"I don't want to see you again," Nola said.

"You won't. I'm going. Sorry," Aaron said, apologizing his way to the elevator. "Really sorry."

And he was sorry. She was a nice woman but not worth getting arrested for, and besides, this could be great news for Bruce. And Aaron couldn't help feeling slightly brilliant for the way he'd pulled that last bit off. What a recovery.

Maybe the CIA could use an architect.

On the way to his car, he texted both Jessica and Elizabeth.

GOT IT! YOU'RE NEVER GOING TO BELIEVE THIS.

3

Just as Elizabeth stepped through the entrance to the Lexington airport, her phone dinged. She fished it out of the side pocket of her bag.

ROBIN PLATT DID WORK FOR RICK WARNER. BUT SHE USED A DIFFER-
ENT NAME: MONA THOMAS! SECRETARY CONFIRMED: THE PIC YOU SENT IS
MONA THOMAS.

Aaron had attached the picture Elizabeth had sent him.

The wheels in Elizabeth's head whirled. Why had Robin used a different name? What was she hiding?

Another text from Aaron came through.

BTW, MONA THOMAS WAS FIRED FROM WARNER GAS FOR EMBEZZLING
TO SUPPORT A DRUG HABIT!

Drugs. That was the connection she was looking for. She thought about the girl who was Robin or Mona and realized her suspicions were right: Drugs were somehow involved. Elizabeth felt she now had the evidence she had been looking for.

She had to get back to that rehab center to talk to the director again.

She wheeled her luggage straight back out and jumped into the first cab she found.

When the cab arrived at the rehab center, Elizabeth asked the driver to wait. She still hoped she could get what she'd come for and still make the plane to Sweet Valley that night.

Elizabeth swallowed her nerves and walked back into the recovery center. She had to find out if Mona Thomas had been a patient there. Aaron had said she'd been fired from Warner Gas for theft to fuel a drug habit. From a quick iPad search in the cab, she'd found Mona Thomas on Facebook, but the profile was set to private and she couldn't get access to pictures. She did, however, see that Mona Thomas had gone to the same high school in Richmond that Robin had.

She walked up to the front desk.

"Hi, I was just here, and I need to see Stacey again, please," Elizabeth said. She noticed the locked gate at the front desk was not quite latched this time.

"I'm sorry," the orderly behind the desk said as he glanced back and saw the director's door, which was slightly ajar. "It looks like the director is in a meeting. I'd be happy to take a message."

Elizabeth looked at the clock on the wall behind him. She didn't have time. She'd need to be on the road to the airport in no more than fifteen minutes.

"No, I'm sorry. I have to see her now."

"I'm afraid I can't let you through. You can wait over there if you'd like."

Elizabeth thought about pushing her way back to the director's office but froze in a moment of nerves. She backed down, going to sit on the bench.

Immediately, she felt like a coward, just sitting and waiting. Her sister, Jessica, wouldn't just take "no" for an answer, would she? Elizabeth stewed for a couple of minutes. She was tired of playing by the rules. Besides, if she was going to help Bruce, she needed to find her courage.

The phone rang and the orderly picked it up. While he was turned away from her, Elizabeth knew what she had to do. She stood and strode purposefully straight past the front desk toward the director's office.

"Hey! You can't go in there!" cried the orderly behind her, but it was already too late. Elizabeth had her hand on the knob. She threw open the door and saw the director sitting behind her desk, a look of surprise on her face. She was talking to a woman with a salt-and-pepper bob and wire-rimmed glasses.

"Excuse me?" Stacey said.

"I need to talk to you." Elizabeth was proud her voice remained firm and in control. The orderly appeared behind her. He put a hand on her arm. She pulled away from him.

"Stacey?" the orderly asked.

"It's okay, Mike." The director nodded to him to let Elizabeth go. "I'll handle this."

"You have answers, and I need them." Elizabeth surprised herself with her own forcefulness. She took out her phone and pulled up the picture of Robin Platt, now Mona Thomas.

"Do you know this girl?" Elizabeth held up her phone almost in the director's face.

Surprise—and clear recognition—darted across the director's face before she could suppress it.

"Mona? How did you—" Stacey began, and then stopped, realizing she might have revealed too much.

"Mona Thomas, right?" Elizabeth finished. "That's what I thought! You need to tell me about her."

"I can't tell you about our patients," the director said quickly.

So, she was a patient here. Bingo, Elizabeth thought.

"You can and you will because your patient is my sister."

"I thought your name was Rachel Platt."

"It doesn't matter what my name is." Elizabeth's voice rose. "You have to tell me about Mona. Now."

"And why do I have to do that?"

Elizabeth swallowed. It was time for her big play.

"Because our mom has terminal cancer, that's why."

Dead silence filled the room as the two women in front of Elizabeth absorbed the shock.

"That's right. I promised *my dying mother* that I'd find Mona. And you need to help me do that. Or I'm going to tell the *Lexington Post* and Channel Five and anybody else who'll listen how you denied a dying woman her last wish."

Elizabeth's voice was loud now, drawing the attention of a visiting family signing in at the front desk.

"No need for that," Stacey said, standing. "We'll help. Please sit. Let's talk about your sister." Stacey walked around her desk and shut the office door behind Elizabeth.

Relieved her ploy had worked, Elizabeth sat down. She glanced at the other woman in the office.

"This is Lee Anne," the director said. "She knew your sister, too."

Elizabeth nodded at the woman. "Tell me: Why did you let her go when you knew she wasn't well yet?"

"She's a troubled girl, but we can't keep people here against their will. And, I'll have you know, she left us with her portion of the bill unpaid. She owes us quite a lot."

"But she needed your help. You failed her. Now my mother is dying and all she wants is to say good-bye to her daughters—both of them."

The director sighed, regaining a bit of her composure and her patience. "I'm sorry about your mother. I am sure this is hard for you."

Elizabeth grabbed a tissue off the director's desk and buried her dry eyes in it. "I just don't understand what happened. We were so close, my sister and I, and now I don't know her at all. I find out through friends she's partying again and . . . I thought I could trust you to make her better. So did my mom. She was devastated when she heard Mona had been released and wasn't any better than she'd been before. And no one let us know."

These words seemed to hit the director hard.

"Look, I know what you're feeling. My brother also had an addiction and it tore our family apart. He lied to us and every time we tried to help him, he would just disappear. Sometimes, the only time we'd even know he was still alive was when he showed up at the ER from an overdose."

"Then you know what I'm going through. The least you could do is tell me why she left. How did it happen? Please."

The director paused and glanced at the other woman in the room.

"You're my last hope to understanding all this," Elizabeth said, continuing her full-court press. "My sister isn't talking to me and I can't find her. The entire family thought she was in rehab, but now we find out she's out on the loose doing God knows what. I don't even know where she is. She could be unconscious on the street somewhere. Please. Give me something. My mom has worried herself sick. Literally. You know what it's like to wait and worry and not know. I don't know how much time my mother has left. I might not even find Mona before she . . ." Elizabeth swallowed. "My worst fear is that my mother will die alone, without either of us there."

The director glanced over at the other woman, who nodded glumly. Then she leaned forward and typed on her computer's keyboard. In a second, she'd pulled up Mona Thomas's file.

"I'm going to deny I ever told you this, but Mona was only in rehab for eight months two years ago. She left us and said she had no intention of ever coming back."

"What was Mona like when she left here?"

"Defiant. If you'd asked me, I would've guessed she'd relapse immediately. She didn't really buy into the twelve-step program at all, and the therapists wrote notes here that she was conniving and was a compulsive liar. Lying, of course, is a big problem for addicts."

"I know." Elizabeth nodded. "The worst part is that she had such talent."

"Talent?" The director looked confused.

"She was an artist."

"Really? We never saw that here. Not at all. We even have special art-therapy sessions with some of our patients. Mona hardly participated and when she did, I wouldn't say her drawings were very inspired."

"That's surprising." But not if Robin Platt and Mona Thomas were two different people entirely, Elizabeth realized. And Robin Platt was the real artist and Mona Thomas just stole her identity.

The more Elizabeth talked to the director, the more she got the impression that Mona Thomas was the woman who was trying to convince the world she was Robin Platt. This was huge.

But that revelation only created more questions.

Did the two women know each other? It was a small town. They could have gone to the same school. But why had Mona taken Robin's identity?

"Did Mona have any friends she talked to while she was here? Anyone who might know where she is now? I need to track her down. I have to find her."

"I can answer that," Lee Anne said. "She had one visitor who came to see her maybe a couple of times. A young woman about Mona's age. I think they'd gone to school together."

"Do you remember the name?" Elizabeth hoped beyond hope she could connect Mona and Robin. "Was it Robin?"

Lee Anne appeared thoughtful for a moment as if trying to remember. Elizabeth felt her hope rise.

"It could've been. Honestly, I just don't recall," Lee Anne said, shaking her head.

"Is there a record?"

"There was, but we don't keep the paper logs of visitors for more than a year, so we wouldn't have it anymore."

Elizabeth couldn't help feeling disappointed. A record linking them would help Elizabeth prove the identity theft.

"Can you tell me what you remember about the girl who visited?"

"Well, she seemed nice. The one thing I do remember that was unusual was that she was always bringing in drawings to show Mona. She liked to draw clothes, I think, like she was studying to be a designer or something. She was pretty talented."

Elizabeth felt a flicker of hope. The girl had to be Robin Platt, the *real* Robin Platt, the artist. This was starting to come together.

"What about what she looked like? Can you remember anything?"

"She had red hair, kind of a boyish cut, even shorter than mine." She touched her bob. "And she didn't wear any makeup. That much I remember. Honestly, I actually thought she was a boy the first time she came."

"Why is that?"

"Just her build and the way she dressed. I think she was . . ." Lee Anne's voice trailed off suddenly, and Elizabeth was sure the left out part had to be "gay." And she thought about what Robin Platt's high school boyfriend had said about her. Was she a lesbian after all?

"Did she have any other friends or visitors?" Elizabeth asked.

"No, not that I remember," Lee Anne said. "Sorry I can't be of more help."

"No, this is great. You have no idea how *much* you've helped. Thank you."

Elizabeth rushed out of the rehab center to her cab, but by the time she got to the airport, she'd just missed the last flight out to California.

No matter. She took a cab to a nearby hotel in Lexington. She was too excited to care about missing her flight.

In her hotel room, she could barely contain her excitement. She had discovered there were two women, Robin and Mona, and the one claiming to be Robin wasn't Robin. She had to be Mona. Somehow Elizabeth had to prove that. And to do that, she had to find the real Robin Platt.

But where had she gone? She'd left Richmond, the small Kentucky town where both she and Mona had grown up. She had to have gone somewhere. Elizabeth pulled out her iPad. She mulled over everything she'd discovered this afternoon.

Where would the real Robin Platt have gone? Not to Los Angeles, Elizabeth thought. Mona wouldn't have taken the chance of stealing the name of a person who lived close by. That would just be too dangerous.

Lee Anne said she liked to draw and maybe was studying fashion design. And if she was, the best place to go would be New York.

Elizabeth Googled "Robin Platt" and "New York" and "designer," but couldn't find the redhead she was looking for. She tried "R. Platt, designer," and instantly, Robert Platt popped up. But he was clearly a man. There was a small write-up in the most recent Fashion Week coverage, mentioning his name. Robert and Robin were the same age and, apparently, both were from Kentucky. Elizabeth was getting more and more excited.

There were no photos, so she searched Facebook for Robert Platt, the designer. The instant she pulled up the fan page, the puzzle was solved: Robert's picture showed him, a slight-of-build young man with short-cropped red hair. Despite the hint of a five-o'clock shadow, Elizabeth knew this had to be Robin, a.k.a. Robert Platt.

The rumors about Robin Platt being a lesbian weren't exactly right. She was actually a he. Sometime between when she'd left Kentucky for

New York and now, she had undergone a sex change and had become Robert Platt.

Obviously, this was the person she was looking for.

Elizabeth's writer's imagination began to run wild, and she came out with a scenario that was so plausible she was convinced it had to be the truth.

If Robin Platt in Los Angeles—the alleged attempted rape victim—was really Mona Thomas, the drug addict who had fled rehab and gone to California, she might have found a job working for Warner Gas. The only problem was that her paycheck would never have been enough to finance her habit. She'd have had to look for another way out, like finding someone with money. Nola had talked about her "sleeping with somebody in upper management," and there was no one higher up than Rick Warner himself.

Elizabeth knew enough about the natural gas tycoon to know that he liked women. He was always in the gossip columns with good-looking girls. Blondes, usually. And Robin was pretty and young and blond.

But maybe her addiction had gotten worse and even he couldn't protect her when her stealing became obvious and habitual. Addicts are reckless, and maybe in the end, he had no choice but to fire her.

But just suppose it didn't end there? Warner was such a lowlife; he'd sink to anything to get even with an enemy who happened to be, this time, Bruce Patman. He'd done underhanded things before to destroy his competitors.

Elizabeth let her mind run with it. Just suppose the attempted rape was a scheme Warner had come up with to smear Bruce's reputation. Mona would be his weapon. He knew she had to feed her habit and he had caught her stealing, so he could have turned her in anytime. She was trapped. She would have to do anything he asked.

The timeline made sense. Mona was fired several months before Bruce was accused of attempted rape. Once Warner put his plan together, there would have been enough time for her to go undercover as an intern at Bruce's company. That was crucial.

All she had to do while she was there was to avoid Bruce, which wouldn't have been hard since he really wasn't much involved with the interns.

There were lots of them and they were always changing. All she had to do was make sure to duck into the ladies' room or just out of the way when he made his rare visits. She could have been almost certain that he wouldn't recognize her when she approached him at the bar. That's when she'd set him up.

If he recognized her, she'd just walk away. But if he didn't . . .

But why the new name? Why did Mona become Robin?

Elizabeth knew that Rick Warner was a careful man. He couldn't take the chance that someone might find her on the books at Warner Gas. As an investigative reporter, she herself could have found that information in a minute—any good reporter could have. And with a little more digging they would have uncovered the drug background, and that would have been the end of Mona's credibility as an accuser.

In order for the plan to work, she'd have needed a backstory that was solid and irreproachable. And she'd found it in Robin Platt, her friend from her hometown who had dreamed of going to New York, nice and far away, and becoming a fashion designer. It would have made a perfect cover. And they wouldn't have had to worry about people finding Robin Platt on Facebook or anywhere else because there was no Robin Platt anymore. Mona knew that Robin had planned to become Robert Platt when she got to New York.

If that was true, all Mona had to do was take Robin's name and from there it would be in Warner's hands. He'd have to come up with some kind of story that would discredit Bruce enough so that he could grab the land back from Patman Social Impact Group. For a man like Warner, who would stoop to any low level to get what he wanted, that part would almost be easy.

Even though this was all only in Elizabeth's mind, it made perfect sense.

That's it. Elizabeth practically jumped up from the bed. She was certain she had it, but only part of it. She needed more.

She needed to know how Mona had set up the attack if it had never happened. How did she manage to fake it in a crowded bar, surrounded by other people? How did she even get Bruce into that back room where the attempted rape allegedly happened?

For a fleeting second, Elizabeth wondered if Bruce, seeing the pretty blonde, had gone willingly.

She shut out the thought. No, she was done doubting Bruce. Her uncertainty had been the reason she'd lost him in the first place. She'd been so very wrong about Bruce, and it had cost her his love. There had to be another explanation, and she was going to find it.

From Mona herself. If she had to trick or even threaten her, she would get the truth. And she'd find that bartender, too. He was the only other witness that night. Nothing was going to stop her now.

She pulled out her phone to text Jessica.

I REALLY HAVE SOMETHING GOOD HERE. I'VE CONFIRMED WHAT AARON FOUND AND DISCOVERED MORE. NOT A WORD TO ANYONE. I'LL BE HOME BY EARLY AFTERNOON TOMORROW.

When she got back to Sweet Valley, she'd figure out just how Robin, now Mona, had faked the attack. She'd unearth all the dirty details of the scam Warner had pulled on Bruce. And there would be no holds barred. Down and dirty. No matter what she had to do, she would save Bruce and give him back his life. And maybe he would find it in his heart to forgive her.

He might even love her again.

4

"Even the French papers are turning against me," Bruce Patman said, sighing as he dropped the newspaper on the antique tile coffee table in his villa in the south of France.

Annie Whitman glanced up at him, worried. "It's just one column," she pointed out, even though she, too, had noticed the slight turn of favor in the French media recently. While the French were notorious for forgiving men in power for indiscretions, Bruce's case had begun to try their patience. Even some French journalists had begun to question whether Bruce was really innocent of attempted rape, and whether France should be so eager to hide America's alleged criminals.

"That's one column, but there are hundreds more online and everywhere else." Bruce slumped on the couch and put his head in his hands, feeling defeated. Jessica Wakefield, talented as she was, seemed to be losing Bruce's PR campaign battle back home, too. Not that there was anything she could do as long as Bruce was out of the country. Bruce knew it, too. Annie had been on him for weeks to go home. Only the guilty flee, she said. But, loathe as he was to admit it, he was scared. He was fighting an enemy he couldn't see with weapons he didn't have. If he didn't beat this, he could spend years in jail. And his billions weren't going to help.

"Maybe we should talk about going home," Annie said quietly. "The case is still circumstantial. There are no direct witnesses to the attack and no DNA. The prosecutor's case is weak."

"Even with the problem of 'guilty men run'?" Bruce asked, quoting the headline of the op-ed piece on the table in the English-language *Herald Tribune*.

"We can explain it," Annie said. "You had urgent business abroad. Something. We can figure it out."

"Can we?" Even Bruce was starting to believe his own bad press. How was he going to defend himself in court with his self-confidence this shaken? That's what scared him the most: Even he couldn't be a hundred percent sure he didn't do it, didn't try to force himself on that girl, his former intern. He'd blacked out and had little to no memory of that night.

The phone at the villa rang, and Bruce jumped up. Annie could almost see the excitement flicker across his face. She knew why: He thought the call might be from Elizabeth. Only she and Jessica had the number at the villa.

Despite having officially broken up, Bruce still held on to some hope that there was something left. They'd been in love, deeply, for these last three years. But for him, it had started long before that. It had been years of longing for her and now it was like a piece of his body had been torn off. He missed her so much.

Bruce leaped to the phone and grabbed it on the second ring. "Hello?" His shoulders slumped in visible disappointment as he heard the voice on the other end. "Oh, Jess. Hi. What's up?" He could always tell them apart instantly.

Bruce walked over to the minibar in the room as he shifted the phone, cradling it between his ear and shoulder. He went right for the crystal Scotch decanter and poured himself a generous drink. He raised it to his lips.

"Hey, Bruce, I know it's late there and you sound bad. But you're going to sound great in about ten seconds."

"Yeah, right. You're going to tell me it's all been a dream."

"Not quite, but we may have found the connection."

"Robin Platt and Warner?"

"That's right."

Bruce froze, cocktail in hand. He set it back down on the bar, fearing that he hadn't heard correctly. "You found something on Robin Platt?" Bruce echoed. In the room, Annie sat up straighter on the couch, all ears, as she watched him intently.

"It's too early to say, but we might have something good."

Bruce slammed his flat palm down on the bar, making the glasses jump.

"I knew it! That guy was out to get me. Unbelievable. Elizabeth said that right in the beginning. What is it? Was he paying her to smear me? What?"

"It's too early to get into all the specifics, but it looks like she's not who she said she was at all. I think you really should think about coming back to Sweet Valley. I can't do anything for you when you're in hiding."

"It's a risk." Bruce glanced at Annie. He ran a frustrated hand through his dark hair. His blue eyes looked troubled as they met Annie's. "What if it's too late?"

"It's not too late." Jessica's voice was firm and determined. "We can fix this."

"I'm not so sure anymore."

"Just stop being a jerk," she said in a tone that implied she was only partly kidding. Only Jessica, who'd known him forever, could talk to him like that and not offend. "Come home, Bruce. It's time."

"What if your Warner-Robin lead doesn't pan out?"

"It will because you're innocent and the truth is ready to come out." Jessica sounded so sure, so confident. Bruce wished he could borrow some of her assurance. There were days when he suspected she believed in him more than he did.

"You've been fabulous, Jessica, and I'm really grateful." Her loyalty was so unexpected; he only wished she could lend some to her sister. The second that snide thought about Elizabeth entered his mind, he pushed it aside. It was too painful to think about Elizabeth. Too heart-wrenching to think about how easily she'd abandoned him when he needed her most. How could she have betrayed him that way? She'd turned into his enemy, finding Robin Platt and then hiding her. How could she? She was supposed to have loved him. He never would have done that to her.

"Please come home, Bruce."

"I'll think about it."

"Trust me. That's all I can ask."

"Thanks, Jessica. For . . . everything."

"My pleasure," she said, trying to lighten the conversation. "As long as you know you owe me a week in that villa after you're acquitted. Annie can't have all the fun there."

"This is not exactly a fun vacation for anybody." He knew his response was a touch too strong and defensive, but Jessica couldn't have known why.

"That's not what Caroline Pearce thinks."

Obviously, from her gossipy response, Jessica had no clue about what had really happened on Annie's first night in France when Bruce had drunk too much wine. He relaxed, realizing she had to be referring to Caroline's blog and tweets, her relentless campaign to imply Bruce and Annie were romantically involved. Bruce had read the posts. He couldn't help reading them since Caroline filled his in-box with them every day. Honestly, the woman needed to get a hobby or adopt a dog or something. She had far too much time on her hands.

Then again, maybe the rumors rubbed Bruce the wrong way because it reminded him just how desperately he had failed when it came to Annie and the night she'd flat out rejected him.

He'd had too much wine and had come on hard. Annie had turned him down, and the rejection still stung a little. He had to think that if his life weren't such a horrendous mess he would never have even done such a thing in the first place.

"Since when does Caroline Pearce get anything right?" Bruce asked. "She's a liar."

Annie's ears perked up at the mention of Caroline Pearce. Annie had read the posts, too.

"Yeah," Jessica said, "I know she lies. But she can really make it sound true. That's what makes her so dangerous."

"You don't believe her?"

"Of course not. Forget about Caroline. You can set her straight later. It's time to come home anyway. In fact, it's crucial."

"You make a persuasive argument."

"That's my job."

Jessica hung up. Bruce looked at the receiver in his hand and then plunked it down. He glanced over at Annie, who was looking at him expectantly. "What did Jessica say?"

"To come home. They think they've found something on Robin."

"What?"

"She didn't want to give me too many details until she could confirm, but it looks like Robin Platt isn't who she says she is."

"This would be the break we're looking for."

"Or just another wild goose chase."

"You have to have faith." Annie smiled at him. She looked particularly fetching today in her camel-colored tunic and leggings. She sat on his couch with her slim legs crossed at the knee. Back in the day they used to call her "Easy Annie," but he'd come to know that she wasn't anything like the insecure high school girl who craved approval from any boy who'd give it to her. She had grown into a beautiful, complex woman.

Bruce felt a pang of guilt. That night he'd come on to her, he'd treated her badly. It was no wonder she'd turned him down. He'd behaved like a stupid teenager. And he really wasn't that Patman anymore. He'd thought that being his old self could give him strength. He'd thought if he was a big enough jerk, he could bluster his way through the fear that ate at his confidence daily.

But he'd just made a fool of himself instead. Annie had stood by him, and her legal expertise was unparalleled. She deserved better than that.

"I'm sorry," he told her then.

"Sorry for what?" A curious expression crossed Annie's face.

"For . . . that night."

Annie's eyebrows shot up in surprise. She knew exactly what he meant. "Bruce, you don't have to—"

"No, I want to, Annie." Bruce took a seat beside her. "I shouldn't have been so . . . crass. I've just been under pressure and . . . you deserve better from me. I'm sorry."

Annie looked at him a long time.

"It's okay," she said at last. "Really. I understand."

For a second, a current of promise ran between them. The spark, the attraction, was still there and both of them could feel it. And neither one was drunk this time.

For Annie, it was pure attraction complicated by feelings she knew she shouldn't have. But for Bruce, it was even more convoluted. There was a physical attraction to this beautiful, smart, desirable woman who might be able to save him. Of course he wanted her. Plus, he was a man in love with a woman who had betrayed him, abandoned him, and even deceived him, so it should have been easy. But it wasn't. Bruce had loved Elizabeth for so many painful years, yearned for her when she was hopelessly out of reach and then finally, when they did come together, it was amazing. Those were the happiest three years of his life. That he should even be considering Annie at all showed how much damage had been done.

But maybe it wasn't beyond repair.

Or was it?

"Annie . . ." Bruce began.

Across the room, Annie's iPhone dinged with an incoming message. She jumped up, her face flushed. "I probably should get that," she said, avoiding looking him in the eye.

"We need to talk, Annie."

"Do we?" Annie met his eyes. In them, he saw confusion and struggle and something more. "Not now, Bruce."

"When?"

"Maybe never." Annie turned away from him. "But there is something I'm going to ask you to do for me."

"What is it?"

"Fly back to Sweet Valley first thing tomorrow. It's time for us to go home. I can't guarantee it will be easy for you, but we have to do this. It's time."

Bruce nodded slowly. She was right. "Okay," he said. "I trust you, Annie. I'll do it."

The next morning in Sweet Valley, Jessica felt a little bit lighter as she sat down at her desk after fetching a cup of coffee from the break room. Aaron was a genius for finding the Robin-Mona link, Elizabeth had dug up more dirt at the rehab center, and now it would only be a matter of time before the entire story came out.

And last night, Elizabeth had called from her hotel to fill Jessica in on what she'd found. Jessica still had a million questions about Robin Platt— now Mona Thomas—but Elizabeth would be home in a few hours to answer them.

The news even made work a little more bearable. Jessica glanced up, and her eyes locked with Michael Wilson, vice president of VertPlus .net. Michael looked away quickly, his face blank and stoic. Not so long ago, Michael's face lit up with happy surprise anytime he saw Jessica, and his enthusiasm only increased after they'd gone on a series of hot and heavy dates. Now Michael wouldn't acknowledge her at all. As much as she'd turned the whole period over in her mind, Jessica still couldn't explain why he'd gone so cold.

Just like she didn't know why Lila Fowler, one of her oldest and dearest friends, wasn't returning her phone calls. It had been weeks since Lila had replied to even a simple text message. Jessica knew Lila had a lot on her plate, what with her fake pregnancy turning out to be real, but enough was enough already. She couldn't even text?

And then there was Cal, the guy she'd met at Steven's law firm. They'd gone out once, and then he'd never called her back.

Jessica had begun to feel like a pariah.

At work, hardly anyone spoke to her these days. Michael had taken away all her clients and Jessica was shut out of anything important. Her own assistant, Emily, the too-much-makeup-wearing redhead, sabotaged her at every turn.

Most days, she just felt like she was waiting to be let go.

Just then, her phone dinged with an incoming message from Liam O'Connor.

I NEED TO SEE YOU. LUNCH?

Jessica sighed. She didn't want to see Liam. He might have been one of *People*'s sexiest men alive and the hottest actor in Hollywood at the moment, but she had decided to break up with him.

In fact, the last time they'd had lunch she'd tried to end things with Liam but couldn't quite get the words out. He had been so perfectly nice and Jessica just couldn't seem to find the right time to bring up the delicate subject. She knew their relationship wasn't going anywhere, and she thought she needed to end it, but she wasn't quite sure how. In the meantime, she'd been guilty of avoiding him.

NO, CAN'T, Jessica texted back. And she couldn't. She planned to spend her lunch hour talking to Elizabeth about Mona Thomas.

Immediately, her phone rang. She sent Liam to voice mail, but then he called again. She knew from experience he'd just keep calling until she answered, filling up her voice mail and becoming more and more irate. Eventually, she decided to answer.

"Why not lunch?" Liam's voice came over the line, plaintive and pouty.

"Liam, I . . ."

"It's important, Jessica."

"I know, but . . ."

"I know you don't have plans," he interrupted, his Irish lilt sounding unusually grim. "You said last week nobody at work will go to lunch with you anymore."

"Liam!" It might have been true, but she didn't like it thrown back in her face. She knew the rest of the office looked at her like career kryptonite. She couldn't blame them.

"Look, they're daft for not seeing what an amazing woman you are."

Jessica perked up at the compliment. This was why it was so hard to let Liam go. She knew she needed to do it, but she hated to lose the last member on her cheerleading squad.

"And I need to talk to you. Lunch?"

"I was going to meet Elizabeth," Jessica said.

"She's your sister. She'll understand if you cancel. And besides, I'll meet you at your place. I can be there at one."

"Liam, she found something in the Bruce case and—"

"Look, I won't keep you long. I promise. You can talk to her after. There'll be time."

"Well . . ." Jessica hesitated. She knew Liam, and she knew he wouldn't give up until she'd said yes. Maybe she did need to deal with him first.

"I'll be there at one," Liam said.

"Fine," Jessica sighed. Liam first, then Elizabeth.

Lila Fowler Matthews was standing behind her immense island in her giant kitchen in Sweet Valley. The granite countertop just hid her emerging belly bump from the *True Housewives of Sweet Valley* cameras, set up at opposite sides of the kitchen.

This was a big day. It was a special live broadcast of *True Housewives*. When she'd told the producers about her pregnancy, they couldn't have been more congratulatory, probably because they knew they had just landed a ratings bonanza. They'd asked her to put off telling the rest of the wives and had decided to shoot a live show at her house to capture the big announcement. This would be the first time she revealed the emerging baby bump. Until now, she'd mostly been wearing baggy clothes that disguised everything.

Under different circumstances, Lila would've been thrilled. This was the kind of attention she'd been craving her whole life. Unfortunately, nearly all of the attention she'd received on the show so far was negative.

Lila was still the most hated housewife in Sweet Valley, and she had no doubt her pregnancy news would do nothing to change fans' reactions.

Not after what they'd already learned.

She'd faked her first pregnancy and her miscarriage, all for some ratings and to win back her husband from that evil Ashley Morgan, who'd tried to steal Ken away practically in episode one. She'd gotten Ken back all right, only to lose him again when he found out that she'd never been pregnant at all. Ken saw the whole drama as one big publicity stunt.

Lila could still see the heartbreak on his sweet face. Normally, she didn't let things like that bother her. Maybe it was the pregnancy hormones, but she felt bad about it. Even she knew she'd gone too far.

She put her hand on her belly and sighed. She felt the little rise of a bump and still couldn't quite believe she was going to be a mother.

In fact, she nearly wasn't.

She'd only just decided to keep the baby. She'd struggled with what to do through nearly the whole first trimester. She'd stayed up many nights wondering whether she was really ready for motherhood or whether she should just march down to the clinic and make everyone's lives a little easier.

She wasn't even sure she wanted to be a mother. She had never been the maternal type, never even wanted to have kids who might, after all, steal some of the spotlight meant for her. But she came to realize that as self-centered as she sometimes was, this was one time she couldn't actually put herself first. As much as it would make life simpler, she just couldn't do it. Every time she made the call to set up an appointment at the clinic, she would hang up right after the receptionist answered and cry.

Sure, it was probably the hormones rushing through her veins, but she also believed that the baby growing inside her might just be a gift. After all, the baby was her very last link to Ken. He might never forgive her and they might never be together, but she'd always have this baby.

And, with a baby, she'd never be alone. Not the best reasons to be a mother, probably, but they were the ones she had. So she went with them.

She sighed, took a drink of ice water and glanced around at the other Housewives chatting at the kitchen table. Ashley looked curvaceous as usual in a clingy miniskirt. Devone was dressed in a yellow maxi-dress, which made her cocoa-colored skin glow. Marina, sitting on the edge of her chair, pursed her lips and channeled her inner Eva Longoria as she took a sip of her martini. Marina and Devone chatted away about some recent club opening both had attended.

Still hidden, standing behind the counter, Lila knew the other wives had no idea what was coming. She suddenly felt very alone and very pregnant. She wished her *real* friends and family were here, not the fake ones. She missed Jessica, frankly. But ever since reading those mean and completely below-the-belt messages Jessica had sent on Facebook, Lila wasn't even sure if they *were* friends anymore. Jessica had written "You've been selfish your whole life and now you've finally gotten what you deserved." Lila's feelings were beyond hurt.

Lila felt like the world was suddenly a place with too many sharp angles. She just wanted to sit somewhere cozy and soft, in clothes with elastic waistbands, surrounded by people who cared about her.

People like Ken. Her old Ken. The one who adored her.

That's who she really missed. Sweet, caring Ken. Being with him was the closest Lila ever came to loving anybody.

Lila glanced up and got the cue from the producer. It was time to do the big reveal.

It was now or never, Lila figured. Already, the Twitterverse was alive with rumors she was putting on weight.

And frankly, announcing she would likely be a single mom was better than being fat. Anything was better than that.

Lila was wearing a loose-fitting sweater and leggings with the waistband tucked underneath her growing belly. She'd have to get maternity wear soon, but for now, she was still squeezing into regular clothes. She had on a formfitting tank beneath the loose sweater. Everyone would be able to see how pregnant she looked when she took off the sweater.

And that was the point.

"Ladies, I'm so glad you could come to my house today," Lila began. "I've got an announcement to make. . . ."

⌒

Ken Matthews sat on the couch in the shabby apartment he'd hastily rented after moving out of the mansion he had shared with Lila. Ken had picked the first open rental near the football stadium and he hadn't even bothered to furnish it other than to throw in a futon and a big flat-screen TV.

He'd been devastated and hurt and all he cared about was getting as far away from his wife as quickly as possible. Where he lived or how he lived didn't really matter anymore.

Luckily, the guys on the team hadn't given him too much grief. He was still their quarterback, still the guy they looked to as team leader. None of them made jokes, at least where he could hear, and he appreciated that. Lila had humiliated him in the worst possible way. He felt like such an idiot for believing anything she'd ever told him.

The worst part was that part of him still loved her. Maybe part of him always would. He hated that.

He had practice later, but for now, all he wanted to do was chill out. He popped open a can of Coke and took a sip as he pulled up the guide to see what was on. Instantly, a new episode of *True Housewives of Sweet Valley* popped up. On the bottom of the screen, the message "Live Special!" blinked. What was so earth-shattering that they needed a live show to announce it?

He shouldn't have cared.

He should've changed the channel instantly, but something made him hesitate. Maybe it was the shock of seeing Lila right there, front and center, looking so pretty it physically hurt him. Why did she have a right to glow like that? Her looking so good felt like she was just twisting the knife—again.

Turn the channel! a voice inside his head told him. *What are you doing watching this trash? Why do you even care what she's doing on that stupid show?*

But part of him did care. He hated to admit it, but it was true. Just seeing Lila wasn't enough. He wanted to hear what she was saying. He turned up the volume and took another deep swig of his drink.

He was just in time to hear the words "I'm pregnant" come out of Lila's mouth.

Excuse me? Ken put down the Coke can. He kicked up the volume another notch. He couldn't have heard right.

The other Housewives—Ashley, Devone, and Marina—all laughed.

"I'm serious," Lila said as she shrugged off her sweater. There was what looked like a small bump under her tank top, but Ken wouldn't believe his eyes. "This time."

"No way that's true," Ken muttered, shaking his head. "She's got padding under there. God, there's no stopping her!"

"Go on, feel it," Lila offered to Devone. But before she could, Ken jumped up and turned off the TV.

Hurt and anger bubbled up inside Ken as he paced his small apartment. All the dark emotions surrounding Lila's first fake pregnancy and fake miscarriage came rolling back, knocking him down. How dare Lila do this to him *again*? Did she really think he was dumb enough to fall for that a second time?

Was she so desperate for sympathy and affection that she'd stoop *this low* again? Lila had to be loved, no matter the cost, and she just couldn't help trying to get his attention.

Well, she got it, all right. And this time she wasn't going to like it, either.

He grabbed his car keys from the counter and stomped off to his car. He was in such a fury, he flung open the door of his precious Porsche 911 convertible, almost cracking the hinges, jumped in, and with his foot to the floor screeched out of his parking space. He would show everyone what a liar she was. No way was he going to let her get away with this trick again.

Not ten minutes later, Lila heard the front door open and slam shut. Everyone heard it. All the wives looked up at the entrance to the kitchen, waiting. But they didn't have to wait more than seconds for a very angry Ken to burst into the room.

"Ken!" cried Lila, surprised. She hadn't expected him. Not at all. "What are you doing here?"

"I still own half this house," Ken ground out. "And I saw your little stunt on TV."

"You were watching?" Lila's voice carried just the slightest bit of hope.

"By accident," he said as he looked at her very pretty, very magnetic eyes. He never could resist them. She was beautiful to him. And she looked so pretty. Why did she have to look so pretty?

Focus, Ken, he told himself. Don't be sucked in. Not this time.

"There's no way I'm letting you get away with this, Lila," Ken growled, finding his anger again. "I know you're lying."

"I'm not, Ken. I swear. Not this time." Lila held out her hands as if to show she wasn't hiding anything. "I know this sounds ridiculous, but back when I was faking, remember when you couldn't keep your hands off me? Well . . . turns out I became pregnant."

"No way."

"It's true."

"Are you going to stand there and listen to this drivel?" Ashley Morgan got up from the table, hands on her hips, glaring. Lila shot her a look that would slice through glass.

Devone and Marina exchanged solemn glances as the cameramen silently filmed.

"No, I'm not going to believe it and no one else will, either," Ken said as he took a step closer to Lila. She didn't move. He reached out and grabbed the hem of her tank and pulled it up. "Fraud!" he declared, turning her to the cameras. Everyone else in the room gasped.

Lila really was pregnant. There was no hiding that little rounded naked belly that was clearly one hundred percent baby sticking up over the rolled-down waistband of her leggings.

Seeing the stunned reaction of the other wives, Ken turned around to look at Lila. "What . . . ?"

Ashley whipped her head back and cackled. "Unbelievable. *Now* you're pregnant? God, Lila, is there anything you don't screw up?"

"That's enough," Devone said, stepping in front of Ashley. "We are not going there. Marina? Help me."

Devone took one arm and Marina took another, and with a quick nod to Lila, Devone said, "We're stepping outside now, Ashley. To give Ken and Lila a minute."

"Get your hands off me!" Ashley struggled, but Devone and Marina had tight grips.

"You go nicely, Ashley, or I will *personally* pull out every last one of your extensions," Marina threatened.

"And I'll take care of that padded ass!" said Devone, pulling at her arm.

"You wouldn't!"

"Try us."

One look at the determination of her fellow wives, and Ashley knew she had no choice. Defeated, she followed them outside to the patio.

Ken hadn't moved. He was still staring at Lila's belly. The skin was taut and a little bit firm. He reached out tentatively and touched it.

All anger seemed to drain away in that second. All the hurt and the grief of betrayal and losing the one thing he realized he wanted most in the world—a baby with his very flawed wife with whom he was hopelessly in love—melted away. Here, beneath his fingers, this tiny bump was a possibility that it could all be okay again. He never thought it would be, ever again, but now he allowed himself the hope.

"Is this . . ." Ken couldn't form the words.

"Our baby, sweetheart," Lila said, her voice soft and full of affection. She covered his hand with hers and their eyes met. "*Our* baby."

Tears sprang to Ken's eyes. Tears of relief and joy and happiness. Some might have called him a fool in that moment for letting the happiness in and releasing the anger and hurt and suspicion. But at his core, Ken was not a complicated man; he just wanted to be with his pretty wife and have cute babies crawling around on the rug. That's all he'd ever wanted, really. He'd give up nearly anything for that, so a little bit of pride didn't seem like a huge sacrifice. Not when everything he'd ever wanted was right in reach.

Ken let go of Lila's tank top and pulled her into his arms, hugging her fiercely. Lila returned the hug, slipping her arms around her husband's back.

Ken lifted up Lila, hands on her rapidly disappearing waist, and twirled her around their kitchen. Lila giggled and Ken did, too.

"I missed you so much, baby," Lila said.

"I missed you, too," Ken said as he put her down gently. He dipped his head and their lips met. The cameras zoomed in, but neither one of them cared.

They were in their own world now, and the future was full of promise.

7

Elizabeth's plane landed and she took her carry-on luggage and went straight for her car, which was parked in the garage.

Armed with the new knowledge that Bruce's accuser, Robin Platt, was really drug addict Mona Thomas, she planned to confront Mona and get some answers.

In less than a half hour, she was standing on Mona's porch, ringing the bell. No one answered. She slipped open the screen door and banged on the door. She waited, listening.

Elizabeth heard no one inside.

She glanced through the window to the side of the door but couldn't see anyone moving inside.

What now? Elizabeth ran through her options. She needed to get to the bottom of this. The next best thing to confronting Mona might be to talk to the only other prime witness in Bruce's case: the bartender. He'd sworn Bruce was coming on to Mona in the bar.

But if Mona had been put up to it by Rick Warner, maybe the bartender had been, too.

Elizabeth got back in her car. The bartender, Jackson, no longer worked at the bar where the attack supposedly took place. Now he took shifts over at Friday's on Riverhead. That's where she'd found him before. She drove there and walked into the restaurant, asking the tall, slim hostess for Jackson.

"Sorry," she said, and shrugged. "He's not on shift right now, but he should be here in about an hour or so."

"But it's very important. I need to talk to him now. Do you have a number?"

The hostess eyed her cautiously. "No, sorry, we don't give those out. But I could get him a message."

"No, forget it. I'll be back."

She called Jessica, but her cell phone went straight to voice mail. When she called work, Emily, Jessica's assistant, picked up the phone.

"She's not here," Emily said matter-of-factly. "I guess she's still at lunch."

"Do you know when she'll be back?"

"No. She just left. But knowing her, I'm sure she'll take her time."

"Maybe you should be more careful about what you say about your boss," Elizabeth chided. She knew all about Emily, Tracy's spy, and she didn't like her one bit, either.

"Would you like to leave a message?" Emily's tone was mildly annoyed.

"No, thanks."

Elizabeth hung up. Weird, she thought, glancing at her watch. It was after one, and Jessica should have been back around now. Jessica wasn't answering her cell, which was strange, and she wasn't at work. Maybe she'd taken Jake to the doctor? He was always coming down with an ear infection. Still . . .

Elizabeth was distracted, and didn't have a lot of time to dwell on it. She called Jessica's cell again and left a message saying she was going to grab lunch at Friday's on Riverhead and wait for the bartender to show.

She swung back to Friday's and grabbed lunch. But the bartender never showed.

She approached the hostess again. "Do you know when Jackson's coming in?"

"Oh, he's not coming," the hostess said curtly. "He canceled his shift."

"You told him someone was waiting?"

"Yeah, I told him."

"What did he say?"

"Nothing. He just canceled."

Elizabeth could have kicked herself. She should have come up with some kind of story. Instead she'd spooked the bartender. Now the danger was that he'd tip off Mona. She had to get to Mona's place—fast.

She texted her sister and told her she wouldn't be able to make lunch, but she'd explain why later.

She decided to loop back one more time to Mona's house, to see if she could catch her there. If the bartender had vanished, maybe Mona was clearing out, too. Elizabeth couldn't let Mona slip away. Not now.

On a whim, she pulled around to the back instead of the front, and that's when she saw Mona dragging a huge suitcase out of the back door.

Elizabeth put her car in park and jumped out.

Seeing her, Mona froze mid-step, a guilty look on her face.

"Mona?" Elizabeth said.

Shock and fear crossed Mona's face, and Elizabeth knew she had her. "Just where do you think you're going?"

Mona dropped her suitcase on the porch. She ducked back inside, but Elizabeth sprinted to the steps and caught the door before she could shut it.

"We need to talk," Elizabeth said.

When Jessica pulled up to her town house to meet Liam, she was surprised to see him playing with Jake in the yard. Technically, not playing. Liam was trying to coax Jake to open some large, new gift he'd brought. Liam was always bringing gifts, but usually Jake didn't like them. Jessica didn't know exactly why. His father, Todd Wilkins, believed Jake was afraid of Liam. Or more likely, it was Todd who didn't like Liam and was influencing Jake. Whatever.

Jessica thought Jake was just a little shy. Liam was one of those guys who wanted to win over everyone in the room. He just pushed a little too hard with Jake.

Like now, when he was trying to pressure Jake to play with the giant robotic dinosaur he'd brought. It made a loud, almost too-scary roar, and Jake didn't like it. Jessica glanced around the yard, wondering where Liza the nanny was.

"Mommy!" Jake cried, seeing Jessica. He jumped up and catapulted himself into her arms.

"Hi, honey," she said as Jake nuzzled his head right under her chin. "Where's Liza?" Jessica asked Liam.

"I told her she could go."

"Excuse me?" Liam had no right to do that. Jessica hated this controlling part of Liam's personality. He always entered a place thinking he owned it. "I have to work this afternoon! Who's going to watch Jake?"

"Don't worry. I told her just to go for lunch. No big deal."

"Oh." That wasn't as bad as she'd thought, but still, she fumed. Liza worked for Jessica, not Liam. "You should ask me next time."

Jessica wouldn't have agreed; she wasn't sure leaving Jake alone with Liam for even a short time was a good idea. Todd didn't like Liam, and he'd have a fit if Jake told him. Not to mention, Jessica had planned to end things with Liam, maybe today. Having Jake get too attached would not be a good thing. Not at all.

She needed to tell Liam now, before this got any more out of hand, but she didn't want to do it in front of Jake.

"Hey, Jake, do you want to watch *Thomas the Train*?" Jessica asked. Her son rarely got to watch TV with Liza, so it was always an unexpected treat.

"Yeah!" Jake cried and pumped his fists in the air. Jessica walked him into the living room and clicked on the TV. She turned up the volume a little, hoping he would be distracted enough that he wouldn't hear what was going on in the kitchen.

"Liam, we need to talk."

"We do," Liam agreed.

"You've been a great friend to me, really. But I just don't think this is going to work out." The minute the words were out of her mouth, Liam's face fell. The heartbreak shone in his eyes. She knew he loved her; he'd said so repeatedly, but now she saw just how much. This was harder than she'd thought. "You're amazing. You are, but I just don't think we should see each other anymore."

"Jessica, I love you."

"I know you do." Jessica had broken dozens of hearts before. That was nothing new. But something about the pain in Liam's eyes, the devastation written on his face, hit her hard. Maybe it was because all along she knew she'd never cared for him all that much. She had been using him like a salve for her bruised ego. Todd had left and she wanted adoration from someone. Now, she realized, she did feel badly. Liam had thought this whole time their relationship meant something. She'd known all along it didn't.

And no matter what anybody said, she wasn't heartless.

"No," he said. "You're not finished with me. You can't be. Jessica, I love you too m-much." His voice broke at the last bit, and Jessica felt terrible.

She swallowed the lump in her throat. She had to do this. Ending it now was the most merciful thing to do. Maybe she'd let him get too attached, and maybe he was already in too deep, but prolonging the inevitable would only make it worse.

"Liam, please. I'm sorry. I am. But it's just not working."

"Really? Because no one loves you like I do, Jessica. No one. Did you see how Michael dropped you without a word?"

"But . . ."

"And what about Lila? She's not returning your phone calls, either. What kind of friend is that?"

Jessica felt the barbs of what he was saying. They were true.

"Liam, that doesn't mean *we* work together."

Liam pulled at his hair, desperate. "But what about that guy Cal? What about him?"

Jessica's mind went back to the one date she'd had weeks ago. Liam wasn't supposed to have known about it.

"How did you know about Cal?"

"I know everything about you, Jessica." Liam's voice went flat, and for a second, Jessica felt a cold stab of dread in the pit of her stomach. What did he mean he knew everything? She'd never told him about Cal. "I know you and Michael made out in that parking lot. I know you and Cal kissed, too. I saw it all, Jessica."

"How . . . ?" Oh, God. Liam had her followed! He was out of control. Just like Elizabeth had said.

"It's not important! Cal, Michael, Lila—they don't really love you. One bad word and they abandon you." Liam was pacing the kitchen now.

"What do you mean 'one bad word'?" Stunned, Jessica tried to process what she'd heard. Liam had had her followed. He'd watched her on her dates. Had he been the one to sabotage her relationships with Michael and Cal and Lila?

"All it took was a fake Facebook account. They all fell for it. All of them."

"What did you do?"

"I copied your account down to your same profile picture. You weren't friends with Michael and Cal, so it was easy to fool them. And I figured Lila was so self-absorbed she wouldn't really click through to your profile to check whether it was really you. I was right."

"You created a dummy account?"

"I copied everything. Even your likes and dislikes. And from there, I just sent messages."

"What did you say?"

"I just wanted to test them, Jessica. I tested their loyalty because I care about you, and they all failed."

"Oh, my God. You may have ruined my career! Are you insane? How could you do that to me?" Jessica pressed her palms to the sides of her head. She couldn't believe this. She itched to get to a computer, to find the fake account, to do some kind of spin control if it wasn't already too late. But Liam was pacing, growing more agitated by the minute.

"How could I do that to *you*?" His voice was low, almost a growl. "Because I'm protecting you. I'm the only one who *truly* loves you, Jessica. The only one!" Liam slammed his fist down on the island in her kitchen, causing the container of serving utensils nearby to topple, spilling oversized stainless steel spoons with a loud clatter on the floor.

Jessica saw the wild look in Liam's eyes and for the first time began to get scared. Lizzie was right about him all along. He really was a stalker. And stalkers could be dangerous.

"Mommy?" The soft, concerned voice of Jake, her beautiful baby boy, came from the kitchen doorway. He'd come to see about the noise and because his stomach was empty. "Mommy! Want mac and peese!" Jake hadn't quite mastered the *ch* sound, yet. *Peese* was as close as he got to *cheese*.

Jake's expression instantly went somber as he felt the mood in the room. All thought of mac and peese quickly vanished.

"Sure, Jake. One second," Jessica said, her voice soft and monotone, her eyes never leaving Liam for a second, as if he were a poisonous viper poised to strike. She slid over toward Jake, trying to put her body between her toddler and Liam.

"You can't do this," Liam said, ignoring Jake altogether.

"Liam, this isn't the best time." Her eyes darted to Jake. "I think you should go."

"No."

"Please, Liam. You need to leave." Jessica knew Liam could be stubborn, but this was something else.

"I'm not leaving here without you."

"Liam . . ."

"Mommy?" came Jake's plaintive voice again. Jessica could hear the growing worry in it as the little boy's eyes flicked from Jessica to Liam and back again.

Jessica's heart pounded. Her maternal instinct was in full swing. She wanted Liam out of there. She didn't want Jake to witness any more of this argument, and if Liam did go crazy, she didn't want Jake anywhere near him.

"We can talk about this later."

"No, we can't. You are going to see reason," Liam said, clenching his jaw.

"Mommy!" cried Jake, more worried this time.

"*Shut up!*" snapped Liam, throwing the full force of his bubbling rage at the little boy. "Your mom and I are talking!"

Jake's eyes welled, and his lower lip began to quiver. Jessica flew over and instantly scooped him up in her arms.

"Liam! You need to go. Now!"

"Not a chance," Liam said, and moved in front of her, blocking her way to the exit.

Clutching her baby boy, Jessica's thoughts instantly flew to all those horrible news stories about mothers and their children killed by husbands or ex-boyfriends, men who lost their minds in jealous rages. Were Jessica and Jake about to become another headline?

She sent up a little prayer as she clutched Jake to her.

Please, God, no.

9

Clutching Jake to her, Jessica took a slow breath as she watched Liam seething on the other side of the kitchen. Jessica's attempt to end things with Liam had backfired. He was furious and, Jessica realized, very likely dangerous. And she and Jake could be at his mercy.

Calm him down, she thought. *Talk him back from the ledge. You can do this.*

Jessica took three deep breaths and pulled up a calm face, hoping it didn't look as false as it was. "Liam, let's talk this through."

"I don't feel like talking," Liam ground out, his eyes still ablaze with fury.

"Liam, I'm sorry. Let me just get Jake's mac and cheese and we'll work this all out. I promise." Liam's face softened a bit. Jessica, still holding Jake on her hip, moved through the kitchen quickly under Liam's watchful eyes. She popped the instant mac and cheese in the microwave, then tucked Jake into his booster seat at the table. In seconds, he was devouring his lunch.

Jessica glanced at the front windows, thinking, *Where is Liza?* Liam had told her to go for lunch more than forty minutes ago. Maybe even close to an hour. Surely, she had to be back soon.

All I have to do is keep Liam calm until then.

With Jake happily eating in the dining room, Jessica moved back to the kitchen, where Liam was leaning, arms crossed, against the refrigerator.

"You can't break up with me," he growled. "I won't let you."

"Liam," Jessica began. "Look, all I need is a little break, okay? Let me organize my life and then . . ."

"You had no right to lead me on." Liam's voice belied a level of hostility Jessica had never heard before. His eyes were flat and cold, like stone.

The hairs on the back of Jessica's neck rose a little as she realized that Liam might be capable of something seriously violent. Liam stood wearing his black T-shirt and dark-wash jeans, his muscles tensed, like a cobra ready to strike.

But she might still be able to calm him with the right words.

"I didn't lead you on, Liam," Jessica said, trying to soften her words with a soothing voice. "But if you thought I did, I am very sorry. I never wanted to hurt you. I need you."

Liam scoffed, a rough, doubting sound at the back of his throat.

"I just need a little more time, okay?" Jessica offered. She decided she'd say anything to get him to calm down and to leave. She moved a little closer to him. "I'm in the middle of a divorce. I need to work through this before I can really give you what you want. But once I'm free—truly free—then we can be together. Just like you want. There won't be anything standing in our way then. I can be focused on you and not distracted by the divorce and everything else in my life. Think about that! After this craziness is behind me, we can really be together. Maybe even take a trip. Wouldn't that be nice?"

"No." Liam shook his head slowly. His blue eyes were cold, and the chill reached her, too. She'd almost rather see anger there than this dead nothingness. The eerie calm scared her even more than his show of temper.

She glanced at the clock. *Where was Liza?*

"I want to be together now." Liam's voice was monotone and lacking real emotion.

"Hey, I have an idea," Jessica said, grasping at another tactic. "As soon as Liza gets back, I'll head to the office, clean up the loose ends at work, and we can have dinner tonight. You and me. We'll talk about everything. We can fix this."

Liam shook his head slowly. He didn't buy it for even a second, and the quickness with which he dismissed her idea frightened Jessica a little. He wasn't budging. Not even an inch.

"No," he said. "I told Liza she could take the whole afternoon off."

"What! But you said just for lunch."

"I lied."

Jessica felt anger and indignation bubble up. *How dare he?* But she quickly swallowed it. Showing her anger was too dangerous now. Jessica felt the room spin. The idea of Liza as her savior quickly vanished. This meant Jessica was truly and completely on her own. No one was coming to save her from Liam. It was just her and Liam and Jake, innocent Jake, happily eating his lunch of mac and cheese in the next room, blissfully unaware of the danger.

Jessica realized this situation was spinning out of control quickly. She needed to change the dynamic and quickly. She needed to get Jake safely *somewhere*.

"Hey, that was a good idea," she said brightly, flashing Liam a smile she hoped looked real. "With Liza off, and since we're all together, why don't we go to the park after lunch? Just the three of us?"

The neighborhood park was always overrun with kids—and their parents or nannies—at this time of day. If she could just get out in public, she might be able to diffuse whatever was going on with Liam. And if not, she could get help. Plus, there was a fire station right across from the park. If need be, she could take Jake there to be safe. She doubted Liam could be any match for six or seven firefighters. The thought calmed her.

"No." Liam shook his head calmly. "Let's stay here instead."

"But it's a beautiful day. Jake would love to get out, and so would I!"

"This is Sweet Valley, California. Every day is a beautiful day." Liam's dead calm rattled Jessica more than anything else could. "We'll do the park another day."

Jessica glanced at the clock. She'd been gone from work much longer than a normal lunch. People in the office would notice.

"Okay, well, while we figure out a plan for this afternoon, I need to call Emily at work, let her know I won't be back this afternoon."

Jessica glanced casually around the kitchen. Where had she left her phone? In the living room, she remembered, where she'd put her purse down by the TV when she'd turned it on for Jake. She needed to get closer to that phone.

"Let me just get my phone and I'll call Emily."

Liam stepped in front of her, blocking the way to the living room.

"Emily hates you. Why would you call her?"

"Tracy, then. My boss."

"She hates you, too. Why would she care?"

"I . . ." Jessica thought fast. "I have a meeting at three. I need to call and tell them I won't be there."

"They'll figure it out when you don't show." Liam's face was hard and immovable, like granite.

"I have to call. I'll be fired."

"From all you've told me, you're probably going to be fired anyway."

That last part stung. He was right, but still.

"I need this job, Liam," Jessica said.

"No, you don't, Jessica. I told you. I have more than enough money for us. And that job is getting in the way of us. We're more important than any stupid job."

Jessica was beginning to feel a little bit clammy. Every new tactic she tried, Liam wasn't having. He was just twisting everything she said. It all came right back to him possessing her.

It scared Jessica. Her heart pounded in her chest. Cold sweat broke out at the small of her back. She felt trapped like a rat in a maze, and no matter where she turned, she couldn't find her way out.

"Okay, so I won't call work," Jessica said. "But Todd's coming this afternoon to see Jake."

"It's not his day," Liam said. "I checked."

"How do you know that?" Jessica couldn't hide her suspicion.

"I called the *Tribune*. He's covering basketball practice, checking up on that injured player. He's probably at the arena right now. And after, there's the game to cover."

Jessica felt her heart sink. Liam knew far, far too much about her life. *He's a stalker!* Elizabeth had said it. And she was right.

Jessica glanced at Liam's hands and pockets. Did he have a weapon? Surely not. He put one hand in his pocket and pulled out his cell phone, which he plunked on the counter. Otherwise, his hands were empty and his pockets seemed flat. She glanced over at the carving knives sitting in the wooden block behind him. He could easily get one, she thought.

Jessica suddenly felt very exposed and very vulnerable. Liam was a big man, tall and broad and nearly all muscle. She probably wouldn't be able to fight him off, if it came to that. And with Jake here, she had zero chance of winning. She realized the hopelessness of what could happen. She wouldn't be able to protect herself or Jake.

She only had one chance: to keep talking.

"Liam, I know we have issues to work out, and we will, I promise." Jessica's hands were trembling. She quickly crossed her arms across her chest, tucking her hands in.

"Jessica," Liam began, taking a step closer. Jessica froze. "I don't want you to be afraid of me."

"I'm not," Jessica lied quickly. She wasn't quite able to reach his eyes.

"Jessica, I love you. You know that."

"I know, but, Liam, you're making me uncomfortable." Maybe honesty was the best policy at this point. Maybe if he could see that he was scaring her, he'd back off. If he really loved her, he'd not want to hurt her, right? Jessica felt a tiny burst of hope. Maybe this was her way out.

"Yes, but can't you see how uncomfortable you made *me* going out with other guys? Like Cal and Michael?"

She felt a cold shiver run down the length of her spine. *Keep talking,* she told herself.

"Look, Liam, those dates didn't mean anything."

"Don't lie to me, Jessica." Menace laced Liam's voice. "I saw you."

"What do you want?" Jessica was desperate. She couldn't keep the note of fear out of her voice.

Liam's mouth settled in a thin line of determination. "I want what we had that night in the hotel room."

"What do you mean?" Jessica asked, but she already knew.

"I want you to make love to me. The way you did in that hotel room. I want to have you again like I did that night."

Jessica swallowed, her throat suddenly dry. "It's not possible," she whispered. "Jake is here."

Liam glanced up at the kitchen clock. "It's nearly his nap time. I know he naps every day around now."

Jessica started. "How do you know that?" her voice was low.

"You know how." Liam met Jessica's eyes, and then she knew for sure. Liam had been stalking her—not just following her, but tracking Jake as well. Did he stake out her house even when she wasn't there? Had he been watching Liza and Jake? The thought made Jessica nauseous. "I told you I know everything about you. Everything you care about, I know about. Everything."

Before this moment, Jessica had been nervous—anxious, even, but now she was scared. She felt the tingling sensation of panic shiver down her spine. Liam was dangerous. He was unbalanced. He was crazy.

Sane people didn't stalk their girlfriend's son and nanny. Sane people didn't sabotage their girlfriend's friendships.

Liam had gone too far.

Jessica glanced over to the living room, where she thought she'd left her cell phone. She didn't see it, either on the coffee table or near the DVR. Where was it? She needed that phone. She saw Liam's on the counter, but he was right by it. No way could she get to it.

"Okay, you're right," Jessica said, trying to be calm. "Let me put Jake down for a nap. Then we can talk."

Jessica walked into the dining room, trying not to run. Jake had finished his mac and cheese. At least a third of it was on his shirt and the floor.

She scooped Jake up, hardly even caring that a smudge of mac and cheese got on her shirt. "Let's clean you up," she said, and took him to his room. She wanted to get him as far away from Liam as soon as possible. She climbed the stairs.

The happy Thomas the Train decal on Jake's wall met her with its usual smile as she walked into Jake's room. She grabbed some wet wipes from a container on his shelf and busied herself cleaning his face and hands. Her own fingers shook.

What am I going to do?

"Nap time," she said to Jake.

"Ap!" Jake repeated.

"Time to lie down," she told him. She hoped he wouldn't fuss. She had no idea how Liam would react if Jake made a scene. It might just push him over the edge. "Time to be quiet, sweetie."

Jessica put Jake in his crib. He sat there quietly. He knew the routine. Some days, though, he didn't like to nap and let her know it. Thankfully, today he didn't seem to mind. In fact, he seemed to want to play with one of the pockets of his overalls. He probably had a Thomas the Tank Engine stashed there. She decided to let him have whatever it was. Anything to keep the peace, because today his life might just be at stake.

"Sweet dreams," Jessica said, backing out of the room. As she went, she noticed the baby nail scissors sitting on the top of the bureau. They weren't much of a weapon, but something was better than nothing. She grabbed them and put them in her pocket and then closed the door behind her.

As soon as the door shut, Jake pulled out the toy he'd been hiding in his pocket: Jessica's phone.

He knew she was always using it, and therefore, it was his favorite thing to swipe. Whenever she left it anywhere in his reach, he would take it.

As he held it in his hands, it began to vibrate.

"Mine!" he cried, as he touched the screen, answering the call. He'd seen his mom do this a million times. It was a piece of cake.

"Hello? Jessica?" Jake heard his father's voice.

"Hi!" he squealed. "Hi! Hi! Hi!"

"Jake?" came Todd's hesitant voice.

"Jake! Jake! Jake!" the little boy mimicked. "Jake has a new toy!"

"Jake, where's your mom?" Todd asked.

Jake ignored the question. He was far too excited to have his mother's phone. "Jake has a new toy! Jake doesn't like the toy man."

"Who?" asked Todd.

"The toy man! He's scary. The toy man is scary!"

"You mean Liam? Is Liam there?"

"I don't like the toy man."

"Jake, can you put your mom on the phone? Where is she? Is she with Liam?"

"Bye-bye!" Jake clicked the front of the phone, hanging up.

"Wait!" Todd cried, but it was too late. The line went dead. Todd tried calling back, but Jake didn't answer. The call went straight to voice mail.

At the stadium where he was covering the basketball practice, Todd looked at the phone in his hand. He felt his annoyance rise. He'd specifically asked Jessica not to have Liam over when Jake was there. She was free to see whomever she wanted when Jake was with Liza or him, but he'd warned Jessica that Jake was afraid of Liam. Now here was Jake, clearly unsupervised with Jessica's phone, while she and Liam were doing God knows what.

Todd could only imagine them kissing or cuddling or something far worse while Jake, his two-year-old son, was left loose to run through the house. What was Jessica thinking? What if she and Liam were having sex? Right now? In the house with Jake there?

He tried to call again, but again the phone went straight to voice mail. Todd grabbed his laptop bag. He had a couple of hours before the game started. The new stadium was actually much closer to Sweet Valley than the old one. He could get to the town house and back in plenty of time.

He only got angrier as he strode out into the bright sunlight of the parking lot. How could she do something so careless? She was about to get the surprise of her life. And Liam, too. He was going to give both of them a piece of his mind.

10

"I don't have anything to say to you," Mona said to Elizabeth as she crossed her arms defiantly across her chest.

"Yes, you do." Elizabeth shut the door behind her. "Come on, sit down."

Mona backed into the living room but didn't sit down. She glared at Elizabeth.

"I don't care what you think, you know. I'm not talking." Mona shook her head.

Elizabeth realized she wasn't going to get the answers she wanted by playing it straight. She had to shock Mona into telling the truth.

"Well, if you don't talk to me, you'll have to talk to the police," Elizabeth said.

"I don't think so."

"You're wrong. The real reason I'm here is that the true Robin Platt, Robert Platt as you know him, has been murdered. And you're the prime suspect."

Shock temporarily silenced Mona. She was genuinely stunned.

"No! Never! I'd never hurt Robin. I haven't seen her since I left Richmond, I swear. I'd never hurt her. . . . She was my friend. I really liked her. She was great. And she was talented and wonderful." Mona's knees gave way and she sank into the couch. "I only took her name, I swear."

"I don't believe you. And I doubt the police would, either, with your record of addiction."

"But it's not true! Yes, I have a drug problem, but that doesn't have anything to do with anything." Mona sounded desperate, trapped, and then trying to please Elizabeth, to get her on her side. "Look, I'm sorry about Bruce and everything. I didn't want to hurt anybody. I really didn't. Rick Warner, it was his fault. I had no choice. He was blackmailing me."

"How?"

"He caught me stealing. He knew about my drug problem. He threatened to send me to jail for embezzlement and for the drugs unless . . ."

"Unless what?"

Mona swallowed, her eyes brimming with tears. "Unless I went along with his plan to accuse Bruce Patman of attempted rape."

"Did he say why Bruce?"

"He said something about a land deal. Something about getting Bruce off the board of his company so the other board members might sell the land to him."

"So how did you do it? How did you set up Bruce?"

Mona hesitated. The shock was wearing off; now she was beginning to think. "I never left L.A., so I couldn't have murdered Robin."

"But who knows that you were here all this time?" Elizabeth didn't wait for an answer. "Me. I'm the only one who knows where you were."

"But you wouldn't—"

"Look, if you tell me everything, I'll help you. Otherwise, do it on your own."

"But I need you."

"Let's start with Warner. If he really is the one behind this rape charge, I have to know."

Mona nodded and took a deep breath.

"It was a setup. All Warner's idea, and he had the bartender in his pocket. The spilled drink on Bruce was on purpose, so that he'd go to the restroom to clean up and I'd be waiting when he got out. I had a story to tell him about my dad abusing me. I cried a lot."

Elizabeth sat up straight. This was exactly how Bruce said things had happened. That the girl had been upset and Bruce had offered to help.

"He was actually really nice. He didn't come on to me at all. I felt bad about it, but what could I do? Warner had me. Bruce bought me a Coke and he got a club soda from the bartender, who'd already slipped something into his drink. It made him dizzy and nauseous, like food poisoning. And then the bartender helped Bruce lie down in the back. He was out for about an hour."

It was all exactly as Bruce had originally said. Drugs! Why hadn't Elizabeth thought about the possibility that Bruce had been drugged? Bruce had just assumed it was food poisoning, but it was much more. Elizabeth couldn't believe she'd ever doubted Bruce's word.

"After the bartender laid him down in the back room, then I could leave. All I had to do was go to the priest, make the confession."

"Was the priest in on it, too?"

"No, he wasn't. Warner had me go to the church a month in advance so I could build a relationship with him. The priest thought I was telling the truth. I begged him to go to the papers because I said I was afraid. They had to keep my name out of it. Of course, he believed me."

That would explain why he seemed so sincere when I interviewed him, Elizabeth thought.

"That was horrible." Elizabeth shook her head, disgusted.

"I know I did a terrible thing. I can't even bear to think about how I hurt him, but I had no choice. You have to believe me."

"Why should I believe you, Mona? You've lied to me again and again. And now you've almost destroyed Bruce. He's a good man and you've trashed his reputation." *And ruined our relationship, perhaps forever. Bruce can never forgive me now,* she thought.

He had been right all along. Elizabeth felt the truth cut through her like a sharp knife. If only she'd trusted him from the start. If only she'd believed in him. He had been telling the truth.

"You have to understand, Warner made me do it. And he made me . . ." Mona choked back a sob.

"Made you what?"

"Made me *do* things with him." Mona shuddered. The girl clearly didn't like Warner. "He wanted sex. Lots of sex. He insisted if I didn't do what he wanted when he wanted, he'd have me arrested."

Elizabeth was struck silent for a moment. For the first time, she saw just how frightened Mona really was. Elizabeth knew Rick Warner was conniving, but she hadn't realized how manipulative and abusive until that moment. She put her hand on Mona's shoulder. Now she realized why Mona had been able to act the part of the traumatized victim so well. She had been one. Only it hadn't been Bruce who'd caused it. It had been Rick Warner.

"Mona . . ." Elizabeth's anger at the girl faded. She was a victim, too, just like Bruce. Unless she was lying again. "You've lied to me so often. I don't know what the truth is anymore."

"But . . . I . . ."

"Do you have proof of anything you're saying? I need proof."

"But you have to believe me. I am telling the truth."

"How can I? Do you have any evidence Warner framed Bruce?"

Mona shook her head slowly. "No, I don't." She shifted uncomfortably. "I know I've lied. But this time I am telling the truth."

"I need some kind of proof. Anything that can corroborate your story."

"Wait . . ." Mona straightened her shoulders. "I do have one thing. I don't know if you can consider it proof. Warner liked to tape us when we . . . you know." Mona rubbed her arms like she was cold and couldn't look Elizabeth in the eye. "Sometimes he talked about Mr. Patman. It was like it turned him on. Warner doesn't know I have a copy; he thought he deleted them all, but I managed to steal this one yesterday."

"Yesterday?"

"I saw him at his house. I was freaking out about everything and he left me alone in his office for a minute. I managed to copy one of the files from his home computer. Laura, Elizabeth, whoever, I swear I never hurt Robin. You have to help me."

Elizabeth covered Mona's hands with hers. "I know you're telling the truth. I know you haven't been out of L.A., and if you give me that tape, I promise to do everything I can to get you help. If you've been honest, Warner is the one who's going to jail."

Tears slid down Mona's cheeks and she wiped them away furiously.

"Are you willing to show me part of the tape?"

Mona nodded. The recording was an electronic video file on her laptop. She booted up her computer and pulled up the file. It was grainy and dark, but Elizabeth could distinctly make out Rick Warner and Mona. Neither one had clothes on.

"What . . . is this just a sex tape?" Elizabeth couldn't help sounding skeptical.

"No. Keep watching. There's more."

Mona looked miserable, like a girl being forced. She really was a rape victim. And then Warner spoke.

"So, if the police ask, Patman did this to you . . . and this . . ."

"No, please . . . Rick . . . You're hurting me," Mona pleaded.

"And this . . ."

"Oh, my God." Elizabeth felt disgusted. Warner was acting out the alleged rape that Mona was supposed to pretend had really happened. "I've seen enough." Elizabeth clicked off the video.

Mona was silent for a moment. "But . . . Robin? Tell me. How did she die? She was such a great person. I really liked her. She was so nice to me. And she was going to be so happy going to New York and changing her life. What happened? Who did it?"

Elizabeth looked at Mona and saw a devastated friend. Whatever Mona was guilty of, she had truly cared about Robin. She braced herself to admit the truth.

"Mona." Elizabeth took in a fortifying breath. "I'm truly sorry, but I had to lie. At least it was a good lie, if there's such a thing, because Robin is alive and well in New York."

"What?" Mona's face was a blur of emotion: relief, surprise, and then, most of all, outrage. "You *lied* about that? You're just like Warner. How could you do that?"

Mona moved to go. Elizabeth grabbed her wrist.

"Mona, wait. I needed to get the truth to save a man's life and it was the only way I thought I could get it."

"Still, it was terrible. And I'm leaving. You people are all crazy."

"You're right. It was crazy, but I had to take the chance. And it's going to be good for you, too. Don't you see? You're free now. What you have in this video is enough to put Warner away. We have to go to the police."

"And testify against Warner? No way. I'm not going to risk my life for anybody. I'm getting out of here."

"Mona, I can help you."

"Yeah, right."

"I can get you into the best rehab facility in Los Angeles. Not that rinky-dink place in Kentucky. Mona, if you leave now and you don't face this addiction, someone else will just use it against you. Aren't you tired of being used?"

Mona paused a moment, letting the truth sink in.

"Yes," she said softly. "But I can't do it. I tried, more than once, and failed."

"But this time you won't be alone. I'm here."

"You're going to help me through rehab?"

"I will. I'm your friend, Mona. I really do want to help you."

Mona looked into Elizabeth's earnest face and believed her.

"I don't know if I can do it."

"You can. This time you'll make it. I know it. And I'll be there for you. All the way through." Elizabeth squeezed the girl's hand, and Mona squeezed back, giving her a faint smile.

"What do I have to do?"

"Testify against Warner and, I promise, I'll help you recover. You can have a life free of drugs, and free of people like Warner."

Mona nodded slowly. "But Warner is a powerful man . . . and he swore he'd have me arrested."

"No, he won't. We're not going to let him. I told you, you're not alone anymore. And we're powerful, too."

Mona hesitated for a moment.

"Trust me, Mona. I promise you that bastard is finished. That's what you want, isn't it?"

"With all my heart."

"Well?"

"Okay, I'll testify."

"Good. And we've got the best attorney in Southern California on our side," Elizabeth said as she pulled out her phone and dialed Annie's number. She tried to calculate what time it was in Cannes but wasn't sure. "We're going to fix this. You're going to be all right, Mona, I promise you."

Annie answered on the first ring. Elizabeth had expected to hear the soothing sounds of the Bruce's villa in the background, but instead heard the bustling sounds of an airport.

"Annie, where are you?"

"At LAX, getting my baggage," she said. "We just flew in from Cannes."

"With Bruce?"

"Yes."

"Don't tell him who told you, but I've found out everything. Robin Platt's name is really Mona Thomas and she was working for Rick Warner and being blackmailed by him, which is why she's made up the charges against Bruce. They're all false."

"Are you sure?"

"She's willing to swear to it. And she has an incriminating video."

"Okay, then I have to call the D.A. and set up a meeting at the police station. Colton will need to know his star witness is a fraud. He might even drop the charges. Can you bring her there?"

"Can you protect her?"

"If it's blackmail, I think I can get her immunity. Meanwhile, let me tell Bruce."

"Wait! Bruce can't know I'm involved."

Annie hesitated on the line. "Are you sure?"

"He can't, Annie." Elizabeth's tone left no room for argument. "Promise me."

"If that's what you want."

"Thank you." Elizabeth hung up. She speed-dialed her sister, hoping Jessica would be the one to take Mona to the police station. Elizabeth didn't want to take a chance of Bruce seeing her.

Jessica's phone went to voice mail—again.

Where was she?

11

Jessica put Jake down for his nap, closed his door, and walked down the stairs. Liam was waiting for her in the living room. Her mind raced, trying to come up with something—anything—to distract him. His cool blue eyes watched her every move. He looked the same as he always did, close-up ready, with his dark, nearly black hair worn a little bit shaggier than usual for his new movie role as a mob hit man.

Jessica had never seen Liam as dangerous before, but now, sitting in her living room, he looked like a man who could be violent. She swallowed her fear. He was still upset. His calm expression did nothing to mask the anger and frustration Jessica could see simmering under the surface.

"Is he asleep?" Liam asked her, his eyes giving her body a slow sweep up and down. She regretted wearing her fitted pencil skirt and heels. She wished she were wearing baggy old sweatpants. Maybe then Liam wouldn't be looking at her like she was on the menu.

"Not quite," Jessica said. "It takes him a few minutes to settle down."

Liam sat on the couch. "Come here," he said, his arm stretched out on the back of the sofa like he owned it.

Jessica hesitated.

"Come here," Liam said, shifting and patting the seat next to him.

"I think we need to talk first," Jessica said, hoping to delay and keep as much physical space between them as possible.

"We can talk when you're sitting. Sit." Liam knitted his eyebrows, his impatience clear.

"Do you want something to drink first? Coffee? Tea? Wine?" Jessica edged to the kitchen door.

"Jessica, you know what I want, and it's not a drink."

Jessica felt her stomach lurch. He wasn't going to be dissuaded. But he had to be.

"Liam, I . . . I want that, too." She'd say anything, she decided, to calm him down and get him out of her house. What she needed was for him to leave. She could figure out everything else later.

"You do?" Liam sounded skeptical.

"Of course I do."

"Then come here."

"But Jake . . ."

"Is sleeping by now."

"Maybe. Even if he is, I can't enjoy it when Jake's here. Besides, I want to go out to dinner tonight. Have some wine, and then we can go to your place. Really take our time. Doesn't that sound nice?" Jessica couldn't believe the lies coming out of her mouth. She hoped they sounded convincing. She was never going to be with Liam ever again. As soon as she got him out the door, she'd never let him in again. That much she knew.

He watched her carefully.

"No," he said, shaking his head. "I've waited long enough."

"Liam . . ."

"You've kept me in limbo for months, Jessica."

"I know, Liam, and I'm sorry. I was just confused. The divorce and Todd . . ."

"Don't mention his name!" Liam's voice suddenly rose to a furious shout.

Jessica froze. Liam jumped up from the couch, agitated again, running his hands nervously through his hair.

"I don't *ever* want to hear his name again, do you understand me?"

"Of course. I'm sorry, Liam." Jessica did her best to look contrite.

"You damn well better be sorry," Liam fumed.

"Hey, I have an idea." Jessica tried to keep her voice light and bright, as if Liam hadn't just exploded for no good reason. *Ignore the crazy, just pretend everything's fine and maybe it will be.* "Why don't we go back to the restaurant where we had our first date? We could go back to that hotel, re-create that night together. That night we *both* enjoyed so much." When they'd had quick, furious sex.

Liam glanced up at Jessica and their eyes met across the living room. For a split second, Jessica thought she might have convinced him.

"Let's start over," Jessica said in her most soothing voice. "That night together was perfect, wasn't it? Let's go back there, to that wonderful night in the hotel."

Liam broke eye contact and looked away.

"We could get it all back, Liam. It's not too late. Let's do that night all over again."

"That night?" Liam's voice sounded flat.

"Yes, that perfect night."

"That night you made love to me? Yes, that night was perfect, wasn't it?" Liam's voice sounded wistful. Jessica thought she had him. Now all she had to do was to seal the deal.

"Yes, let's do it again. At that same hotel. Tonight. You go home and get changed, and I'll call Liza and it'll be just you and me, Liam. All night long."

"That night." Liam let out a little scoff and shook his head, his mood suddenly changing again. "That . . . night. The night you made love to me, gave yourself to me, and then ran away from me, crying."

"What?" Jessica felt her hope slipping away again.

"That night, at the end, you don't remember? You wouldn't even let me hold you afterward. You just wanted to leave that room as fast as you could. You made me drive you home, and on the way, I couldn't even hold your hand. It was like I disgusted you. You made me feel like you'd used me."

"No, Liam, that's not true." But even Jessica knew that it was true. She *had* used Liam. She'd used him this whole time.

"And then, and then . . . you wear these sexy clothes to taunt me." He gestured to Jessica's outfit. "And then you string me along and you barely even let me touch you. What is that, Jessica?" Liam's eyes shone with pain and frustration. The old, tender Liam was back for a fleeting second.

"I'm sorry, Liam. I am. I never meant to lead you on. I never meant to hurt you."

Liam just shook his head, the tenderness in his face gone now. He moved closer to Jessica, one slow, deliberate step at a time. "It's too late for apologies. I'm tired of your words. I'm tired of you trying to convince me that your torturing me is okay. It's not okay, Jessica."

"I see that, I do. I understand."

"I followed you night and day; I hardly ever let you out of my sight, and what thanks do I get for that? I get delays and excuses."

Jessica felt a cold chill run down the small of her back. Liam was obsessed. Beyond obsessed. Crazy. For the first time, she really believed that she wouldn't be able to make him see reason. There might not be a rational part of him left.

"What do you want, Liam?" The words came out as a hoarse whisper, fear choking her.

"You know what I want," he said.

Liam was right in front of her now. Jessica realized she had two choices: She could have sex with him, here and now, and hope that afterward he would just leave. Or she could fight him. She had the small cuticle scissors in her pocket. Her fingers curled around them, feeling the cold metal. He had no weapon that she could see. Jake was safely tucked away upstairs.

Give in.

Or fight.

She'd had sex with him before. Would it really be so bad to do it again? She didn't remember much about that night, so how bad could it have been? The breakup with Todd had been so fresh, all she had thought about when she'd been with Liam was all the many ways he hadn't been Todd.

Liam put his hands on Jessica's shoulders and she stayed very still. He pulled her close to him and dipped his lips down to meet hers. She stayed completely still as Liam kissed her. She smelled the familiar scent of his cologne. This was Liam, the man she'd been dating, the man who'd listened to her problems all these many weeks. He'd been patient with her and kind. Shouldn't she just give in?

And yet . . .

The way he touched her now, the way his lips felt on hers, made her feel queasy and nauseous. She hated him touching her. She'd hated it for weeks but hadn't been able to admit it even to herself. She'd hoped that at some point she would feel the same way about him that Liam felt about her, but that moment never came. She wasn't attracted to Liam. She never really had been. His touch felt oily and wrong. She wanted him to stop.

And that wasn't all. If it had been just a lack of attraction, Jessica could probably have shut her eyes and gotten on with it.

But there was so much more.

She was angry. Angry that he'd been stalking her and lying to her about it. Angry that he'd been interfering in her life, ruining her career and chasing away her friends and trying to control everything she did.

Well, he wasn't going to control her anymore. She realized she'd been living her life passively for weeks. She hadn't been her real self. She'd just been some shell-shocked version of Jessica, someone who let other people decide things for her.

Those days were over.

Liam didn't get to decide whom she saw or whom she slept with. Nobody did. She was her own person. This was her life, and she was tired of letting him live it for her.

"No," Jessica said, pushing Liam away. Taken by surprise, Liam stumbled back a step. "I don't want that."

"Jessica." Liam's voice carried a warning, and his eyes went cold.

"No. Get out, Liam. Now." She was angry and let him see it. If he cared about her at all, even the least little bit, he would leave now. "I want you out of this house!"

"Jessica . . ."

"Get out! I want you out, Liam. Go!" She slipped her hand into her pocket and felt the cold metal of the cuticle scissors. She clutched them. If he wasn't going to go, she was going to make him.

She couldn't believe things had gotten this bad. Liam O'Connor was a bona fide movie star. His picture currently graced the cover of *Us Weekly*. Millions of women would kill to date him, but he was obsessed with her. In this instant she knew she hated him. He wanted her? Too bad. Let him find someone else.

Except if he really was obsessed. Maybe even mentally unbalanced. Still, Jessica hoped he would come to his senses. Wasn't there a sane bit of him left?

"No," Liam said, shaking his head, his eyes flat. "I'm not leaving, Jessica. I'm not ever going to leave."

He stepped forward and grabbed her by the arms. He moved so quickly she wasn't prepared. She fought him and tried to pull the scissors from her pocket, but he had her by the arms and he was bigger and stronger. He pushed her down on the couch and then fell on top of her, his weight pinning her down.

It was suffocating as he pressed the air out of her lungs. She still had her hand curled around the little scissors, but her arm was pinned between Liam and the couch. She couldn't budge.

"No, Liam! Get off." She struggled, but he was too strong, too heavy. She desperately wanted to scream, but she couldn't, not with little Jake upstairs. She hoped he was sleeping. He mustn't wake up. Even now, in the struggle, she didn't want to draw Liam's attention to her little boy. She had to keep him safe, no matter what happened to her.

"No!" she growled, pushing at him, clawing at him. She scratched his arm, but he didn't even feel it. His eyes were blank, his pupils dilated as if he wasn't quite himself.

"Stop fighting me," he told her. "We were meant to be together. We're going to be together. Forever."

"No, we're not." Jessica squirmed; her right arm was coming free. She clutched the scissors. If she could just get them out . . .

Liam's face was above hers now, and he dipped down, kissing her roughly, his stubble scraping her chin. She could feel the desire he had for her as he ground against her, and it made her feel sick.

Jessica squirmed and struggled and then bit his lip.

"Ow!" Liam cried, pulling back, shock and hurt in his eyes. He lifted himself up just enough that her right arm came free. She pulled out the scissors.

"We're not ever going to be together," Jessica declared, and she jabbed the small scissors in his neck as hard as she could. He shrieked in pain and clutched at her wrist. She didn't get a chance to stab him again. He grabbed the scissors from her hand and threw them far behind him, well out of reach.

She used the distraction to knee him, hard, in the stomach. A little whoosh of air escaped and she slid out from underneath him. She landed on the living room floor with a hard bump and tried desperately to crawl away.

"You little bitch," he hissed, recovering and furious, as a tiny trickle of blood flowed down his neck. He dabbed at it with one hand, staring at the blood on his fingers in dull surprise. The sight of the blood just made him angrier. He grabbed her leg and Jessica swallowed a scream.

She kicked at him silently, one shoe flying off. He had a solid grip on her ankle. "Let go," she hissed, her voice an urgent whisper.

"Never." Liam's face was flushed red, his eyes dull. The Liam she knew was long gone, and in his place was a monster: vicious and determined. He yanked her leg and pulled her back to the couch. When she tried to claw at him, he grabbed her wrists and pushed her back down on the couch.

"You're hurting me."

"I don't care."

Liam held both of her hands in one and then ripped her blouse. The top three buttons popped off.

"No! Liam." Her voice was low, but inside she was screaming. He couldn't do this. Distantly, she couldn't believe any of this was happening.

She got one arm free and scratched at his face with her nails. He slapped her hard. Instantly, she tasted blood in her mouth. Tears sprang to her eyes.

That's when he yanked up her skirt so hard the side seam ripped. His hands were rough as he grabbed at her underwear.

"No, please, Liam!" She was ready to beg him to stop. But she knew he wasn't going to stop. Liam was going to do what he wanted, and Jessica couldn't prevent him. No matter how hard she fought.

Tears slid down her cheeks.

"Liam, please!"

"You want this, too," he murmured, throwing her underwear on the floor. "I know you want this."

"I don't, Liam! Stop it." Her foot connected with his chest, but he just pushed it away roughly, hardly fazed.

"I love you, Jessica." Insanely, he began kissing her even as she squirmed and struggled against him.

He pulled back long enough to reach down and undo his pants with one hand.

Jessica redoubled her efforts, but he had her arms pinned and her legs couldn't do much against the weight of his body. She could feel his knee spread her legs apart roughly. She squeezed her eyes shut as if she could somehow make this nightmare end.

The front door banged open then and Todd suddenly burst into the room.

"What the hell?" Todd cried, surprised. He took in Jessica's swollen lip, her torn clothes, the tears in her eyes and mascara running down her face, and Liam holding her wrists above her head. In that moment, Todd lost coherent thought. Everything went red.

"Get off her!" In a rage, Todd grabbed Liam and flung him against a wall. Liam hit with a sickening thud.

Jessica sprang up, scampering off the couch as fast as she could as she clasped the ends of her torn shirt together. She ran to the kitchen and grabbed Liam's phone that he'd left on the counter. She used it to call 911, her heart pounding.

"Help! I need help! Please!"

Meanwhile, in the other room, Liam, recovering from hitting the wall, shook his head to clear it. He looked up and saw Todd waiting for him. "You don't want to do this, Todd." Liam gave him a slow, confident smile.

"Yes, I think I do." Todd's face flushed red with anger and his chest heaved. He'd hated Liam from the start and he'd been looking for a reason to punch him for months. Now he finally had one and he wasn't going to let it go. He'd hurt Jessica—the love of his life—and Liam was going to pay.

"I've had six weeks of intensive martial arts training for my latest movie," Liam said with a smooth confidence. "Do you know martial arts?"

"No," Todd said, rage still bubbling in his blood. "But I do know how to kick your ass."

Todd lunged, his shoulder connecting with Liam's chest as Todd rammed him against the wall.

Liam raised both fists and smashed them down against Todd's back. Todd stumbled and Liam kicked him, sending Todd flying backward across the coffee table. Todd jumped to his feet quickly, hardly feeling anything, adrenaline and rage fueling his body, a fighting instinct that went deep for a man who would do anything to protect his family.

Todd came back swinging, and connected three times. Liam stumbled back, knocking over a lamp and breaking it. Glass shards scattered across the tiled entryway.

Liam picked up a piece of the lamp and flung it at Todd, who felt the shard of glass nick his upper cheek as it flew by. He didn't care. He couldn't feel the pain. All he could think about was making Liam hurt as much as he'd hurt Jessica.

He'd pay. Todd would make sure of it.

Liam might have known technical fighting moves, but Todd had heart and determination on his side. Soon, Liam was on his back foot, just trying to defend himself against the dozens of blows Todd rained down on his head. Liam's hands were shielding his face, but his knee was free and with all his might he jammed it into Todd's stomach, sending him flying back against the couch. For a moment, Todd was helpless. Liam threw himself in for the final blow. Just then Jessica appeared in the room clutching the matching lamp. She swung it hard, connecting with the back of Liam's head. He crumpled like a paper doll, out cold at her feet. She glanced at the lamp in her hands.

"Nice hit," Todd said, and smiled at Jessica.

Suddenly overwhelmed, Jessica let the lamp drop to the floor as if her arms had just given out. She stumbled a little. Tears slid down her cheeks.

"Jessica," Todd cried, leaping to her side. "Are you okay? Did he hurt you?"

He had his hands on her face, tracing her bloodied lip with his finger and swiping away her mascara-laden tears. Jessica couldn't speak. Her whole body trembled.

"I'm here. It's okay," Todd said. "Everything's going to be okay now."

Jessica, tears streaming down her face, glanced up at Todd even as a sob escaped her throat. Todd wrapped her up in his arms.

"Police!" shouted a man outside before the front door was thrown open and police swarmed in, guns drawn.

"There," Jessica said, pointing to Liam, the man on the ground. "That's the man who tried to rape me."

Liam was just starting to come to, sitting up and holding his head.

"You're under arrest," said one officer, who grabbed Liam's arm and hoisted him up. "You have the right to remain silent. Anything you say or do . . ."

Liam struggled, his face twisted in anger and pain, but he stayed silent. He wouldn't even give his name. The only thing he said was a furious threat thrown to Jessica: "You'll pay for this!"

Jessica flinched and buried her face in Todd's chest, and he wrapped his arms protectively around her.

"Get him out of here," Todd said to the cop holding Liam, who obliged.

One of the officers took down a quick statement from Jessica, who held Todd's hand the entire time. As the police were leaving, Jessica heard one of them say, "He looks just like that actor, Liam something."

"Naw," the other one said, and they were gone.

Jessica stood in the middle of the living room, still numb with shock. Todd brought her a glass of water, and she took a shaky sip.

"I can't believe this," Jessica said, even as her hands shook. Todd took the glass from her fingers gingerly and set it on the table, then wrapped his arms around her.

"It's okay now. He's gone. And he won't bother you anymore. I doubt he'll even be able to show his face in Hollywood after the police and the paparazzi get through with him."

"I was so wrong," Jessica murmured into his chest. "I was so wrong about everything."

"Shhhh. It's okay, now. Everything's okay."

"Todd, I'm sorry. For everything. You tried to warn me about Liam. Elizabeth did, too. I should have listened. I'm sorry. Can you . . . can you forgive me?"

"I already have," Todd said, kissing the top of her head. "Jessica, I love you. I always have. I always will."

She pulled away from him and met his eyes, hope brimming there with the tears.

"I love you, too," she said, as if it were a revelation. "I always will."

Todd's heart soared. It was all he had ever really wanted to hear. What was this whole thing about? Her career? What was he? Crazy? Standing in her way. This wasn't that spoiled high-school girl with a new fad every month; this was a woman who knew what she wanted. And there was nothing Jessica wanted that she couldn't do. He saw that so clearly now. And he also saw that nothing else mattered except that Jessica, the mother of his son, loved him.

"What about Sarah?" Jessica asked, swiping at her face.

"I never loved her," Todd said. "I always loved you."

Jessica threw her arms around his neck and reached over to kiss him. Todd returned the kiss, and in that moment, everything was right in the world again.

Suddenly, Jessica pulled back. "Jake!" she said, suddenly remembering her little boy. The two stared at each other in surprise and then both bolted up the stairs. Jessica swung open the door, and found their little Jake, peacefully asleep, cradling Jessica's phone in his little chubby hand like it was a teddy bear.

"He slept through the whole thing," Todd exclaimed, amazed.

"I wonder if he'll keep sleeping," Jessica said as she pulled Todd out of Jake's room and gave him a kiss.

Todd's hands found her waist and pulled her close as he returned the kiss. He vowed to be there for Jessica. After months of agony and loneliness apart, they both realized there was no choice; they had to be together.

They'd both come home at last.

12

"Here she is," said Elizabeth as she handed Mona Thomas over to Annie Whitman in the secluded parking garage near the police station.

"And here's the video." Elizabeth handed Annie a Memory Stick.

Annie took it and glanced over at Mona. Annie didn't like lurking around in the shadows here, but Elizabeth had insisted.

"I'm Annie Whitman. I can help you, Mona. Are you ready to do this?"

"I'm ready to do what I need to do," Mona said, looking determined.

She had her blond hair pulled back in a ponytail and wore a simple blue sundress. Wearing hardly any makeup, she looked even younger and more vulnerable than her twenty-three years.

Annie glanced at Elizabeth, who was already turning back to her car.

"Are you leaving already? You should come in. Tell the police how you found out the truth," Annie said. "And Bruce is already inside. He'll want to know it was you, Elizabeth."

"No," she said, shaking her head slowly, her hand on the door of her car. She swung it open and slipped into the driver's seat. "I've done enough to hurt him. I don't want Bruce to know."

"But he'd be so happy to know you fixed this. That you didn't give up on him."

"But that's the problem, Annie. I did, right at the start." Elizabeth stared dejectedly at her lap. "Doing this was the least I could do, but it doesn't make up for what I did to him. Nothing will. Please. He can't know."

"What should I tell the police?" Annie leaned in to the driver's side, resting her arm on the door.

"Just tell them Mona came forward. That's all. She's agreed to say that."

"But what do I tell Bruce?"

"Just tell him his family and his friends pulled together to exonerate him, but leave my name out of it."

Mona nodded her confirmation.

"Elizabeth—"

"No. My mind is made up, Annie."

Just then, Elizabeth's phone rang. She fished it out of her purse.

"It's Jessica," she said. "I've got to take this call. You two go in."

"Okay, if this is what you want." Annie began walking to the police station, Mona following. Elizabeth shut the car door.

Once inside the police station, Annie steered the girl into the conference room where Tom Colton, the district attorney, was waiting.

Mona had grown quietly nervous as they walked into the room.

"It'll be all right," Annie told her. "Just tell Tom the truth."

"Where's Mr. Patman?" Mona asked, glancing around the room.

"He's waiting in another conference room," the D.A. said. "Don't worry about him. We've got two officers keeping him company."

"That's not necessary, Tom." Annie led the girl to a chair opposite Tom and sat down next to her, putting her briefcase to one side.

"I'm just trying to cover my bases, Annie. Besides, are you really trying to tell me he's *not* a flight risk? Seriously?"

"He came back here on our own volition, Tom."

"Right. So tell me what the big news is all about." Tom motioned for Mona and Annie to begin.

Mona proceeded to tell the D.A. what had really happened that night of Bruce Patman's alleged attack. While she explained, Tom's face went three different shades of gray, finally settling on a color duller than ash. Rarely was Annie able to shock a D.A. to quite this extent, and she had to admit, she rather liked it, especially since Bruce was completely and one hundred percent innocent.

Mona left out no detail, and when Annie produced the Memory Stick, holding the video that would offer the corroborating evidence, Tom shook his head.

He watched some of the tape, fast-forwarding it to where Warner acted out Bruce's alleged rape.

"Wow," he said. "Incredible." Tom Colton's case against Bruce Patman had just disintegrated. There'd be no selling Patman's guilt to any jury, anywhere. It was over.

"The real villain isn't Bruce at all," Annie told him. "It's Rick Warner. I'm not trying to tell you how to do your job, but I think you should drop the charges. Your star witness was blackmailed and admits to making it all up. And I think she was coerced into sex, but not by Bruce. By Rick Warner, who is the real rapist."

Tom sat down and ran his hands through his hair. One of his biggest contributors for the fall campaign was also a blackmailer extortionist who had clearly forced a girl on tape to have sex with him. He had no choice. When his opponent got wind of this news, she'd have a field day in the campaign ads. The only way he could hope to come out of it would be to hit Rick Warner and hit him hard. But even then, his reelection bid looked grim.

"What are you going to do?" Annie asked.

"I'm going to issue a warrant for Rick's arrest," Tom said. "And the bartender, too."

"And Mona?"

"No charges and immunity, providing she'll testify for the prosecution," Tom said, his face growing red.

Mona's face lit up with relief, and she sent a grateful look to Annie.

"And Bruce?"

"Dropping the case against him. He's free to go," Tom grumbled.

Annie felt like jumping up from the table and shouting, but she managed to keep calm as she walked briskly from the room to tell Bruce the good news. Still, she couldn't quite keep the smug victory smile from her face.

13

The next day, on the front porch of Bruce's immense mansion, the paparazzi and reporters had gathered to get Bruce's official statement. By now, they'd all reported the news that the D.A. had dropped the attempted rape charges against him and arrested Rick Warner.

Beyond just the usual reporters and paparazzi, Bruce's supporters stood shoulder to shoulder. It looked like a mini Sweet Valley High reunion, familiar faces dotting the crowd.

Alice and Ned waited with Elizabeth and Jessica. They'd cut their latest trip short when they'd heard about Liam's attack on Jessica.

"Are you sure you shouldn't be resting?" Alice asked Jessica. Both parents hovered near her, protective of their youngest daughter. Jessica had been checked out at the hospital the day before and had officially filed charges against Liam at the police station. Liam was in jail.

"That's what I told her," Todd said. He was carrying Jake on his shoulders and holding on tightly to Jessica's hand.

"I just have a few scrapes, nothing that won't heal," Jessica said. "I'm fine. Thanks to Todd."

The two of them exchanged a loving look.

"If only I'd listened to you sooner, Lizzie," Jessica said, turning to her sister.

"No second-guessing," Elizabeth said, throwing an arm around her sister. "It's not allowed!"

Elizabeth had been shocked to hear the day before that her worst fears about Liam had come true. Even she hadn't realized Liam could be dangerous. She'd never liked him, but she'd also never predicted he could do what he did. She was glad he was locked up and hoped he stayed there a long time.

"Who could've guessed that such a hot and famous actor would be so crazy?" Lila asked. She stood nearby with her husband, Ken.

"Not me," Ken said. He wrapped an affectionate arm around his pregnant wife.

"Well, I'm glad everyone is okay," said Steven Wakefield. He was carrying little Emma in his arms. Aaron, his husband, stood nearby.

"Me too," Elizabeth said. She glanced at her sister and saw pure happiness on her face. Now that she was back with Todd, she was the old Jessica again. Liam's attack was the furthest thing from her mind.

Elizabeth smiled at her sister. As she stood with her friends and family, she realized she was the only single person there. Jessica had Todd. Ned had Alice. Steven had Aaron. Even Lila had Ken.

Everyone was one-half of a perfect couple. All except Elizabeth. Would it be this way forever? Would it be just her, alone, in a sea of soul mates? Hers always just out of reach?

Because, as of now, it was just Elizabeth and . . .

Missy LeGrange.

The socialite and Bruce's old snobby friend snuck up on her when she wasn't looking.

"I'm surprised to see you here," she sniped, her voice a low whisper. Missy was drenched in diamonds. As usual, she was sticking her nose where she wasn't wanted.

She stood close enough to Elizabeth for them to bump elbows.

"I'm here to support Bruce," Elizabeth said.

"Better late than never."

Missy was referring, of course, to the day Bruce was arrested. Missy had been there by his side, a steadfast supporter, when Elizabeth hadn't.

Elizabeth wished Missy would just go away. She hated that Missy was a walking reminder of how she'd failed Bruce.

Maybe it had been a bad idea for Elizabeth even to come today.

When Annie had called her that morning to invite Elizabeth to the press conference, she'd almost said no. After all, she blamed herself for the case against Bruce dragging on for so long. If she'd seen things clearer earlier, if she'd never doubted Bruce, this case might have been over weeks ago.

But in the end, it had been Jessica who had guilted her into coming. "I'm going. You can't wuss out on me," Jessica had said. "And this day is about Bruce being vindicated. He wants friendly faces in the audience and he deserves the support."

Elizabeth couldn't argue with that. Showing up was the least she could do.

Suddenly, Bruce's front door opened, and Annie stepped out. Bruce followed, and they were together standing at the hastily put-together podium.

"I'd like to get everyone's attention, please," Annie said into the microphones attached to the podium. A few boom mics danced in the air above their heads. "As you all know, Bruce Patman has been exonerated of all charges. And he's here today to give his statement. I'll now turn the floor over to Bruce."

Annie stepped back and Bruce moved forward. Elizabeth thought he'd never looked so handsome. Gone were the furrowed brow and slumped shoulders brought on by the months of worry over these trumped-up charges. He looked confident, energized, and unstoppable. His dark hair was perfectly combed; his blue eyes shone.

Elizabeth felt a lump in her throat. She was proud of him. He'd weathered this storm and come out stronger than ever before. That took character. She loved him for it.

Bruce nodded at the audience, seeing more supporters than reporters, the adoring looks of his friends, and began.

"Before I get to my statement, I want to say that there are so many people I have to thank. People who cared for and helped me . . ."

Next to Elizabeth, Missy LeGrange puffed herself up a bit, nodding to Elizabeth as if saying *He's talking about me.*

Elizabeth tried to ignore her.

Bruce continued in a softer voice, a voice brimming with emotion. "But the one person who has done more to save me than anyone else, who has tirelessly worked to prove my innocence . . ."

Elizabeth glanced over at Jessica.

Is it possible? Did Bruce know she'd been the one to get Mona Thomas to confess?

But how? The only people here who knew were Annie, Jessica, and Aaron. And she'd sworn them to secrecy. Elizabeth glanced over at her sister. It would be just like her to try to play matchmaker—promise or no promise.

"You said you wouldn't tell him anything," Elizabeth whispered to Jessica, barely able to contain her happiness. Jessica shook her head and shrugged silently. *Play dumb,* Elizabeth thought. *It doesn't matter. All that matters are the words coming out of Bruce's mouth.*

Could it be . . . she'd been forgiven?

Did Bruce love her again? If so, she would be the lone singleton in the crowd no more. She was meant to be with Bruce. She didn't realize just how much she'd missed his love until this moment, when she would finally get it back. She would be whole again. She'd be with the man she truly loved.

"Without her tireless work, day and night, this travesty of justice never would have been uncovered . . ." Bruce looked out to the crowd. For a second, his eyes lighted on Elizabeth. Her heart leaped. This was happening. It was really happening. She felt overcome with emotion. Her hands shook.

". . . and the real criminals punished. And I would have lost everything. . . . Not just material things, but more importantly, my name, my reputation, and the respect and love of people I love."

A small smile played on Elizabeth's lips. Happiness lighted her eyes, and she felt like she was glowing. This was the moment when she would finally be redeemed. Could it really happen?

Elizabeth looked at her loving sister, Jessica, who had the same hope in her eyes. She squeezed Jessica's hand and mouthed the words "Thank you."

Her heart, bursting with emotion, felt like it was going to explode.

"There is no one to whom I owe more . . ." Bruce said.

Elizabeth held her breath. She saw grateful tears glinting in Bruce's eyes and immediately her throat closed up. All the suffering, all the pain—it would all go away in this next moment. She felt like the luckiest girl in the world.

"I would like to thank the woman I love . . ."

Tears of joy and happiness slid down Elizabeth's cheeks.

". . . Annie Whitman."